PRAISE FOR
Handsome Harry

"*Handsome Harry* is Blake's most buoyant and polished novel yet. . . . Sassy, stubborn, funny, and resilient, his women are one of the delights of his novels. . . . Among other things, this is a great love story." —*Entertainment Weekly*

"*Handsome Harry* is a humdinger. . . . Blake brings this character to life so powerfully that we can't help but find him an entertaining and somewhat sympathetic companion." —Otto Penzler, *New York Sun*

"[An] engrossing novel . . . filled with hoodlums who are violent but honorable . . . capturing the attitudes and outlooks of the populace." —*USA Today*

"Blake at his edgy best . . . seductively violent." —*Atlanta Journal-Constitution*

"A beguiling, hurtling digression into a new voice for Blake." —*San Francisco Chronicle*

"The gutsy Blake mimics a true criminal marvelously while telling an alluring story." —*St. Louis Post-Dispatch*

"Blake's dialogue is fast, funny, and often raw. . . . A fast-paced novel that will pull readers into a world of violence, vendettas, and revenge. . . . Blake's telling is oh, so good." —*Fort Worth Star-Telegram*

"Blake writes with a bare-knuckled intensity that crackles with relevance and truth. Make no mistake about it, Blake is a master at his craft and his *Handsome Harry* is one of the best crime novels of the year." —*Tucson Citizen*

"Underpinning scenes of bank robberies, jailbreaks and bloody shootouts is a surprisingly intimate story of friendship, honor and desperate love. . . . A masterful social commentary on Depression-era America."   —*BookPage*

"Harry's voice is the smooth, almost affectless vernacular of a hardened con [in] this 'ripped from the history books' adventure as seen through Harry's lens of tough verisimilitude."   —*Publishers Weekly*

"A brilliant portrait of the real-life Pierpont. . . ."   —*Milwaukee Journal-Sentinel*

"Easily the year's best crime novel."   —*Clarion-Ledger* (Jackson, MS)

"The novel cooks harder than sly narrator Pierpont does when he meets his inevitable appointment with Old Sparky. . . . Blake brings this gin-soaked era back to life."   —*Booklist*

"Irresistibly compulsive reading."   —*Library Journal*

"Blake has created one charming gangster [and] tells the story with humor, finesse, and deftly paced action. . . . *Handsome Harry* is a kick."
                              —*Tucson Weekly*

"To categorize *Handsome Harry* merely as a 'crime novel' would neglect the solid characters and quality of Blake's writing. . . . He keeps readers enthralled with the skill of a master storyteller."   —*Oxford Town*

"The exuberantly unrepentant Harry Pierpont relates his story with power and raw vivacity."   —*Book Folks*

"Pierpont manages to seem both clever and good-natured even as he revels in the brutal things he's capable of doing. This is a violent rogue's memoir."
                              —*Arizona Republic*

Maura-Anne Wahl

About the Author

Handsome Harry is JAMES CARLOS BLAKE's eighth novel and ninth book of fiction. Among his literary honors are the Los Angeles Times Book Prize, the Southwest Book Award, the Quarterly West Novella Prize, and the Chautauqua South Book Award. He lives in Arizona.

Handsome Harry

A NOVEL

JAMES CARLOS BLAKE

wm

WILLIAM MORROW
An Imprint of HarperCollins*Publishers*

A hardcover edition of this book was published in 2004 by William Morrow, an imprint of HarperCollins Publishers.

HarperCollins books may be purchased for education, business, or sales promotional use. For informa-tion, please e-mail the Special Markets Department at SPsales@harpercollins.com.

FIRST PERENNIAL EDITION PUBLISHED 2005.

Designed by Renato Stanisic

The Library of Congress has catalogued the hardcover edition as follows:

Blake, James Carlos.
    Handsome Harry : a novel / James Carlos Blake.— 1st ed.
        p. cm.
    ISBN 0-06-055478-9
    1. Pierpont, Harry, 1902–1934—Fiction. 2. Dillinger, John, 1903–1934—Fiction.
    3. Middle West—Fiction. 4. Criminals—Fiction. I. Title.

PS3552.L3483H36 2004
813'.54—dc21   2003053991

ISBN 0-06-055479-7 (pbk.)

15 16 17 18 ❖/RRD 10 9 8 7 6 5 4

*C*onscience is but a word that cowards use,
Devised at first to keep the strong in awe.
Our strong arms be our conscience; swords, our law.
—WILLIAM SHAKESPEARE, *RICHARD III*

Foremost we admire the outlaw
who has the strength of his own lawfulness.
—ROBERT DUNCAN, *ROOTS AND BRANCHES*

I never knowingly harmed a fellow creature
that didn't get in my way.
—NELSON ALGREN, *A WALK ON THE WILD SIDE*

You run out of everything when you run out of luck.
—ANONYMOUS

Contents

Handsome Harry

OCTOBER 16, 1934

Now all the gang's dead except for me and Russell.

At least Russell can hope for a better tomorrow, since a guy doing life can always try another break. Me, they're going to finish off in the morning.

They wouldn't have to bother if they had simply let me die. They say I took seven bullets, including one to the head and one in the spine, but I remember being hit only once. The rifles were firing and firing and I saw Fat Charley's grin burst in blood and the next thing I knew I was lying on my face and couldn't move. I could feel the life draining out of me, and I knew another minute would be all she wrote. But they hustled me into the hospital and the doctors outdid themselves.

So. Here I am, half-crippled and my head still feels like it's got a rail spike in it. But they did it. They saved me for the executioner.

When I awoke from the surgery, the warden was in the room, glaring at me with a kind of furious satisfaction. He said Thought you could cheat the chair, didn't you, Pierpont? Well, I'm here to tell

you, mister, you're gonna burn—and keep on burning for all eternity.
The warden's a devout Christian, and he gave me a little sermon elab-
orating on the eternal tortures I was bound for. I have to admit he's
got a flair for description. When the warden finally left the room, the
hack posted at the door brought his hands up like they were strapped
to the arms of a chair and said *Zzzzzzztt* as he went big-eyed and grit
his teeth and shook like he was getting the juice.

Laugh a minute, the hacks.

The warden had it right, though. I *did* figure that if the break
went bad they'd shoot me dead, which would be a lot better than
what they were planning for me. I mean, the things you hear. Your
brain bakes and your eyes pop and your waste steams out of your
mouth. Your blood turns to tar. . . .

Oh man.

They've kept one nurse or another in my room around the clock
and doctors check on me several times a day. I so much as clear my
throat and they come running in a panic.

The nurses aren't supposed to talk to me, but three days ago a
leggy one with bold green eyes whispered Happy Birthday as she
changed the sheets under me. It took me a minute to understand I
was now thirty-two. She'd been reading up. I gave her a wink and she
glanced toward the open door, then kissed her fingertips and touched
them to my lips.

So many women have bandit hearts. This one would've joined us
in a wink.

A few hours ago they put me on a stretcher and lugged me down
here to the ready cell, next door to the death chamber. And they've
still got a nurse watching me through the bars and a doctor on hand
down the hall. It's really funny—both ha-ha and peculiar—that
they'll go to so much trouble to keep a man alive just so they can fry
him. Even if they have to carry him to the chair.

I mean to tell you, the Law's notion of justice is more cold-blooded
than any outlaw I ever knew. And I mean *outlaw,* not criminal. *Crimi-*

nal doesn't distinguish between guys like me and the guys who own the banks and insurance companies and stock markets, who own the factories and coal mines and oil fields, who own the goddamn *law*. I once said to John that being an outlaw was about the only way left for a man to hold on to his self-respect, and he said Ain't that the sad truth. The girls laughed along with us because they knew it wasn't a joke.

Speaking of John . . . I want to make something clear right off the bat. There was never any rivalry between us for leadership of the gang. There's no question he was boss of the gang he rounded up after breaking out of Crown Point—that bunch of cowboys including Van Meter and that lunatic Nelson or Gillis or whatever the runt's name really was—but if anybody in *our* gang could be called the leader, it was me, and even John would've said so. Not that any of us needed a leader. Each of us was his own man and could've gone his own way and done all right for himself. It just so happened the five of us made a smooth team and we could trust each other to the bone. You don't pass up luck like that.

I'll grant you that John was the coolest of us. He had cool in spades—except when it came to women, anyway. Russell and I had tempers like guard dogs and we had to work at keeping them on a tight leash. But not even Red and Charley, who were pretty unflappable guys themselves, could match John for coolness on a job or under fire. I'll also grant you that Charley was the brainiest and Russell had the brute strength on us all and nobody was tougher than Red. Nevertheless, when it was time for a deciding say-so, it was always yours truly they turned to.

John got the publicity because he loved it. He played up to it. They say that in his last few weeks he wasn't taking much pleasure in the limelight anymore and was wishing he looked like anybody but himself, but I wouldn't know about that. What I can tell you is that while we were together he carried on like the whole thing was an adventure movie and he was Douglas Fairbanks. He wanted to be a *star*. That's how he was.

Not me. I never even liked having my picture taken. All *I* ever wanted was to show the bastards who own the law that it didn't mean they owned me.

Anyhow, I want it understood that I never competed with John about anything, I never envied him about anything, and that's the truth.

Or rather, it was the truth until recently. Given my present situation, I certainly envy him now.

I envy him the way he died.

I envy Fat Charley and Red for the same reason. I'm most jealous of Russell, naturally, since he's still in one piece and can try another escape—although, sad to say, I doubt he will. But as far as dying goes, I'd trade deaths with John or Charley or Red in a Shytown minute.

Of course none of them would go for the swap. They'd laugh and tell me to go to hell. And I'd laugh along with them and say After you, gentlemen, after you.

Which is pretty much the way it's worked out.

I doubt it will make any difference to those who think they know everything about us just because they know some of the facts, but, between you and me, *this* is how it was. . . .

I

The Joints

It was grand.

Every single time it was grand. I loved the moment when you announce the stickup and everything suddenly goes brighter and
sharper and the world seems to spin faster. You show them the gun
and say hand it over and there's no telling what's going to happen in
the next tick of the clock.

I always expected somebody to say Not on your life, Mac, and go
for his piece, but it never happened—not counting the time I told the
sheriff to hand over John. It never happened with money. They always
handed over the money. That was the easy part. Then you had to get
away. That's when things sometimes became very intense indeed, and
the notion of *present moment* took on meanings you felt in your blood.

I've never understood how somebody could simply hand it over
and leave it at that. If somebody ever stuck a gun in *my* face and said
give me the money, I'd say sure thing—and then the minute the guy
took his eyes off me I'd yank out my piece and pop him. Any man
who doesn't keep a gun handy to protect himself and what's his is a

fool. Deeds and titles and bills of sale be damned, nobody really owns anything in this world except what he can keep others from taking away, and I mean robbers, bankers, judges, or government agents.

Even if I didn't have a gun on me and somebody tried to hold me up, as soon I saw a chance to jump him I'd do it. I'd let him have it with whatever was at hand—a chair, a bottle, a fork. I'd go at him fists, feet, and teeth.

You can't let a guy rob you without putting up a fight. It isn't self-respecting.

• • •

Even before I went to the joint for the first time I'd stolen so many cars I'd lost count. It was a snap. I swiped my first when I was sixteen—a spanking new Model T roadster, a nifty little thing. A pal named Eddie Rehnquist and I went rambling in it all over three counties before it somehow ended up in the Wildcat River. After that first one, whenever I needed a car to get somewhere, I'd pick one out and take it. If I had a date with some special girl I wanted to impress, I'd grab a Packard or a Buick or a Cadillac, something classy, even though fancy cars were easier for the cops to track down.

Like the Packard I was driving when I had my first close call with a stolen car. It was the same shade of smoky yellow as the hair on the honey snugged up beside me and saying she wished her friends could see her now. Then a cop car came up behind us and turned on its flash. I'd snatched the Packard a few hours earlier on the other side of town but had been in too much of a hurry to swap the plates. The girl took a gander at the cops and asked me if we were speeding. I said we are now—and floored the accelerator and we barreled past a stop sign, just barely avoiding a collision. We went tearing through the streets, making lefts and rights that had us leaning one way and then the other. The girl was shrieking and citizens were gawking from the sidewalks. When I didn't see the cops in the mirror any more I slowed down and made a nice easy turn and stayed under the speed limit for a few blocks so we wouldn't attract further notice, then pulled into an alley and stopped. The girl was crying so hard she could hardly breathe. I gave her my handkerchief and a kiss on the ear, then got out and hopped over a fence and made myself scarce. The next day's newspaper carried a report about the chase. The cops had found the Packard a few minutes after I amscrayed, the girl still sitting in it and bawling her eyes out. She ratted me right away, telling them I was Len Richardson, which was the name I'd given her, and that she'd known me for only an hour, which was true. The report included a photograph of her in the backseat of the police car, her face turned directly toward the camera. She didn't seem to be wishing her friends could see her now.

Not that I ever needed a fancy car to get a girl's attention. My looks could always do the trick. My mother said that the minute she laid eyes on my newborn self, on my fair hair and baby blues, she knew I'd never lack for female notice. She was right.

However, every jewel has its flaw, and in the interest of total honesty I have to confess that mine was in my feet. I was born with the second and third toes on each foot grown together. The toe tips were small but distinct and each one had its own nail, but there was only a bare hint of a groove where the toes should have separated from each other. Siamese toes, Red Hamilton would call them. My parents never made much of this abnormality and so neither did I, nobody did—until one summer day in Muncie when I was fifteen and a bunch of us were playing baseball in a park by the river.

I was playing barefoot like always because I could run faster without shoes. And this kid named Sorenson, whom I'd seen around but didn't know very well, suddenly points at my feet and hollers Hey, you guys, look here! Look at the *freak!*

Sorenson was at least a couple of years older than me but he wasn't much bigger. I was always big for my age. He was still point-

ing at me and saying Freak, freak, when I punched him in the face
and put him on his ass. He grabbed a ball bat as he got up and the
other kids all jumped back. I ducked under his first swing but he
caught me on the side of the head with the next one. I staggered and
saw stars but I didn't go down. Instead of hitting me again he stood
there gawking like he couldn't believe I was still standing. That was
all the chance I needed to grab the bat away from him. He tried to
fend with his arm against my swing and the bone cracked like a fence
picket and he let out a hell of a howl. I got him in the ribs with the
next one, then gave him one to the head that laid him out. I was
about to club him again when Eddie Rehnquist said Oh shit, Harry,
you killed him.

Blood was running out of Sorenson's hair. I checked closer and
saw he was still breathing. Then I saw the way the other kids were
looking at me and I was suddenly aware of my own blood hot around
my ears and on my neck. I touched my scalp and the huge lump there
and my hand came away red. I was enraged but still thinking clearly
enough to know that another knock to the head would probably do
him in and I'd be looking at a murder rap. Still, it didn't feel finished.
So I took out my dick and pissed on him—which really made the
other guys whoop. Then I went home. An hour later the cops were at
the front door and I was under arrest.

I'd been in plenty of fights but this was the closest I'd come to
killing anybody, and I was lucky I didn't get sent to the reformatory.
When we went to court, several of the other kids testified that Sorenson had hit me with the bat first, and my mother wept as she told the
room what a good son I was. The judge said he was troubled by some
of the details of the case but decided that a clean-cut boy like me was
worthy of another chance.

Mom hadn't known all the details until they came out in the
courtroom, and on our way home she said, Land's sake, Harry, you actually . . . *voided* on that fellow? What will people *think?*

Shortly afterward we moved away to Indianapolis. As for Sorenson, I heard that when he got out of the hospital he had a permanent walleye and walked kind of funny.

Like some kind of freak.

• • •

*I*t was a fancy car that got me sent up my first time, although not for auto theft. I was nineteen years old and hadn't worked at a legit job in almost six months, not since I'd beat the daylights out of a loudmouth foreman at the gravel pit where I was a truck loader. I got thirty days for it but it was worth every minute. Since then, I'd been making my way as a stickup man—or as Fat Charley would call it, an independent fund-raiser. I'd pulled more than a dozen robberies but nothing you could call big. Grocery stores, pharmacies, filling stations, a few greasy spoons. My biggest take was 130 bucks, and most of the others didn't get me half that.

Anyway, what happened was, I needed a car to go see a college girl I'd met at a dance in Bloomington the week before. Annie Macsomething, a creamy brunette with wet dark eyes and a build like a modern-day calendar girl rather than most of the flat-chest flappers of the day. I could tell she was keen on me, which was no surprise, and she didn't object to the liberties I took with her person while we were dancing cheek to cheek in a dark corner of the floor. But she was with friends and had to leave before I could get her out to the car I'd swiped in Indy and bang her in the backseat. She gave me her address and phone number and said to come see her sometime, and I said I'd be up next Saturday. I figured I'd steal a car and pull a stickup on the drive up there so I'd have enough cash to show her a really swell time and book us into the best hotel in town.

Come Saturday morning I went out looking for a car that struck my fancy and I spotted a shiny new Buick on a side street. I've always had a soft spot for Buicks. I was bent under the hood panel and was clipping my jumper to the coil when I heard somebody say, Hey Jack, what the *hell* you doing to my car?

Before I could run for it the guy had an arm around my neck from behind and was strangling me. He was my size and no slouch and I was sure he was going to kill me if I didn't get free of that chokehold quick. I managed to get my hand on the .32 in my coat pocket and turn it so the muzzle was pressed against his thigh, and *bam*, I let him have it, and he hollered and fell down. I was so wound up I accidentally squeezed off another round through my coat and it glanced off the street and hit him in the same leg and really got him wailing.

As luck would have it, a squad car had come around the corner while we were at it and the two cops inside saw the whole thing. The car screeched up and they jumped out with their guns pointed at me, yelling drop it or else.

So I dropped it—and the gun hit the sidewalk just so and went off again, *bam,* and we all flinched as the bullet glanced off the building and smacked the side of the Buick. It's Christ's own wonder those jumpy cops didn't shoot me then and there.

The guy I shot bled pretty impressively but he wasn't in any real danger of dying, and an ambulance took him away. I was booked on attempted murder, but my mother hired a good lawyer who got the charge reduced to felonious assault.

The lawyer did the best he could to persuade the judge that I was a high-spirited youth who meant no real harm and deserved nothing worse than a period of probation. I was wearing a new suit and was freshly barbered and looked every inch the college boy headed for a career in accounting. My bearing was attentive and respectful, my manner amiable and confident in the wisdom of the court. But the prosecutor had to go and bring up the business about Sorenson and the baseball bat back in Muncie. He insisted I was a violent personality in need of a severe rehabilitation of attitude.

The judge agreed. He gave me two to five in the state reformatory at Jeffersonville.

• • •

There isn't much to tell about J-Ville, as we called it. According to the rules-and-regulations booklet every inmate received on his arrival, the reformatory's purpose was to help young offenders become useful citizens through vocational training and character guidance. In truth, the inmates were little more than slave labor for the private companies that contracted with the state to provide work inside the walls. J-ville had a small factory for making shoes, plus a carpentry shop and a garage for teaching auto mechanics. I'd heard plenty about the reformatory from guys who'd been there, so I had some idea of what to expect. Still, it took some getting used to, the constant whine of machinery and electrical saws and steam whistles, the smells of sawdust and exhaust smoke and disinfectants.

I'd only been there about two weeks when I got jumped. One minute the shower room was full of naked guys and the next there was nobody there but me and the three hardcases who came at me. Their intention, as one of them so explicitly put it, was to break the cherry in this pretty boy's ass. They must've fixed it with the guards, because the fight lasted a while and we weren't quiet about it, but not a hack showed his face until I got a grip on one guy's balls and twisted as hard as I could and he screamed like he was on fire. That's when the hacks came running and found him folded up on the floor and bawling like a baby. One of his pals was down too—I'd rammed his head against the wall and he was out cold. The third guy took off before the hacks showed up.

I had a broken nose and what felt like cracked ribs and a shiner that almost closed my eye, but I'd retained my rectal virtue. None of us finked and the superintendent gave us each three days in solitary confinement, although the other two couldn't serve their punishment till they got out of the infirmary.

The solitary cells were in the guardhouse basement under the mat room. The mat room was large and windowless but brightly lit and didn't have any furnishings except for a few chairs for the guards and a dozen straw mats arranged in a wide circle in the center of the room, each mat two feet square. Commit a minor infraction and you were brought in here and made to stand on a mat for six hours in your underwear and with your hands cuffed behind you. Step off the mat without permission and you got a beating and a stretch in solitary. But the two fastest ways into the hole were by fighting or trying to escape.

The hole cells were along the rear wall of the basement, which was always chilly and smelled of piss and shit. Of the guys I'd known who'd been in J-ville, only one had done time in solitary, and he said it was no big deal. He was right. They made you strip naked but they gave you a small blanket, and the cell was big enough to stretch out in. The door had a small window that admitted some of the hallway's light, and there was a big can of drinking water, and at noon you got a plate of beans. That was a reformatory's idea of harsh punishment—making you sleep on the floor and piss in a can, eat beans and be alone. It was nothing like the holes I'd heard about from guys who'd been in real joints like Joliet or Michigan City. I could've done a month in J-ville's hole standing on my head.

When I was let back into general population I had a lot of new friends. The three guys who'd ganged on me had been regarded as the toughest mugs in the place and they'd been lording it over most of the other inmates, who were glad to hear I'd settled their hash. Guys came around to introduce themselves and ask if I needed anything.

One of the older fellows said he could set my busted nose, so I said go ahead. He positioned his thumbs on either side of my nose and told me to brace myself. It took him three tries to get it right and I couldn't keep the tears from running down my face, but he did a good job. There you go, kid, he said, Handsome Harry rides again.

The other guy who'd jumped me in the showers, the one who got away before the hacks showed up, was named Kruger. He'd been the leader and the one to make the crack about busting my cherry. I hadn't been able to give him anything worse than a shiner and some loose teeth. Now he was being careful to keep his distance from me, and he kept a pair of goons at his side for protection. I affected indifference to him for more than a month before he started to lower his guard. Then one morning in the mess hall I made my move.

At my signal, a handful of guys started a sham fight in the food line to draw the hacks over there and get everybody's attention. Some other guys closed up around the two goons, blocking them off from Kruger, who was at the far edge of the crowd and up on tiptoes trying to get a look at the fight. I came up fast behind him and gave him a roundhouse to the kidney with all my might. He made a sound like he'd been stabbed and I was walking away as he fell. By the time they broke up the crowd and saw Kruger curled up on the floor I was already out in the yard.

They took him to the hospital but there were complications and in another two days he was dead. Internal hemorrhaging, they said. Because the brass had no idea who'd done it or even how, they wrote it up as a factory accident in order to cover themselves.

I'd heard that a kidney punch could be lethal but I'd had my doubts. I'd figured I would hurt him plenty but hadn't expected to kill him. Still, I can't say I was sorry when I got the word. I've never been given to casual use of vulgar language—unwarranted profanity implies mental laziness—but there's no other way to say this: A guy tries to fuck me . . . well, fuck him.

A few inmates had seen the whole thing, and the story got around J-ville fast, but nobody ever ratted me. Just like that, I was one of the top hardcases in the joint. Now even more guys were eager to get on my good side, including the two apes who'd been with Kruger.

The trouble with a hardcase reputation, of course, is having to hold it against all comers. The toughest of them was a guy named Joe Pantano, a big curly-haired Wop out of Jersey. The day we slugged it out in the laundry even the hacks were laying down bets. The smart money was on me and it paid off. I broke Pantano's nose, then put him down and cooled him with a kick that raised a knot big as a

plum behind his ear. We both got a week in solitary, but I was now
the top dog in the reformatory and everybody knew it. Only the occasional true fool ever took me on the rest of the time I was there.

My first job in J-ville was in the garage. I didn't mind it too
much since I'd always liked cars. But after a few months they transferred me to the shoe shop, where I was taught to operate a machine
that attached the sole to the rest of the shoe. I stitched soles all day
long. It was stupefying, mindless labor that could drive you insane if
you didn't have something to think about while you were at it. And
what I thought about, month after month, was busting out. But my
mother and the lawyer had never quit trying to get me released, and
near the end of my second year behind bars, just as I was putting the
finishing touches on an escape plan, they came through and I was
paroled.

• • •

I returned to Indianapolis and went to work at a garage job my
parole officer arranged for me. I did oil changes and lubes, in-
stalled batteries and fixed flats, now and then tuned a motor.
I still loved cars—the look and sound of them, the feel of driving
them—but I'd come to hate working on them. I hated being smeared
with grease and skinning my knuckles and breathing gasoline fumes
all day. I hated being within earshot of the morons I worked with. At
the end of the day I'd wash my hands so vigorously with detergent
soap that they'd burn and turn red, and I'd *still* smell oil and gas on
them, still feel like there was grease under my fingernails even when
they were spotless. The only difference between this joint and Jeffersonville was that I could go home at the end of my shift. I had sworn
I'd never work for wages again, but I was determined to bite the bullet until I settled on a solid plan. I didn't want to go back to robbing
gasoline stations and grocery stores. That was small-time stuff for
kids and suckers lacking in self-respect.

Banks were the thing. But all I knew about robbing a bank was that only a fool would try it single-handed. What I needed was a partner.

The only partner I'd ever had was Earl Northern. We'd known each other for a couple of years before I went to J-ville, and he'd been with me on half my stickups. He was a husky guy with a badly pitted face, a little older than me, and he'd been in the reformatory twice, doing a year for car theft the first time and then six months for parole violation. He'd been arrested more than once in the time I'd known him, but he'd managed to avoid being convicted again.

I'd received a letter from him while I was in the reformatory, a half-page in uneven script in an envelope with an Urbana, Illinois, postmark and no return address. He said he was sorry to hear of my bad turn of luck and that he'd recently had a close call himself, but of course he didn't give any details, not in a letter he knew would have to get by the censors. He hoped I was doing good and said he would write again soon, but I heard no more from him before I was paroled. When I'd got back to Indianapolis I searched for him high and low but nobody knew where he was. His family had moved from their old neighborhood and left no forwarding address. That wasn't too surprising, since Earl's stepfather was constantly on the lam from creditors. He's a *step*father, all right, Earl once said—always a step ahead of the bill collectors.

With no idea where Earl might be, I'd been on the lookout for another partner. I'd talked to a few guys but none of them struck me as having the right stuff. I'd been working at the garage for almost three months—and knew I wouldn't be able to take it much longer—when one sunny morning a brand-new Franklin roadster pulls up to the pumps and there's Earl behind the wheel.

Fill 'er up, Junior, he said, grinning around a toothpick and adjusting the brim of a fedora that nicely complemented his new blue suit. I'd always been something of a natty dresser myself when I could afford it, but I'd never seen Earl looking so spiffy, and I was impressed.

I smiled back at him and leaned on the car door and said in my best flatfoot voice Pardon me, sir, but I wonder if I might see the registration and title to this vehicle?

Registration? Earl says. *Title?* We snickered like school kids sharing a dirty joke.

He told me he'd been in Illinois for the past ten months. The close call he'd mentioned in the letter happened while he was robbing a filling station in Martinsville. He took his eyes off the attendant for a second and the man swung at him with a tire iron and missed his head by a whisker. It scared Earl so bad he shot the guy. He didn't kill him, but he thought it wise to absent himself from Indiana for a time, just in case the fella was able to give the cops a solid description. He'd gone across the state line to lay low for a while but ended up staying longer than he'd planned.

I said I'd bet the longer stay had to do with a girl. It did, he said, but it wasn't what I was thinking.

He'd been faring all right, getting by on small stickups and an occasional break-in, and then one night he met a sweet young thing in a speakeasy in Effingham. She told him she was recently divorced, and they hit it off so well she took him home with her at closing time. Earl couldn't believe his luck. He knew he wasn't the best-looking guy in the world, plus he'd never had a smooth way with the ladies, and things like this didn't happen to him.

He and the sweet thing were in the middle of hitting it off even better when her husband came charging into the room and started doing some hitting of his own. Earl said it was like fighting a jackhammer in the nude. They fairly well tore up the room—breaking the bed frame and busting lamps and bringing down the curtains, everybody punching and kicking and cursing. The neighbors must've thought murder was going on and called the police because the next thing Earl knew the cops were pulling them apart. They slapped the cuffs on hubby and let Earl put his clothes on before cuffing him too. The sweet thing took her time about picking out some underwear to put on but the cops didn't mind at all. She had a knockout body, Earl said, and not a modest bone in it, and she tried on two different outfits before deciding to go with the first. It was a swell show and everybody enjoyed it except for hubby, who called her a cheap-ass whore and got smacked by a cop who told him it was no way to talk to a lady. Then they all got hauled to the station.

It turned out that hubby worked the night shift at a cement plant and got a call from a buddy who'd seen his wife leaving the speak with some stranger. Sweet thing was irked with hubby because of his recent misconduct with an office girl at the cement plant and was getting back at him by way of Earl. There was a lot of finger-shaking and loud assertion of having each other's number and singing different tunes and what's good for the goose and so forth, till the cops got tired of it and let them go with a warning not to disturb the peace again. Earl, on the other hand, wasn't going anywhere except in front of a judge, not after the cops checked out his car and discovered it had been stolen on the other side of town earlier that day.

The judge seemed sympathetic on hearing the details of his arrest and even remarked on the treachery of unfaithful wives and the misery they caused. His honor's bitter tone made Earl suspect the man was speaking from personal experience. He asked if Earl had damaged the stolen vehicle in any way, and Earl swore that he had not, that he had cared for the car as if it were his own. Rather than send him to the penitentiary—which is what Earl expected, considering the state's introduction of his previous conviction for car theft in Indiana—Judge Nicefellow fined him a hundred dollars, then reduced it to forty-two because that's all Earl had to his name, and gave him six months on the county work farm.

I said he'd been lucky to get such a light sentence on a second car theft conviction. Earl said if he was lucky he never would've run into that no-good Effingham bitch.

Anyhow, that's where he'd been, on an Illinois work farm, slopping hogs and shoveling pig shit until about three weeks ago, when he was released a few weeks early for good behavior. They took him to the bus station and bought him a ticket to Terre Haute just over the state line and told him Bon Voyage, grifter, and don't come back.

Earl figured the filling station shooting in Martinsville was ancient history by then and it was safe to come home, so as soon as he got off the bus in Terre Haute he scouted around for suitable transportation and settled on the Franklin roadster. He was ten miles down the road before it occurred to him that he didn't have a red cent. The Franklin was already low on fuel and he supposed he'd have to steal a car with a lot more gas in it. Then he thought to take a look in the door pocket and, oh baby, there's a wallet, and it's holding 132 bucks. He stopped off in Greencastle and bought himself the spiffy suit and fedora and treated himself to a steak with all the trimmings before swapping license plates with a car parked in an alley. Then he went to Kokomo to visit a certain cathouse he'd heard a lot of good things about, and the place had lived up to its reputation. Since getting back to Indy he'd been working at a lumberyard, but he hadn't gone by to see my parents and say hello till this morning. Mom gave him the news of my parole and the job at the garage.

He was in the middle of telling me more about the Kokomo cathouse when my boss, Larkins, stuck his head out the office door and hollered for me to quit flogging the dog and get back to work.

I went over to the office and told Larkins I was quitting and wanted the pay I had coming. He said I was making a big mistake and would be sorry, but he counted out eleven dollars and handed it to me. He said Mr. Hollis wasn't going to like this. Hollis was my parole officer. I said to give Hollis my regards, then went back to the roadster and got in and said Let's go.

● ● ●

I accepted Earl's offer to let me move in with him, but before going to his place we stopped at my parents' house so I could get my clothes, and Mom insisted on fixing us lunch. She didn't blame me for breaking parole. She didn't think it was fair that somebody of my intelligence and charm should have to work in a dirty garage under threat of getting sent back to the reformatory. My mother's name is Lena. She's bright and well spoken and doesn't take guff from anybody, and it's safe to say she has ever and always been devoutly partisan in disputes involving her Harry.

My father sat at the table and ate with us and as usual didn't say much. He's a man of intelligence and a good egg, but by his own admission he'd never been in a fight, not even as a kid, and he's always been content to let Mom wear the pants. In all his life he's probably never said anything more often than Yes dear. His name's Gilbert. I have a brother too, Fred. Unlike my mother, who nobody could've stopped from taking up the spear for me, neither my dad nor my brother got mixed up in any of my misdeeds—I want that understood—and I'll leave both of them out of this as much as I can.

I was packing a suitcase in the back room when Hollis pulled into the driveway. I knew Larkins would call him about me quitting and I figured he might show up soon, which was why I'd had Earl park the Franklin out of sight around the corner.

My mother greeted Hollis at the front door but didn't invite him in. Earl and I stood out of sight in the hallway and listened as he told her I'd walked off the job and he'd see to it my parole was revoked quicker than she could say King James if I didn't present myself at his office to talk things over no later than noon tomorrow.

She affected vast motherly alarm at the news and told him that the minute I showed up or got in touch by telephone she would insist that I go see him immediately. She stood out on the porch till he drove out of sight, then came back in and said, Good Heavens, what a sorry specimen of a man. She gave me a kiss and admonished me to be careful.

Earl knew he'd been holding on to the stolen roadster for too long already, but it was a sweet car and he hated to part with it. Still, Larkins had seen it and for sure given its description to Hollis, and the Franklin would be hotter than ever. So we went to a certain repair garage not too far outside of Indy, a place run by an ex-con named Elmore Brown who accepted fine-quality cars of unspecified ownership in exchange for a car of less worth but with a legal title. We arrived at Earl's place in a well-used Maxwell coupe.

He lived in an industrial neighborhood, in a garage apartment behind the house of an old Swedish couple named Carlson. His mother lived in an apartment house a few blocks away. He had so many brothers and sisters even he had lost the exact count, but the only ones still living with his mom were a pair of teenage sisters, Mary and Margo. His stepfather, a guy named Burke, was doing a stretch in the county slam for some kind of fraud, and Earl's mother had been forced to take a job in a tire factory. His sisters worked too, when they weren't in school. Mary did housecleaning and laundry for the elderly Carlson couple, and Margo, who was three or four years younger, earned a few bucks a week at babysitting jobs.

Earl's apartment was small but clean. It was equipped with a stove and an icebox and it had a bath with shower and hot water. Earl had the tiny bedroom, but the sofa was comfortably firm and large enough for me. It stood under a big window flanked by a maple tree that gave good shade against the afternoon sun.

There was some bootleg beer in the icebox and we opened a quart bottle to toast our reunion. And to our new career as bank robbers.

We'd talked it over in the car. When I told him I was through with nickel-and-dime stickups and wanted to hit a bank, he said Oh man, Harry, I don't know. He thought it was a hell of a risky step up the ladder. Filling stations didn't have armed guards or robbery alarms. They didn't have teller cages or vaults or a whole bunch of witnesses standing around. The way he saw it, banks were strictly for guys who knew what they were doing, guys with experience at it.

I said the only way to get experience at something was to do it.

We batted it back and forth a while, but my mind was made up. Listen, I said, which is it—in or out? If he'd said out, I would've had him drop me off at a hotel and figured my next move from there. But he said Ah hell, man, of course I'm in.

We talked late into the night and came up with a basic plan. The Indytown banks were out of the question. They were sure to have the most money, but they were also the best guarded and would be the hardest to make a getaway from. And common sense told us it wouldn't be smart to rob a bank in the same town you lived in. We spread open a road map and picked out a dozen towns inside a forty-five-to-seventy-five-mile radius of Indianapolis. During the next few weeks, while Earl was working at the lumberyard to earn the rent and keep us fed, I'd go visit all twelve towns and make a note of every bank that didn't have a guard and was well situated for a getaway. When I finished making the list, we'd decide which bank to hit. As for weapons, Earl had a four-inch .38 and he said he could get me one for a good price from the same source.

And so we were settled on a course of action. Earl fetched us a nightcap beer from the icebox and clinked his bottle to mine and said Big time, here we come.

• • •

On my second morning in the apartment I woke to Earl's muffled snoring behind the bedroom door and an excited shrilling of birds. The room was full of sunlight and the heat of the summer day was already building. I flung the sheet off me and stretched, feeling grand. My usual morning stiffie was poking out of my undershorts and I was casually fingering it when I turned toward the window and saw a young red-haired girl perched on a maple branch and grinning at me. I snatched up the sheet but she was already shinning down the tree, laughing her head off.

I recognized her as Earl's sister Mary. I remembered her as a short skinny kid with plum-red hair who used to come to the front door and wave to me whenever I'd pull up to their house and honk the klaxon for Earl. He'd recently mentioned that he still called her

Shorty because she wasn't five feet tall and it looked like she never would be.

I didn't see her again until the following week, on a hot Saturday afternoon at a riverside park swimming hole. There were ropes attached to tree branches overhanging the river and kids would swing out on them and drop into the water. The air was full of their shrieks and laughter and the aroma of meat roasting on open grills. Earl was trying to make time with some girls sitting in the shade of a tree and pretending to be experienced cigarette smokers, but none of them was pretty enough to hold my attention. I was lying shirtless and sweaty on the grass at the edge of the river and staring up at the clouds when a squirt of water hit me in the chest. I flinched at its coldness and sat up fast. And there she was, a few feet from the bank and treading water as easily as a duck, wearing a white bathing cap and laughing at me. She had a scattering of freckles across her nose and upper cheeks.

Daydreaming again, huh? she said. Better not do out here what you were doing the other day or you'll get arrested. She waggled her brow and grinned.

I felt my ears go hot and I said they should've named her Tom instead of Mary.

Why's that, she said. Because I'm a tomboy?

Because she was a Peeping Tom.

She said she was no such thing, all she was doing was climbing a tree to get some exercise. How was she supposed to know I'd be lying there playing with that big ugly thing?

What would she know about men's *things,* I said, she was just a child. I didn't care for her calling it ugly but I was secretly pleased she called it big.

She said she was certainly not a child and she knew plenty and I ought to keep the shade pulled down if I was going to engage in self-abuse. That's the phrase she used, self-abuse, and it made me laugh.

I said she had a pretty smart mouth for a kid and asked how old she was, anyway—fifteen?

She said she was sixteen and way too smart for me—then gulped up another mouthful of water and spouted it at me, catching me on the ear.

I scrambled to my feet and was going to jump in and give her a good dunking, but before I could kick off my shoes she shot away with a few strong strokes and then surged up onto the bank about ten yards downstream, coming out of the water in a silvery rush, the thin blue swimsuit pasted to her nipples and lean belly and small round bottom shaped like an overturned heart. She snatched up her towel and gave me another wag of her eyebrows and ran off, brown legs flashing. She sprinted past Earl and the tootsies and disappeared where the lane to the bathhouse curved around through the trees. And took a good bit of my breath with her.

The next time I saw her was a few days later when she came over to clean the old couple's house. She came speeding down the driveway on her bicycle and slid neatly off the seat and let the bike go crashing into the backyard fence. She was wearing her hair chippy-fashion, long and loose to her shoulders. As she started up the steps to the Carlson kitchen she saw me at the apartment window and smiled. When I smiled back she stuck her tongue out at me, then laughed and went inside.

Over the next few weeks I saw her only on those days when I happened to be home and she came to tidy the Carlsons' place or do their wash. On laundry days she wore shorts cut so high they would've had my mother shaking her head and remarking on the shamelessness of young girls today. When she hung the clothes on the outdoor line, she'd work with her back to the garage, and each time she bent to get another piece of laundry from the basket the shorts rode up high and snug on that perfect little bottom and I'd feel my dick take a deep breath. She always knew I was watching—I knew she did because she'd never even glance toward my window. On the days when she did housecleaning she'd wear one of Earl's old shirts that was so big on her the tails reached almost to her knees and I had to wonder if she was wearing shorts underneath or just her underpants. She'd always leave the top buttons of the shirt undone, and whenever I'd hear the screen door screech open I'd go to the window and watch as she leaned over the porch rail and shook out the dust mop. The shirt would bag wide open and even at that distance I'd catch glimpses of her small round tits. As she damn well knew I would.

She was sixteen going on thirty is what she was.

One laundry day she didn't show up. When I casually remarked on it to Earl that evening he said she had quit school and taken a full-time job as a waitress in a café.

* * *

My list had seven banks on it. We discussed the pros and cons of all of them and narrowed the possibilities down one by one and ended up choosing the Mid-State Bank in Marion. It seemed to be doing good business and stood right at the edge of town for an easy getaway. The road out of town went winding through woods and came to intersecting highways not more than two miles beyond the city limits. If anybody came after us and didn't have us in sight before we hit the intersecting roads, they wouldn't know for sure which way we'd gone. On top of that, the police force didn't look like much, and its cars were Model Ts. Whatever car we stole for the job would outrun them easily if they came after us.

Earl gave his boss at the lumberyard a song and dance about having to appear in traffic court in Anderson on the Friday we were going to pull the heist. On the morning of the big day, I swiped a Lincoln from the south side of town. Earl followed me in his car to Anderson, where we left the Maxwell parked near the edge of town.

We got to Marion a few minutes before noon. It was sunny and windless and chilly enough so that people's breath showed like thin smoke. There was a scattering of cars parked at an angle, nose to the curb in front of the bank, and we found a spot close to the building. There wasn't a cop car in sight. We'd picked the noon hour for the job because most people, including the cops, would be having dinner, and street traffic would be at its lightest.

We wore dark glasses and pulled our hat brims low. Even if they saw our faces, nobody in that town knew who we were. All they could do was describe us, and most descriptions fit so many people they're fairly useless. We checked our pieces and slipped them back into our waistbands, then grinned at each other and I said Let's do it.

We went in and pulled our guns and Earl took a position next to the door. In a voice as commanding as if he'd done this a dozen times before, he shouted All right, people, this is a stickup! Stand fast!

He was tickled pink later when I said he'd sounded so scary I almost put *my* hands up—just like some of the customers did, although nobody'd told them to do it.

There were only six or seven citizens in the place, all of them staring at us with their mouths open, including a woman who was wearing what looked like a pot of flowers on her head and stood at the only open window at the teller's cage. Three guys were waiting in line behind her. They all backed away as I came up and told the woman Pardon me, lady, I'm cutting the line.

She moved aside and I stepped to the window. The teller was a skinny guy wearing horn-rims and a red visor. I took a folded pillowcase from my coat and shook it open and slid it across the counter through the bars and said Put the money in there, pal, and make it snappy.

His eyes rolled up in his head and he keeled over off his stool and hit the floor like a sack of stove coal.

I thought Jesus H. Christ and pulled myself up on the window bars high enough to see him flat on his back in a dead faint with his glasses hanging off one ear.

The only other person inside the cage was a woman at a desk. She was staring at the guy on the floor like he'd done something to offend her.

You, I said, wagging the gun at her, Get over here.

She wore wire-rim specs and her chestnut hair was in a bun at the nape of her neck, but when she stood up I saw she was nicely put together.

Christ sake, woman, *move,* I said.

There's no call for swearing, she said. Her eyes were dark blue. She took up the pillowcase and began putting money in it. She wasn't wearing a wedding ring.

We'd been expecting an alarm but so far it hadn't sounded. A well-barbered fat guy with pink hands and wearing a pinstriped suit sat with a man in faded overalls at a big desk under a wall photo of President Cal. I figured Pinstripes for the boss and probably the guy with the alarm button. Earl had him spotted too and was pointing his revolver at him from ten feet away and Mr. Pinstripes was staring at Earl's gun like a guy in a trance. If he had a button he was too scared to push it.

Miss Blue Eyes took the last of the money from the till and put it in the pillowcase and shoved the bundle to me. *Here,* she said. Now go away.

But I'd seen that the vault behind her was open, and I went to the cage door and said for her to unlock it.

It *is* unlocked, she said. Sarcastic as hell.

Let's get a move on, buddy boy, Earl said.

The teller on the floor had come around and was starting to sit up as I came into the cage. Then he saw me and up rolled his eyes and down he went again.

Miss Blue Eyes shook her head and looked so disgusted I thought she might spit on him.

The vault contained cabinets and lockers of various sizes, steel bookcases, stacks of ledgers. The light in there wasn't very good and I was tempted to take off my sunglasses but didn't. I turned around just as the woman was putting her hands to the vault door and I read her eyes and knew what she was thinking. I pointed a finger at her and said Don't try it.

You won't shoot *me,* she said, which I guess meant because she was a woman. I didn't know if she had nerve or was plain foolish. What did she think Earl would do if she locked me in?

I pointed the .38 at her and cocked it. If you've never heard a revolver cock inside a bank vault, let me assure you that it is a very serious sound. I said Don't bet your life on it, honey. Now get in here.

She took her hands off the door and came in. I wondered what she looked like without the glasses and her hair down and her clothes off. My money would've been on very nice.

I asked where the cash was and she pulled open a drawer filled with packets of greenbacks so new that a smell rose off them like some fresh-baked treat. I laughed and I handed her the bag and said to put it all in.

Let's *go,* brother, Earl called out.

I came out of the cage with the pillowcase wrapped snugly around the money and tucked under my arm like a football. The citizens were all exactly as before, their eyes still on Earl's revolver. The power of the gun—*wooo.*

Earl was as charged up as I was. If I hear an alarm go off, he said loudly, I swear to Jesus I'll run right back in here and shoot all you goddamn Hoosiers. Starting with *you,* fatso!

He wagged his pistol at Mr. Pinstripes, who shook his head and made all sorts of jittery gestures to let us know he wouldn't dream of giving the alarm.

We slipped our pistols under our coats and went out and headed for the car at a quick walk. I whispered Easy does it, easy does it, and Earl whispered back I know, man, I know—and then said What the hell's *this?*

Directly behind the Lincoln, blocking it in, stood an idling Templar coupe. The driver was leaning out his window and gabbing with the driver of a pickup truck facing the other way. A pair of locals chewing the fat in the middle of the street and in no hurry about it because there was no waiting traffic behind either of them.

As we got to the Lincoln, Earl said Hey you! Move it!

The driver of the Templar turned to squint at us through the passenger window. Say now, mister, he said, you could try asking a little more polite.

I slid behind the wheel and cranked up the motor as Earl took out his piece and pointed it at him and said How's *this* for polite, you stupid hick! Now *move it!*

Their eyes got *this* big and the other driver hunched down behind the wheel and his truck went rumbling off. But the guy in the Templar was so rattled the car bucked hard and stalled.

Oh God, mister, the guy shouts, don't shoot! And puts his hands up.

I said *move* that fucken thing! Earl yells. But the guy's too scared to do anything except put his hands higher and beg Don't shoot me, *please* don't shoot!

Watch out, I said to Earl. I yanked the gearshift into reverse and gunned the Lincoln backward and—*pow!*—I sent the little coupe screeching sideways farther into the street, its windshield falling apart and the driver's hat flying off. But it was still partially blocking us in, so I pulled forward again, put it into reverse once more, and *pow!*—I rammed the Templar even harder, spinning it halfway around and out of our way. The little car's side was demolished and the driver wasn't in sight.

Earl hopped in as I wheeled the Lincoln around. People were flocking out to the sidewalks to see what all the crashing was about. I stomped on the gas pedal and we tore off down the street as the bank alarm started sounding.

Why, that fat sorry bastard, Earl said, glaring back toward the bank. Then we flew past the city limit sign without any cars behind us and we were both laughing like hell.

We weren't laughing two hours later when we were back in the apartment and found out the money was mostly small bills. The take came to $2,285—more than either of us had ever had our hands on, to be sure, but there was no denying Miss Blue Eyes had pulled a fast one on us. We read all about it in the next day's paper. Her name was Helen Something-or-other and the report hailed her as a fast-thinking heroine who had outfoxed the robbers by foisting the small bills on us and saving the rest of the cash in the vault. More than four thousand bucks.

Earl was so furious he wanted to go back to Marion and fix her wagon. For days afterward he muttered about that no-good crooked bitch. Not me. I admired her pluck—not to mention those sexy eyes and sweet curves. Ten to one she ended up marrying some banker and they bought a nice house and had a bunch of kids and she lost her figure and every day of her life is the same as every other day and will be until she's too old for it to make any difference anymore. But I'll bet you anything that every now and then she remembers staring down the barrel of my pistol and how her breath went deeper than it ever did in her life and how her blood sped up and she had absolutely no idea what would happen next.

* * *

I bought a four-year-old Buick in good condition and went to the best haberdashery in town and got myself a new wardrobe, including three custom-tailored suits and a pair of Italian shoes. And then one evening I drove over to the Copper Kettle Café where Mary was waiting tables.

I hadn't seen her since she'd quit her job with the old couple. She was busy taking an order and didn't notice me when I came in and took a booth at the rear of the room. I held a menu so she couldn't see my face until she came to the booth and said, What's yours, mister?

I lowered the menu and smiled big. How's the caviar in this place, I said.

Well now, she said, look at *you*.

I said I happened to be in the neighborhood and thought I'd drop

in for a bite before taking in a movie. She asked what I was going to
see and I said there was a Chaplin playing a few blocks away. Say, I
said—as if the idea had just come to me—would she like to go to the
flicker with me when she got off work?

She gave me a strange look, then said no, which I never expected.
And which surprised me with how much it irked. Then she smiled
and for a second I thought she'd seen the disappointment on my face,
but she said what she'd really like to do was go to the carnival over at
the river fairgrounds. She guessed I wasn't really dressed for a carnival, though, in my nice suit and all.

I told her my clothes were no problem. What time did she get off
work. I said I'd already asked Earl if he minded if I took her out and
he said no.

She said it was a good thing Earl didn't mind, because even
though he was her big brother and she liked him a lot he wasn't her
keeper and did not tell her what she could and could not do. She gave
me that funny look again and said How old are *you*, anyway? You
never said.

Twenty-one, I said—that too risky for you?

She laughed and said Oh brother, you really think I'm a sap for a
dare?

Actually, I said, Earl told me your momma might not like the
idea of you going out with an older guy.

Actually, she said, she wouldn't.

I said it seemed to me that anybody who worked at a grown-up
job and was helping to support her family like she was doing was en-
titled to make her own decisions.

She said men were always encouraging girls to make their own
decisions as long as the decision might involve taking off clothes.

Nice talk, I said. What kind of a guy you take me for?

She waggled her brow and said she wasn't sure. Then said there
was no need to worry about her mother because she was working
nights at the tire factory and didn't have to know about me. As for

her little sister Margo, the girl was devoted to her and knew how to
keep her mouth shut.

And so, when she got off work an hour later, we went to the carnival.

I hadn't realized how short she was until we were walking out to
the car—the top of her head didn't reach my shoulder. It was a cool
clear night, perfect for being outdoors. She was crazy for the rides, the
wilder the better. She claimed she'd been on scarier roller coasters
than this one, but she was pleased with the Whip, which had arms
that bobbed up and down even as they swung round and round and
the seats at the end of them spun constantly. Her favorite was the
Bullet, which looked like two rocket ships, one at either end of a long
whirling arm that first wheeled in one direction and then in the
other, while the rocket you were belted into spun like a top. The first
time we went on the Bullet all the change fell out of my pockets and
went pinging all over the rocket. It was all I could do to keep from
heaving up my supper, but she loved every minute of it, ya-hooing
and laughing and clutching tight to my arm. Her stomach was a bot-
tomless cast-iron wonder. I didn't see how somebody so small could
eat so much. She put away a spool of cotton candy and a bag of popcorn, a foot-long hot dog with the works, a candied apple as big as a
softball—and never showed a sign of queasiness, not even after our
third ride on the Bullet. I was feeling green around the gills by then
and close to losing my supper. She must've noticed and taken pity on
me because when I asked if she wanted to go on the Bullet again she
said no, she'd had enough of whirling upside down. I was silently
thankful when she suggested the Ferris wheel. We gently rode it
round and round, rising high above the blaze of fairway lights and
seeing way off into the shadowy countryside under the pale bright
moon. I held her close and she snuggled against me and we were at
the very top of the turn when the wheel made its first stop to begin
letting off passengers. She said This is really nice, and put her hand
to my face and kissed me. In a minute we got our tongues into it.

When I put my hand on her breast she put her hand over mine and held it there. She wasn't wearing a brassiere and I felt her nipple stiffen under my thumb. I figured I had a sure thing and couldn't wait for us to get back to the car.

The Buick was parked at the edge of the lot, in the shadows of the trees. As soon as we were inside it I drew her to me and kissed her again. She helped me unbutton her blouse. There was enough light from the fairgrounds for me to see the freckles on her breasts like a sprinkling of cinnamon. I put my mouth to her nipple and she made a sound like a cat purr. She didn't object when I ran my hand under her skirt and stroked her legs and bottom. But when I tried to lay her down on the seat she pushed me away and said Whoa there, mister.

She said she was a virgin and intended to stay that way until her wedding night. I said she could've fooled me. She said she wasn't trying to fool anybody but she meant what she said about waiting.

Well hell, I said.

She snugged up to me again and kissed me and put my hand inside her blouse. Don't you like what we're doing, she said. Don't you think it's fun?

Sure, I said, it's just . . . well. . . .

Oh, she said. She slid her hand up my thigh and closed it around the erection bulging in my pants. My breath hissed through my teeth. I could see her grinning in the dim light.

She unbuttoned my fly. Goodness, she said, and stroked me gently.

Then she bent and took me in her mouth. I was stunned breathless. I felt it building fast and tried to pull away, but she moaned and held me with both hands and I shot off. She attended to me a while longer, then sat up and kissed me.

I've done a fella with my hand, she said, but not this. This was my very first time, I want you to know.

I said it was truly grand and thank you very much—and we both laughed.

That's how it went every time we got together. Sometimes we went to the movies, sometimes we went dancing—her arms up high around my neck, her head against my chest. From across the room, we probably looked like a daddy dancing with his daughter, but after our first few turns I quit being self-conscious about it, and I don't think she ever was. Whatever we'd do for fun on our dates, we always ended the evening with our clothes off, either in the car or, if we knew Earl wouldn't be back for a while, in the apartment. She'd let me do anything except put it in. She liked me to rub it on her breasts, on her bare ass, she loved squeezing it between her thighs. We were on my sofa the first time I used my tongue on her and she was so loud I was afraid the old couple would call the police.

Somewhere along in there she said she loved me, and I guess I said it back, since saying so is a good way to keep a girl in the right mood. But she was serious about not doing the full deed until she got married, and marriage was a subject I preferred to avoid. And so, whenever I got worked up to the boiling point, she'd always finish me with her mouth.

It was swell, of course, and I had no complaints. But as marvelous as these intimate attentions were, they weren't always enough. Sometimes a man has to get laid full and proper.

For that particular pleasure I had Sandra Deloro.

We'd met in a movie house one evening. She came up beside me at the concession stand and remarked in a lovely Southern accent that it was a shame everything on the shelves was so bad for a person's teeth. She was lean and remarkably tall for a girl, only a few inches shorter than me, with a black pageboy and eyes as pale green as a Tom Collins. Her clothes were expensive but the only jewelry she wore was a little gold crucifix on a fine necklace. I figured she was slumming. She said she loved adventure movies like the one showing that night, *The Thief of Baghdad*. She was alone, so I asked if she'd like to sit with me and she said sure. Fifteen minutes after the houselights darkened we were kissing and I had a hand under her dress. Her perfume was some exotic thing that might've come from jungle flowers. Half an hour into the movie we left for her apartment.

It was large and extravagantly furnished and there was a framed picture on her dresser of an earnest-looking young guy in an army uniform, but she didn't tell me his name and I didn't ask. She might never have asked mine if I hadn't volunteered it. She had smooth honey-colored skin and she was strong and went at sex like it was a wrestling match.

Beyond her name she told me nothing about herself except that she wasn't married, she didn't have to work for a living, and she spent most of her time in Indianapolis even though she owned a country estate on the Ohio River, just this side of Louisville. She'd inherited the place a year ago when her parents were killed in a car crash. She said we should spend a few days in it sometime and I said all right. We'd been together several times since then, and for the most part we hardly talked. It was a fine arrangement.

* * *

By early spring the weather was still gray and chilly, the trees still mostly bare, and I was nearly broke. Earl and I were already thinking about which bank on the list to hit next when Pearl Elliott offered us a job too good to pass up.

Pearl owned a Kokomo poolroom called the Side Pocket. She ran a speakeasy in the basement but her real money came from the cathouse on the second floor, the one Earl had raved to me about. He had been patronizing the place for the past couple of months, and he and Pearl had become pretty chummy. As I would come to find out, she had an adventurous nature and a history of shady dealings beyond her speakeasy and whores. She also had a reputation for being trustworthy and knowing how to keep her mouth shut. Bootleggers and other felonious types often used her as a money-holder and a go-between. A few years earlier, in East Chicago, Indiana, where she had her first house, she'd taken a fall for receiving stolen property. She would've pulled a suspended sentence if she'd named the people she was fencing for but she dummied up and the judge gave her eighteen months. By the time she got out she'd lost the house, but the guys she'd stood up for told her they knew of a robbery team looking for a woman driver and asked if she was interested. The stickup guys were glad to have her—she was good at the wheel and a woman driver made for a better cover. As soon as she had enough money she opened another house, this one in Kokomo, where things weren't quite as intense as in East Shy. But she still kept her hand in an assortment of other enterprises. Which is how she came to offer us the job.

Earl drove me up to meet her one night, saying she had a proposition, but he wanted me to hear it from her personally. We were about to enter the place through an alleyway door when it abruptly swung open and in the sudden cast of light a guy got the bum's rush past us and went sprawling on the pavement. Somebody handed the bouncer a hat and he sailed it at the evicted guy and said Don't come back. The guy struggled to his feet and said he'd been thrown out of better places. The bouncer laughed and said Shit, you've never even been allowed *in* better places. Then he saw us and said Hey, Earl, how goes it?

Pearl met us at the bar and Earl made the introductions. He had told me she was about forty years old, and she looked it to me, with lines around her neck and crow's-feet at her eyes. But she was nicely groomed and had fine strawberry-blond hair, and although she was a little hefty for my taste, she had some nice curves on her. She gave me a bold once-over and said Goodness, aren't you a cutie, then took us into her private office.

She poured us a drink and explained the situation to me. An acquaintance of hers—Let's call him Moe, she said—had learned that a certain bank in town would on a certain day be holding ten thousand dollars of payroll money for several local factories. Moe had found himself a partner and they had then recruited her to be their driver for 20 percent of the take. But then two days ago—only four days before the job—Moe got in a fight in a west side speakeasy and was hauled off to jail where they found out he was a parole violator and wanted for questioning in a St. Louis jewel heist. That was it for Moe.

The partner—whom she called Ted—had only lately been paroled from a prison back East. He had never worked in the Mid-west, and he didn't know anybody he could call on to replace Moe. He was desperate not to let this fat job slip away, so he asked Pearl if she knew somebody who might want in. She knew several somebod-ies, but they were all seasoned pros and nobody she talked to would take the job on such short notice for less than 50 percent, a cut that was out of the question, since Ted was set on 40 for himself and she was in for 20, no matter what. Then she thought of Earl. Without having gotten too specific, Earl had told her that he and a partner had recently hit their first bank and were looking to do more of them. So she'd offered him the job, but he'd said he wouldn't do it unless his partner was in on it too.

If Earl and I would settle for a 40 percent cut to split between us, she said, we were in. We could meet Ted in the morning and he'd give us the lowdown and we'd do the job the next day. Did we have a deal?

I looked at Earl and he gave me a wink. Sure, I said.

Next morning we all met for coffee at a downtown diner. We sat across the table from Pearl and Ted in a back booth and she intro-duced us as Harry and Earl and said she thought it would be smart if we kept our acquaintance to first names only. That was fine all around—the less a guy knew about you, the less he could tell the cops if he got collared. I didn't mention it but it crossed my mind that only Pearl knew who everybody was.

Ted was a beefy guy with a nervous tic in one eye and a habit of sucking his lips like he was trying to get rid of a bad taste. He had yardbird written all over him.

It was a simple enough plan. We'd rent three cabins for two nights at the Happy Trails Motor Camp about ten miles outside of

Kokomo. We'd leave Earl's Maxwell and Ted's Chrysler there in the morning and come into town in Pearl's Model T, which looked exactly like every other black Ford sedan in the country but would be carrying license plates off a junkyard car. Another of Pearl's sidelines was the sale of license tags. She got them from a variety of sources in a variety of states, and there was never a shortage of buyers.

We would hit the bank as soon as it opened. Ted described the layout and assigned me to the door and gave Earl the job of disarming the guard and keeping everybody in line while he himself collected the money from the vault. When Ted gave me the high sign, I would go out and signal Pearl to bring up the car and we'd all hop in and get gone. Back at the motor camp we'd divvy the loot and everybody go his own way.

Did we have any questions?

I said it sounded like a solid plan to me, and Earl nodded.

Well then, Pearl said.

It'll go smooth as oil, Ted said.

* * *

And it did—right up to the part where we were all supposed to get gone.

As soon as Ted came out of the vault and gave me the nod, I stepped outside and beckoned Pearl, who had the Ford idling at the end of the street. She was wearing sunglasses like ours and a man's hat with her hair tucked up under it, and she wheeled up in front of the bank, fast and slick. I jumped into the front seat and Earl zipped into the back.

But Ted wasn't behind him.

He was at the bank door, struggling with the guard and some other guy, the guard with an arm around Ted's neck from behind and the other guy trying to get the gun out of his hand. There was yelling and shrieking and the alarm started shrilling and Earl said Oh shit. The sack of money was on the floor by the doorway. The three of them staggered back into the lobby like drunk wrestlers and fell down, still grappling for the gun. I jumped out and ran over and snatched up the money as the pistol went off—*blam*—and people *really* started screaming.

I dove back into the car and yelled *Go!*—and Pearl stomped on the gas and hauled us out of there.

• • •

She was as good behind the wheel as she'd claimed to be. In minutes we were well out of town and rolling along on an isolated farm road that circled back to the highway and the motor camp, no sign of anybody behind us.

I should mention here that Earl and I had already decided we weren't going to stand for a measly 20 percent apiece, not with Ted getting 40. We intended to make our position clear to him when we got back to the cabins to cut up the take. Pearl would get her 20 all right, but the rest of the money would get evenly cut three ways. If he didn't care for the new arrangement, too bad—there was only one of him and two of us. But, seeing how things turned out, there wouldn't even be any argument about it.

As we were heading for the cabins, Earl said maybe God was telling us the split should be between him and me and to total hell with Ted.

Pearl cut her eyes at him in the rearview, then at me, then back to the road.

I'll confess I was sorely tempted. But I said no, if we deserved an equal share, so did Ted.

Earl said he didn't much like it that the sonofabitch had tried to cheat us.

He didn't try to cheat us, I said. He just hadn't been fair with us. There was a difference.

Well hell then, Earl said, did we have to be *fair* to him?

The take was less than we'd expected—$8,900. In appreciation for bringing us in on the heist and doing such a good driving job, we gave Pearl two grand, a little more than she'd bargained for. Then Earl gestured at the rest of the money still on the bed and said Well?

I said we'd be fairer to him than he'd been willing to be to us. I counted out $2,400 for Earl and the same for me, leaving $2,100 for Ted. If he had any complaints, he could sue us. I gave his share to Pearl, who would get word to him that she was holding it. He'd probably need the dough for a lawyer.

It was only midmorning but Pearl got a flask from her bag and we had a drink to celebrate. Earl told her he'd come back to the Side Pocket later in the day to see her. He didn't say it like a buddy but like a guy who was getting ideas. She said she couldn't promise she wouldn't be busy. Earl said he'd take the chance.

While he was outside putting the real plates back on her car, Pearl said it broke her heart when the wrong guy got sweet on her. Then she gave me a kiss on the mouth and said she'd wouldn't be busy if I came to see her.

I said I appreciated the invitation and thought she was aces but she wasn't my type. How do you know till you try me, she said. She kissed me again, this time with plenty of tongue in it, and I have to say the woman knew how to kiss. She smiled and patted my cheek and said the invitation was always open. Then went out and thanked Earl and left.

Earl followed me to Tipton, where we ditched Ted's car. As we rolled on to Indy, he asked if I thought he had much chance with Pearl. He knew she *liked* him, but he had a feeling that was as far as it went. Did I think she might give him a tumble?

I didn't see the need to make him feel bad about it any sooner than he was going to, so I said Sure man, why not?

· · ·

As soon as we got home I gave Sandra a call, and she talked me into going to her river house for a few days. I asked if she could get a friend for Earl and she said certainly, but she

wanted the two of us to enjoy a private supper first, so I should tell
him not to show up till after nine o'clock. Earl was excited about the
whole thing and thought the plan was perfect, since it gave him
enough time to go up and see Pearl first. Maybe he'd get lucky, he
said, and get it from two women in one day. He knew how to dream
once upon a time, Earl did, I'll say that for him.

Sandra and I were leaving right away, but she'd given me the address to give to Earl. I taped it to the icebox and stuck my head in the
bathroom where he was singing in the shower and told him where it
was. Then I was out the door.

The drive was a little more than two hours, and the afternoon
turned gray and chilly. Her house was the nearest thing to a mansion
I'd ever been in—a huge two-story with gables and balconies and
three chimneys. She wasn't sure how many rooms the place had. A
middle-aged couple lived in an efficiency off the kitchen and took
care of the house. The fireplace mantel was lined with dozens of pho-
tographs of distinguished-looking men and women, some of the men
posing in front of factories. The house was on a bluff, and boats and
barges chugged by on the misty river below. You could see downtown
Louisville.

Her bathroom was equipped with a Roman tub. She lit a few
clusters of candles for mood and drew us a hot bubble bath that
smelled of violets. At hand was an ice bucket with a bottle of brandy.
We did it in the bubbles and then dried each other off and did it
again on her bed, which was big enough to take up most of Earl's living room. I napped briefly while she saw to supper, then she woke me
and we went downstairs to a meal of broiled sole, asparagus, and a
bottle of Chablis. She said what she liked best about me were what
she called my dangerous blue eyes and that I didn't ask questions. I
said what I liked best about her was everything.

We were back in bed and about to have another go-round when
we heard loud but indistinct voices downstairs. It wasn't even seven
o'clock yet but I figured Earl might have arrived sooner than planned.

Sandra wasn't happy about it and was practically growling as she put on a robe and went downstairs to investigate. I never saw her again.

I was sitting up in bed and smoking a cigarette when the door crashed open and two gorillas barged in. One pointed a pistol at me and the other stuck a shotgun in my face and said Harry Pierpont, you're under arrest for bank robbery.

* * *

When they told me Ted's true name was Thaddeus Skeers, I laughed out loud, but it proved to be his real moniker, all right. There'd been warrants on him for breaking parole and for two drugstore robberies back East someplace, and there were witnesses in both holdups who could identify him. He was facing the big bitch—a mandatory life sentence on the habitual criminal law for a third felony conviction. The only way he could avoid the bitch was by giving up his partners in the bank job.

The bastard had been plenty willing to finger me and Earl, but he didn't have much to bargain with, since all he could tell them was what we looked like and our first names, and for all he knew they weren't true. For some reason he didn't rat on Pearl. The cops thought she was another guy, and Skeers let them go on thinking it. He said he'd never seen the driver before the day of the job and all he knew about him was he called himself Jackson. The cops were ready to throw the book at him, but Thaddeus had a hole card. He must've been used to things going wrong and had learned to prepare for that eventuality, because he'd taken the precaution of writing down the plate numbers on Earl's car. The cops were floored when the plate turned out to be legit. They went to the address of record for Earl Northern and there he was, all dressed up and about to leave for Kokomo. Five minutes later and they would've missed him. Half an hour earlier and they would've had me there too.

They found the bank money and Earl's guns, then took him to the station and told him to save himself a hard time and give up the other two partners. Earl said he didn't know anything about us, including our names. Like Skeers, he was facing life on the habitual law, but he wouldn't finger me or Pearl, even though they really gave him the business. Then the head cop sent a guy back to Earl's place for another look-around and there was Sandra's river house address on the icebox exactly where I'd left it.

They took me back to Indytown for the night, then drove me to Kokomo the next day and booked me into the Howard County jail. When they took me downstairs to the central lockup, we passed by Skeers in his isolated cell. I pointed my finger at him like a gun and said Your days are numbered, *Thaddeus,* you sorry son of a bitch. He wouldn't even look at me.

Earl was stretched out on a bunk, his face bloated and black-and-blue. His ears looked like clusters of purple grapes. He said he'd been about to take the address off the icebox and put it in his pocket when the cops busted in. I told him he was a backbone guy and I was proud to know him. He said I shouldn't talk too soon, that if they'd given him the business another five minutes he would've caved in.

We'd been in the clink two weeks when Pearl showed up for a visit. She signed in as my sister Gladys and showed a birth certificate to prove that's who she was. She told me she'd arranged for a lawyer for us but it wouldn't do much good, not with Skeers's turning state's evidence. She said Skeers hadn't finked her too because he knew she was friends with Sonny Sheetz, the Indiana mob boss up in East Chicago, and nobody with an ounce of brains wanted trouble with Sonny. I said she didn't have to worry about me and Earl keeping our mouths shut, but it wasn't because we were scared of Sheetz or anybody else. I'd heard of Sonny Sheetz, but to tell the truth I was still ignorant of how much clout he really had. Pearl said she knew Earl and I were backbone guys and she appreciated it and that we could always count on her to help in any way she could.

Earl's jury was moved by the testimony of his mother and his sister Mary and refrained from recommending the habitual criminal sentence. Instead, he got twenty years at the state penitentiary at Michigan City. As for me, the prosecutor insisted that I was a hardened criminal who deserved the state pen no less than my partner. But Mom again came through with a good attorney. He made an eloquent argument that I was a young victim of bad company, that I never would've broken my parole or become involved in a bank robbery if it hadn't been for the nefarious influence of Earl Northern, and that, given a chance at rehabilitation, I would yet prove a lawful and productive citizen.

Let's hope so, the judge said—and packed me off to the new reformatory at Pendleton, saying I could be out in three years if I walked the straight and narrow while I was there.

It took a few hours for it to fully hit me that I was headed back behind bars, and then I was in such a rage I was afraid to open my mouth for fear I'd start howling and never be able to stop.

• • •

The Pendleton superintendent was a bigmouth named Miles. He liked for everybody to call him Boss. He was at the reception building to look me over when I arrived. He made a little speech about having read my Jeffersonville file and how he was convinced the court had made a mistake putting me back in a reformatory when my crime warranted the penitentiary and that I better not think I could get away with any monkey business at Pendleton and blah-blah-blah. When the processing clerk at the desk asked my name—as if he didn't know—I said Millard Fillmore. I refused to sit in front of the mug-shot camera, so Miles ordered the hacks to force me into the chair and hold me there. Each time the guy was ready to take my picture, I shut my eyes or turned my head or stuck out my tongue and he'd have to take another one. After more than a half-dozen tries, Miles said the hell with it and told the clerk to use the best of the lot.

A pair of hacks yanked me up out of the mug chair and one of them said Real hardcock, ain't you?

I said That's exactly what your mother told me, only she was smiling.

I dodged his wild punch and gave him a knee in the nuts and down he went. Then down *I* went as the others laid into me with their canes. Miles wrote me up on the spot and told them to put me in the hole.

As the hacks dragged me out, he said I don't believe you'll be with us for long, Mr. Pierpont.

Me neither, I said, but my mouth wasn't working quite right and he might not have understood me.

. . .

endleton was a larger and more modern version of Jefferson-ville. Like J-ville it had a clothes plant, a bigger one, and its laundry was about twice the size of J-ville's. It had a shop for making furniture and cabinetry, and a foundry for producing all kinds of ironwork. And just as at J-ville, all of it was operated for profit by a bunch of private bloodsuckers using inmate labor.

I was in solitary for two weeks before they assigned me to the fur-niture shop. The other inmates were respectful of me right from the start. Fight the hacks in front of the superintendent on your first day in the joint and nobody fails to understand that you're not afraid of punishment and are not to be trifled with. But there was more to it than that. In any prison, everybody knows everything that's on every-one else's record, and a hell of a lot that's not. By the time I came out of solitary every guy in Pendleton knew why I was there and had heard a lot more.

On my first day in the yard there were whispers all around me everywhere I went.

That's him right there . . . Handsome Harry . . . Robs banks, *man. . . . Shot a man in Indytown . . . Killed a guy in J-ville with his bare hands. . . .*

And so forth.

I won't deny the pleasure I got from all the talk, from the looks I drew. I never would care for public recognition out in the free world, but in the joint all you've got is the reputation you make for yourself and the balls to back it up. In the joint recognition is everything.

The first time I went to the mess hall, I picked out a table by the wall, where three guys were already sitting. I set my tray down and stood there staring at them. One didn't lose any time picking up his tray and moving to another table. The other two looked at each other and then back at me and for a minute I thought they'd make a stand. But then they got up and moved too. It was my table from that day on and everybody knew it.

I'd been out of solitary less than a week when three guys came over at lunchtime one day and asked if they could join me. Two of them, Timmy Ross and Joe Pantano, I knew from J-ville. I'd never seen the other one before. I gave them the okay to sit down.

Ross introduced the third guy as John Dillinger. He pronounced the last syllable of his name the way John himself always did—*grrr*, like a growl, and not *jer*, the way everybody in the country would be saying it one day.

John offered his hand and I shook it. He said he was glad to know me, he'd heard a lot about me and so on. He was dark-haired and short, not much over five and a half feet, but he had a limber way of moving, like a boxer or a dancer—I would come to find out he'd been a good semipro baseball player—and he had a hell of a grip. He was only a year younger than me, but at the time he struck me as hardly more than a kid. There was nothing in particular about him to make you think he'd ever be the stuff of headlines. He was one of the few married guys in the place—I think he'd been married a year or so at the time—and he was dippy as hell for his wife. Beryl, her name was.

It was his first time in stir and he'd gotten a raw deal. Every guy behind bars says the same thing but in John's case it was true. He and some stumblebum a lot older than him had robbed a grocer, and in the course of things John gave the grocer a good whack on the head. It wasn't long before they got pinched and were charged with felonious conspiracy and assault with intent to rob. The prosecutor assured John that if he pled guilty the judge would go easy on him as a first-time offender. So he went to trial without a lawyer and pled guilty—and the judge hammered him with ten to twenty years. His partner hired a lawyer for his own trial and even though he had a record he only got two to fourteen.

That's the Law for you. Its promise isn't worth spit. There's never been a day I haven't heard or seen something about the Law to make me hate it even more than I did the day before.

Anyhow, John worked in the clothes factory, and I heard he could operate a sewing machine like nobody's business. As I came to find out, he was a whiz with anything mechanical. He could listen to a car motor and tell you why it was running rough. Show him some gadget he'd never seen before and in ten minutes he could tell you how it worked. One morning at breakfast this guy came up to our table and handed him a pocket watch, saying he'd won it in a bet but it wasn't running and he wondered if it could be fixed. John put it to his ear and shook it slightly, then fiddled with the stem and said yeah, he could fix it. The guy asked how much he'd charge, and John said Hell, buddy, let's call it a favor. The guy couldn't thank him enough.

That's how he was. Everything you've heard about his charm is true, never mind some of his blowups with Billie. And nobody was a better friend, take it from me. Ask Russell. Charley and Red would've told you the same. Of course, we were a pretty special bunch. His later friendships were obviously another story. I mean, I don't know much more about what happened at that Chicago movie house last July than what I read in the papers and heard through the grapevine, but I know what went wrong. He trusted those two whores is what went wrong. He thought they were his friends.

Then again, I never did understand why he made some of the

friends he did. Like that clown, Homer Van Meter. They got to be pals when we were all at Pendleton and they worked on the shirt line together. Van Meter was a real fumbler, and John was always helping him meet his work quota. From the day we met, that guy and I had it in for each other. It happened one morning when John and I and a few other pals were in the yard exercising with the punching bags and dumbbells and jump ropes. The other inmates were keeping their distance from us, as always, but then this goofy-looking guy with a stupid grin comes ambling over as casually as if he'd been invited. He was at least six feet tall but he was skinny as a cue stick and his smirky manner irritated me the minute I laid eyes on him.

He walked up behind John, who was skipping rope and unaware of him, and stood watching the rope whipping around and then suddenly stamped his foot on it, stopping it short. The rope handles slipped out of John's hands and for a moment he was whirling a rope that wasn't there anymore. He said What the *hell* and spun around, ready to start punching, then saw the goof grinning at him. He said Homer, you asshole, and they both laughed.

John started to introduce him all around, but before he could tell him my name, Van Meter said, Wait, don't tell me, I know who this guy is—he's the famous big-time bank robber. He snapped his fingers a few times like he was trying to recall my name. Then he made a scared face and held his hands up and pretended to be trembling and said, Oh my God, it's Jesse James!

If it had come from somebody else, I might've smiled to be sociable, but not from this creep. John saw my face and said Ah hell, Harry, he's just being funny.

He's funny, all right, I said. Funny looking.

Funny *looking!* Van Meter says, and goes into a big loud show of phony laughter, holding his belly and slapping his thigh, saying Boy, that's a *hot* one, all right! Funny *looking*—whew!

That did it. I pulled off the bag gloves and said Beat it, clown.

And what's that fool do? He makes a face of exaggerated ferocity and starts shuffling around me with his fists up in the old-time way of John L. Sullivan or somebody. Mocking me.

I hooked him good on the jaw but he scrambled right back up and came at me like a bulldog and we went down snarling and punching. The bastard was tough, I have to give him that. He was skin and bone but he was strong and his fists were like rocks. The hacks pushed through the crowd and pried us apart and hauled us off to the solitary cells. A week later they made the mistake of taking us out at the same time. We shoved the guards aside and got into it again right there in the isolation block. While we were beating on each other the hacks were beating on us. Van Meter got another week in the hole and I got ten days.

John couldn't understand why Van Meter and I disliked each other so much. I couldn't understand how he could tolerate the dopey son of a bitch. He said Van Meter wasn't as dopey as he made out, he just liked to clown around. John was sure the two of us would get along if we got to know each other. I told him Look, you want to be his friend, that's your business, but he comes near me again I'll break his scrawny neck.

He said okay, have it my way, but he stayed friends with both of us. From everything I've heard, Van Meter was loyal to him to the end, which is good to know. But it doesn't change the fact that he was a goofy bastard and I couldn't stand him.

For the rest of the time I was at Pendleton—only another few weeks—the scarecrow kept away from me, but we'd still see each other now and then, almost always at a distance. And every time we did, he'd make a stupid clown face and do his old-timey pugilist act, trying to get my goat. I was aching to kick the hell out of him. By then, however, I had something much more important than him on my mind and I didn't want to jeopardize it by getting put in the hole for fighting.

I'd smuggled a six-inch piece of saw blade out of the shop, and every night after lights out I went to work on the bars of my cell door.

I knew some of the other guys could hear the rasping, but it couldn't be helped. Then Boss Miles ordered a shakedown and the hacks found the saw in the lining of my mattress and discovered where I'd cut almost all the way through two of the lower bars. Somebody had finked on me, but no telling who, the place was so full of finks. At any rate, it was all Miles needed to get me out of his hair. I was in solitary for the few days it took them to complete the paperwork, then I was taken to Miles's office, where he was waiting for me with a smart-ass smile and the news of my transfer to the pen at Michigan City.

Pantano was being transferred too, and on the following morning the two of us were chained together and taken out to the prison van. A bunch of inmates were gathered at the fence to watch us. I spotted John among them, and he saluted me with a raised fist.

I wouldn't see him again for four years.

I saw Van Meter a lot sooner than that. Not long after I got to M City, as it was known to everybody there, another few guys were transferred from Pendleton and he was one of them. He hadn't been there a week when we crossed paths in the yard and got into it on the spot, rolling on the ground and trying to strangle each other. We both got a week in the hole. Then we were assigned to separate cell blocks and rarely saw each again. Whenever we did, we pretended not to.

. . .

Somebody once said that stone walls do not a prison make, but as Fat Charley pointed out, you throw in a few dozen armed guards and a general lack of the social amenities and by Jesus you've got something.

Most of the unpleasant things about imprisonment are fairly obvious, but, believe me, if you've never been inside the walls you can't begin to imagine the boredom. The days plod one after the other like prisoners on a chain. You can *see* time going by on a calendar, you can see it in the change of seasons. You can *feel* the time passing. But you're doing the same things day after day, and so there's nothing to distinguish one day from another. Red used to say he'd been sentenced to only one day in prison, but the catch was that the day would be twenty-five years long.

One way to break the monotony of prison routine is to refuse to cooperate with its rules. Refuse often enough and strongly enough and they label you an incorrigible. At M City the incorrigibles were called Red Shirts, and not only was I one of them, I was the youngest and the best known, if I do say so myself. We went out of our way to make things tough for the hacks and didn't care that they could make things even tougher for us. The worst punishment they could give you was a beating and a stretch in solitary. They'd hit you with radiator hoses or some thick book like a catalog or a dictionary so as not to mark you up too badly in case you died on them and some outside doctor should happen to examine your remains. At M City just the threat of a beating was enough to keep most cons in line, and for most of the guys who ever went to the hole one trip was enough.

That's how it was for my old partner Earl. He'd been in solitary at M City only once—he got two days for talking during a silent period and then arguing with the guard who wrote him up—and he told me he'd do whatever it took to keep from ever going into the hole again. That's when I realized how much the beating at the Kokomo jailhouse had taken out of him. He was trying to be a Good Convict and make an early parole. I can't deny that Earl was a disappointment to me at M City, but he'd been a loyal partner and that counts for plenty, and so I always stuck up for him if he got in a scrape with other convicts. Besides, he was Mary's brother.

Speaking of Mary, I'd exchanged one or two letters with her while I was at Pendleton and she continued to write to me after I went to M City. She came to visit me and Earl as often as she could, which was only every six weeks or so, since she had to take a day off from her job, plus scrape up the dough for the long bus trip and a hotel room for the night. Her mother had kicked out her bum husband Burke and filed for divorce, and money was tighter than ever. On every visit she brought me goodies of some kind she baked herself. But every now and then when she'd show up, Earl would have to tell her I couldn't see her because I was in the hole, and she'd be furious with the prison.

My mother and father had also often driven up from Indianapolis during my first year in the pen. Then they moved to a farm a few miles outside of Leipsic, Ohio, which was even farther from M City than Indytown was. After they made the trip twice in a row only to find out I was in solitary both times, I persuaded them not to come anymore. I told my mother to settle for writing me letters, and she did, twice a week without fail.

The only other visitor I had was Pearl Elliott. She came to see me and Earl every two weeks and always saw to it that neither of us was short of money for cigarettes and stuff. The Side Pocket was turning a steady dollar and her trade in license plates and phony documents was going well, and so she'd quit doing driving jobs, figuring they weren't worth the risk anymore.

It didn't take long for Earl to realize I was the main reason Pearl came to visit. He told me he'd never seen her look so down in the mouth as whenever he had to tell her I was in the hole.

* * *

The hole—oh man. I got put in the hole more often than anybody else and I did the longest stretches. Name a rule and I broke it.

Those solitary confinement cells felt like coffins in comparison to the regular six-by-nine cages in the main cell houses. The only way a guy my size could lie down was curled up, which is how you would've done it anyway, to try to keep warm, because you were naked and without a blanket. There was a low-watt bulb in a steel-mesh recess in the ceiling and they kept it turned on twelve hours a day. The other twelve hours you were in darkness as black as a tar pit. There was a tapered hole in the concrete floor for you to do your business in.

That hole in the floor is what you never forget about solitary confinement at M City. Each time you went in the hole the stink seared your throat and made your eyes water. After a few days you'd almost get used to it. Then the next time you got sent to the hole the stench seemed worse than before.

They gave you a small half loaf of bread and a quart of water a day, shoving it in through a little gate at the foot of the cell door. Rather than eat the bread, some of us would use it for a pillow. A lot of people would be surprised at how long you can go without food, and how easily. Once you get past the first few days, you even stop being hungry. It's mostly a matter of will. You will yourself not to break, no matter what.

There were two main tricks to doing time in the hole. One was to occupy your mind with some particular thing the whole time you were in there—naming the players on every major league team, trying to remember the exact detail of some house you'd lived in, things like that. The other, which was harder to do but often more effective, was to think of nothing at all, to go into a kind of trance for as much of the time as you could. There were occasional distractions of course, mainly the cockroaches and the rats that came up out of the waste hole to get at your bread after the light went out.

I'd been to the hole a half-dozen times before I managed to catch a rat. The bastard bit me good before I crushed it to death and my hand swelled up like I was wearing a winter glove. I thought I'd get the plague or some god-awful thing, but after a week the hand didn't hurt anymore, and a week after that it was almost back to normal size. Anyhow, the day after I got the rat, when the guard opened the little gate to pass in my bread and water, I said Here's a snack for *you,* pal, and shoved the thing out through the gate. Its eyes were bugging out and its bloody mouth was open and full of blue gut. Judging by the sound, I'd say if the hack didn't puke he came close to it.

That was your trump card, see—showing them you could take

anything they dished out. Each trip to the hole was another chance to show them you could take it better than *they* ever could.

• • •

*M*y longest lockups were for trying to escape. M City had a rep as a tough joint to break out of. I saw guys try all sorts of ways but only twice did anybody make it beyond the walls. In the first case three guys busted out and a few days later were spotted running into a cornfield. The cops set the field on fire and drove them out and recaptured them, one with half his face burned off. In the second instance two cons went over the wall and were found in some hick burg three days later. They were breaking into a hardware store in the middle of a Sunday afternoon when a pair of cops showed up. They tried to run for it and the cops shot them dead. The cons were still in their prison grays. After each of those breaks, M City of course made changes to prevent the same sort from being repeated.

My first attempt was really dopey. I hid in a truckload of laundry. They laughed at me for a fool when they checked the truck at the gate and found me. I got a beating and a week in the hole.

The next time, Joe Pantano and Russell Clark were with me. We jumped two guards outside the tin shop, gagged them and wired their hands behind them, and then Russell and I put on their uniforms and led Pantano toward the administration building like we were escorting a prisoner. We were halfway there when one of the hacks we'd trussed up came running in his underwear, squealing through the gag like a pig at slaughtering time, his hands still behind him. We kept on walking and the guards on the wall yelled for us to halt and *bam-bam*, here came the warning shots. One of the bullets ricocheted off the walkway and hit Pantano in the throat, and he went down. They yelled to put our hands up or they'd blow our heads off. We stood there with our hands up high while the guards came running and Pantano lay there quivering with his hands at his bloody neck, making gargling noises for about a half-minute before he died.

They hauled me and Russell off to the guardhouse and beat each of us in turn and clapped us in solitary for two weeks. There was talk that the warden was going to try to get us charged with murder, saying we were responsible for Pantano's death, but nothing came of it.

I didn't get another chance at escape until a bunch of inmates tried to pull a work strike. This was around the time of the stock market crash, when guys in suits were jumping out of thirty-story windows because they couldn't bear to go on living without being rich. The hacks went charging into the strikers with their clubs swinging, and in the midst of the brawl Russell and I snuck away and made it to the roof of one of the factory buildings. We figured we could jump from building to building until we got to the wall. But as we ran across the first rooftop we were spotted by the tower guards and *bam*, a round glanced off a chimney near my head and a brick fragment hit me in the eyeball and turned it red as a tomato for a month. A hack with a bullhorn said to drop down on our bellies or we were dead.

We got another beating and another stretch in the hole, except this time Russell managed to break loose of the guards holding him against the wall and he gave them a fight to remember. He broke one hack's arm and knocked out another's front teeth and nearly throttled another before the whole crew came running in and pinned him down. The day captain of the guards—a huge liver-lipped bastard named Albert Evans who weighed nearly three hundred pounds—then banged on Russell so bad I thought he'd killed him. Russ didn't regain consciousness for two days.

Evans had given me my worst beatings too. The inmates called him Big Bertha behind his back, but Russell and I called him that to his face. Russell swore he was going to settle Evans's hash, but I said not unless he beat me to him.

● ● ● ●

word about Russell. He was always a tough number, one of the toughest at M City. *Today* . . . well, let's say he's changed, but I'll get to that later.

He was a little older than me and nearly as tall. He had thick black hair and was impressively strong. He was doing a twenty-year stretch for bank robbery. He said he grew up in Detroit and joined the Marines when he was a kid, but some sergeant kept getting on his back and he'd had to clobber the bastard—and accidentally blinded him in one eye while he was at it. He did six months in the brig and got booted with a dishonorable discharge. He had a job in a car plant for a while, but it wasn't long before he'd had enough of working for wages and being bossed around by fools, so he took up the gun and went into business for himself.

He had a longtime girlfriend named Opal Long who lived in Chicago and often came to see him at M City on visiting days. Her family name was Wilson but she'd got married young to a guy called Long and kept his name when they divorced. I saw her for the first time when Russ and I were seated next to each other in the visiting room one time and he was talking to Opal through the grill while I talked to Mary. She was a big hefty girl with darker red hair than Mary's and one of the best smiles I've ever seen. It was also Russell's first look at Mary, and after the visit he said he was surprised a guy as homely as Earl Northern could have such a pretty sister. I said I thought Opal had a pretty face too. He said yes she did, even though she was never going to be mistaken for a calendar girl, not with her build. He sometimes called her Mack, short for Mack Truck. In days to come, he'd now and then grab that ample ass of hers with both hands and say how much he liked a woman with some meat on her. She loved it when he did that, and she'd laugh along with the rest of us and wag her big behind like a happy dog.

A couple like Russ and Opal is one more example of how funny life can be. Russell's a good-looking guy who could have his pick of gorgeous girls, and yet he's been with Opal ever since I've known him. As far as I know, he's never cheated on her and I'm not saying that to cover for a pal. Now he's doing life and isn't likely to get paroled anytime soon, if ever, and I hear she still comes to visit him every week. No doubt she'll wait for him as long as it takes.

Which by the way Mary did not. Wait, I mean. While I was in M City she got married. I hadn't had a letter from her in more than a month and hadn't seen her for almost two, and I was getting worried. Then one Sunday she showed up to tell me she'd married some guy named Dale Kinder.

All I could think to say at that moment was *Dale?*—what the hell kind of name for a guy is *Dale?*

To make it even more unreal, the Dale guy's father was an Indianapolis police sergeant. The wedding had taken place two weeks earlier and she'd already given the news to Earl in a letter, but she'd asked him not to say anything about it to me because she wanted to tell me herself.

I won't deny the news hit me hard. She was wearing a blue dress and her hair was shorter and lighter than the last time I'd seen it. She looked so gorgeous I could hardly breathe. Until that moment, I hadn't realized how much she meant to me.

She wanted me to know she'd married Kinder because he'd asked her to and she didn't want to wither on the vine, as she put it, and which, at the rate I was going, was what would happen to her before I ever got paroled.

I didn't say it, but I had to wonder how much her decision had been influenced by the fact that her little sister had already been married four years—never mind that her hubby hadn't been around for the past three-and-a-half. At sixteen Margo had got hitched to some strong-arm who a few months later went to prison on a ten-year jolt. Jesus, those Northern girls could pick them.

Mary said I'd never given her cause to think she should wait for me. Oh sure, I'd said I loved her, but that's not the same as asking somebody to wait.

I said yeah, when she was right she was right.

What did I expect her to do, she said, a girl has to watch out for herself.

I told her I understood and no hard feelings, and I wished her the best of luck. I really thought I'd never see her again. When I got back to the cell house I threw up.

• • •

The next break I tried was with a skeleton key I'd made on the sly in the welding shop. It was month after month of trial and error on my cell door lock, of constantly reshaping the key and trying it on the lock again. Then one night I put my arm through the bars and tried the key for the millionth time and . . . *clunk* . . . the lock opened.

Oh baby, I heard Russell whisper from his adjoining cell.

I relocked the door and hid the key in a corner crevice of the cell, and the next day Russ and I talked things over with Red and Fat Charley and some of the other guys in our bunch.

There were a few hardcases at M City who rarely got in fights or caused any trouble but who everybody knew you didn't chivvy with, and Red and Charley were prime examples. Charley was from Ohio. He was in his early forties and looked like everybody's favorite uncle—short and round and with the sociability of a born salesman. He was missing the tip of his left index finger and had a habit of keeping that hand half-closed to hide the mutilation. We'd been friends for months before I ever noticed it. When I asked what happened he was reluctant to say, so I took off my shoes and socks and showed him my toes. Born that way, I said. He smiled and said all right and told me he lost the fingertip because of the first girl he ever fell in love with. He was sixteen and she was beautiful but cold of heart and he knew it but he couldn't help himself. She was constantly demanding that he prove his love, getting him into bad fights over her and so on. One day she said if he'd cut off his finger she would be his forever. So he went and got a straight razor and did it right in front of her.

She was, to use Fat Charley's word, aghast. She called him crazy and refused to ever see him again. The story he gave his mother was that the finger got caught in a machine at the bottling plant where he worked after school. He'd had his share of women since then, had even been married for a few years to a nice woman whose face he could no longer envision, and he'd enjoyed them all, but he had never again fallen so profoundly in love.

Lucky for you, I said.

Lucky for me, he said, the wench didn't ask for my peter.

In addition to looking harmless and well intentioned, he spoke like a college professor, and it tickled all of us that once upon a time he'd been an insurance salesman. One day when he was giving his routine spiel to a prospect, telling him about the importance of having insurance because as much as we hate to think about it life is awful short and even worse it can come to an unexpectedly abrupt end and so on and so forth, it struck him that everything he was saying was true *except* for the part about needing insurance. Fat Charley said he suddenly saw his own life as so unspeakably dull he felt like he was committing slow suicide. He asked the customer to excuse him a moment and then slipped out the back door and got in his car and left. A week later he was running hooch for a bootlegging bunch in Cleveland. Shortly after that he made the jump to what he called the exhilarating trade of the brigand. He was in the third year of a ten-to-twenty for bank robbery and said his only regret was having been caught.

Because Charles Makley was the absolute picture of the happy fat man, he was often able to get out of a tight spot without having to resort to rough stuff. His looks and manner also made it easy to underestimate his capacity for self-defense. Out in the yard one morning I saw a bohunk named Markowski backing Charley against a wall as a bunch of other cons were looking on. Markowski had had it in for Fat Charley ever since losing all his cigarettes to him in a crap game a week earlier. I couldn't hear what they were saying at that distance, but Markowski was poking Charley in the chest with a finger and running his mouth hard. Charley was talking calmly and apparently trying to keep things from getting out of hand, but I knew he wasn't going to take too many more of those pokes.

As I started toward them, Markowski jabbed him one time too many. In a blink Charley snatched him by the shirt and the hair and spun him around and rammed his head into the wall so hard it must've rattled the paperweights on the warden's desk over in the next building. Even as the bohunk dropped to his knees and fell over, everyone was moving away from him like ripples from a splash, moving in that deceptively fast-walking way of convicts. In a matter of seconds, there was nobody within twenty yards of Markowski as he lay there with his brains oozing out his ears. Red and I covered Charley's flanks and back as we headed for the other end of the yard, in case any of Markowski's pals might want to make it their fight too, but nobody made a move on us.

We mixed into a crowd of convicts and looked back to see the yard hacks converging around Markowski. Charley looked almost rueful. He said it disturbed him deeply when a man refused to listen to reason. He said reason was the bedrock of orderly human relations.

Goddamn right it is, Red said. Anybody wants to argue the point I'll kick him in the nuts.

That was Red Hamilton for you. His real name was John. He'd come to M City a year or two after I did. A beefy, big-boned guy with rusty-red hair and huge hands, he was only two or three years older than me but he looked closer to Charley's age. He'd worked his way up the robbery ladder to bank jobs and was doing fairly well until one night when he was on his way to a date with some girl and realized he'd left his wallet at home. So he decided to pull a filling station stickup to get some quick cash. He was holding his piece on the attendant with one hand and rifling the till with the other when two

police cars pulled into the station to gas up and the cops saw what
was going on. Next thing Red knew he had four guns pointed at him
and the jig was up. He still hadn't gotten over the embarrassment of
being taken down on such a two-bit job. It was his second robbery
conviction and he got twenty-five years.

Little on the harsh side, if you ask me, he said. There was only
twenty-two bucks in the till. That's more than a year for every fucken
dollar.

He had Charley beat in the missing fingers department, lacking
part of both the index and middle fingers of his right hand. Naturally
some of the guys called him Three-finger Jack. He said he'd lost them
in a sledding accident when he was a kid, but some of the stories that
followed him into M City told it differently. One version had it that
he'd been a bagman for the mob in Kansas City, got caught skimming and paid for it with the fingers. According to another, a St.
Louis gambler caught Red putting the blocks to his woman and
opened fire on both of them, killing her and clipping Red's fingers
before he got hold of his own piece and shot the gambler through the
wishbone.

When I told Red the St. Louis story he laughed and said it was a
new one to him but he liked it and might start using it. Those hands
of his were so large he could still work a trigger with the stub of his
index finger.

He wasn't one to talk about himself very much, but he did di-
vulge that, like Charley, he'd been married once. He was still somewhat bitter about the divorce settlement. If the bitch had fucked me
as good in bed as she did in court, he said, I never would've divorced
her.

As dangerous as they were, Red and Charley were basically cool
types and usually managed to avoid trouble with the hacks. Charley
thought the Red Shirts were courageous fools to fight so openly
against the system. The way he looked at it, the more attention you
drew to yourself the worse your chances of ever breaking out. We had

talked a lot about escape, but every plan I came up with had too many holes in it to suit them. They weren't afraid to take chances but neither were they reckless, which is what my breakout plans always seemed to them. On the other hand, they hadn't been able to come up with a worthy plan either.

My skeleton key took them by surprise. I'd been making it on the QT and now that it worked I had every intention of using it.

Fat Charley said the key was a nice piece of work but it didn't constitute an escape plan. All it did was get us out of the cells. *Then* what?

Then we cut the bars out of a cell house window with the saw blade Russell had swiped from the tin shop. We'd let ourselves down on sheets tied together and sneak over to the admin building and jump a guard or two and disarm them and take them hostage. We'd force the hacks posted on the doors to open up and let us out or we'd shoot their pals.

It's a plan, said Red. Risky bitch but it's a plan.

Charley said it was too hastily conceived, there were too many unknown factors. Some of the inmates on the row might've been aware of me trying the key on my door night after night and one of them could've finked us already.

I said if somebody had finked the warden would've come down on me by now.

Not necessarily, he said. Could be the warden was only waiting for us to try the break so he could hit us with everything in the book. In any case, the wall guards would be sure to spot us as we went down 'the sheets like a bunch of cartoon convicts.

No, they wouldn't—the wall under the window we'd cut through was the only one not in view of any of the towers.

It felt great to have all the answers. I mean I was *ready*. I let every man have his say, then said I was going out that night and whoever wanted to come with me was welcome.

Russell said count him in. Everyone else nodded except for Red and Charley. Red ran his three-fingered hand through his hair and sighed, then said What the hell, me too.

Charley looked glum. He said his intuition told him the plan was folly but that we'd caught him in a moment of philosophical weakness. To paraphrase Socrates, he said, the unrisked life is not worth living. I'm in too.

Who's Socrates, John Burns wanted to know, some outlaw you partnered with? Burns was doing life for murder. Sounds Mexican, he said.

Sounds like a guy with no use for insurance, Red said, winking at Charley.

Charley always did his best to be patient with the untutored. He told Burns that Socrates was most definitely an outlaw, a true enemy of the state who had been executed.

Tough break, Burns said. What state was he enemy of? Texas I bet. They're quick to fry your ass in Texas.

Even Charlie couldn't resist. Oklahoma, he said.

Oh hell, Burns said. Them Okies are just as bad.

I'd be the last one to call myself an educated man, but it's always been fairly obvious to me why most guys in prison are in prison.

* * *

That night I unlocked my cell and then let out the others. Russell and I took turns with the saw blade, working like we were in a contest, while some of the guys started rolling up bed sheets and tying them together to make shinny ropes.

We'd almost finished cutting through the first bar when the guards came charging in, all of them armed with shotguns, yelling for us to drop on our bellies and put our hands behind our heads— *Now now now!* By chance, Red and Charley had just gone into their cells to get their sheets to add to the shinny rope. When they heard the hacks come crashing in they shut their cell doors before the guards even looked their way. Like I said, very cool customers Red and Charley.

Charley's hunch had been right—somebody on the row finked, and the warden had been waiting to catch us in the act. A lookout in an adjoining building had been keeping an eye on our tier through the windows.

Every man caught outside his cell was punished with a beating and a month in solitary. Except for me. The warden knew about the cell key and he instructed Captain Evans and his apes to give me an extra-special treatment before clapping me in the hole for two months. Big Bertha smiled like he'd been given a present.

I'm sure the warden thought I wouldn't come out alive, and he wasn't the only one. I was conscious enough to hear the guards making bets on it as they dragged me down to the solitary cages. My vision was blurred for days and I pissed bloody fire for more than a week and it was longer than that before my ears stopped ringing, but I never doubted I'd make it.

I admit I wasn't looking my handsome best when they took me out of the cage at the end of that stretch. I was the color of the newly dead and my skin was scabby and felt loose on my bones. It would be another week before I could walk right again. As a pair of hacks were helping me across the yard toward the cell house, I saw the warden watching us from his office window, and in a crackly voice I started singing "The Best Things in Life Are Free." I could faintly hear inmates laughing from the cell house windows. One of the guards said to knock off the shit but the other one told his partner to take it easy. The warden's mouth looked like a tight little scar and then he yanked the drape closed.

While I'd been in the hole, Red found out who ratted on us about the key and had attended to the matter. The warden had tried to protect the fink's identity by transferring him among two dozen other guys from our cell house to another. But Red still learned who it was, and he put out the word to some friends in the guy's new block. A few days later the fink somehow went tumbling over the second-tier railing and his head shattered on the concrete floor. More than a hundred inmates had been out on the tiers at the time but none of them witnessed what happened. We heard that the warden was in a fury but there was nothing he could do except write it up as an accident.

· · ·

*B*y that time, John had been at M City for about three years. He'd been transferred from Pendleton a few months before the inmate labor strike, when Russell and I got caught trying to escape by way of the rooftops, but he was never a part of any of my attempts to bust out. Not while he was *inside* the walls, I mean.

He'd arrived a few days after I'd been given two weeks in the hole for I-forget-what, so I didn't know he was at M City until I came out of solitary. Russell and I were crossing the yard and I spotted him tossing a baseball with some of the guys on the prison team.

I went over and said Well now, look what the cat dragged in.

I was so skinny and beat-up it took him a second to recognize me—then he grinned and we shook hands. Christ, Harry, he said, it looks like they really gave you the business.

I said I'd be right as rain in no time and introduced him to Russell. Physically, he didn't look too different from the way he had at Pendleton, maybe a little huskier. But he had a little more twist in his smile and a lot more iron in the eyes. I asked what kind of trouble he'd made at the reformatory to get sent to M City, and he said no trouble, he'd requested the transfer.

Russell said You *asked* for the pen? Goddamn, man, how long you been brain-damaged?

John gave him that cocky smile.

Later on he told me his request for transfer actually had to do with a couple of things that happened almost back to back. First of all, his wife divorced him. During the first three years he was in Pendleton she'd often gone to visit, but then the visits began to fall off, and her letters became long complaints about being lonely and feeling that she was wasting her youth and so on. He wasn't surprised when she filed for divorce, but it hurt like hell just the same. He said he hadn't known what loneliness was until he got the divorce papers. He couldn't put out of his mind that she was still so geographically nearby but was as removed from him as the moon.

A month after the divorce, he got another kick in the gut. He'd already served about five years of that ridiculous ten-to-twenty he got for a first-time conviction on a minor stickup and assault, and although he'd caused his share of trouble in his first two or three years at the reformatory, his record since then had been pretty good. What's more, his partner in crime had been paroled two years earlier. John thought his own parole would be a cinch. It hit him hard when the board said no dice.

It amuses me that so many people like to think he would've gone straight if either his wife hadn't left him or if he'd been granted parole at that Pendleton hearing. People are always saying If only this had happened, if only that, if only, if only. . . . That's parlor-game stuff. The only thing that matters is what actually happens, not what should've or would've or could've. Like Fat Charley used to say, in any endeavor that's over and done with, what *could've* happened . . . *did*.

John was convinced the Pendleton parole board had it in for him on account of his early troublemaking in the joint, and he was sure they'd turn him down again next time. He figured if he transferred to M City he might get paroled sooner. His official reason for requesting to go to the penitentiary was that it had a better baseball team than Pendleton's and playing for it would boost his chance of becoming a pro when he got out. Boss Miles thought John was being foolish, but he okayed the transfer.

● ● ●

t didn't take long for him to pass muster with Red and Charley and Russ. He also started buddying with Van Meter again, but my attitude toward the scarecrow hadn't changed

and never would, and John knew better than to bring Van Meter anywhere near me.

He tried hard to stay out of trouble with the hacks, and all of us
encouraged him to keep his record as clean as he could. He would go
before the parole board much sooner than any of the rest of us, and if
he stuck to the straight and narrow he stood a good chance of being
let out. But in a place where there were rules against nearly everything, it was hard for him not to break one now and then. It was usually for something petty—having a cigarette lighter in his cell,
having a razor, gambling, stealing tomatoes from the garden house. I
don't think he did more than a one-day stretch in the hole until he
was caught putting it to one of the cell house punks. That episode got
him three days.

It wasn't the first punk John put it to and it wouldn't be the last,
and I was always disappointed in him about that. Red and Charley
and I were among the few guys I knew at M City who never used
punks. Russell used them only to get sucked off, but as far as I was
concerned any kind of sex with a punk was degrading. Whenever I
got so worked up that the urge couldn't be ignored or willed away,
I'd lie in the dark with my horn in my hand and think about Mary's
ass and *bang,* in less than a minute it was done with. Beating off isn't
the best sex in the world but it beats—ha ha—using a punk. John
used to give me a song and dance about how if he didn't have frequent
sex he'd get terrible headaches. He claimed that jerking off didn't
help, only sex with somebody else. He made it sound like doctor's orders. I always thought it was a lot of hooey.

As long as we're this close to the subject, it's as good a time as any
to say how sick and tired I am of being asked about John's dick. Ever
since he was put on display in the Chicago morgue, the rumor's been
going around that he had one like a smokestack, and I've been asked
a hundred times if it's true. I hear there's even a Tijuana Bible about
him and Mae West in which he lugs his hard-on around in a wheel-
barrow. Jesus. I wish I'd done what Russell did one time when a re-

porter who was interviewing him from a chair at his cell door asked how big John's dick really was. Russ stood up and pulled out his pecker and held it through the bars in the guy's face and said It was about like this.

The reporter jerked away from the bars so fast he fell over in the chair. He ended up writing that Russell was a degenerate personality and had the look of a born criminal.

Ten to one that none of the guys who have written about John's dick ever saw it with his own eyes. Well *I* did, and I mean at full mast. Mary did too—she was with me at the time and I'll get to that part of the story when I get to it. Suffice it to say for now that John's tool was, to use Mary's word, impressive. However—and as much as I hate to toot my own *horn,* ha ha—I have to be completely honest and say that he had nothing on yours truly. As you may have heard, the guys in the gang called me Pete, and why do you suppose? Because one Sunday afternoon at M City I'd been napping and dreaming about fooling around in a swimming pool with Norma Shearer and Greta Garbo, the three of us naked as jays, and I woke up to find Charley and Red and Russell at my cell door and grinning at the erection sticking out of my shorts. Russell and Red applauded and Charley said Good heavens man, that's no peter that's a nine pin. He always called a dick a peter. So they took to calling me Big Pete for laughs. After a while it was just Pete. Later on when Mary asked how I picked up the nickname and I told her, she waggled her brow and said she should've known. With her, though, I was always Harry.

As I was saying, John found it a lot harder to toe the line in M City than he'd thought it would be, but like Red and Charley, he was able to stay out of serious trouble. And being the easy guy to like that he was, he had a lot of pals.

One of them was a kid named Jenkins who was doing life for murder. The guy was friendly and a pretty good singer but there was something about him that struck me as a little off. I asked around and came to find out he'd hustled pansies on the outside. There was a rumor he was punking for John but I didn't know if it was true—I didn't ask John and he didn't say. In any case, Jenkins had a swell-looking sister, and the minute John saw her picture he went ga-ga. Jenkins said she was married but unhappy about it and would soon be filing for divorce. So John started writing to her. Next thing I knew he had his own snapshot of her taped on his wall. Like I've said, the man was cool in all things except women. He once said it himself: his dick was his weakness.

. . .

*J*ohn got his early education in the ways and means of bank heists from me and Red and Charley and Russ—and then a couple of rough characters named Walt Dietrich and Oklahoma Jack Clark came to M City and we all learned even more about the business. For the previous two years they'd been part of the Herman Lamm gang, the best band of bank robbers ever.

The way Dietrich told it, Lamm had been an officer in the German army until he got in some kind of bad fix just before the war and amscrayed from Europe to the USA, where he took up the time-honored occupation of holdup man, and if anybody can be said to have made a true profession of bank robbery, Lamm's the guy. Until he came along, bank robbers had been operating in much the same catch-as-catch-can fashion since the days of Jesse James. You picked out a bank and went in and pulled your piece and told everybody to stand pat, you bagged all the cash you could lay your hands on, and then you made a run for it. Lamm regarded that technique as primitive Wild West stuff. He believed a bank job should be a clockwork operation, as well planned as a military raid, and he worked out a system of operation.

The first step was to become thoroughly familiar with the bank he was going to hit. He learned its routine and found out how many employees there were and what their jobs were, who the manager was and what kind of safe or vault the place had. He made a map of the layout and every member of the gang memorized it. He found out if the cops regularly patrolled the bank's neighborhood, and if they did, he learned what the patrol schedule was. He studied street maps of the town and road maps of the region, then made his own map and noted on it the precise distances and speed limits and travel times from point to point on the getaway route. He'd do the same with a backup route, in case they'd have to use it. Every man in the gang had a specific job and every job had to be done with perfect timing. Timing was the key. Lamm would figure to the exact second how long a job should take from the moment they entered the bank until they came out again, and he never deviated from the timetable by a hair, not even if it meant leaving some of the money behind.

But there's an old saying in the criminal trades—when you set out to pull a job there's a hundred things that can go wrong, and if you can think of fifty of them you're a mastermind. Even the best-laid plans require a lot of luck. Lamm sure had his share of it to last more than a dozen years, which is a hell of a long run in the robbery business. His luck ran out in Clinton, Indiana, when the getaway car blew a tire in front of the bank. They grabbed another car but it couldn't go faster than thirty miles an hour, and Dietrich later read in the paper that the car belonged to an old man whose son had slyly rigged the throttle so his daddy couldn't speed. The gang switched to still another car but it ran out of gas inside of ten miles. You run out of everything when you run out of luck.

Two hundred cops and vigilantes caught up to them and opened fire. Lamm and two others in the gang were killed. Walt and Okie Jack considered themselves blessed that they'd been allowed to surrender. They'd come to M City on life sentences for big bitch convictions.

There was no denying the beauty of Herman Lamm's system. All it required was a smooth and well-disciplined team, and we knew that team was us. I think it's safe to say it'll be a good long while before anybody robs banks as . . . *artfully,* that's the word for it . . . as artfully as we did.

• • •

I hadn't heard a word from Mary, not that I'd expected to, since she'd told me she'd gotten married, but I never did stop thinking about her. She stayed in touch with Earl, however, and he kept me informed of how things were going for her. Almost from the start they hadn't gone well in her marriage. It turned out that her husband, the Kinder guy, was a small-time stickup man. Yep, the son of the police sergeant. They say the apple doesn't fall far from the tree, but every now and then an apple will take a big bounce when it hits the ground and some will roll a long way down the hill. Earl said Mary hadn't been specific, but reading between the lines he got the impression Kinder was a boozer and sometimes smacked her around. What I wouldn't give for five minutes with that guy, Earl said. I didn't say anything, but my gut was tight as a fist.

They hadn't been married very long before Kinder took a fall for armed robbery and was sent to M City. Earl found out from Mary and his first impulse had been not to tell me until after he'd had first crack at the guy. But he'd been suffering for weeks from some kind of respiratory infection, coughing almost constantly, and he wasn't sure he was in shape to give Kinder what he deserved. So he came to me and told me the news. Imagine my glee.

Red and Russell went with me to Kinder's cell house one evening before lockdown. I wanted them along to keep away witnesses, but when the other cons on the row saw the three of us coming they all ducked into their cages and stayed there. Red positioned himself on one side of Kinder's cell and Russell on the other, and I went in.

Kinder was on his bunk but jumped up when he saw me. His cellmate wasn't there—maybe he'd seen us coming, maybe he was just lucky.

Who the hell are *you*, Kinder said, giving me a hard-guy look he'd probably picked up from the movies.

He was shorter than me but thicker and heavier. To tell the truth I wouldn't have taken it any easier on him if he'd been a midget.

Got a message for you, I said. From Mary.

His expression got curious. My wife? What's *she* want?

I gave him the first one in the solar plexus so he couldn't yell out, then held him against the wall with one hand and punched him with the other for a while before I let him fall. I kicked him in the face until his nose was a bloody ruin and some of his teeth were on the floor and his lower jaw was turned at an angle you wouldn't believe. I stomped on his hands until they were bloated and purple and some of the fingers pointed in different directions. See how many women he could beat up with those.

He was curled up on his side and moaning low, his breath gargly, when I bent close to his ear and said Don't call her your wife again, you yellow son of a bitch. And don't even dream about fingering me. You do, you're dead.

As Red and Russ and I walked back down the row, not a con was out on the tier and nobody said a word to us as we passed the cells.

Not long after that I got a letter from Mary saying Earl had told her what I'd done, although he'd been skimpy on details. She thanked me for taking up for her. She called herself the biggest dope in the world for marrying Kinder. She'd known he wasn't very smart but she'd had no idea he was so stupid or such a bully. Talk about stupid, she said, look how stupid *she'd* been to think it was so god-awful important to wait till she was married rather than indulge herself with me—that was how she put it—while she'd had the chance. I rue my mistakes, she wrote. She placed a bright red lipstick kiss at the end of the letter, and below that she wrote Thinking of you.

She came to see me on the next visiting day and brought me a batch of fudge. The scooped neck of her dress exposed the sprinkle of freckles along her collarbone. I had an aching erection the whole time we talked.

She thought she must be awful bad luck for the men in her life,

seeing as she had a husband *and* a brother *and* me all in prison. She
didn't care that she was bad luck to Kinder, but she was sorry
about me and Earl. She thought a curse ran in the women in her
family. Her mother's most recent ex-husband, Burke, had been
killed in a car crash a week before their divorce was to become
final. He was on his way back to Indy from Cleveland after phon-
ing her and saying he wanted to talk about the two of them giving
it another try. God only knew what was in store for her mother's
new husband, a car mechanic named Jocko who'd already had a few
scrapes with the law.

Her mother's problem wasn't that she was bad luck for men, it
was that she took up with men who were no good, and I told Mary
she'd made the same mistake with Kinder. She wasn't bad luck, I assured her, not for me.

When our time was up we touched fingertips through the wire
mesh and she looked like she might cry and laugh at the same time.
She whispered Oh baby how I wish. And blew me a kiss as she got up
to go.

* * *

That winter the wind came off the lake and over the dunes
even harder than usual. It ripped through the prison
grounds every day like an icy sandblast. I'd walk in the yard
with my collar up and my hands deep in my pockets, my eyes stinging, and I'd think and think. By winter's end I'd come up with an escape plan.

It was different from my others in that it was long-range and
called for patience, never my strong suit. Still it was a plan we all
agreed on. *We* was only six of us to begin with—me, Red, Charley,
Russell, Walt Dietrich, and Okie Jack.

It was my plan, but in fairness I have to give a lot of credit to Fat
Charley. He always insisted that a plan should be simple as possible.
The more complicated the scheme, he said, the more things that can

go wrong with it. The way he saw it we needed only one thing to try a break—guns. With guns and a little luck we might be able to take hostages and use them to get past the gates to the outside.

When Charley had first mentioned this idea to the rest of us, Russell smacked a palm up to his forehead and said *Guns*, of course—why the hell didn't *I* think of that? Then he laughed in Charley's face.

Red said That's a pretty simple plan all right. Why don't we just ask the warden if we can borrow the keys to the place? That's even simpler and it's got about as much chance.

That was the problem in a nutshell—how to get the guns into the joint. Months crawled by and none of us could think of a way. Then there was a major change in inmate job assignments and Dietrich was made the supply clerk in the shirt factory. That's when the answer to the gun problem came to me.

I didn't say anything about it right away. I wanted to have the thing worked out as much as possible before running it by the guys. I grilled Dietrich like a cop about the supply procedures in the shirt factory. And then I had a talk with Pearl Elliott. I needed her to convey a proposal to a Mr. Williams, the shipping manager of a certain trucking company in Chicago. She was gone for a week before coming back and informing me that the deal was acceptable to Mr. Williams, but he'd have to have his money in advance. No tickee no washee was how he'd put it to her.

The following afternoon out in the windy yard I laid it all out for the other guys. The whole thing depended on John and on the assumption that he would get his parole when he went up for it sometime in the coming spring. I wasn't sure he would throw in with us, and if he hadn't, the plan would've died then and there. But he was as keen for it as the rest of us.

You boys can count on me, he said.

It was a lot of groundwork he'd have to do, I said, and it wouldn't be easy.

He said he could handle it.

Red said that was easy to say, but rounding up the dough to pay for the groundwork would be one risk after another.

John said it wouldn't be as much fun if it wasn't.

Oh man, Russell said, listen to this guy.

I told John it might be fun for *him* because he'd already be out there free as a bird, but we'd still be inside, sitting on our hands waiting for the big day.

Dietrich said John hadn't got the parole yet and we were counting an unhatched chicken there as far as he was concerned.

John said the man had a point. After all, he thought a Pendleton parole was a cinch and it fell through.

I said if he kept his nose clean until he went before the board the parole would be in the bag.

He looked around at the others and said Get a load of who's telling who to keep his nose clean.

It got a laugh. Charley said it was a distinct case of the pot advising the kettle against blackness.

They were right, and from then on I began walking a finer line myself. I couldn't afford to get put in the hole while we were prepping John, and once he was out I didn't want to get clapped into solitary and miss out on anything going on with him.

The only thing John asked for was that Jenkins be in on the break. His correspondence with Jenkins's sister had heated up plenty—whenever he got a letter from her he brought it over so I could smell the perfume—and I guess he felt an obligation to her brother.

It was a minor favor compared to what John would be doing for us, so I said Okay, he's in.

. . .

Smuggling the guns into M City required a five-thousand-dollar payoff to Mr. Williams in Chicago and we didn't have five bucks among the lot of us. But bringing in the guns was the last step in the plan. As I'd come to see it, the trouble with most prison breaks was that the guys didn't plan far enough ahead. Almost all their thinking went into the break and not to what they'd need after they got outside the walls—namely, safe places to stay and enough money to get by on. Guys who don't plan ahead are forced to act out of desperation, and desperation makes for bad decisions. That's why most guys who make it over the walls are caught so soon. My idea wasn't simply to break out but also to have everything else all set up and waiting—two or three separate hideouts with the rent paid two months in advance at each one. Clothes, guns, good cars with legitimate plates. And sufficient cash on hand to get by on until we were ready for our first job.

No telling how long it would take John to round up the money for all those things—on top of the five grand for Williams—and get everything in order, but he had to do it all before smuggling the guns to us. Once we got the guns, we'd have to move fast, before they could be discovered in a sudden shakedown or some fink got wind of them and put the button on us.

Over the next few months we gave John a crash course in the basics of making your way around in what the newspapers love to call the underworld. We made up a roster of guys for him to get in touch with who would make good heist partners. We drew up a list of banks that we knew handled payrolls for factories and other businesses. Charley and Walt made a list of different fences in Indianapolis, Chicago, and East Chicago where John could sell bonds and new currency.

Charley and I also helped him play the Good Convict in preparation for his parole hearing. We kept him on a tight leash and out of trouble with the other cons and made him mind his p's and q's—no gambling or sassing the hacks or fooling around with punks and never mind his complaints about headaches. We edited every letter he wrote to his family. Each one testified to a reformed character and sincere contrition for his wayward youth and was of course meant to impress the prison censors and make it into his board review file. Now and then he'd sound like he was auditioning for a church choir and we'd make him tone it down. Sincere but restrained, I told him, that was the ticket.

Pearl Elliott had agreed to be our go-between once he got out. I made John memorize her telephone number and the address of the Side Pocket in Kokomo. He asked if I was sure she could be trusted, and I said As sure as I am about you. Oh hell, he said, you better keep a damn close eye on her.

We grinned at each other like loonies.

Sometime in there I came to find out Homer Van Meter would be going before the board within days of John's hearing and that he was pulling the same Good Convict act. He was working in the prison hospital and walking the straight and narrow, doing his best to convince the bosses he had finally seen the light. When I asked John if he knew the scarecrow was coming up for parole, he said sure he did but he hadn't mentioned it because he didn't think I'd be interested. I said I'd be sorely disappointed if he took up with the guy once they were both out. He's a damn clown, I said, and you don't have time for clowns. You said we could count on you and we're taking you at your word.

He gave me that wiseguy smile and said the only way he'd ever let me down is if they killed him.

. . .

*I*n May he got the parole. On the morning of his release he shook hands with all of us and said to sit tight and he'd be in touch soon. Then the Indiana state penitentiary gave him five dollars and showed him the door.

Out in the yard a little later that day Russell said that if he was in John's shoes he might have second thoughts. He might wonder why he should risk getting put back in the slam for any reason except robbing banks.

I could tell by their faces that the others had been thinking along the same line. There were ten of us in on the break now. John Burns had thrown in and so had Joe Fox, who was doing life, and Ed Shouse—*that* miserable bastard. Shouse was doing twenty-five years for robbery, but if I'd known back then the kind of guy he really was, he would've received capital punishment. From me.

You might have second thoughts, I told Russell, but you'd come through.

Yeah, Russell said, but that's me.

Charley said he didn't know if John would have second thoughts but it wouldn't be surprising if he was distracted from his mission. After all, he said, the lad hasn't had a taste of the free life in nine years.

Hasn't had any poon in nine years is what you mean, Red said. He said if he was in John's shoes the top item on his things-to-do list wouldn't be us guys, it'd be making up for what he'd been missing. The way he saw it, even if John didn't have second thoughts, it'd probably take him a while to get around to business.

And even when John did get around to business, Dietrich said, if just one job went bad and he got taken down, that would be all she wrote. We'd have no man on the outside and it'd be back to the drawing board.

He'll come through, I said.

Perhaps he will, said Charley, but like all else beyond the immediate moment, it remains to be seen.

He'll come through, I said.

How do you know, Russell said.

I just do, I said.

Well hell, Pete, that's a load off my mind, Red said.

Jesus. I think about it now and I wonder what made us think we had a chance. So *many* things could've gone wrong.

Then again, what could've happened . . . did.

II

The Breaks

It took another four months to pull it off, four months of the same old suffocating routine, never mind that we got a new warden. Wardens come and go, but prison routine never changes. This one was another hardnose but he liked to keep his distance from the cons, and none of us ever got a look at him. We called him Bashful Louie.

Before he'd been out a month, John hit his first bank—in New Carlisle, Ohio—and took away $10,000. Not bad at all, especially for a beginner. Pearl brought the news on visiting day, giving it to me in her expert whisper so the guards in the room couldn't hear. Unfortunately, the bills had been brand new and in consecutive serial numbers and John couldn't risk passing them, so he'd had to fence the bundle. He got a good rate—three for five—but still, that's 40 percent down the rathole. After splitting the take with his partners and covering his expenses, he was way short of what he needed to finance our arrangements. Just the same, it was an encouraging start and we were sure that one or two more jobs and he'd have the necessary grubstake. Then bring on the guns.

New Carlisle, however, proved to be a fluke. We hadn't figured on the damn Depression. It didn't mean much to us inside the walls, but as John quickly came to find out it was kicking hell out of the real world. He'd go to case a bank on our list and as often as not it turned out to have boards on the windows and a padlock on the door. And of the banks still in business, most weren't holding enough cash to make them worthwhile. Pearl told me he had hit some drugstores and a few supermarkets but none of those jobs got him more than pin money. I said to tell him to quit the penny-ante heists, they weren't worth the risk. He could get collared on one of them as easy as on a bank.

Then there was no more word from him. A month went by and Pearl had no idea what he was up to. The absence of news put us all on an edge. Russell got in a fight and beat up a guy for no reason except raw temper and did two days in the hole for it. Charley had a rare case of the grumps and Red was ready to bite off heads. Okie Jack's chronic ulcers were eating him up.

Walt Dietrich said that for all we knew John had been arrested and was cooling his heels in some hick jail. He could've been killed and how would we know? We could be waiting on a dead man, Walt said.

I said that was possible, but more likely he'd met some looker and was enjoying himself for a while.

Russell said it was a hell of a note if John was spending his time dicking the chippies while we were waiting on him to set things up.

As if any of us would not do likewise, Charley said.

He's supposed to be taking care of *business,* Shouse said.

I told them not to worry about it, John would come through.

Red said I sounded like the president of the optimists' club.

Why's that, I said. Because I think every cloud has a silver lining? Because I think it's always darkest before the dawn? That for every drop of rain that falls a flower grows? That he who laughs last laughs loudest?

He who laughs last, Red said, is the dimmest fucken wit in the room.

Charley said his favorite adage about laughter held that a man who can laugh at himself is truly blessed, for he will never lack for amusement.

John Burns chuckled for a moment and then suddenly looked puzzled and asked what the hell *that* was supposed to mean.

Which got a laugh from everybody. Then Burns joined in and we all nearly split a gut.

*   *   *

The next time Pearl came to see me she was smiling when I entered the visiting room, and so I knew John was all right. She said he'd shown up at the Side Pocket one night and told her he'd been in Ohio hunting for fat banks, but he'd only found slim pickings. He'd then come back to Indiana and with a couple of partners hit a bank in Daleville for about three grand.

Three grand wouldn't leave much to put in the breakout kitty, not after the split and expenses. At the rate he was going, I said, we'd die of old age before he got the dough together.

Maybe not, she said. She leaned even closer to the screen and told me she had talked to Sonny Sheetz, her old pal and East Chicago outfit boss. When she told Sheetz that New Carlisle and Daleville had been John's work, he said he might have something for the guy and to send him around.

John's in East Shy right now meeting with him, she said.

I'd learned a lot about Sonny Sheetz in the time I'd been at M City. They said he got a cut of every illegal dollar that changed hands in Indiana between Kokomo and the Michigan border. There wasn't a cathouse or gambling joint or speakeasy in the northern part of the state that didn't pay him for something, if only for protection. The other guys knew about him too. Red said the man was well named, because anybody who got on the wrong side of him ended up under a sheet.

I asked what Sheetz might want with John, and Pearl said he might want to make some banking arrangements with him is what he might want. For a second I didn't know what she meant and she said You know . . . set-ups.

Of course. Fat Charley had explained them to me once, except he'd called them cover-ups. He'd even done one for an old pal who managed a bank in Ohio and was headed for an embezzlement rap until he thought to ask Charley for help. Pearl said Sheetz had people in a number of banks—including one or two in Indianapolis—regularly skimming the books for him or doing some other kind of inside larceny. Usually all it took to cover such theft was a talented bookkeeper. But there were times when even the most creative accounting wasn't going to get past the auditor on his next visit, and the best way out of the jam was to get robbed. Robbery was a swell solution because the bank could claim a loss that balanced its books, plus it got fully reimbursed by the insurance company. Fat Charley said it wasn't unheard of for insurance agents to be included in such operations for a cut of the profits. The only ones left holding the bag were the insurance company itself and the depositors. Of course the insurance company wasn't about to go broke, no matter what, and the depositors, well, they got what they deserved for trusting a bank. The American way of business, Charley once said to me and John, was designed to let the intelligently greedy fleece the stupidly greedy, never mind the plain stupid, and the law was their set of rules for keeping it that way. I said he took the words right out of my mouth, and John laughed and said Me too.

A set-up by Sonny Sheetz, Pearl said, meant that the vault at such and such bank would be found unlocked at a certain hour of a certain day and all the cash would be ready to go. It meant that, under the guise of protecting the customers, certain bank employees would not set off the alarm until the robbers were on their way. It meant that erroneous serial numbers could be reported for the stolen money in case the cops decided to send the numbers out around the state.

And how much of the take from a set-up, I wanted to know, did Mr. Sheetz get?

A third, Pearl said.

Let me see if I got this straight, I said. He skims who-knows-how-much from a bank, then has the bank robbed to cover the skims, and *then* gets a third of the rest of the bank's dough?

And *then,* she said, he goes back to skimming the same bank after it collects on the insurance.

Nice work if you can get it, I said.

She said guys like Sheetz weren't called bosses for nothing, but to keep in mind that the other two-thirds of the take was practically found money for the guys who did the job. The way she figured it, if John got one or two set-ups from Sheetz our financial problems were over.

I didn't get why Sheetz didn't use his own people for the set-ups. Why bring in somebody from outside?

Because strictly speaking, she said, Sonny wasn't in the holdup business. His main dealings were in booze, whores, gambling, and loansharking. Now and then he would also broker certain projects— including an occasional bank robbery—but he never used his own people for those projects because even in a set-up there was no guar-antee that nothing would go wrong. Something could *always* go wrong. And if it did, Sonny did not want the robbers to have any record of connection to himself or his associates. He liked to use stickup men with no known ties to the mob and who could be trusted to keep their mouths shut. John had no mob associations, none of us in the gang did. And because I'd vouched for John to her, she had vouched for him to Sheetz.

I've told him about you, baby, she said. Play your cards right and you can do business with him yourself when you're out of here.

I didn't say anything to that. The way I saw it a boss was a boss, whether he was a prison warden or the head of some outfit, and I was never one for taking orders.

Pearl was a smoothie—before she left she managed to pass me a small wad of paper through the wire mesh without the guard noticing. Back in my cell I saw it was a newspaper report about the Daleville robbery. A young female teller had been the only employee in the place when two men entered the bank and announced a stickup. One of them jumped up on the teller counter and then vaulted over the barrier into the cashiers' cage and started gathering the money. The cashier said she didn't know why he made the leap, since the door to the cage was wide open. Several unsuspecting customers entered the bank while the holdup was in progress and the other robber rounded them up as they came in. The holdup men herded everybody into the vault and made their getaway with $3,500.

That newspaper article was the first time I ever heard of Captain Matt Leach of the Indiana State Police, and we would sure get to know that bastard well enough in days to come. He was quoted as saying he already had a good lead on the identity of the robbers and expected to make an arrest very shortly.

When the other guys read the report, Red said What's with the acrobat stuff? I'm telling you, if he breaks a leg and gets put back in here I'll bust his other fucken leg for being such a dope.

I agreed it was a stupid stunt.

Johnny Fairbanks, Charley said. Our boy has a flair for the dramatic and likes to impress the ladies.

What bothered Dietrich was the business about Leach having a lead on the robbers. He asked Fat Charley if he thought it was true.

Charley said of course not, it was simply a standard police pronouncement. More troublesome to him was the size of the take. He thought it was rather meager, considering the sum John needed to raise.

That's when I told them about Sonny Sheetz and the possibility of John getting a set-up bank.

Man alive, Russell said, a set-up from Sonny Sheetz would be a piece of luck.

Maybe so, Walt said, but he wasn't going to count that chicken till it was hatched.

• • •

The following Sunday Jenkins got an unexpected visit from his sister. I caught a look at her through the screen as I went past them to where Mary was waiting. Sis was a honey, all right, as pretty as her picture, with a dark blond bob and nice-looking tits in a yellow dress. When I had told the guys it wouldn't surprise me if John was spending time with some girl, she was the one I had in mind.

After my visit with Mary I found Jenkins waiting for me in the yard. He was holding a basket of fruit Sis brought him. She had also given him a message for me. John says go to the Crow's Nest, he said.

Go there when?

His sister hadn't specified, but he guessed she meant now. Oh, and she said give you this, he said. It's a present from him.

He handed me a banana. I figured it for some kind of joke and stuck it in my pocket.

Say Harry, he said, what's the Crow's Nest?

I ignored him and went over to the mess hall. They kept the coffee urns full all day on Sundays. I poured a cup and casually ambled over to the bank of north windows. I was aware of the mess guards watching me closely from the far side of the room like I might try to bust the thick glass and wriggle through the six-inch-square grill-work of iron bars and drop two stories to the concrete pavement of the exercise yard below and then run across the yard and scale the twenty-foot-high perimeter wall like a fly in full view of the gun bulls in the towers and drop down on the other side and run all the way to Lake Michigan and swim out of sight.

The windows offered one of the few views a convict could get of the outside world. I'll grant you it wasn't much of a view, which explains why most guys didn't look more than once if they ever bothered to look at all. There was nothing beyond the perimeter wall except scrub grass and dunes and an isolated strip of sandy road. Some of the visitors and prison staff used the road as a shortcut to the old Gary highway. John and I had liked to go to the window after breakfast on Sundays and have a long look. We liked to see for ourselves that the free world still existed and was out there waiting for us, no matter how scrubby it was. I forget which of us named the spot the Crow's Nest, but we'd kept the name to ourselves.

I was the only one at the windows. It was a brightly sunny day and there wasn't a thing unusual about the view. I wondered what I was supposed to see. Then here came a green Chevy roadster with the top down. There was no mistaking John at the wheel or Sis Jenkins in her yellow dress beside him. Another girl was in the rumble seat, a longhaired brunette wearing blue. He stopped the car directly in view of the Crow's Nest. I didn't think he could see me through the window bars, but later on when we talked about it he told me he could just barely make out a silhouette and figured it was me.

He was wearing a white suit and fedora. He turned and said something to the two girls and they stood up on the seats. They were hatless and even at that distance I could see their grins. They raised the hems of their dresses way up high and started doing a sort of clumsy little rumba step in place. Sis wasn't wearing stockings and garters like her friend and her legs were long and pale. My dick swelled in my pants. It was all I could do to keep a straight face and not give the game away to the mess hall guards. The hacks in the corner towers were either paying the car no mind or they were enjoying the show as much as I was. John held his arms toward the girls like a stage host presenting an act and then said something to them and Sis stopped dancing and shook her head no-no-no. The brunette laughed kept on dancing and showing those garters. John turned up his palms to Sis like he was making some special plea while she looked down at him. She tossed her head back and laughed big and he reached up and stroked that long bare thigh. Whatever he said did the trick because the girls turned around and bent waaaay over and pulled their skirts up to show me their panties. The Jenkins girl's were yellow and the brunette's white and, oh man, I wanted to howl like a moonstruck hound. They were waggling their behinds and just as I was thinking the entertainment couldn't get any better John reached up and yanked down Sis's underpants to expose her ass—and I glimpsed a dark patch between her legs. I heard a faint *Woooo!* from one of the guard towers. Sis jerked up and around so fast she lost her balance and John caught her by the skirt to keep her from falling out of the car. She dropped down on the seat and started beating at him with her fists and knocked off his hat. He hunched a shoulder against her assault as he worked the gearshift and got the car rolling. The brunette was sprawled in the rumble seat and looked like she was dying of laughter. As the car pulled away, John raised a fist up high in the air and shook it. And then they were out of sight.

I hadn't seen that much of a woman's legs in nine years—never mind a female rump or a furpatch—and I had a hard-on for the rest of the day. That night I tossed and turned for I don't know how long before I finally quit fighting it and jacked off so I could get to sleep.

Before breakfast the next morning I peeled the banana and bit into it and chewed a time or two before realizing something wasn't right and spitting the mush into my hand. In it was a tightly rolled pair of ten-dollar bills.

I told the others about the money but not about the show John gave me. That merry little incident always stayed between the two of us.

• • •

During the next month he hit two banks, one in Montpelier, Indiana, and the other in Bluffton, Ohio. Pearl said Montpelier was a Sonny Sheetz set-up and went smooth as glass. The newspaper claimed the bandits took twelve thou but the real take was seven.

Blufton was a different story. John did that one because he'd gotten a tip that it was fat, but he'd been misinformed and the take was
only two thousand. What's more, the bank alarm started ringing
while he was in the vault and his partners panicked. They ran outside
and started shooting up and down the street to ward off the curious.
It didn't help their nerves a bit when a waterworks whistle suddenly
started wailing. It did that every day at noon, but John and his guys
didn't know that, though they should have. They shot holes in store
windows and windshields and generally scared the beans out of the
citizens until John came out and they piled into the car and took off.
John told Pearl the job didn't take five minutes but between the bank
alarm and the waterworks whistle and his rattled partners' gunfire it
sounded like a battle in a crazy house.

As she told me all this, I was thinking *Jesus* he's having a swell
time.

Sonny was arranging a fat set-up for him a couple of weeks down
the road and John was sure the take from that job would do the trick.
He'd said to tell me he'd have everything arranged by the middle of
September.

* * *

The set-up turned out to be in Indianapolis. John made away
with fifteen grand, although the bank claimed twenty-five.
He told Pearl to let us know that Harry Copeland had been
with him on most of his jobs, including this one. She hadn't met
Copeland, but Russell and I knew him from years back when he'd
done a short fall in M City. His name had been on the list of contacts
we'd given John. Russell had recently heard from his girlfriend Opal
that Copeland was living in Chicago and dating her sister. Everybody
called him Knuckles because the three middle fingers of his right
hand had been broken so bad they now looked like they had an extra
set of joints. He'd never told any of us how it happened, but Russell
had seen fingers like that before, on a guy he'd known back in De-

troit who once worked as a drop man for the local outfit. One day the guy was late delivering a cash payment of some sort and the tardiness cost his boss an extra day's interest. The boss was so displeasured he had a goon hold the guy's hand in a dresser drawer and then he kicked the drawer shut.

Pearl snuck me a wadded news clipping that described the Indytown job as being skillfully professional. The reporter couldn't conceal his admiration for the bandit who'd vaulted to the top of the cashiers' cage and sat up there cross-legged and with his skimmer cocked over one eye while he held a gun on the manager below and announced the stickup.

Matt Leach was on the case, still promising the public a swift arrest.

When he read the clip, Charley said somebody had to have a serious talk with John about the gymnastics.

I said somebody would, and pretty soon, to judge by the look of things—and I gave them the rest of the news. Pearl had informed me that immediately after the Indy heist John had gone to see our man Williams in Chicago and paid him the five grand. He'd watched Williams put five pistols into a two-hundred-pound shipping crate of spooled thread and then reseal the lid on the crate. On one corner of the lid John carved an X the size of a two-bit piece and he darkened the X with a fountain pen. The mark distinguished that crate of thread from two others in the same shipment coming to the Gordon Shirt Company at the Michigan City penitentiary. The crates would arrive at the shirt company dock on the twenty-fifth of the month.

All right, Russell said, *now* we're talking.

We agreed that if the guns came in on schedule we'd make the break on the first of October, a Sunday. We'd take some of the visitors hostage and use their cars to make our getaway.

I don't know about you boys, I said, but I got my bags packed.

The next time I saw Pearl I filled her in and told her to inform John. She said sure, but she hadn't seen him since right after he did the Indy job and had no idea when she'd see him again. He told her that in addition to the Jenkins girl, who lived in Dayton, Ohio, he was also spending time with a Chicago girl named Billie Something. As far as Pearl knew, he hadn't arranged any hideouts yet, but he had Knuckles Copeland scouting for places.

Up to now I'd kept Mary in the dark about our plan. The only people outside M City who were in on it were Pearl, John, and our man Williams in Chicago. By the time Pearl brought the news about the guns, however, I had decided Mary could be a lot of help, and the guys took my word she could be trusted.

She hadn't been able to visit me in weeks because she'd been put in charge of the Sunday shift at the café, so I wrote a note saying Pearl's a friend and signed it and rolled it into a little wad, and during our next visit I slipped it to Pearl through the screen. I told her to go see Mary at home and lay the thing out. Frankly, I didn't know if Mary would throw in with us or not. But if she chose to stay out of it, I knew she wouldn't fink.

Later in the week I got a letter from her. It was the usual blah-blah about her job and how her mother and sister were doing, but that was all stuff to gull the censors. At the very end, she wrote that Aunt Pearl had dropped by the house to tell her of a vacation visit they would soon receive from distant family members they hadn't seen in a long time. It sounds lovely, she wrote, and I know Cousin Earl is looking forward to it as much as I am.

So she was in. But she should've known better than to think Earl could come with us. His lung trouble had gotten steadily worse, and a month ago he'd been put in the prison hospital. He was still in there, and word had it he wouldn't last another month. I supposed he hadn't let her know how bad off he was.

• • •

Six days before the thread shipment was due to arrive, the warden ordered a lockdown and put the silent system in effect. Except for going to work or to eat we were kept in our cells, and any man caught talking on the job or in the mess hall got put in solitary.

Nobody knew why the crackdown. The hacks were jumpier and grimmer than usual. We whispered to each other without moving our lips, all of us asking the same thing—What the hell's going on? We were sweating plenty, wondering if somebody'd got wind of our plan. We figured the bosses weren't on to us yet or we'd all be in the hole already, but they might've heard *something* and were closing in.

It wasn't until the next day that word came through the grapevine that a package of three pistols had been flung over the wall bordering the athletic field. But the guns were found by somebody other than whoever they were meant for, and the finder ratted to the hacks. The warden still hadn't found out who the pieces were intended for and he meant to keep the crackdown in effect until the malefactors were identified. He had put out public notice that the prison was under lockdown and visitation was canceled indefinitely.

Evidently we weren't the only ones who thought the best way out of M City was with the help of a few guns, but whoever these guys were they had tried to bring them in by more direct means than ours.

At the mess table Russell whispered What're the odds of *this* so close to our move?

Only fucken morons would try a stunt like that, Red said, and nobody argued the point.

There were shakedown inspections three times a day. Every cell house and factory and storeroom in the joint was searched with a fine-tooth comb. The guards never took their eyes off us while we were at work. Walt said he might not be able to sneak the guns out of the crate when they arrived, but even if he did manage it, the sort of shakedowns taking place would sure as hell uncover the pieces, no matter where he hid them. It looked like the plan was headed for a crash.

And then, on the fifth day of the crackdown, three guys from another cell house were tagged for the guns and all of them got put in the hole. The lockdown and silent system were lifted. It was on a Sunday, so we were allowed out into the yard for the rest of the day. But the visiting ban stayed in effect and any visitors who showed up at M City were turned away at the front gate.

The yard was humming with excitement. We sat together in the bleachers and talked things over. The crates of thread were due the next day, but rumor had it the warden was still nervous about the past week and would probably have more shakedowns in the immediate days ahead. What's more, the warden hadn't said when visitation would be reinstated, so we couldn't even be sure there would *be* any visitors the next Sunday for us to take hostage.

The way things stood, we all agreed it was too risky to wait that long.

All right, I said. The pieces come in tomorrow and we go out the day after.

If the pieces come in tomorrow, Russell said.

They all looked at me.

They'll be here, I said.

. . .

Walt was on the loading dock when the shipment arrived. He signed for the three crates of thread and had a dock crew dolly them over to the storeroom. As soon as the crew left, he took a closer look and found the crate with the small circled X. He pried off the lid with a crowbar and started digging through the spools inside. But he couldn't find any guns and he began to panic. Then he pulled out a spool that felt heavier than the others. Snugged deep inside the spool was a pistol. Four other spools had guns in them too. Walt wrapped three of the pieces in a large burlap sack and jammed the sack between the back of a storeroom locker and the wall. The other two guns he put in the lower tray of a tool box.

Three-eighty automatics, Walt said. Full magazine in each.

Woo, Red said, that Johnny boy did it.

I didn't say anything but they could probably all read it on my face: I *told* you.

• • •

The big day began with a chilly sunless morning under a sky the color of iron. It started to rain before we were done with breakfast, the kind of rain that looked like it would last all day. Perfect weather for our purpose.

The shirt factory storeroom was never unlocked until after breakfast, by which time the bunch of us were scattered all over M City at our jobs. We couldn't get together to make our move until lunch brought us back to the mess hall. We made a show of eating and then we went out to the main yard about fifteen minutes before the hack whistles would signal it was time to get back to work. A breeze had kicked up and the guys in the yard were hunkered into their shirts with collars turned up against the blowing drizzle. The puddles looked like shards of dirty glass. We picked our way around them as we casually crossed over to the shirt factory and then went downstairs to the storeroom. It was full of shipping crates and tool lockers, empty cartons and tables stacked with new shirts ready for pickup.

A moment later I was holding a gun for the first time in nine years, and I felt like the world had suddenly turned right-side-up. As soon as the piece was in my hand, I knew that within the hour I'd be free or I'd be dead.

Walt, Red, Charley, and Russell got the other pistols. They looked half-crazed with exhilaration. We checked the magazines and worked the slides, jacking rounds in the chambers.

Oh baby, I *love* that sound, Russell said.

The resonance of authority, Fat Charley said. He was beaming like a jack-o'-lantern.

The hack whistles shrilled outside.

The only one looking unhappy was Okie Jack. His ulcers were

worse than ever and his face was pinched with the pain of them. He caught me staring at him and gave a weak smile. Ah shit, Pete, he said, I'm okay.

Anybody wants out, I said, now's the time.

Go to hell, Pete, Red said.

I grinned back at him. After you, sir, after you.

All right, Walt said, here goes. He slipped his piece into his waistband under his shirt and he and Fox went up the stairs and out the door.

It felt like an hour but probably wasn't ten minutes before Fox returned. As we'd planned, he brought the superintendent of the factory back with him, a guy named Stevens, telling him that Dietrich needed to see him right away about some kind of shipping mix-up. Stevens came down the stairs ahead of Fox and halted at the bottom step when he saw me and Red off to the side, holding pistols on him.

Oh God, he said, and dropped his clipboard.

Easy does it, George, Fox said, you'll be all right.

We made him sit on a carton out of sight of the stairway and told him to keep his mouth shut.

After another eternal quarter-hour Walt got back. I knew who was with him as soon as I heard the voice say This better be good, Dietrich, or your ass is mud.

Albert Evans—the day captain. We'd expected Walt to come back with one of the hacks and here he came with Big Bertha himself. Russell knew the voice too, I could tell by his look. We heard their feet clumping down the stairs and Walt saying Listen, I *found* the hooch down here and I don't want you guys thinking it's mine.

As they got to the bottom of the stairs, I stepped out with my gun raised. Hey there, Bertha, I said.

Evans stood fast and gaped at me. It was all I could do to keep from shooting him in his liver-lipped mouth.

Russell went up to him and pressed the muzzle of his pistol under his chin. You ugly sack of shit, he said, I owe you *plenty*.

Evans's eyes were showing a lot of white. Don't do it, Clark, he said. You'll fry.

Charley put a hand on Russell's arm. Somebody'll hear the shot and we're finished, he said.

We need him, Russ, Red said.

Russell snapped on the safety and stuck the pistol in his waistband. Evans looked relieved.

Then Russell drove a fist into the bastard's big belly and Bertha's breath blew out of him and he fell to all fours, gagging hard, and vomited.

I stepped between them and told Russell that was enough, Red was right, we needed the guy. And not all busted up.

Russell leaned around me to spit on Evans. Fat son of a bitch, he said.

Burns and Jenkins hauled Bertha to his feet. He was pulling hard for breath, his eyes streaming and his face waxy. I said for him to wipe the puke off his chin and pull himself together. I told him and Stevens exactly what I expected from them. I emphasized that if *anything* went wrong for any reason, they would be the first to die.

I told Stevens to pick up his clipboard and look his usual official self. I asked if he was married and he said yes sir, and he had two young children. I said that was real nice and if he did everything right he'd live to see them again.

Sure thing, Mr. Pierpont, he said, you give the orders.

You bet your life, I said.

The guys without pistols armed themselves with small iron bars used for prying the lids off shipping crates. All of us except Stevens and Evans took up an armload of folded shirts. They hid the weapons in our hands. Anybody who saw us would see Big Bertha in charge of a work party transporting an order of goods.

All right, I said, let's do it.

Nobody on the factory floor paid us any mind as we came up from the storeroom and went outside into the chilly drizzle. Stevens was in the lead, me and Red directly behind him, the other guys trailing us in a loose double column with Big Bertha at the rear, flanked by Dietrich and Charley.

We walked slightly hunched over the shirts in our arms like we were trying to keep them dry. Almost the full length of the yard lay between us and the warehouse, which fronted the yard and flanked the admin building. The warehouse was where we delivered shirt orders for local pickup. You'd go into a little sort of alcove off the yard and up to a double-barred window manned by two civilian clerks and a pair of M City guards with shotguns and you'd pass the shirts and invoices through the bars. This time, however, when we came abreast of the alcove we kept on going.

It was still a good twenty yards to the yard gate at the administration building, and as we headed toward it I had a momentary sensation of being in one of those dreams where you're steadily moving toward something but never get any closer to it. At every step, I expected to hear somebody yell for us to halt and the fireworks to begin. I took a casual look up at the nearest guard tower and saw a gun bull watching us. Then he turned away. He'd seen Big Bertha ramrodding us and that made everything jake.

The admin yard gate was a large iron-barred thing that opened onto a courtyard containing the door to the main gate inside. A gun tower loomed over the courtyard and the bull came out on the catwalk with his rifle in his hand. I glanced over my shoulder and saw Bertha raise a hand at him. The bull returned the wave and went back inside.

The guard on duty at the rear gate booth was an old-timer named Swanson. He'd come out of the booth with his rain slicker on as we closed in on the gate. Hey, Mr. Stevens, he said, what's this?

Special delivery, Stevens said. The warden said to bring these shirts over and leave them at the main gate.

I was impressed by Stevens's coolness. I'd been afraid he'd give the game away with his face or voice, but he did fine.

Nobody said nothing to me, Swanson said. He looked past us to Big Bertha and said Hey, Albert.

It's okay, Swanny, Bertha said, open up.

O-kay, Swanson said with a shrug. He took a big key off his belt and worked it into the lock, muttering about the meaninglessness of official procedure and how nobody ever informed him of anything.

The lock clunked open and Swanson grunted as he pulled the heavy door back and we entered the courtyard. It was the first time I'd been in there since the day I'd arrived at M City. My pulse was thumping in my throat.

Don't look like this rain's gonna let up any time soon, does it Albert, Swanson said. He turned toward the building door but Bertha said Lock it back up, Swanny.

Swanson said Ah hell, Albert, you fellas are just gonna come right back out again.

Lock it, Evans said.

I had told Bertha to make sure Swanson locked the rear gate again. If things started jumping I didn't want any of the yard hacks coming in behind us.

Swanson sighed like a man much imposed upon by unreasonable authority and relocked the gate. Then he went to the other door, a huge wooden thing with iron bracings, and pulled it open. We filed into a wide and brightly lit corridor with long wooden benches running along the windowless walls. Bertha closed the door behind us.

A dozen yards down the corridor was the main gate, which was actually two gates—one door at either end of a barred cage the full width of the passageway and some twenty feet long. A few yards on the other side of the cage the corridor ended at a heavy door like the one to the courtyard. Beyond that door was an alcove that gave onto the admin lobby.

Each of the main gate doors was manned by a guard, one inside the cage, one on the far side of it. They had been chatting through the bars when we came in, and they stared narrowly at us as we followed Stevens up to the cage with our arms full of shirts.

The outer guard asked what was going on.

I said *Now,* and we dropped the shirts and I shoved Stevens hard against the bars and pointed my gun at the guard inside the cage and told him to stand fast. Russell had Bertha by the shirt collar and his pistol pressed to the back of his head. Red held his gun at Swanson's ear.

The hack in the cage threw his hands straight up and said Oh God, don't shoot. The other guard started backing away toward the alcove door but Charley aimed at him through the bars and said, Halt right there, my good fellow. And the hack did.

I told the one in the cage to unlock the gate and make it snappy. The guard worked the key and the lock clunked and I pushed the gate open and Russell propelled Big Bertha ahead of him across the cage and rammed him face-first into the bars on the other side. Evans groaned and dropped to his knees with a deep gash in his forehead and blood running down his face. Russell clubbed him on the ear with the pistol and then kicked him in his fat belly for good measure.

I made the inside guard sit on the floor with his hands in his pockets and ordered the other guard to open the second gate. The guy just stood there. You could see in his eyes he was thinking of saving the day. Charley cocked his piece and said Be reasonable, sir.

The hack eased forward and worked his key in the lock, but he was slow about it, and I knew he still had the notion of being a hero. Then the lock turned, and when Charley stepped back to let the gate swing open the hack whirled around and broke for the alcove door. But Red had seen it coming and ran out and caught the guy by the shirt collar before he got to the door, and he slung him around hard into the wall. The hack bounced off and fell on his ass and Red grabbed him by the hair and hit him twice with his pistol barrel and the guy keeled over on his side with his hands over his nose and blood seeping between his fingers.

Charley looked at him like a vexed schoolmaster and said How much the better for you, sir, if you'd simply been reasonable.

I told Shouse to round up the gate keys, then gave Red the nod and he heaved open the corridor door and we all rushed out through the alcove and into the lobby, waving our guns and yelling for everybody to stay right where they were.

A handful of clerks were scattered at various desks and cubicles behind a long counter and they gawked at us like we'd risen from the grave. I said to keep their mouths shut and they'd be fine. There were two enormous claps of thunder back to back and the rain smacked hard against the windows.

Russell went around yanking out telephone lines while Charley and Red ran behind the counter and went from office to office, rounding up about another eight or nine people. We wouldn't know it till the next day when we read about it in the papers, but among those we had in our hands was the warden himself, whom none of us had ever seen and who had the good sense not to identify himself. The alarms hadn't sounded yet and I figured the hacks were either still unaware of what was happening or they knew but were busy locking down the inmates before setting off the sirens. As we'd come to find out, another reason they held off so long with the alarm was they thought we'd taken the warden hostage.

Jenkins patted down the men and took their money, and he found a .32 five-shooter on a guy who said he was a parole officer from South Bend. I pointed to the only two women among the workers and told them they were coming with us. I wanted hostages the hacks could easily recognize as civilians. Charley gently took them aside, saying This way, ladies, if you will. The thunder was steadily booming now.

I felt a sudden rush of cool air and turned to see Walt, Okie Jack, Burns, and Fox going out the front door. That wasn't part of the plan—we were supposed to stay together—but before I could say anything, they were outside and the door closed behind them.

I said for Jenkins to put the other employees in the main gate corridor with Stevens and the hacks. He started ushering them over there, saying Let's go, you Hoosiers, get a move on.

Lagging behind the others was a white-haired guy with a bad limp and a look of disgust. Punks, he said, looking right at Jenkins, nothing but punks.

Jenkins jabbed him in the side with the .32 and told him to shut his yap and get in the corridor. The old man had more nerve than was good for him—he slapped at the gun, saying Don't point that thing at me, punk.

The gunshot was like an electric blast through the room and everybody jumped and the old man fell down and curled up in a ball, holding his side and saying *Jesus, oh Jesus*. The younger woman let out a little shriek and the other one told her to hush up for God's sake.

Goddamnit, Jenkins hollered at the old guy, look what you made me do!

I shoved him aside and bent over the old man. He wasn't hit bad, just a deep tear through the flesh along the ribs. But it was hurting him plenty and he was really cursing us for bastards now.

Hell, he's all right, Red said. He took hold of him under the arms and the old man groaned and swore even louder as Red dragged him over to the hallway door and let the other employees pull the old-timer in with them. Red said anybody who opened the door inside the next half hour would get a bullet in the head, then he shut the door on them.

I took the older of the two women by the arm and headed for the front door. Charley had hold of the young one, who said Please don't hurt me. Charley told her to fear not, she was among gentlemen.

The visitor lot was out in front and we hoped there'd be at least one car there. If there wasn't, we'd have to hustle out to the highway and hijack the first vehicle that came along.

A car was pulling away as we got outside. Looking back at us through the rear window of the sedan were Fox and Burns, with some guy in a hat sitting between them. Walt was driving and Okie Jack was up in the front seat with him. A guy in civilian clothes stood in the driveway watching them go. He said he was a prisoner being transferred from another county by the high sheriff himself, but when they pulled up in front of the building they got surrounded by a bunch of convicts with guns. They made him get out of the car and took the sheriff with them.

The bastards left us, Shouse said.

We'll jack one off the road, I said. Let's go.

I tugged the woman up close beside me and started hotfooting it across the parking lot and toward the highway, the others close behind.

The new transfer yelled What about *me,* and Charley yelled back I hereby pardon you, laddybuck—try to be a better person.

The woman complained she couldn't keep up and I said she'd better. The gun bull in the corner tower was looking down at us through the blowing rain. He held a telephone receiver to his ear with one hand and was jabbing his finger at us with the other, as if the guy he was talking to on the phone could see what he was pointing to.

There was a filling station where the prison road joined the highway and its neon sign shone a hazy orange. We were almost to the junction when the prison sirens started wailing. I heard a pistol shot and I looked over my shoulder as Russell fired two more rounds at the nearest tower. The bull ducked out of sight—as if anybody could've hit him with a handgun from that distance. Russ spun around and came running, giggling like a kid.

The woman was stumbling bad now and sucking air hard. Then down she went and I let her go. Behind me, huffing like a bellows, Fat Charley stopped running and kissed the younger woman's hand and said something I didn't catch, but I heard Russell yell Come on, Romeo, *move* it.

The highway lay empty in both directions as we ran across it but there was a brand-new Ford Phaeton at the station pumps. The attendant saw us coming and left the hose nozzle in the tank and ran away around the corner of the building. The man and two women in the car stared out at us like terrified paralytics. I told them to get out, and Red yanked the hose from the tank. The guy behind the wheel and the woman by the front passenger door were quick to scramble out of the car, but the old lady in the backseat said she most certainly would not get out into the rain and we had no right to take her son's car and blah-blah-blah.

Charley opened the back door and said, Madam, we are desperate men and I implore you to be reasonable. Remove yourself or I will drag you out by the heels. He was wild-eyed and heaving for breath. The old girl quickly slid across the seat and got out by the other door.

And then we were barreling down the highway, the six of us packed in the Phaeton and stinking it up with sweat and mud, laughing like hell. I wiped at the fogged windshield, peering past the slapping wipers at the rainy road ahead as the M City sirens faded behind us.

• • •

The rain was coming down even harder now. I couldn't see thirty feet in front of us but I kept a heavy foot on the accelerator. The Phaeton was one of the new V-8s and it flew through the gloom. Then the road made a sudden curve and the wheels lost their grip and we skidded off onto the soggy shoulder and went fishtailing through shrubs and past trees close enough to spit on and *wham* we clipped one and the left front fender started flapping and banging like crazy. Without ever taking my foot off the gas I managed to get us back up on the road and the fender fell off with a clang and we roared full speed ahead.

Russell hollered *Wa-hoooo!*

Red said, Listen Pete, if you ever wanna borrow my car the answer's no.

I thought I was doing well for a guy who hadn't been behind the wheel in nine years.

Shouse was sitting up front between me and Russell, and he

scanned the dial on the crackling radio for news of the break. We'd been on the road for maybe half an hour and there still wasn't anything on the air about us. We didn't see a cop until we whizzed through some burg none of us caught the name of. Maybe it was our speed or maybe the missing fender that caught their attention, but a police car going in the opposite direction made a U-turn behind us and turned on its flasher. Our luck was running good, though, and when I sped past a stop sign at the city limit, the cop did too—and a truck smashed into him broadside. In the rearview mirror I saw a silver explosion of glass spray off the cop car and it went whirling into a ditch with its doors flapping. The truck veered off the road with steam billowing from under the hood panels.

We cheered like the home team scored a touchdown. Russell said Man, I'd pay good money to see that again.

In another twenty minutes the radio was full of excited blabbing about us, much of it close to hysterical. They were calling it the biggest prison escape in Indiana history. Some reports claimed that fifteen convicts had escaped, some said as many as twenty-five. One said three getaway cars had been waiting for us. We were said to be armed and extremely dangerous, and citizens were warned to stay in their homes and keep their doors and windows locked. A state policeman told a reporter that a posse of five hundred men, both cops and vigilantes, was being organized. He said roadblocks were going up on all the highways in this part of the state and he promised they'd have us in custody, dead or alive, within forty-eight hours.

We knew they would set up blocks on the main routes but it was impossible for them to bar the back roads. I turned off the highway and went zigzagging from one farm lane to another. We kept bearing southward, the windshield wipers steadily slapping and Shouse working the radio as we moved through the broadcast ranges.

The rain kept falling and the roads got muddier. Most of the farms we passed were well removed from each other, and around midafternoon I turned in at the entrance gate of one of them and headed for the house. We pulled up in front of the porch and some old guy in overalls came out and stood there looking at us with a barking yellow Lab at his side. If he'd been holding a weapon it might've gone bad for him, but it so happened he hadn't heard the news. He recognized the convict issue as soon as Russell got out of the car, though, you could see it in his face. Russ told him to hold the dog off if he didn't want it shot, and the old guy grabbed the Lab by the scruff and spoke to it and calmed it down. They all went inside while I parked the car out of sight around back.

The farmer's name was Warren. He was short and wiry but had big rough hands and his face looked hard as oak wood. He put the dog in another room and said there was nobody on the place but him and his wife and the hired man out at the barn. Russell went out and brought the hand into the house and I told them who we were and promised them no harm if they cooperated. I said all we wanted was something to eat and a place to rest until dark when it would be easier to avoid the roadblocks between us and Fort Wayne—which of course wasn't where we were going, but it never hurts to plant a phony lead for the cops. I apologized to the woman for muddying her carpet and the bad smell we'd brought into her home. They were cool, those farm folk. They held their fear well and they didn't ask a lot of questions.

We took turns keeping a lookout from the front window. The woman made coffee and cooked pancakes and scrambled eggs. Shouse asked Warren if he had any beer or booze or cigarette makings. The old man said alcohol and tobacco were terrible evils and he wouldn't allow them on his property. Shouse said he didn't give a shit what the farmer didn't allow. I told him to watch his language in front of Mrs. Warren. I sent Russell and the hand out to siphon gasoline from the farmer's truck and put it in the Phaeton, and while he was at it Russ punctured two of the farmer's tires, just to play it safe.

There was no telephone but they had a radio and we tuned in the news. The speaker hissed and popped with bad-weather static but we were able to make out that the cops had received sightings of us in South Bend, Rensselaer, Lafayette, as far away as Columbia City. Which meant they had no idea where we were. They still weren't exactly sure how many of us were on the loose, but because of the sheriff's prisoner we left behind and the couple whose car we jacked, they knew we'd split into at least two groups and that one group had taken the sheriff as hostage. But that was about all they knew.

We washed up at the kitchen sink and made short work of the food, and the woman brewed more coffee. I had Warren and his hired man fetch us some of their clothes. Russ and I were too tall for either man's shirt or pants and Charley was way too round, but the others guys were able to make do and were glad to be shed of their prison grays.

The rain brought an early darkness. As we got ready to go I told the farmer I was sorry we didn't have any money to pay him for the food and clothes, and he said never mind. I said that was generous of him and then told him to give me all the money he had in the house. He'd been doing his best not to antagonize us, but now his eyes went narrow and his jaw set tight and I thought he was going to draw the line at being robbed under his own roof.

William, his wife said softly. Her eyes pled with him. He let out a long breath and emptied his pockets on the table. I told the hired man to pull his pockets out too. It came to about six dollars, much of it in silver. Russell went through the wife's handbag and found another two bucks. Shouse put a finger in the farmer's face and said he knew damn well there was more money in the house and he better get it from his hidey-hole or else. I pushed him away and said we had all we needed. I apologized to Warren and his missus once again, and then we left.

The rain hadn't slackened at all and the roads were really deep with mud now, and I was forced to hold our speed down. We got mired once and some of the guys had to get out and push the car free, but we didn't come across a single roadblock on any of those back-country routes.

It was getting late when we cut back over onto a main road a few miles north of Kokomo. Our original plan had been to go straight to one of the hideouts John was supposed to have set up—but then came the lockdown and cancellation of the visiting day when Pearl was going to tell me where the hideouts were.

We spotted a telephone booth alongside a filling station and I pulled up beside it. I tried calling Pearl at home but her phone rang and rang with no answer. So I called the cathouse. The woman I talked to said Pearl wasn't in, she'd been gone all day, no telling where or how long before she got back. I said to tell her that Handsome called and she could get in touch with me through Shorty—the code name Pearl and I used for Mary.

Then we headed for Indianapolis.

- - -

Sometime around midnight we rolled slowly into Mary's neighborhood. I parked the car in the shadows of the dripping trees across the street from her place. It was actually her mother and stepdaddy's apartment, where she'd been living with them and her sister Margo ever since Kinder had gone in the slam.

The rain had eased up, but it was still drizzling and the night had turned chillier. The sky was densely black and the streetlamps at either end of the block had hazy halos. I adjusted the pistol in my waistband under my untucked shirt and told the guys to sit tight, then went across the street and up the stoop of the apartment house. It was a two-story building with three upper and three lower apartments and a common front porch downstairs. None of the front windows was showing light.

Her place was a lower corner unit. The screen door was unlatched and I opened it and rapped on the inner door and waited a minute and then knocked again and a light came on inside. A moment later the deadbolt turned and the door opened a few inches and a guy in skivvies peeked out and said Who're you and what you want?

I recognized him from Mary's description—Jocko, the latest step-daddy. I said I was a pal of Earl's and had an important message from him for Mary.

Christ, he said, you one of them that busted out? That chicken-shit Earl send you? Well I got enough cop troubles of my own, you tell him, so he better—

Mary's voice cut in: Who is it, Jocko? Is it Earl?

Jocko tried to close the door on me but I had my foot between it and the jamb. I heard Mary say to get out of the way. He said he didn't need this kind of trouble. *Move,* she said.

The door swung open and there she was, holding her robe closed at her neck and gaping at me, her hair disheveled. Behind her stood a woman and girl, both of them as short as Mary. It was my first look at her mother and little sister, who was no kid anymore but a good-looking young woman. Jocko cursed and left the room.

Mary peered around me into the darkness and said Earl?

He was too sick, I said.

The mother put a hand to her mouth and Margo held her close. Mary stared at me a moment like she was angry, and then her face softened and she sighed and said Oh God, I knew it.

She came out and closed the door and tugged me aside a little ways—then she threw herself against me and went up high on her toes so she could lock her arms around my neck. She said something I didn't catch because her words were muffled against my chest. I stroked her hair and her hip and felt my dick stir, which struck me as a little perverse under the circumstances.

She stepped back and wiped at her eyes and asked what happened, what I was doing there. Pearl had told her the break wouldn't be until Sunday. When she heard the news on the radio she didn't know what to think.

We could talk about everything soon enough, I said, but the most important thing right now was a place for me and the guys to lay low. Where was Pearl? Had she said where the hideouts were?

All Pearl had told her was that a friend of John's named Copeland was arranging for hideouts, but she hadn't said where.

I said I had to come up with someplace quick, the guys were waiting on me.

I couldn't see her face very well in the shadows but I felt her staring hard at me. I know a place, she said. Let me get dressed.

She went inside and closed the door and I waited in the dark. I heard the others all talking at once. I couldn't make out most of what they were saying but I heard her mother screech that she forbid her to go with me. A few minutes later she was back, wearing a long coat over a short dress. The only one still in the living room was Margo, and she wiggled her fingers goodbye at us.

We hustled out to the Phaeton and Shouse crammed himself in the backseat with the others so Mary could sit between me and Russell. I made hasty introductions as I got us rolling. Russell said Hell girl, you're little-bitty enough to carry in my shirt pocket. She said he better not try it if he knew what was good for him.

Woo, Red said, she's a feisty one, Pete.

The car was warmly humid and reeked of our rancid state. The stink must've disgusted Mary but she showed no sign of it. She took several packs of cigarettes from her purse and passed them out, saying she'd swiped them from Jocko's stash, figuring we might be in need.

You sweet angel, Fat Charley said. In a minute the car was so thick with smoke that we had to lower the windows a little and never mind the rain.

I followed her directions toward the west side of town. She was taking us to a friend's house. She said the place was small but well away from neighbors. It also had a telephone, and a garage around back and out of sight of the street. I asked if her friend could be trusted, and she said she thought so. It really didn't matter. Her friend wasn't going to have any chance to fink us while we were there, and once we were gone it wouldn't make any difference.

The first thing I wanted to do when we got there was try calling Pearl again. I figured she'd know how to get in touch with John. I laughed and said I wondered if that Hoosier even knew we'd busted out, or if he'd been so busy making whoopee he hadn't heard the news yet.

Oh God, Mary said, don't you *know?* John's in jail.

● ● ●

He'd been collared in Ohio four days earlier. Mary got the news from Pearl over the phone. Somebody tipped the cops that one of the guys who'd hit the Blufton bank last month was paying regular visits to a certain woman at a boarding-house in Dayton. So the cops staked out the house. Sure enough, John showed up and they nabbed him.

I looked at Jenkins in the rearview. He said Yeah, hell . . . that's where my sister lives.

See what I mean about John and broads? It's one thing to have fun with them, it's another to get so dippy you let your guard down.

When Indiana got word of the arrest, Matt Leach took a bunch of eyewitnesses to Dayton and they identified John as one of the guys on the Indytown bank job. Leach wanted to extradite him, but John refused to sign the papers, and Ohio anyway wanted to prosecute him for the Blufton robbery. He was being held in the Allen County jail in Lima, where he would be tried. Pearl said it would be at least two weeks, if not longer, before his case went to court.

Fat Charley was from that part of Ohio around Allen County and he knew the jail John was in. He said it was a cracker box. No doubt John had thought so too, and that was why he'd chosen to stay there instead of letting Leach take him back to Hoosierland.

I said of course that was why. He knew if we busted out of M City we'd sure as hell come for him, and he was trying to make it as easy for us as he could.

● ● ● ● ●

*B*ut first things first.

Like Mary said, her friend's house was nicely isolated. I cut off the headlights as I turned onto the driveway and drove around to the rear and parked next to her friend's DeSoto. It was after one o'clock in the morning and the house was completely dark. Mary and I went to the kitchen door and knocked until a light came on inside. The curtain in the door window drew back and a guy in a shiny red robe gawked out at us.

Mary said It's me, Ralph, open up. Until then I'd assumed her friend was a woman.

Who's with you, he said, and she said A friend, now let us in.

As he opened the door I gave a little whistle and the others came out of the car. Ralph said something I didn't catch and backed away fast as the guys hustled to the door and tramped through his kitchen and into the parlor, filling his house with loudness and bad smells. He had the smoothest-looking skin I've ever seen on a man. He must've recognized the prison issue and he gawked at the gun in my waistband. He looked on the verge of panic. There was a dining room between the kitchen and the parlor and I told him to sit down at the table and take it easy. Mary saw how scared he was and hurriedly introduced us—his name was Ralph Saffell. She explained things to him, saying she was sorry for the intrusion but we'd had nowhere else to go. She said we needed a place for the night and would be leaving in the morning.

I told Ralph there was no need to be scared, and he nodded and cleared his throat and said All right, okay. I thanked him for his hospitality and told him not to touch the telephone unless it rang and we said he could answer it, in which case one of us would be right at his ear, listening along with him. He nodded and said All right, okay, you bet. He was so eager to please that if I'd told him the moon was made of green cheese he would've said he always thought so too, you bet.

I tried calling Pearl but there was still no answer at her house and she hadn't been back to the Side Pocket. Mary had informed Margo where we were going, so that if Pearl phoned or showed up there she'd know where to find us.

My mother would've heard about the break by now and I knew she'd be worried about me, but I thought it best not to phone her until some of the dust settled and I had a better idea of what my next move would be. Russell felt the same way about contacting his girl. He said Opal was a good soldier and knew he'd be in touch as soon as he could.

Red found two quarts of beer in the icebox and we divvied it up in tumblers, including one for Mary. Ralph said he didn't care for any, thank you. It was common knowledge that Prohibition would be repealed before the end of the year, and Russell said he couldn't wait to step up to a bar again and buy himself a Blue Ribbon and a bump. I raised my glass and said To Ralphie boy, our generous host and a jolly good fellow. Fat Charley said Hear hear. We all touched glasses and Mary said Welcome back to the world, boys.

I drained mine in two swallows, and oh Jesus I still remember it. It was so nice and cold and stung my tongue and I felt it all the way up in my sinuses, in my eyes. Red said Oh man, and smacked his lips. Charley sighed and gazed into his glass like it was a picture of a long-lost love. I've never been a hard drinker or cared to work with those who are—in our trade you always need your wits about you—but I've always appreciated a glass of cold beer. That first taste at Ralph's after nine dry years was unforgettable.

Mary went to the kitchen to make sandwiches and Shouse said he'd help and went with her. The rest of us bunched around the radio and scanned it for more news about the break. Most of the reports now had it right and knew there were only ten of us. Dietrich and the others were also still at large and apparently still had that sheriff with them.

We were talking about where they might be when we heard what sounded like a slap in the kitchen and Mary said I *told* you quit it!

I went in there. Shouse was smiling stupidly and rubbing his cheek, and Mary was glaring. They must've seen something in my face, though, because she quick said It's nothing, it's over with, and Shouse's smile sagged and he said Hey man, it was just a friendly pat, nothing to make a federal case about.

Touch her again, I said, I'll break your fucking arms.

What the *hell*, Pete, he said, shrugging big, playing the puzzled pal. He was about to say something more but I pointed a finger at him and said I didn't want to hear it. He half-raised his hands and said Okay, okay, and eased past me and went back to the parlor.

Goddamn weasel. If half of Indiana hadn't been looking for us at the time, I would've kicked him out of the bunch right then and there. And if I'd done *that* . . .

Ah, bullshit. If, if, if . . .

Mary said there was no reason for me to get so tough about it. She said she knew how to deal with fresh guys and it was only a pinch on the behind and who could blame him after so long in prison. And didn't anybody ever tell me it was impolite to say fucking in front of a lady?

I apologized and said I didn't usually talk that way. She said she already knew that, in case I'd forgotten. If I really wanted to be of help to her, she could use a hand with the sandwiches.

While I was slicing tomatoes and she was carving bologna off the roll, neither of us saying anything, a funny thing happened: She suddenly seemed like somebody I barely knew. Not that she didn't *look* familiar—her eyes and smile were the same as ever, her voice, her gestures. If anything, she'd grown prettier, rounder in all the right places. But it suddenly dawned on me how many years had gone by since she'd been the young girl who so often got naked with me but refused to go all the way, how long it had been since we'd last seen each other without a wire mesh between us. Now she was a woman whose husband I'd beat hell out of for hitting her, who'd touched my fingertips through the visiting room screen and said Baby, how I wish. And yet, at that moment in the kitchen, she struck me as a stranger.

Without looking up from the sandwich she was putting together, she said it was funny, wasn't it, how you could look forward so much to seeing somebody you've been missing for years and you have all these things you want to say, and then you see the person and you don't know what to say or how to act or anything.

She cut her eyes at me and said That ever happen to you?

I shrugged and said yeah, I guessed so. I asked how long she'd known Ralph and she said a few weeks, and why did I ask.

Just wondering, I said. I thought I was being pretty casual about it but she gave me a look and said *Oh?*

I said I guessed she and him had been out on dates, and she said yeah, to the movies one time and then earlier that night they'd gone to a dance.

I said You and him were on a date *tonight?*

That's right, she said, what of it? Something wrong with that?

I became aware that the radio had been turned off and the living room was dead silent. I could picture the guys stifling their giggles and winking at each other as they listened in on us.

I didn't say anything was wrong with it, I said, trying to keep my voice low.

Oh yes you did, she said, not holding her voice down at all. You just didn't say it out loud.

Oh I see, I said, now you're a mind reader. You ought to go on stage, you could make a million bucks.

You're jealous, she said. You're jealous to beat the band.

I said was she kidding? *Me,* jealous? Ho ho, that was rich.

The truth is, brother, she had me cold.

Not that it was any of my beeswax, she said, but she and Ralph hadn't done anything more than kiss, and they'd done that exactly one time. She hadn't done more than that with anybody ever since her lowdown husband went to prison. Not that she *couldn't* have done more than that if she'd wanted to, because she *could've*, with *anybody* she wanted to, because *nobody* was the boss of her, did I get that?

Yeah yeah, I said, I got it. I was thinking how everybody in the house probably got it.

She looked at me like I was some hopeless moron. What the hell did I have to be jealous about, she said. Sweet Jesus, if I'd ever given her a reason, *one* reason, not to see other men, she never would've even. . . . She didn't bother to finish, just shook her head again and gave me one of those looks women use that mean men are *such* dopes.

Is that so, I said.

Yeah, she said, that's so.

I pulled her to me and kissed her. It took her a second to catch up, but then she grabbed me tight and started doing her share. I was getting a stiffie and she pushed herself against it and made a low sound and slipped her tongue in my mouth.

I don't know how long we were like that before somebody said Ahem from the kitchen door and we broke the kiss to see Russell smiling at us. He looked back into the living room and made the OK sign with his fingers and we heard a round of applause.

Listen you two, he said, nobody wants to be a spoilsport, but how long's a man have to wait for a damn sandwich around here?

• • •

After we ate we took turns in the shower. I was the next-to-last to use it and by the time I had my turn the bottom of the tub was coated with grime and the hot water was long gone. But the dirty tub and the gooseflesh were worth it to feel clean again. Charley had dug through Ralph's closet and found a wrap-around smoking jacket large enough for him, and Russell and I made do with a couple of Ralph's terry-cloth bathrobes. The hems didn't reach to our knees and the sleeves ended between our wrists and elbows. We took a lot of ribbing about the way we looked, even from

Mary, but I would've gone buck naked before getting back into those filthy prison clothes.

It wouldn't be long before daybreak and we all needed some sleep. I gave Jenkins the first watch at the window, then Shouse would spell him. Red laid claim to the sofa and Charley and Russell each curled up in armchairs. Shouse made do with a pillow on the floor. Ralph's fatigue had got the better of his fright and he was dozing with his head on his arms on the dining table.

It seemed understood that the only bedroom in the house was mine and Mary's, and we went in there and closed the door. I took off the robe and sat on the edge of the bed and she stood in front of me and I undressed her. Women's underpants had changed in the time I'd been away. She was wearing the sexiest I'd ever seen—baby-blue and silky and they fit her like a second skin. I slid them down her legs and she put a hand on my shoulder and stepped out of them, each thigh rising in turn, her private hair almost in my face and fragrant with her musk. I thought my erection was going to have a heart attack. I'd been nine years without a woman and it was too much to take. She didn't know how close I was, and when she bent to kiss me she took me in her hand. I tried to say No, wait . . . but *bang,* there it came. She looked down and caught a shot under the eye and another in her hair. Before she thought to release me, it was over and done.

I was almost in tears, but she laughed and threw herself on me and we fell back on the bed, tangling arms and legs and rolling this way and that, kissing whatever parts of each other presented themselves, fondling everything that came to hand.

She licked my ear and whispered, Don't worry baby, I'll bet anything that rascal will be up on his feet in no time.

She took hold of me again. Oh look! He's on hands and knees already.

We'd been worried I might hurt her, but our difference in size turned out not to be a problem. She drew a deep breath as I eased into her . . . then sighed and grinned up at me and dug her heels into the backs of my legs and said Oh boy!

Oh boy indeed. As Fat Charles once put it, what a pliant marvel is a woman.

We made love for the next couple of hours, giggling and gasping and groaning and whispering a lot of silliness, pausing now and then to have a smoke and let the rascal rest between rounds. We heard Jenkins singing "What'll I Do?" softly in the parlor. Mary thought he had a sweet voice and that it was nice of him to serenade us. I said it was a tribute to his talent that nobody out there told him to shut up or else.

I wasn't aware of the daylight showing along the edges of the window blind until there was a knock on the door and Russell said Pete, the Elliott woman's here.

· · ·

When I got out to the parlor Pearl had already introduced herself to everybody. She grinned at my undersized robe and said Handsome as ever, Harry, but that's not the nattiest get-up I've ever seen you in.

She gave me a peck on the corner of the mouth and I took a look over my shoulder at the bedroom door. She said Hey, pal, I've met her and I know—she's the one in a million and she's crazy for you. You better treat her right.

She's sure been treating *him* awful right for the past coupla hours, Shouse said, trying for a laugh. Pearl only rolled her eyes at him and I gave him a look that wiped the smirk off his face.

The radio was tuned to a big-band show, low but loud enough so that if the music was interrupted by news we'd know it. The latest word was that roadblocks were still in place in most of northwest Indiana and the police continued to get reports of us being here and there and everywhere. So far so good.

Mary came out in her black dress and she and Pearl greeted each other with hugs, then Mary went in the kitchen to make scrambled eggs for everybody while Pearl filled us in.

She'd been to visit John in the Lima jailhouse, claiming to be Pearl Morehouse, his aunt from Toledo. She had a driving license with that name and address to prove who she was. In fact, she had lots of driving licenses, each one with her description but a different name and address, and she said she'd see to it we all got a few tailor-made licenses of our own. Anyhow, John told her the cops had taken more than four grand off him when they arrested him in Dayton, never mind that they told the newspapers it was only two. That was the money meant to tide us over till we went to work.

Pearl took a roll of bills from her purse and handed it to me. She said it was four hundred dollars and to call it a loan until we got on our feet. She was sorry it wasn't more, but the girl business had been slow and her police payoffs had been jacked up, plus her booze sales had fallen off now that Prohibition was as good as dead and more gin mills than ever were operating in open defiance of a law that had lost its teeth.

I thanked her for the money, which would be enough to get us some clothes and see us through for a short while, but we needed to round up some operating capital fast. They weren't going to keep John in that jail till it was convenient for us to spring him.

Pearl said our luck might be running better than we thought. For one thing, it was certain now that John wouldn't be going to trial till the middle of next month. What's more, the Allen County sheriff didn't consider John anything more than a small-time stickup man and wasn't taking any special precautions to beef up the guard at the jail. And last but not least, Sonny Sheetz had gotten in touch with her to say he was impressed by our breakout. He wanted to meet me. He had a proposition I might be interested in.

Russell said Hot damn, Sonny Sheetz. Now we're talking.

I asked what he had in mind, but Pearl didn't know, I'd have to find out from him.

I looked at Red and Charley. Red said what the hell, there was nothing to lose by talking to the man. Charley said there was no telling how long it might take us to find a lucrative bank, and we had to make haste to liberate John. If Mr. Sheetz had a sure thing to offer, Charley thought we should accept it.

I didn't bother to solicit an opinion from Jenkins or Shouse.

One other thing, Pearl said, taking a folded piece of paper from her shirt pocket and handing it to me. Written on it was the name of Evelyn Frechette and an address. Pearl said she was the tootsie John had been seeing in Chicago. He wanted me to go get her and have her waiting for him when I sprung him.

Well Jesus Whore-hopping Christ, Red said. Anything *else* he'd like? A chauffeured limousine, maybe? With a bucket of champagne in the backseat?

I was tickled by John's audacity. Even before I'd made it out of M City, he was planning on me rounding up his girl and having her standing by when I busted him out of jail. Talk about confidence.

He said to tell you she's Patty Cherrington's friend, Pearl said to Russell.

Small world, Russell said. He told us Patty Cherrington was Opal's sister, who our old pal Knuckles Copeland had been dating for the past few weeks. But to hear Opal tell it, Patty wasn't nearly as keen on Copeland as he was on her.

Ah yes, Charley said, *that* old sad song.

● ● ●

While Mary and Pearl were buying clothes for us, Red and Shouse went off to another part of town and abandoned the Phaeton in a grocery store lot and pilfered another V-8, a year-old Deluxe Ford Fordor.

Around midafternoon Knuckles Copeland showed up. Pearl had phoned him and told him where to find us, and he'd wasted no time driving down to Indy. Poor old Ralph must've felt like his little house had been turned into a hotel lobby. I didn't want him listening in on us so I had Jenkins take him out in the backyard. I introduced Knuckles to the others, and Russell asked him how Opal was doing.

She says to tell you she can't wait, Knuckles said, and wagged his eyebrows.

Russell said *She* can't?

I asked him if he knew a woman named Evelyn Frechette and he said sure, she was John's girl, her friends called her Billie, and it was Patty who'd introduced them. He said he'd seen her the day before yesterday and told her about John getting pinched, but he didn't tell her about the blonde John was with at the time. She seemed almost as angry as sad about the news. She was a hard one to figure, Knuckles said, but man, she was a nice piece of work. He described an hourglass shape with his hands.

Knowing John, I already knew what she was a nice piece of.

Charley cleared his throat and asked if we could dispense with the small talk. He wanted to know if Copeland had found us a place to hide out.

He sure had—a secluded country place in Ohio, a big roomy farmhouse on the Great Miami River, just outside of Hamilton and about fifteen miles north of Cincy. The bad news was that the owners were still finishing up a few repairs on the place and it wouldn't be ready for another two days. Knuckles said not to blame him for the delay. John hadn't given him the job of looking for a hideout till about two weeks ago, and it hadn't made the job any easier that he'd insisted the place be within an hour's drive of Dayton.

Golly gosh, Russell said, I wonder why he wanted to be so near Dayton?

Charley was speaking for all of us when he said a country place was a bad idea. Bumpkins took too much notice of outsiders. They were too damn nosy and loved to gossip. They were too likely to blab to the cops. The best place to hide was in the heart of a large city, where everybody was a stranger and nobody gave a damn about anybody else, including the people next door. Anonymity is our great ally, Charley said. He had assumed John knew that and would get us a hideout in Chicago. As much as he hated to say it, he thought perhaps Johnny Fairbanks's good judgment had been fuzzied by his carnal yens.

I knew there was no perhaps about it, but I said that under the circumstances we didn't have much choice but to go to the country place and we'd see about getting a better hideout later on. We spread a road map on the table and Copeland made a little *x* on it to show where the house was. I made him give us specific directions for getting there, in case any of us got separated on the way.

When the girls got back from shopping and Pearl heard about the delay with the hideout, she said some of us could stay at her house in Kokomo for the two days till it was ready, and she had a trusted friend who could put up the rest of us.

She and Mary did a good job of getting all of us some nice clothes in proper fit. They'd played it smart and gone to a variety of stores, shopping for one of us here, another of us there, so as not to raise curiosity about buying so much men's clothing in a lot of different sizes. It was a wise precaution. The talk in every store was about the Michigan City break. Everybody was wondering where the fugitives might be. People were dreaming out loud about how they'd spend the reward money if they were the first to spot the escaped convicts and tip off the cops.

As we got ready to leave, Pearl said she could kick herself for not having brought a set of license plates to replace those on whatever stolen car we were driving. I said forget it, we wouldn't be driving this one for long, anyway.

I took Mary aside and asked what she wanted to do.

What do you mean, she said.

I mean do you want to stick with us or what, I said.

I can't, she said, I have to go home.

I'd been afraid she would say that, and my chest suddenly felt hollow.

She had to see her mother, she said. She had to talk to her. She needed to take care of things.

Yeah, I said, I get it.

And I need to pack a bag, she said. And then you better pick me up on your way back, mister, and I don't mean maybe.

She giggled at putting one over on me. I couldn't stop smiling even as we kissed.

Ralph didn't know our plans and there was nothing he could tell the police that would do us much harm. We'd already told Mary that if the cops ever got hold of her she should say we forced her to take us to Ralph's. Just the same, I warned Ralphie-boy not to blab to anybody about our visit, and he said he never would, never. Do you swear on the Bible, I said, ribbing him a little, and he said Yes, oh *yes,* I have one in the bedroom, I'll get it. I had to laugh. Never mind, I told him, I believe you.

Jesus, how do guys like that live with themselves?

We left late in the afternoon—Red riding with Pearl in her roadster, Copeland following her in his Olds with Jenkins and Shouse. Russell and Charley were with me in the Ford. We dropped Mary off at home and headed for Kokomo.

It was a short drive, a little more than an hour, and we didn't talk much on the way, Russ and Charley and I. The rain had quit and the low sun was shining bright. It was a pleasure simply to gawk at the broad, flat countryside passing by.

At all that free and open world.

*   *   *

*P*earl owned her house under the name of Dewey, the same name she used for her telephone listing, and of course had a driving license in that name too. Dewey was her Good Citizen identity.

I hid the Fordor in her garage and then she phoned the friend she'd mentioned, Darla Bird, who agreed to stash some of us for the next two nights and said she'd be right over. Pearl said we could trust Darla to keep things under her hat. Besides being Pearl's friend, she was the most popular girl at the Side Pocket, and when she showed up it was easy to see why—she was a blond knockout, far prettier than most women you'll find in a cathouse. Pearl said she was one of those rare working girls who knew how to manage their money, which was how she'd come to own a two-story house on a large piece of wooded property on the edge of town. She lived by herself except for three cats. Her house was bigger than Pearl's, so Red and Shouse and Jenkins all went with her, and Charley and I stayed put. Copeland and Russell had gone to Chicago together to spend some time with Opal and Patty before rejoining us for the drive to Ohio.

The next day we laid low and caught up on our sleep and Pearl arranged a meeting between me and Sonny Sheetz. After supper I telephoned my mother. She was elated to hear from me. She said the police had been there early that morning and searched for me over every inch of the place. She said she should've been an actress, she'd wept so convincingly as she told the cops how much heartache I'd caused her with my criminal misdeeds. Two of them stayed in the house most of the day in case I showed up or telephoned, and she made sandwiches for them to show what a good citizen she was, but it was all she could do to keep from putting rat poison on the salami. A car finally came and got the two cops, and she'd waved goodbye to them even as she was wishing they would all be killed in a crash. She had me laughing and I said Easy does it, Killer. She wasn't sure if they had anybody watching the house but she intended to take a long walk all the way around the property twice a day and see what was what. She said for me not to go see her until she gave the all clear. I said she was a champ and I'd call again in a few days.

Pearl and Charley were playing double solitaire and drinking wine at the kitchen table. I said goodnight to them and went off to the guest room with its comfortable twin beds. When I woke in the morning I saw Charley's bed hadn't been slept in. I found him and Pearl still in the kitchen, only now they were wearing fresh clothes and Charley's thin hair was wetly combed. Pearl said good morning and went to the stove to fry me some eggs. Charley was smiling *very* big.

I sat down and glanced at Pearl's back, then grinned at Charley and raised my brow in question and lightly tapped the top of a fist against my palm. His own grin got even wider and he nodded, and we both tried to stifle our snickers with our hands.

Without turning around, Pearl said I *know* what you guys are giggling about—you sound as silly as schoolboys, I swear. Then she gave us a scolding look and all of us busted out laughing.

• • •

An hour later she and I were on our way to East Chicago in her roadster. I wore a rube's straw boater and plain-lens eyeglasses she'd bought for me at a novelty store, and we wore matching wedding bands. If we should be questioned by the cops we would say we were Mr. and Mrs. George Elliott of Kokomo. Pearl could produce a driving license and automobile registration to verify the Elliott name and address, but I couldn't because I'd recently been assaulted and robbed of my wallet while taking a stroll in the park—and where were the police when you needed them, anyway? Despite our careful preparations and cover story, I was a little jumpy about going back to the region I'd fled less than two days earlier. But we must've looked respectable enough because we were waved through without questioning at both of the roadblocks we came to.

Sheetz's headquarters was in an old three-story building with the paint peeling off and a sign saying INDIAGO INDUSTRIES. It was flanked by a smoky refinery on one side and, on the other, by a dark green canal that ran out to the lake. Sheetz's office, however, was nicely appointed with dark leather armchairs and sofa. His bare desktop gleamed like brown glass. I sat across from him, and Pearl made herself at home on the sofa. Also in the room were a nervous, portly man named Hymie Cohen, whom Sheetz introduced as his associate, and a big guy with a black goatee who looked like a well-dressed pirate and whom nobody introduced. He stood next to the door and his nicely tailored jacket almost hid the pistol bulge under his arm.

Sheetz was perfectly groomed, every hair in place, his fingernails buffed to a shine. He was one of those guys whose age was impossible to tell by his looks—he might've been thirty years old or fifty. He had a diamond in his stickpin and another in his ring. His manner was casual but his eyes were constantly on the prowl. He thanked me for coming to see him and said he appreciated the risk involved in doing so, although the events of the day before had made it clear I wasn't any more afraid of risk than our mutual friend John. He said he had enjoyed his dealings with John, which had been fruitful for them both, and he was sorry to hear of his predicament in Ohio. He hoped things worked out for him.

I said I hoped so too, and we left the subject of John at that.

As I'd expected, what he had for me was a bank, only it wasn't a set-up. Like a lot of other banks around the country in these hard times, this one had been officially closed down, but it was still serving local business in such matters as lease and deed contracts and so forth, transactions that called for little cash beyond service fees. Through one of his sources, Sheetz had learned the bank would soon be reopened, and that a few days before then it would receive a large shipment of cash from the federal mint. Between ten and twelve thousand dollars, according to the source.

I asked what was in it for him and he said a third. I said that was a hell of a cut for just pointing me to a bank that wasn't even a set-up.

He said he ought to take more than a third *because* it wasn't a set-up. This wasn't one of the banks he got skims from. The only money he'd ever see from it was a cut of the take.

I said it was still a big slice for nothing more than steering me to
a bank.

He said I was free to say no and go find my own jug to rob, see
how easy it was to find a fat one.

He had me over a barrel. I'm sure he knew I meant to get John
out of jail and I needed some fast cash to work with.

All right, I said. Deal.

· · ·

t took a while for Fat Charley to realize I wasn't joking when
I said the job was the First National Bank in St. Marys, Ohio.
Gadzooks, he said, my old sweet home.

Which all of us except Pearl and Mary had already known. Naturally we ribbed him plenty about it. Russell said it was a pretty sad
state of affairs when a man celebrated his homecoming by robbing the
town bank. Red wondered how a community with a sacred name like
St. Marys could have produced such a lowdown individual as Charles
Makley. And so on. For all the kidding, though, our excitement was
like electric charge. Three days out of M City and we had a score
lined up. *Wooo*.

The only drawback to the job was that St. Marys was so close to
Lima, little more than twenty miles between them, Charley said.
There was bound to be a hullabaloo after we hit the bank—cops all
over, probably some roadblocks, the locals all worked up and wary—
and so the smart thing to do would be to let things cool a little before we set out to spring John. The way Charley saw it, the delay
would actually work to our advantage. Once the excitement about the
robbery died down, the locals would relax their guard even more than
usual, simply out of relief. If we waited a week or so between the bank
job and John's deliverance, we'd stand a better chance of catching his
keepers with their pants down and have an easier time of it.

The way *I* figured it, John wanted out of that cell as soon as possible, but Charley had a point and we all knew it.

Copeland and Russell had got back from Shytown shortly after Pearl and I returned from East Chicago. Knuckles had picked up a .38 revolver for Shouse, so now all of us had a piece. Pearl added even more to our arsenal when she got me a sawed-off twelve gauge from her office at the Side Pocket. There's nothing like a shotgun to ensure everybody's full attention and prompt cooperation in a holdup.

That night we all took supper together at a café, then said so long to Pearl and Darla and left for Indianapolis to retrieve Mary before heading to the Ohio hideout. Shouse and Jenkins went with Copeland in his car. Russ and Charley and Red rode with me.

On the drive down, Russell told us about his two days in Chicago. He said Opal shared a one-bedroom apartment with her sister Patty Cherrington, and the girls flipped a coin to see who got the bedroom. Opal won the toss, so Knuckles and Patty made do with the foldout sofa bed in the living room. But Knuckles got drunk and started accusing Patty of cheating on him, and Russell finally had to get out of bed and tell him to knock off the yelling or go home. Copeland said to look who's talking, that Russ and Opal sounded like feeding time at the zoo when they were humping. That got a good laugh out of Opal, but Patty'd had enough of Knuckles' ranting and told him to get the hell out. The next day he telephoned her and they had a long talk and he must've said the right things because Patty relented and said okay, she'd go spend the night at his place. Russell didn't see them again till it was time to get back to Kokomo.

As for himself and Opal, Russell said, they never left the bedroom in those two days except to go to the bathroom, and all they had to eat was cheese and crackers.

Truth to tell, we didn't really care all that much about eating, Russell said, if you get my drift.

Red said if crackers and cheese was *all* Russell ate, then he wasn't treating his lady friend as well as he ought, if he got *his* drift.

Fat Charley said he thought the conversation would be better

served if we didn't speculate about Mr. Clark's skills or lack thereof
in the perverse sexual arts.

Fuck you guys, Russell said.

Now *that* would be perverse, Red said.

Charley said he was sure what Mr. Clark meant to say was that he
and his lady had nourished themselves almost exclusively on love.

Exactly right, Russell said.

Red said that on their first night at Darla's house Shouse made a
pass at her and she said nothing doing. Shouse then offered to pay her
but said she'd have to put it on the cuff since he didn't have any
money. She said she never did business on credit or in her own home.

She says to Ed, I *live* here, mister, Red said, and man, you could've
chilled your drink with her tone of voice.

Jenkins was polite the whole time they were there, but he generally kept his distance from Darla. Red thought the little fruit was
scared of her. He himself got along with the lady just swell. He
mowed the lawn and helped her re-pot some plants, and after they
did the supper dishes they danced to music on the radio. Shouse tried
to cut in, and Red was willing, but Darla told Shouse Sorry, my dance
card's full up for the night.

I guess he'll think twice before offering a working girl money
under her own roof again, Red said.

He and Darla danced and talked until Shouse and Jenkins turned
in, and then she took him to her room. He slept with her on the second night too. In the morning he'd asked her if she'd like to come
along with him and live the exciting life of an outlaw-ette. She said
it sounded like fun, but no thanks, her life was satisfying enough as
it was. Satisfying wasn't the same as exciting, Red told her, and she
said he was right about that, but it tended to last longer.

He understood and so did we. He'd only asked because he didn't
want to have to wonder the rest of his life if she might've said yes.

• • •

*W*e were almost to Indytown when an announcer cut into the radio music to report all excited that Oklahoma Jack Clark had been captured in Hammond, about thirty-five miles east of Michigan City.

A taxi driver Jack had asked to take him to Chicago turned him over to the cops instead. According to the report, Jack was having terrible stomach pain and said he was glad he'd been caught so he could get medical treatment. I didn't doubt it. What's more, the old sheriff they'd taken hostage, Sheriff Neal, had shown up out of nowhere at the Gary police station. Everybody thought he'd been killed, but he was only a little worse for wear and had caught a bad cold.

Sheriff Neal told reporters he'd been abducted in his car by four escapees from the Michigan City penitentiary. They'd gone about a dozen miles when the car slid off into a ditch and broke an axle. The fugitives figured the highway would be full of cops any minute, so they took to the woods, hauling him along as a hostage. They spent two days tramping through the boondocks, chilled and wet and hungry, drinking from ponds and mud puddles. Neal said Dietrich was the leader of the bunch and gave Jack Clark a gun and the job of keeping an eye on him. But Neal and Clark were both in a bad way and had a hard time keeping up with the others, and yesterday around noon they'd been deserted.

After another miserable night in the woods, they'd stumbled onto a highway and hiked into some burg. Okie Jack made the sheriff give him his overcoat to cover up his prison issue. The other convicts had taken the sheriff's wallet, but Neal had a few dollars in his pocket and they got a bite in a café. Neal said he didn't think Jack was the sort to shoot him, but you never know, so he thought it best not to let on to anybody in the place that one of the fugitives in the news was right there among them. They then rode an interurban to Gary, where Jack wished the sheriff well and left him. And Neal went to the police station.

There was no word on the other three convicts, nor on the six of us. The announcer promised more details as they became available.

Poor old Okie Jack, Russell said.

Yeah, Red said. But don't it sound familiar, Dietrich leaving a buddy behind?

• • •

We turned onto Mary's block and everybody piped down and kept a sharp eye out for cops. I drove slowly down the street and past her apartment house, Copeland trailing me by a few car lengths. The coast looked clear, so I signaled Knuckles to pull over, and I parked at the corner and left the motor running while I went to get her.

Margo answered the door and smiled big when she saw me. It's him, she called out, and gave me a hug. Mary came into the living room with a small suitcase in hand and her mother at her heels, looking none too pleased. Jocko wasn't around. I'd find out from Mary that he'd been gone since the day after I showed up, none of them knew where to, or cared. Mary gave her mom a peck on the cheek and said to take care of herself. She hugged Margo and they said something to each other in whispers. Then Mary hooked her arm around mine and we hustled out of there.

I had Jenkins and Red switch cars because Jenkins was the smallest of us and could ride up front with me and Mary without crowding her, then Copeland followed me to the east-west highway and we headed for Ohio.

We'd barely cleared the city limits when I looked in the rearview and saw a car swoop around Copeland's Olds and come up fast behind me. The silhouette of its rooftop bubble showed against the glow of Knuckles' headlights.

Cops, I said.

Russ turned and looked through the back window. Two of them, he said. One's checking something in his lap with a flashlight.

I'll wager it's a list of plates, Charley said.

They stayed close behind us for about another mile, then hit both the red light and the siren.

I said Here we go, and stomped on the gas and the Ford jumped forward like a dog let off a leash.

Whatever the cops were driving, it was pretty speedy too. I passed a farm truck at sixty-five and the cops stayed right with us, only a few car lengths behind. Through the rumble of the motor I heard a muted pop-pop and glanced in the mirror as the one leaning out the passenger window fired again with a yellow spark and there was a thunk against the rear of the car.

I said Get down, and Mary ducked her head below the top of the seat. Jenkins was hunched low against the shotgun door with his hand on the revolver in his waistband.

They wouldn't be shooting except they know it's us, Russell said. He bent down to get the sawed-off from under the seat and I heard Charley work the slide on his .380.

Not yet, I said. Hang on.

I'd spotted a junction road up ahead and we were almost to it when I tapped the brakes and cut the wheel hard. We swerved into the turn with the tires skidding and the left side of the car started lifting as we went off on the shoulder and I thought we were going to roll. I heard the shotgun door snap open and Mary gave a little shriek and I managed to steer the car back onto the road and we sped on. I glanced over and saw the flapping door and no Jenkins and then looked in the rearview and saw the cop car sliding off the shoulder in a haze of dust and *wham* it hit a rail fence I hadn't even known was there and knocked posts flying and lost a headlight and came to a sideways stop with the one light shining across the road. Copeland's car wasn't behind us anymore.

Then Russell and Charley were looking out the back window and blocking my view. Holy shit, Russ said.

I don't see him, Charley said.

My God, Mary said, he just . . . *sailed* out. She flung a hand to show how Jenkins left the car.

I eased off the gas but Charley said it wouldn't be smart to turn back. Those cops were shooters and we had Mary with us and for all we knew Jenkins had broken his neck.

He's right, Pete, Russell said.

I stepped on it again.

We ditched the Ford in an alley in Shelbyville and swiped a pair of sedans, Russell grabbing a Hudson and me a Studebaker. In Greensburg we swapped plates with a couple of cars in a diner parking lot.

We had a tough time finding the hideout house in the dark but eventually did. Knuckles greeted us at the door with a drink in his hand. It was obvious he'd been hitting the sauce hard.

Jesus, he said, I thought they had you guys.

Shouse and Red were playing rummy and drinking beer at the table. Red said What kept you?

• • •

The house was clean and roomy enough for all of us, affording everyone his own bedroom except for me and Mary, who shared one. The place had a nice view of the river and was as secluded as Knuckles had said. You couldn't see the house from the passing highway, and we made sure to keep out of sight of the road whenever we went outside to stretch our legs. To play it safe, we didn't even buy our groceries in Hamilton, which was only a little way up the road, but sent Knuckles to Cincinnati for them. He brought back some newspapers too and we read all about Okie Jack's capture and the continuing manhunt for the Michigan City fugitives. They were calling Sheriff Neal a hero.

Our first full day in the house was a Saturday and we mostly lazed around. Mary and I took a stroll along the riverbank and found the head of a toy wooden soldier. It was about the size of a strawberry, and because I've been a pretty good whittler since I was a kid I carved it into a little heart for her. She loved it and had me make a small hole at the top of the heart so she could wear it around her neck on a fine gold chain. Then it was her turn to surprise me by proving to be a first-class cook. She fixed a big supper of fried chicken that night and everybody said it was the best they'd ever had. When we were done with it, there was nothing left but bones. Charley and I and Russell did the dishes afterward.

We had just finished up in the kitchen when the report came over the radio that Jenkins had been killed by a bunch of farmers in some two-dog burg near Indianapolis. There'd been a shootout and he wounded some yokel before another one let him have it with a shotgun and took off half his head.

The news put a damper on the rest of the evening and everybody went to bed early. Mary didn't say much about it, but when we made love I felt how tense she was. Afterward, as we lay there in the dark, I said that what happened to Jenkins could happen to any of us, even to her, if she should have the bad luck to be too close to me at the wrong time. I said she better give a lot of thought to what she wanted to do.

I couldn't see her face, and she didn't say anything for so long I'd thought she'd fallen asleep. Just as I was about to nod off, she hugged me tight and said I'm *doing* it.

• • •

The next day we all went up to St. Marys in two cars. It was a pretty morning of crisp air and soft autumn sunlight. St. Marys was a trim little town, nice and quiet except for the church bells, with red and gold trees shedding leaves along the streets. We cruised around and got acquainted with the place. The cop station had only two cars in the lot. We drew a street map of the bank's neighborhood and we made our own road map of the surrounding region, including every farm lane not shown on a regular map and marking the exact distances between every road and intersection. Then we went back to the river house and made copies of the map for each of us to study until we had them memorized.

On Monday morning Russ and Charley and I went back to St. Marys to case the bank itself. I was wearing my phony-lens spectacles, and Russell was cultivating a mustache that was coming along nicely. We wore seersucker suits, white skimmers, and green bow ties and looked every inch like yokel businessmen. Take it from me, a simple disguise is the best. The only one of us who never used any kind of disguise at all was Fat Charley. He looked so thoroughly common, so ordinary and benign, he didn't need one.

We took turns going into the bank on different pretexts—to break a large bill, to ask directions to some local address, to pick up an application for a checking account—and each of us took a good look at the layout. We then put our heads together and drew a diagram of it while we had lunch in a rear booth of a café. We went back to the hideout by way of one of the getaway routes we'd decided on, making a stop at a hardware store in Greenville to buy two large cartons of roofing nails. That was my own embellishment on the Lamm method. If they came after us we'd dump the nails behind us. See how far they chased us on flat tires.

That evening we had a light meal of soup and sandwiches and went over the plan until everybody had his job down pat. The only hitch was Copeland, who'd started puking before supper and would keep at it, off and on, for the rest of the night. He'd picked up a case of beer and a couple of bottles of whiskey from a bootlegger in Cincinnati and had been taking nips from one of the bottles all afternoon. He wasn't drunk but he was sick as a dog, and it was Charley's guess that he'd gotten a batch of bad booze. I wasn't sympathetic. He wouldn't have been so sick if he didn't have such a taste for the stuff.

His condition caused us a problem. The plan called for three guys in the bank, one on the street, and a pair of drivers—one for the heist car and one to wait with the switch car outside of town. Without

Copeland, we'd either have to leave the switch car unattended, never a good idea, or go in the bank with only two guys, which we could do, but it was always best to go in with three. Lamm had thought so and I did too.

When Mary said she'd be willing to take Knuckles' place with the switch car, we all stared at her for a minute. I could see she was serious. There were grins around the table.

She gets an equal share, I said.

I should say so, Fat Charley said.

Red said Holy smoke, Pete, you been smooching it up with a damn *bandit*.

Mary just beamed.

. . .

We pulled it off a little before closing time. I hadn't been sure the other guys would share my disdain for masks, but they did.

Masks or not, Fat Charley said, they'll know who we are.

Russ said Who cares? They got enough on us already to lock us up forever. A hundred more robberies ain't going to make it any worse.

Fuck 'em, Red said. I *want* them to know who I am.

Mary was waiting in Copeland's Oldsmobile at a small picnic park not far from a highway intersection and about three miles west of town. Russell was at the wheel of the Hudson, parked halfway down the block from the bank and with a clear view of the doors. Shouse had the street. Red and Charley and I did the inside work.

The manager and an assistant were at their desks and a single teller was in the cage. Charley paused inside the door and checked the time on the bank's wall clock and pretended to set his watch. Red unfolded a road map and went over to the manager to ask if he knew the best route to Bellefontaine. I strolled up to the cage.

The teller didn't seem to recognize me from the day before when

I'd gone in to get change of a twenty. I shoved a flour sack across the counter and brought up the sawed-off from under my coat. I told him to empty the drawers into the sack and be quick about it.

He went white, and I thought Not again, remembering my first bank job ever and the teller who fainted off his stool. Luckily, this one managed to stay conscious.

I heard Red tell the manager not even to dream about touching a goddamn alarm button. He had his gun to the guy's head. A few customers came in while I was scooping up the cash in the vault, and Charley got them together all nice and quiet. When I came out of the vault we ordered the bunch of them in there and Charley told them to stay put until the manager had counted aloud to five hundred.

I'd figured it for a five-minute job but we were out of there in a little over four. Russell pulled up in front of the bank and we got in the car and he drove us off nice and easy.

Oh man, Red said, oh *man*.

The alarm still hadn't sounded as we eased around the corner and then all of us were laughing like we'd just heard the best joke in the world.

Somebody tell me, Russell said, *how* long we been out of M City?

We have been at large exactly one week today, Charley said.

World, watch your ass, Red said.

In minutes we were at the picnic spot and Mary smiled big at the sight of us. I took the shotgun seat beside her, and Charley and Red got in back. She drove us out of there nice and smooth, and Shouse and Russell followed along.

We were all still pretty pumped up from the job, and Red said Boys, we are one *fine* fucken team if I do say so myself. Then looked at Mary and said Pardon my Turkish, honey.

She looked at him in the mirror and said I think you speak it quite fluently, Jack, and got a big laugh. She always called him Jack, ever since finding out some of the cons had called him Three-finger Jack.

At the next highway intersection, Mary turned south but Shouse kept going west. He and Russ wouldn't get back to the hideout till an hour after us—in a brand-new Chrysler they'd stolen in Celina. They ditched the Hudson in the woods along Grand Lake.

We made the next day's newspapers, of course. And of course there'd been a to-do—cops all over, roadblocks, the usual routine. The bank employees had looked at mug shots and put the finger on us. Matt Leach came over from Indiana and told reporters he was hot on our trail. They probably laughed at him as hard as we did.

The haul was twelve thousand, a convenient sum for cutting into shares. Four thousand would go to Sheetz, and everybody in the gang got $1,050, including Mary. She said she'd never expected to see that much money in her hand in her life. She got to hold even more when we named her the keeper of the common kitty and gave her the left-over $650 bucks to hold.

Copeland was a little sheepish in accepting his cut, saying he felt like he hadn't done much to earn it. Shouse said he could say that again. Mary said Oh hush, Ed. I told Knuckles he'd done plenty in getting us the hideout house and letting us use his Olds for the switch car. Besides, all that mattered was he was in the gang, and as long as I had anything to say about it, every member would get an equal share of every job.

The only problem we had with that job was the money itself—it was too new. You could smell it all through the house. It looked so unreal Russell said if he didn't know where it had come from he'd swear it was counterfeit. The bills were perfectly smooth and they crackled when you balled them up and no matter how hard you tried to smooth them out again they stayed so stiffly crinkled it was hard to stack them neatly. With money that new, the cops were sure to circulate the serial numbers and alert every business in the Midwest to report all transactions in which they received brand-new currency.

Nobody was for selling the cash. We all hated fences—a bunch of thieves who rarely paid more than fifty cents on the dollar. We figured the thing to do with the money was age it.

We put the bills in a big sack and took turns beating the sack against a tree truck for a while and then walking back and forth on it. We filled a large bucket with damp dirt and mixed in a touch of lard for that slightly greasy feel paper money gets over time and we worked the cash around in the dirt by the handfuls. Then we rinsed the bills under the tap and spread them on cookie sheets and put them in the oven at low heat. We took them out again while they were still damp and balled up each bill and then opened it up and passed it to Mary who pressed it flat with a clothes iron. It was a day's work, believe me, but at long last the money looked and felt and even smelled a little like it had been around a while.

Before we did all this, we set aside Sonny Sheetz's cut. If he wanted his money aged he could do it himself.

* * *

Late that afternoon a man and two kids wandered across the rear of the property, carrying fishing poles and a bucket and stringers of fish. Russ and Red watched them from behind the curtain and figured they were taking a shortcut home from the river. The man and kids all had a good look at the cars and no telling who they might talk to about them. That night we all slept in our clothes and took turns keeping watch out the window. The next morning we cleared out of the river house and moved to Cincinnati.

* * *

Mary and I rented a furnished two-bedroom in an apartment building two blocks from the Ohio. We were Mr. and Mrs. Harold Wahl. The other bedroom would be for John and his Chicago girlie—if I was able to find her. Russell and Charley took a two-bedroom in the same building and down the hall from us, and Red and Shouse rented a place a few blocks away.

Copeland had gone off to his own place in Chicago and to be with Patty. I told him Russ and I would see him there in a few days.

We stored the stolen Chrysler and the Studebaker in a downtown garage and then we all went out and bought ourselves some legitimate cars. Mary and I went to the Ford place, me in my phony specs and my skimmer and green bow tie, and I bought a new V-8 Victoria. The car had a radio, a clock, leather seats, dual wipers and horns, whitewall tires—the works. I told the salesman the Vickie was a fifth-anniversary present for my wife and gave Mary a big hug and a pat on the rump and she blushed fetchingly and told the sales guy I was the best husband a girl could ask for. We then took in a movie, and then went shopping for clothes and I bought some tailor-made suits for myself and a pair of red shoes and some pretty dresses and underthings for Mary. In one store, she held a sheer nightie in front of her and said Pardon me, but can you see through this?

It was a line from the movie we'd just seen in which Jean Harlow asked a salesgirl the same question. I smiled and answered with the salesgirl's line: I'm afraid you can, my dear.

In that case, Mary said in Harlow's line, I'll take it.

We had supper with Russ and Charley that night in a restaurant down the street from the apartment house. They'd gotten themselves some dapper new duds too, but I was the sharpest dresser in the bunch and always would be, if I say so myself. Charley had bought a Terraplane roadster with a rumble seat and was happy as a kid with a new toy. He said the car was a rocket, just like the ads claimed. Russ said a Terraplane was a fine car, all right, but it tended to draw attention, which was why he'd got himself a plain Essex sedan. Charley ribbed him about that, saying a young man like Russ ought to have a sporty car with which to impress the ladies, not some crate better suited for a fogey.

Take it from one who knows, my boy, he told Russ, youth is fleeting.

I know it, Russell said, and I'd prefer it to fleet into old age instead of an early grave.

We had a fine time, the most relaxed we'd been since the break-out. The night was cool, and as we strolled toward home the air smelled faintly of the river and burning leaves. Mary said fall had always been her favorite time of year. Charley gestured at the city lights all around us and said *This,* ladies and gents, is a proper refuge—among the urban multitude.

Cincinnati's all right, Russell said, but I'll take Shytown any day.

But of course, mon ami, Charley said—*there's* the best of all multitudes to hide among.

Chicago soon enough, I said.

• • •

The next day Mary telephoned home and her sister Margo gave her an earful of big news. The night before, a dozen state and Indytown cops armed to the teeth had stormed into the apartment. A dozen more had surrounded the building in case anyone tried to get away. The street out front was full of flashing red lights and the whole neighborhood was in a hubbub. The cops ransacked the place, emptying dresser drawers and closets onto the floor, overturning beds, using flashlights to search up on the roof and down in the crawl space. We'd been ratted by Ralph Saffell, supposedly because he was afraid we were going to harm Mary. The guy in charge of the raid was Matt Leach, the Indy state police captain whose name I was already sick of hearing. He threatened to arrest both Margo and her mother if they didn't tell him where Mary was. Mrs. Northern was so scared she was a blubbering mess, but of course didn't know anything to tell except that Mary had run off with me. Margo came through like a champ, though, telling Leach she was partly deaf and asking him to please repeat his questions and speak a little louder, constantly interrupting him to ask if he'd like a cup of tea or maybe a cookie, all in all just exasperating the bejesus out of him with a lot of harebrained doubletalk.

Mary was laughing so hard on the phone she was in tears and had to blow her nose. After she hung up she said Margo wanted me to know that Leach had a bad stutter that got even worse when he was in a state.

Margo said the m-m-madder he gets, the f-f-funnier he talks, Mary said.

Pearl showed up at noon with a half-dozen driving licenses for each of us, two apiece from Indiana, Illinois, and Ohio. Everyone's licenses carried correct physical descriptions—hair and eye color, height and weight—but each license was of course in a different name. From the common kitty I repaid her the four hundred she'd lent us and threw in another hundred, which at first she wouldn't accept. She said she didn't charge interest on loans to friends and the licenses were an inexpensive favor, since she had a plentiful supply of them. She finally took the money when I told her I'd burn it otherwise. She had lunch with us and then headed back to Kokomo.

That night I called my mother. She said the cops had showed up at the farm two days in a row after my last call to her, but they hadn't been there since. She scanned the woods and roads all around the property with her field glasses several times a day but hadn't spotted anyone keeping surveillance on the place. She said my father and my brother Fred had cut a clearing behind the barn to make a good hiding place for our cars. I told her I'd be seeing her the next day, and she said all right, but to call her again for a report before I got too close.

It was a pleasant drive, cool and sunny, and the Vickie ran smooth as a Swiss watch. Russ and Charley followed us in Charley's roadster. Mary sat huddled against me and sang along with the radio. The past two nights had been the first we'd spent in complete privacy, just the two of us under one roof, since before I'd gone to prison, and naturally we'd made the most of them. She was still feeling giddy from the good time we'd had. We stopped for lunch at a barbecue joint in Sidney and I called my mother from a phone booth there. She said the coast looked clear, but be careful just the same.

Lima was on our way and I wanted to have a look at it. Russell and Charley weren't crazy about the idea. They thought the risk of being recognized by somebody in Lima wasn't worth taking until we were ready to spring John, and we had agreed to wait at least a week to let the dust settle. Charley had also convinced the rest of us that we didn't even need to case the town—it was little more than twenty miles from St. Marys and he'd been familiar with the place since boyhood. He even knew the layout of the jail. Back in his insurance days, one of his clients had been the Allen County sheriff, and he'd visited the jail more than once to discuss the sheriff's policy. According to Charley, that man had been a hard case, and we might've had our work cut out if he was still alive and in office. The present sheriff, on the other hand, was some guy who'd sold used cars until a few years ago when the Depression ruined his business and he decided to run for office. How much trouble could a car salesman give us?

Russell agreed. And they were right, of course—there was no need to go into Lima until we went there to deliver John. But it didn't seem right to be so near the jail that was holding him and not even go by and *look* at it. What if he happened to be looking out the window at the time and he and I saw each other? I could give him the high sign—Hang on, brother, I'm coming. He'd done as much for me with the girlie show under the Crow's Nest. But how do you explain something like that without sounding a little sappy? I said I only wanted to have a quick look for myself and I'd wear my specs and with Mary at my side we looked like some ordinary couple and I wouldn't even get out of the car.

It's unwise, Pete, Charley said, but. . . . He gestured like Have it your way. I could see that Russell was displeased too. They said they'd wait for us at a small café down the road.

I drove through town slowly. At the courthouse, a guy in a suit was sitting on a bench next to the entrance and leafing through a magazine. We circled the block slowly. Attached to the rear of the building was the jail—a sort of annex with a side-door entrance to the sheriff's office, exactly as Charley had described it. The annex contained the sheriff's private living quarters as well as the jail.

I stared hard at the barred windows of the annex, straining to see if anybody was looking out, but I couldn't tell. Just in case John was taking a gander I stuck my arm out of the car and held a fist up high and shook it.

Cop, Mary said.

I jerked my arm back in as a police car turned the corner up ahead and came our way. To our right was a house with a FOR SALE sign and I slowed the Ford to a crawl and pretended to point out some aspect of the house to her, trying for an impression of young marrieds shopping for a home. She nodded and pointed at the house too and then glanced past me as the cop went by and she whispered that he'd slowed down and was giving us the eye.

All in a heartbeat I imagined the *way* he was looking at us—like *he* had all the authority in the world because he had a badge, and like *we* better watch our step or else.

Those bastards and their goddamn badges!

I suddenly saw red. I stopped the car and was going to give him a look of my own and let's see what he did about it, but Mary flung her arms around my neck to keep me from turning and said No, Harry, and kissed me hard. We had our eyes open and she was watching the cop over my shoulder. We stayed like that for a while and then she pulled away and let out a long breath.

I turned and saw the cop now more than a block away and still going.

Let's scram, baby, Mary said. This burg gives me the willies.

* * *

We parked the cars in the clearing in the woods behind the barn. I was halfway to the house with a suitcase in each hand when Mom came running out the kitchen door, saying *Harrrr-eeee*. She hugged me for dear life and kissed my face all over and laughed as happy as a child when I picked her up and swung her around. My father and Fred came out and smiled shyly at Mary and ducked their heads in greeting at Charley and Russ as I introduced everybody all around.

As I said before, as far as my mother was concerned, her Harry could do no wrong. Whoever stood against me was her bitter enemy and whoever was my friend was her bosom pal. She took an immediate shine to Russell and Charley, of course, and they both thought she was a pip. I'd been a little leery about Mom's reaction to Mary, though, since she'd never thought any girlfriend I'd ever had was good enough for me. When I'd told her about Mary on the phone, she'd said Yes, well, she sounds very nice—and there was no mistaking the skeptical coolness in her voice.

I'd told Mary that my mother might seem a little standoffish and not to take it seriously, but it turned out there was nothing to worry about. My mother was no dope, and as she told me later, the minute she saw me and Mary together she knew it was the real thing for both of us and that Mary would be protective of me. They adored each other.

Mom made one of my favorite meals for supper—spaghetti and meatballs, with vanilla ice cream for dessert. We sat around the table for a good while afterward, smoking and sipping coffee and talking about everything except prison, which Mom didn't want to hear a word about. When we called it a night, Mary was tickled pink to find out my mother was no prude and had prepared a room for us to share. When we were alone at last, she said That's some momma you got there, pal.

We stayed for two days, sleeping late in the mornings and eating huge leisurely breakfasts. Fred showed Charley and Russ his shotguns and his hunting rifle, and the guys showed him their .380s. Fred wanted to shoot the pistols, and they were willing to let him, but we decided not to take a chance on pistol shots being heard by the wrong ears. We had a picnic one afternoon in the woods way behind the house, and when Mary went wading barefoot in the little creek I was reminded for some reason of the time she'd spouted water at me at the river park in Indytown.

All in all, it was a good visit. As we got ready to leave, Mom fixed us sack lunches to take with us. She made Russell and Charley swear they would always consider her home their home, and she hugged Mary tight when they said goodbye.

At the cars, I kissed Mary goodbye and she got into Charley's Terraplane and they started back to Cincy.

Russell and I headed the other way.

• • •

Northern Indiana—Indian country, we'd started calling it— was very risky ground. According to the latest news, the state police were convinced we were hiding somewhere in the region. The highways were full of police patrols, and we ran into two roadblocks before we got to East Shy. We were wearing our usual road disguises and carried driving licenses identifying me as Len Richardson and Russ as Douglas Gould. On the backseat were a pair of briefcases and a scattering of real estate brochures. We were ready to duck down and floor it if a cop went for a gun, or even if we were asked to step out of the car, but at both roadblocks a cop simply gave us the once-over through the window, looked at the stuff on the backseat, and let us by.

Sheetz wasn't in when we stopped by his office, so we left his money with Hymie Cohen. He said Sonny was pleased with how well things had gone in St. Marys and he had another deal for us. I asked what it was and Cohen said he didn't know, I'd have to talk to Sonny, who wouldn't be back for a few days. I said maybe I'd be in touch.

When we got to Chicago we squirreled the Vickie in a downtown garage and then headed over to Opal and Patty's apartment, trading smiles with the goodlookers on the sidewalk and keeping our eyes on every passing cop car. Russell said the safest he'd felt since we'd

busted out of M City were the two days he'd spent in Chicago with
Opal the week before. All those strangers on the streets, all that wonderful big-city indifference. Perfect for guys on the dodge.

I'd been in Shytown before, of course, plenty of times. My first
visit was back when I was sixteen and a buddy and I went to a
cathouse near the Loop. We'd heard it was one of the best in town,
and I have to admit the girl I had was fine-looking and good at her
work. But the whole experience was like going to a friendly clinic for
treatment of a minor medical condition. It was . . . *efficient,* I guess
you could call it, but no more satisfying than getting a haircut. I
never patronized a whorehouse again.

I told Russell about that memory and he said he knew what I
meant, that he'd never taken much enjoyment in whores either, except for one time in Detroit when he'd had a Chinese girl who was
fresh off the boat and couldn't have been more than sixteen. He described her as a real beauty with not a hair on her snatch, although
he'd been disappointed to discover that it wasn't sideways, like he'd
always heard it was on Orientals. I chuckled at the old joke, and I said
I'd always heard that the only trouble with Chinese girls is that half
an hour later you were horny again.

He hadn't told Opal he was coming. When she answered the door
and saw who it was she squealed in surprise and threw herself on him
and nearly knocked him down. She was a Mack truck with a terrific
laugh.

Copeland and Patty showed up around noon and we all took
lunch together at a restaurant down the street. Like Opal, Patty Wilson Cherrington was divorced. She was a leaner version of her sister,
with the same pretty face and wonderful smile but with brown hair
and a lot sexier build. She was working in a nightclub, mostly as a
hatcheck girl, but she was a fine dancer and sometimes got to fill in
for a regular member of the club's troupe. She had a quicker tongue
than Opal and wasn't one to take anybody's guff. It was obvious she
was too good for a mug like Knuckles, but most strong women don't

have it easy finding a man worthy of them, and I figured she was simply marking time with Copeland till the right guy came along. None of us knew it yet, but Patty's right guy was just around the corner.

Because the sisters' place was a one-bedroom with twin beds, Patty and Knuckles went to his apartment to give Russ and Opal their privacy. I slept on the foldout sofa, and Copeland hadn't been kidding about the ruckus Opal and Russ made in bed. She *whinnied* as they went at it, and when she hit her climax, Christ almighty. Russell sounded like a man getting strangled and fighting for his life. If the only thing you knew about sex was how it sounded when people like Russ and Opal did it, you'd never bother to lose your virginity.

The next day Russell and I went to a riverside junkyard that was a front for a black market in guns and we bought three .45 army automatics. One for me, one for Russ, and one for John, who'd always said it was the gun for him. A .380 is plenty of pistol, but a .45, well, suffice it to say that it was specifically designed to stop even crazy demons like those Moros in the Philippine war. The way the old soldiers tell it, those fanatical little ragheads would keep coming at you with their machetes even after being shot more than once with a .38. But not even a Moro could stand up to a battle ax, which is what the .45 hits like.

We had lunch with Opal and then I went to the address Pearl had given me, a five-story apartment house a few blocks over from the El. The name Evelyn Frechette was on the foyer mailbox for apartment number twelve, third floor. I went up and knocked on the door but got no answer. A rummy-looking janitor replacing a pane in a window at the end of the hallway said he hadn't seen her since she'd left for her job the afternoon before. He claimed not to know where she worked, only that she was a checkroom girl somewhere. I borrowed a sheet off his work-order pad and wrote her a note saying I was a friend of John D's and to give me a call. I put down Opal's number and signed it Pete and folded it and slid it under the door.

She called at three in the morning. The phone was next to the sofa and its ringing woke me from a sound sleep. She had a smoky sort of voice and sounded a little drunk. She wanted to know what news I had about Johnny.

I suppose I could've explained things to her on the phone, but I was irked about being jolted awake in the middle of the night, and it chafed me all the more that she was tipsy.

I said I didn't want to talk about it on the telephone, no telling who might overhear her end of the conversation, so why didn't she name a place where we could meet in the morning?

I figured the crack about being overheard might get her goat, and it did. She said You think there's somebody else here? Some *guy?*

I said How would I know?

Listen you, she said, I know your real name and it isn't Pete. And I know about the crate of thread, you get me? I know things because Johnny trusts me. So get this straight—there's nobody here but me, and don't go telling Johnny any different.

I would've laughed at stinging her so good if I hadn't been pretty stung myself at learning John told her about how we'd pulled the break. I would come to think the world of Billie once I got to know her, but at that point I didn't know Billie Frechette any better than I knew Billy the Kid. For all I knew, she was one more bimbo John had taken a passing fancy to, and I couldn't help thinking he'd been a dope to trust her.

I said I'd talk to her at breakfast, to name a place where we could meet at eight o'clock. She said she didn't eat breakfast and never got out of bed before noon, so why didn't I just tell her what I had to say? I said she could either meet me in the morning or forget the whole thing, it didn't matter to me one way or the other.

She gave a big exaggerated sigh and muttered something I didn't catch, which was probably just as well, then said she'd see me at Paulie's, a café about a block east of her place. I told her I was a tall good-looking blond guy and she couldn't miss me. Yeah yeah, she said, and banged the receiver in my ear.

At a quarter to nine I'd had two cups of coffee and three cigarettes and she still hadn't showed. I was about to say the hell with it, let John fetch her himself, when she came through the door. She was coatless, wearing a black suit and cloche hat. Copeland hadn't lied about her looks. She spotted me, and as she made her way across the room every eye in the place was on the swing of her caboose. She was a few inches taller than Mary and her cheekbones were a work of art and the hair curling out from under the little hat was black as crow feathers. She slid into the seat across from me in the booth and I wondered why somebody with such a pretty face would bother with so much makeup. Her eyes were bright and quick but a little bloodshot, no doubt from the booze I'd heard in her voice the night before.

Without so much as a hello, she took a cigarette from her purse and held it in front of her mouth like the Queen of Sheba expecting some flunky to light her up. I thought about not doing or saying anything until she *asked* for the light, then immediately felt ridiculous, like she was gulling me into some stupid kid's game. I struck a match and fired up her fag.

She took a pull and blew a stream of smoke at me. Okay handsome, she said, you got me up with the roosters—now what's the word?

I kept it brief, telling her that John expected to get out of confinement in a few days and would like it if she was on hand when he did.

For a moment she simply stared at me and I couldn't read a thing in her face. Then she said You busting him out?

Ask no questions, I said, I'll tell no lies. You coming or not?

Christ, she said, you *still* don't trust me. She made a big production out of snuffing out the cigarette. Then said He really wants me with him?

Why else would he send for her?

I knew it, she said, I knew he wouldn't forget me.

I told her to be all packed and set to go by noon, but it didn't sur-

prise me that it was nearly two o'clock before she was ready. We gave
Opal and Patty enough money to rent three downtown apartments
while we were gone. I told them to get two-bedroom places, each in
a different apartment house, to make sure each building had at least
three exit doors on the ground floor and fire escapes at every hallway
window. We wanted places we could get away from fast if the need
arose.

* * *

I drove and Russell rode shotgun and Billie sat in the back and
talked our ears off. She said she was half French on her daddy's
side and half Indian on her mother's.

Do tell, Russell said. He leaned over the seat and gave her a good
once-over and asked which half was which. She laughed along with
us and said she could see she was among rascals.

She said she got the name Billie when she was a kid because she
was such a tomboy. She'd grown up on a Menominee reservation in
Wisconsin. Smallpox nearly did her in when she was eight. She'd
gone to an Indian school and hated the place with a passion. When
she was sixteen she ran off to Milwaukee, and two years after that she
moved to Chicago. She took up with a guy named Sparks, a stickup
man, and why she married him she'd never know. Sparks's partner
was Bobo Cherrington, and Bobo's wife Patty became her best friend.
Patty's marriage was no better than Billie's, and when their husbands
got convicted on a mail robbery rap and sent to Leavenworth neither
girl shed any tears. Billie never once went to visit Sparks and they'd
never exchanged a letter. She didn't care if she never saw him again.
She said Patty felt the same way about Bobo.

Russell said So you're divorced?

She said As far as I'm concerned.

For the past year she'd been working in the coat room of the same
club as Patty. They were better buddies than ever and liked to go
dancing in speakeasies. One night about a month ago Patty's latest

beau, Harry Copeland, showed up at a club with a friend he introduced to them as Johnny.

The minute I laid eyes on him, Billie said, brother, that was it.

I kept our speed slightly under the limit for the whole trip. We
didn't want to attract attention, especially not with a satchelful of
pistols in the trunk. Whenever we spotted a police car, Russell and I
would eyeball it on the sly until it was out of sight. The first time it
happened, Billie kept right on chattering behind me and I thought
she hadn't even noticed the cop. But the next time I spied one, I
glanced at her in the mirror and saw that even as she talked she was
watching the cop car too. That's when I knew Billie Frechette was no
greenhorn.

We got into Cincinnati around ten o'clock. It was a pretty
night—a nearly full silver moon, the air chilly and tinged with river
odors. I've never forgotten that town's lovely fall evenings.

We found Charley and Mary playing rummy and drinking beer at
the dining table. When I introduced Billie, Charley kissed her hand
and said You are exquisite, my dear.

You smoothie, she said, I bet you say that to all the girls.

Mary gave her a big hug and said Welcome to the club, honey.

• • •

What happened in Lima two days later—on Columbus
Day, to be exact—was in all the papers, it made the
newsreels, and five months down the road it all came
out at my trial. But the way things are reported in the news or presented in a courtroom is hardly ever the way they really happened. At
best, what you get in a newspaper or at a trial are some of the facts,
but facts are never the whole story. There can be a big difference between what happened and what *happened,* if you get my meaning. As
far as most people are concerned, *what* happens is all that counts, not
the whys and wherefores. Actually, I tend to agree. Just the same, I'll
tell you what *happened.*

But first I want to set something else straight. There was a hick-head Lima lawyer who claimed that Russell and I went to his office that afternoon and tried to arrange for John's *sister* to visit him in his cell. He said he told us he'd have to discuss it with the sheriff, and that even though he didn't know who we were at the time he was sus-picious, and that he tried to tip off the sheriff but the man didn't take him seriously. Well, that shyster's a liar. I never met him in my life. He's one more guy who used us to get attention for himself. His story doesn't even make sense. We didn't need to get anybody in to see John. What for? To sneak him a gun? To check the layout of that shoebox jail? Christ, all we had to do was exactly what we did—walk in and take him. The whole thing was easy as pie.

Except of course for that business with the sheriff.

We got to Lima a little after six in the evening. We were in the stolen Chrysler and Studebaker and had left our own cars in Dayton. There was hardly anyone on the streets, which of course was why we'd chosen the supper hour to do it.

Red parked the Chrysler in front of the jail office and kept the motor idling. Half a block behind us, Copeland pulled the Stude-baker to the curb. He left the motor running too and Shouse got out and lit a cigarette and leaned on the fender. His job was to watch the street behind Red. Red's job was to watch the jail door.

I had a .45 in a holster under my arm and a .380 tucked under my belt at my side. All right, I said, let's do it.

Charley and Russell and I got out of the car and they followed me up the walkway and through the office door.

The sheriff was at his desk and looked up from some papers when we entered. He was portly and his thinning hair was slicked with oil—and his eyes told me right off the bat he was no pushover. I thought Oh hell.

Two others were in the room, a woman in a chair with a folded newspaper in her lap, and a lanky deputy playing with a pup on a couch. Against the far wall was an iron-barred door that Charley had said opened onto a short passageway to another barred door, the one to the cells. The deputy was unarmed, but a gunbelt with a holstered pistol hung on a hatrack next to the couch. There was a large round clock on the wall, and in the momentary silence I heard its clunking tick.

Evening gentlemen, the sheriff said, can I help you?

The badge on his vest had been polished to a gleam. He was smiling but his eyes were sizing us up. He eased his roller chair a little nearer to the corner drawer of his desk, and I figured that's where he kept his piece.

I told him we were state officers from Indiana, working the Michigan City break. He had a prisoner named Dillinger who was a friend of the fugitives and we wanted to have a word with him.

The sheriff said sure thing, just sign the register and show him some credentials and we could talk to the prisoner all we wanted.

I pulled the .380 and said Here's my credentials, mister, now open the lockup.

The woman said Oh my God. Russell told the guy on the couch Stay put, Mac, and I heard the hammer cock on his piece.

Be reasonable, sir, Charley told the sheriff, there's brave and there's foolish.

The wall clock seemed to hold its next tick like a breath while the sheriff stared at me with a sort of sadness, like he knew what was coming and it was already as good as done for the plain and simple reason that he was who he was and I was me. Then the clock ticked and his eyes went bright and hard as his badge and he said You bastards can't do this. And he turned and grabbed at the drawer.

The man gave me no choice. That's the simple fact of it.

In those close quarters the gunshot sounded like the slam of an iron gate. He spasmed and slid off the chair and the woman cried out *No*.

There was hollering in the cellblock. The sheriff cursed and sat up and groped for the drawer again.

Charley said You *stupid* man and whacked him on the head with his pistol—and accidentally fired a round that glanced off the cell house door and hummed past my ear and thumped into the wall.

But the guy was an ox and he clung to the desk. Charley was wild-eyed now and cracked him with the pistol again, harder, and that did it. The sheriff slumped to the floor with blood running out of his hair. There was a thick red stain on his side.

The woman yelled *Stop* it, *stop,* and threw herself on top of the sheriff.

I opened the drawer and took out a .38 revolver and put it in my coat pocket. Russell had the deputy's gunbelt over his shoulder and his gun to the deputy's head. The pup was nowhere in sight.

Charley rifled the desk but couldn't find the keys. I told the woman to get the keys *now* and she said yes, yes, only please don't hurt her husband anymore. She hurried into the kitchen and retrieved a big key ring and gave it to me.

I opened the outer door and went to the inner one where John was already in his hat and coat and adjusting his tie. Some of the other inmates started crowding him at the door and saying they wanted out too and he tried to elbow them back. I fired into the ceiling and they jumped away from the bars and shut up.

I unlocked the door and John scooted out and slapped me on the shoulder and said About time, brother.

I gave him the .45 and he checked the load in the chamber. Russell brought in the woman and the deputy and put them in the cell and I locked them in. The woman was crying hard and the deputy had his arm around her. He gave John a hard look.

John said I'm sorry, missus, but if she heard him she gave no sign of it.

We hustled out to the office and I tossed the keys behind a filing cabinet. John's face pinched up when he saw the sheriff on the floor, breathing hard and holding his side. He was a lot bloodier now and his eyes were shining with pain but not really focused on anything. The blood was bright red and we all knew what that meant.

Some car salesman, Russell said.

I went to the window and took a peek past the curtain. The coast looked clear except for an old couple talking to Shouse down the street. Whatever he told them did the trick, because they went strolling off around the corner.

Then we were in the cars and tearing past the city-limit sign and out onto the highway.

That's what happened in Lima.

III

The Sprees

John said he couldn't wait to see Billie but he sure wouldn't mind a cold beer first. So, after switching from the stolen jobs over to Red's and Russell's cars, we stopped at a roadhouse speak a few miles south of Dayton.

The parking lot was jammed with vehicles and hazy with raised dust. Inside, the place was dim and smoky and crowded, raucous with laughter and loud talk and a steady blare of jukebox music. We were better dressed than most of the patrons and thought our suits might attract too much attention, but nobody paid us much notice. Three young couples at a secluded table in a corner accepted my offer to pay their tab in exchange for the table. The girls were all lookers and they knew it, and they put a lot of nice sway into their walk as they headed for the bar with their fellas. Red watched them and said what he wouldn't give to take a little bite out of any one of those sweet rumps.

Big bite, John said.

Russell told our waitress it looked like everybody was jumping the gun on the end of Prohibition. She said Honey, where've you been? That poor horse is dead every which way but official.

We yakked and laughed it up over bottles of beer and bowls of roasted peanuts, everybody butting in on everybody else to get a word in, to clarify a point or ask a question or crack wise. John wanted to hear everything about the M City break and about the heist in St. Marys. He told us about the jobs he'd pulled with Copeland and some other guys—we'd already heard about them from Knuckles, but John told the stories better—and about the girls he'd been sporting with. He got a lot of chuckles when he told about being at the Chicago World's Fair with Jenkins's sister and getting a policeman to take snapshots of them.

I knew it, Russell said. There we were in M City, sitting on our thumbs and waiting on this Hoosier to set things up, and there *he* was, dicking with the chippies.

It wasn't easy having fun while you boys were still suffering the tortures of the damned, John said, but I did the best I could.

He'd heard about Okie Jack and Jenkins. He wasn't surprised Jack gave up so easily, what with his bad stomach, but when he heard Jenkins had been killed he got a little worried that the rest of us might have to lay so low we couldn't risk trying to break him out of Lima.

But hell, I knew you bums wouldn't let me down, he said, and slapped me on the shoulder.

Red said the bad news about her brother must've hit Jenkins's sister pretty hard. John supposed so but couldn't say for sure since he hadn't seen or heard from her ever since he got arrested in her parlor. They'd been looking at some Kodaks from their Chicago trip when the landlady announced herself at the door and next thing he knew he had shotguns in his face and his sweetie was down on the carpet in a swoon. He'd written her from the Lima lockup but his letter came back unopened with a note scrawled on it that she no longer lived at that address.

Fat Charley said those police shotguns had probably dimmed her enthusiasm for outlaw adventure.

I guess, John said. But let me tell you boys, she was really something.

Red said he knew that. He hadn't forgotten the picture of her on John's cell wall.

I said she was a tough one to forget, all right. John gave me a wink and we both snickered, remembering the Crow's Nest coochie show.

Well, that Billie girl ain't exactly a hag, Copeland said. He was drinking faster than everybody else. He'd twice had the waitress bring him another bottle while the rest of us were still on a round.

John wiggled his eyebrows at Knuckles and said She's an eyeful, ain't she?

Then that jackass Shouse had to pipe up and say *he* sure wouldn't mind having a go at that squaw.

John gave him a smile that didn't have any amusement in it at all and said not to call her a squaw or even dream of having a go at her.

Shouse said he didn't mean anything except Billie was a goodlooker, that's all.

John said Okay then, Ed, if that's all you meant.

Somebody mentioned Matt Leach, and John said Leach had come from Indiana to interrogate him at the Dayton jail. He described him as a tall skinny guy who was so full of himself that even other cops didn't like him. According to the Dayton cops, Leach was a big believer in psychology as a crime-fighting tool.

I told John what Margo said about Leach's stutter and he laughed and said she was right. When Leach grilled him, John shrugged at all his questions and said over and over that he had no idea what he was talking about. Leach got so mad he was stuttering like a rattletrap Model T and John could hear cops laughing in the other room. I'd pay money to hear him when he gets word I busted out, John said.

The waitress came over to collect empties and see if we wanted another round. She smiled at our high spirits and asked if we were part of the policemen's convention taking place in town.

For a second we all went mute and simply stared at her—and then everybody was grinning big and Charley said why *yes*, we certainly *were* policemen, how did she know?

She said You kidding? I can spot a cop a mile away.

• • •

*I*t was late when we rolled into Cincy and all of us were ready to call it a night. We agreed to meet at my place for a late breakfast in the morning and put our heads together about our next move.

The girls had been dozing on the sofa but they woke up when John and I came in. Billie let out a little yip and ran to John and jumped into his arms, locking her legs around his waist and kissing him all over, her short nightie riding up and exposing a fine ass in pale green underpants. John spun her around and said How's my favorite squaw? She said she better be his *only* squaw.

Mary planted a big welcome home smooch on me and I hummed a few bars of "Happy Days Are Here Again" and danced her around the room. John set Billie down and gave Mary a hug and said he was happy as hell to see her. She said there was coffee made and beer in the icebox, but it was obvious what John was in the mood for the most, and he and Billie said goodnight and hustled off to their room.

They weren't as noisy about it as Russ and Opal—nobody was— but we could hear them as we undressed in the adjoining bedroom. Mary giggled and said Isn't it nice? Then we were in bed and going at each other and all I heard was her breath in my ear. She didn't ask about Lima and I didn't bring it up.

I woke in the morning to her mouth on me. She teased and played and made the pleasure last a long time until I couldn't hold back any longer. Then she kissed her way up my belly and chest and snuggled

close and said Happy birthday, baby—how's it feel to be thirty-one?
I said the way she celebrated it, it felt just grand.

We didn't get out of bed till almost nine, but John and Billie
were still asleep. I told Mary the other guys were coming for breakfast and she started some coffee brewing and began slicing bacon. I
put on my hat and fake specs and headed out for the newsstand at the
end of the street.

It was another beautiful day, the air sharp and cool, the sky cloud-
less and deeply blue. Bad news always seems extra bad when it comes
on a pretty day. Our pictures were on the front page, John's and
mine—and the sheriff's. John's was a mug shot from Dayton, mine
from M City.

I was steamed. I *hate* having my picture in the papers. People who
wouldn't dare look you in the eye in person can study your photograph to their heart's content. It's a kind of spying is what it is. I've
detested cameras from the time I first had one pointed at me, back
when I was a kid in Muncie and my mother took me to a studio for a
portrait. The framed faces on the walls made me think of mounted
animal heads. When the photographer bent behind the camera to
focus the lens, I felt like he was sighting a weapon. Before he could
snap the picture, I jumped up and ran out of the place. I thought
Mom would scold me but she didn't. A few years ago I read about
some South American Indians who killed a photographer because
they believed that in taking their picture he was stealing their soul.
They burned his camera along with his corpse. A lot of people called
them stupid savages. Not me.

The sheriff's name was Sarber. He'd lasted about an hour before
croaking in the hospital. His son was a policeman too and said he
wouldn't rest till his father's killer was brought to justice.

Justice . . . Christ. The man would still be alive if he'd done what
I told him. I wasn't robbing him, I wasn't about to harm his wife, I
wasn't being unreasonable. He had a cocked pistol pointed at him and
the fool *still* went for his gun. The newspaper called him courageous.

My ass. He was a fool and his foolishness is what killed him. If there was any true justice in the courts or any real honesty in the press his death would be called a suicide.

They hadn't been able to find the cell keys so they'd had to use an acetylene torch to free the sheriff's wife and the deputy. The two of them picked me and Charley and Russell out of a mug book. All the main roads in the region were blocked, and vigilante posses as well as an army of cops were conducting a manhunt all over the northern borderland of Ohio and Indiana.

When I got back to the apartment, John and Russell and Charley were at the kitchen table having coffee and laughing it up. Charley tapped his spoon against the rim of his cup to get everybody's attention and said All right, boys and girl, *me-me-me*.

They sang "Happy Birthday" as Charley waved his spoon like a conductor's baton and I stood there smiling like a dope. Then they applauded and Russell said in a singsong voice And *ma-ny mooorrre*.

Mary ratted you out, John said.

There was a platter of crisp bacon on the counter and Mary was now frying chopped potatoes. The smell was wonderful. I asked where Billie was and John said she was still snoozing. That Indian can sleep like nobody's business, he said.

Mary said Red had phoned a few minutes ago to say he and Shouse were on their way over.

I dropped the newspaper on the table and they all stared at the photos and the headlines. Mary stepped over to have a look and her face went funny for a second, and then she went back to tending the potatoes. I poured a cup of coffee and stood sipping it at the counter.

John didn't like the picture of himself. He said it made him look like a banker, the kind whose bank you'd go to rob only to find out the son of a bitch had already cleaned it out himself with a lot of crooked bookkeeping.

Russell said he'd been hoping the sheriff would pull through even though it had been obvious he wouldn't.

Charley cleared his throat and glanced at Mary at the stove. She turned around and looked at us and asked if she should leave the room.

I said Let's both leave the room for a minute.

She took the potatoes off the burner and turned off the gas. We went into the parlor and I shut the kitchen door.

So? she said.

I told her she had a right to know how things stood. We weren't just prison escapees and bank robbers anymore, at least not me and Charley and Russ. They'd have murder warrants on us now, and the worst kind—for killing a cop. They'd never quit hunting us. We'd always be on the run, always be looking over our shoulder. I didn't have plans beyond tomorrow and there was no telling if I'd ever have the chance to make any. And the thing she absolutely had to understand was that *I didn't care*. I couldn't imagine what it'd be like to *not* have the cops after me. What it came down to, I said, was that she probably ought to get out while the getting was good. If the law put the arm on her when she went home, she could say we'd kidnapped her. Every man of us would back her story.

She hardly blinked the whole time I talked. When I finally shut up, she asked if I was telling her to go.

I told her I didn't say that. I only wanted her to know how things stood so she could decide for herself.

Well, we'd already had this conversation, she said. When the Jenkins boy was killed. Had she done or said anything to make me think she'd changed her mind?

I said I'd seen how upset she was by the headlines.

Well of *course* she was upset, mostly by the thought that *I* might've been hurt, or even worse. Of *course* she wished I hadn't killed that man, but she knew I'd only done what I had to do.

I jabbed a finger at her and said That's right, that's right, and no telling what I might have to do tomorrow or the day after that.

I was surprised to feel my hand trembling and I quick put both hands in my pockets and tried not to show how scared I was that she might choose to leave.

She said she knew the way I had to live and she didn't care. She said she loved me and did I understand *that*.

I said yeah, and did *she* understand that as long as she was with me she'd never have any kind of a normal life?

She made a face of mock horror and put her hands to her cheeks and said Oh *noooo*.

I said Ha ha, you know what I mean.

She gave me a thin-eyed look and now it was her turn to point a finger. She said to listen good, Handsome Harry, she'd had about all of so-called *normal* life she could stand and she would thank me most kindly not to ever let her have any more of it. She said she wanted me to promise her she'd *never* have a normal life with me.

I had to laugh. I said it was like asking water to promise to run downhill.

Promise, she said.

All right, girl, I said, I promise.

She went up on her tiptoes and pulled my face down to hers and kissed me hard.

Mary Northern, ladies and gentlemen . . . the one and only.

* * *

When I told John that Sheetz wanted us for another job, he was hot to go for it. I didn't like Sheetz, but unspecified dislike wasn't much of an argument against the fact that he'd been on the square in his deals with both of us. The only hard objection I could make to doing further business with him was the one-third cut he'd taken from the St. Marys job.

John agreed it was excessive, but pointed out that we'd still cleared eight grand, which was nothing to sneeze at.

I said okay, we'd set up a meeting and talk to him, but I'd be damned if I'd cut him in for a third again. If he insisted on a third, I'd tell him to piss up a rope. John said good enough.

That was fine with the other guys too. Whatever John and I agreed on would always be fine with them.

Once that was settled, Russell and I went to a pharmacy down the street and made some long-distance calls from a booth in the back corner. Russ called Opal and found out that she and Patty had rented three apartments, each with two bedrooms and all of them ready to move into. John and I and the girls had already decided we'd go on living together. Opal and Patty would move out of their little place and share one of the other apartments with Russell, and Red and Charley would share one. Shouse would move in with Knuckles.

I called my mother and she sang me "Happy Birthday" before telling me that an army of cops had come charging into the house the night before, waving warrants and badges and guns and carrying on like marauders. They turned the place upside-down even worse than the last time, and were fit to be tied not to find any sign of us on the property.

I asked if one of them was an Indiana cop named Leach, and she said Oh golly, yes, how did you know? She described him as a tall, skinny man with piercing eyes and a sour expression like he'd eaten something that didn't agree with him. He'd warned her that he'd have her put in jail if he found out she'd been helping me in any way.

It enraged me that the bastard had threatened my mother. But she could always sense exactly what I was feeling, even over the telephone, and she said not to worry, she wasn't the least bit scared of Captain Matt Leach, and made me promise not to do anything rash. They were watching the farm again, she said, and she didn't want me to even think about going to visit her anytime soon. But she promised to bake me a belated birthday cake the next time I did.

Then I called Sheetz. He wasn't in, but I got Cohen on the line and we arranged a meeting for two days later.

• • •

*T*he next morning we cleared out of Cincy. While the rest of the bunch headed straight for Chicago, John and Charley and I went up to northern Indiana and robbed a police station.

A *police* station! *Wooo!* How many times you heard of somebody heisting the *cops*—and right in their own jail? Well, we did it. And it wouldn't be the only time.

Some guy John met in the Lima jail had once done thirty days in the lockup in Auburn—a burg about twenty miles above Fort Wayne—and he'd told John the place had a Thompson submachine gun in its gun case. The guy couldn't believe a hick force of a half-dozen cops would have a tommy. It didn't seem right to us, either. We had a lot better use for it than a bunch of rube cops did.

We went in my car and stuck to a crisscross route along the Ohio-Indiana border. If we got recognized by cops on one side of the line we could quick cut over to the other side where they couldn't follow. We didn't see but three cop cars on the way, however, and none of them gave us a suspicious look. John's cheek bulged with a chaw of tobacco and he was hatless, and with his hair plastered on his scalp and parted down the center he looked like a hayseed from the turn of the century. He added to the disguise when we stopped in at a five-and-dime in Fort Wayne and he bought some plain-glass spectacles like mine. We had supper in a café and lingered over our coffee till nightfall, then stole a license plate off another black Ford and put it on my Vickie. Then drove up to Auburn.

We parked at the curb in front of the courthouse and directly across from the jail. It was a Saturday night but you'd never know it by the nearly empty streets and the hush of the place. The only sounds were of leaves stirring in a light wind and a dog barking in the distance. Charley said they ought to change the name to Snoresville.

Fat Charles manned the front door while John and I took care of business. There were two cops on duty, both of them at the desk and reading funnybooks. They were nothing more than farmers with badges, and their jaws dropped when we walked up with our pieces in our hand.

As we locked them in the holding cell, one of them asked Who *are* you fellas?

I said I was the fella who was going to shoot him in the teeth if he said another word.

The rube nodded real quick and made a little twisting motion with his fingers at his lips like he was turning a key on them. I don't know if he was a nervy guy or just simple, but it was all I could do to keep from laughing.

We made fast work of cleaning out the gun case. There was a Thompson, all right, with both a fifty-round drum and a standard twenty-round magazine. And a pair of bullet-proof vests. Imagine— bullet-proof vests for a two-dog-town police force. They were nicely made and looked like blue serge suit vests with pockets and every-thing, but they were heavy as overcoats. The rest of the stuff in the case was a mix of weapons that had probably all been confiscated from local troublemakers. A few rifles and shotguns of different types and a half-dozen handguns, and none of them in very good shape except for a .30-06 Enfield rifle. We took it all simply to shame the cops even more by cleaning them out to the last bullet. Except for the Enfield, we later sold the whole kaboodle to a street gang on the South Side.

We spent that night at a motor court in South Bend, and next morning—John and me wearing our phony glasses—we had break-fast in a little café that was buzzing with talk about the cop station robbery. The few tables were all taken so we sat at the counter. We were ready to scoot out of there at the first suspicious look we got, but once again we were pretty much ignored. The fact is, most peo-ple are too self-conscious or wrapped up in themselves to pay much attention to anybody around them.

A radio was playing music next to the kitchen pass-out window, and the harried counterman told us the robbery news had been repeated every fifteen minutes since the station came on the air at dawn and he was sick of hearing it. He no sooner said it than the music was interrupted and here came the report again. He was about to switch it off, but I told him I wanted to hear.

The announcer's delivery was so breathless I couldn't help getting a little excited myself. He said one of the robbers had been positively identified as John Dillinger, recently set free from the Lima, Ohio, jail by gunmen who murdered the high sheriff in the process. It was suspected that the same accomplices had been with him in the police holdup.

You could tell the radio guy liked saying John's name. It's a dramatic name, bold and dangerous-sounding, and people love to say it. Back in Pendleton, John used to complain that nobody pronounced it correctly, but by the time he left M City he knew it sounded better the wrong way. I told him once that he never would've gotten so famous if his name had been Patterson or Bratkowski or Jones. Or Clark, Russell said. Charley agreed that there was much in a name. Take Pierpont, he said, that's a name for a railroad baron or an oil man. Yeah, I said, Pierpont sounds like one of the biggest robbers of them all.

Three locals claimed to have seen us exit the station house with a bagful of firearms and drive out of town. They couldn't agree on the make of our car—one said a Ford, the other two said an Olds and a LaSalle, for Christ's sake—but they all agreed that we were snappy dressers.

A bony waitress with rat-nest hair came over to hand in an order as the counterman was saying it was a hell of a note when even the cops got robbed. Charley said he couldn't agree more, things in this country had certainly reached a new low.

Maybe so, the waitress said, but doggone if that Dillinger wasn't a *bold* sonofagun—a *police station,* by God.

John said he'd always heard that the jails and the graveyards were full of bold sonofaguns.

You got a point there, mister, the counterman said. It's the cocky ones get it the soonest, that's for sure. He and the waitress moved off to other customers, and the three of us fought down our snickers.

We were in the news that morning in another way as well. The paper carried a report that Sheriff Jess Sarber's funeral had been held the day before and was attended by three thousand mourners. I put my finger on the three thousand number for John and Charley to see, and I whispered Bullshit. I wasn't about to believe so many people would *mourn* the passing of a damnfool car salesman.

John said maybe he owed them all money.

• • •

That afternoon we were in East Chicago, meeting with Sheetz. As usual, Hymie Cohen was there and smiling his nervous smile. The guy with the black goatee was there too, at his post by the door, but I'd never seen him smile at all. John agreed he looked like a pirate and said he'd never been introduced to him either. Between ourselves we called him Captain Kidd.

Sheetz had a set-up for us. It's a fat one, he said. In fact, it might turn out to be obese.

A bank he'd been skimming from by way of its chief accountant was in need of being robbed before a state audit scheduled for next month. The bank would of course claim a loss sufficient to balance its books, Sheetz said, but the heist would be good for an actual fifteen to twenty thousand bucks of bank money.

I said that was fat, but I wouldn't call it obese.

I haven't finished, Sheetz said. He went on to say there was a small outfit in St. Louis run by four brothers named Quarry who had prospered in the bootlegging business and come to own several river-front speakeasies. Now that Prohibition was about to end, they were moving over to gambling. But the gambling in St. Louis was locked up by an outfit with tight ties to Chicago, and while the Quarrys had a reputation as a rough bunch, they had gotten as far as they had by being careful not to get crosswise of the Shytown mob. So they'd moved into southern Indiana, which was open territory to anybody with the capital to set himself up. The Quarrys now had controlling interest in two gambling joints in Terre Haute and two others in Indianapolis.

I take it they know who runs things north of the Kokomo line, John said, since they're staying well south of it.

Sheetz said he would presume so.

I asked what the Quarrys had to do with the bank set-up, and he said If you'll permit me to continue, Mr. Pierpont, I'll clarify that point.

My deepest apologies, I said, by all means proceed. John snorted.

It so happened, Sheetz told us, that one of the managers in the bank under discussion was a cousin of the Quarrys, and for the past seven or eight months they had been using the bank to transfer gambling profits off-the-books back to Saint Lou. The bank was convenient to both Terre Haute and Indy, and on the second and last Monday of every month, shortly after noon, couriers from both towns made cash drops to the Quarry man at the bank. A few hours later, just before closing time, a courier from St. Louie would arrive to collect the money.

But those fellas don't know about *your* man in that bank, John said, and he got wise to the drops. That it?

Sheetz smiled.

And, I said, you figure we might as well help ourselves to the Quarry dough while we're balancing the bank's books.

Sheetz said the amount of the drops always varied, but the Quarry money could be anything between twenty and sixty grand.

That's on top of the bank's money, he said.

John cut a look at me and said *Could* be obese.

I asked Sheetz what his end would be.

The usual, he said, a third.

Out of the question, I said.

He gawked at me like I'd spoken in a foreign language. Cohen cleared his throat and shifted in his chair.

Sheetz then gave us the same song and dance I'd heard from him before about the scarcity of fat banks, especially banks *this* fat, and how long we might have to look before we found one on our own, and how we ought to keep in mind that a bird in the hand was worth two in the bush, and how we better think pretty fucken hard about passing up such a sweet deal as this and yakkety-yak-yak.

I waited till he got it all out, then told him again that a third was too high, especially for this job. We were famous, I said. Our pictures had been on every front page in the country. We were going to be recognized the minute we stepped in that bank. Even if we wore masks, which we never did, everybody was going to know it was us—including the Quarrys. There were certain risks to every bank heist, but they didn't usually involve making enemies of another outfit.

John said I was right, while on the other hand the deal worked out well for Sheetz all the way around. The Quarrys wouldn't connect him to the heist. They didn't know about Sheetz's man in the bank and they didn't know Sheetz knew us.

What they're gonna figure, John said, is *their* man set them up for us. Poor bastard of a cousin is in for a bad time.

If you want us for this one, I told Sheetz, you'll have to settle for fifteen percent.

He said *Fifteen?* You guys have me confused with a charity organization.

He wanted us bad and we knew it, and we wanted that big payday and he knew it. But there was no telling exactly how much Quarry money we'd get, so we haggled for a while longer before reaching an agreement that if the total take was less than forty grand Sheetz would get 15 percent. Between forty and fifty, he'd get 20. Over fifty and he'd get a quarter.

We shook on it.

• • • •

O pal and Patty did a great job picking apartments. All three places were in the Loop and only a few blocks from each other, but they were all in new apartment houses full of residents too busy with their big-city lives to pay much attention to their neighbors. The surrounding streets were heavily trafficked and the sidewalks teemed with pedestrians. Like Charley said, the easiest place to go unnoticed is in a daytime public crowd.

The apartment we moved into with John and Billie was spacious and nicely furnished, with a large kitchen and lots of windows. The other guys were just as pleased with their digs. Opal and Patty had even made a list of other good downtown rentals, in case we had to make a fast change in residence.

The gang of us celebrated our first night together in Chicago at an Italian restaurant with a back-room speak, and the next morning John and I got busy planning the job.

It was the Central National Bank and Trust in Greencastle, about thirty-five miles west of Indianapolis. We drove there in the Vickie and cased the place inside and out, checking all the roads in the area, making layout drawings and getaway maps. Even with a set-up, you had to be ready for anything, and we approached it in the same way we would any other heist.

The only thing I wasn't sure about was using Copeland on the job. I was fed up with his boozing and didn't care that he was singing the blues because Patty had given him the heave-ho. What happened was, she'd finally met the right guy when she met Red Hamilton. As soon as they were introduced on the night we all gathered at the Italian place, they started making eyes at each other and didn't care who saw it. Patty later confided to Mary that she and Red played footsie all through dinner. A couple of hours into the evening Red excused himself from the table to go to the gents, and then Patty left for the ladies room, and that was the last we saw of either of them that night. The next day Charley was fixing himself breakfast when Patty came into the kitchen wearing Red's robe and said good morning and poured two cups of coffee and took them back to Red's room. Knuckles had been on a self-pity jag ever since and drinking even more than usual. I told John how I felt about it, but he had a soft spot for Copeland because they'd been partners, and he wanted to give him one more chance to pull himself together. So we had a private talk with him and he swore he'd ease off on the hooch.

Shouse was another irritation, a different sort, but John's displeasure with him was no less than mine. Ever since the business with Mary at Saffell's house, Shouse had been a perfect gentleman toward her, but I still didn't like him and I guess it showed, and he stepped carefully around me. He wasn't as cautious around John, maybe because John did such a good job of concealing what I knew was a lingering irritation over Shouse's crack about Billie. But you didn't kick a partner out of the gang for making a pass at your girl, and certainly not for saying he'd like to. You warned him away like John had done Shouse, or you slugged him, or you shrugged it off and let the girl decide for herself—but you settled it one way or another and that was that. It's how those things worked and everybody knew it, even Knuckles, who I'm sure wanted to take a poke at Red but didn't do it because he was too scared. Red would've handed him his ass, of course, but there are times when you have to go in swinging anyway, even when you know you're going to get busted up. If you don't, then you've got the worst kind of problem you can have, which is called cowardice. It must be a terrible thing to realize you're yellow. Maybe that's why Knuckles was a drunk.

• • •

few days before we hit Greencastle, Russell got hurt. The cause of his injury wasn't one you could call common. It happened on the day after John and I got back from casing the bank, when the bunch of us drove way out into the boondocks to test-fire the tommy gun and the Enfield rifle I'd got in Auburn.

The Thompson was a potent piece of firepower and we all got a kick out of shooting it. The thing has a lever for setting it on either semiautomatic fire, so that you have to squeeze the trigger for each shot, or full automatic, so that the bullets come blasting out for as long as you hold down the trigger. As soon as we got used to the feel of it, none of us had any trouble hitting the tree trunk we were aiming at, even on automatic and even without the shoulder stock, which we took off to make the piece easier to hide under an overcoat.

Anyway, after we tested the tommy we decided to check out the bulletproof vests. None of us had ever worn one or known anybody who had, but we'd all heard how well they worked, and we were curious to see it if was true. It didn't seem possible that something so flexible could stop a bullet. So we wrapped one around a tree trunk and I fired three .45 rounds at it from about ten yards away and the bullets all flattened on the vest without passing through.

It was impressive, but Russell said a man wasn't nearly as hard as a tree and he couldn't help wondering if the vest would work as well on a real live person. We all believed it would, but there was only one way to find out. We drew straws and Russell pulled the shortie, which got a big laugh from everybody but him. He said Me and my big mouth, then put on the vest and stood like a guy facing a firing squad.

Charley said he was reminded of William Tell, except the vest wasn't on top of Russell's head.

Russell insisted I stand a lot closer to him than I'd been to the tree so I'd be absolutely sure not to miss the vest and hit some unprotected part of him, like his head.

I don't blame you, Russ, Red said, if I was in your shoes I'd want a bulletproof face.

I walked up to within six feet of him and asked how that was. I

was just being funny but he said that was about right, so I shrugged
and said okay, but I felt silly standing so close. I said I could hit him
with my eyes shut from there. He said don't even joke about shutting
my eyes.

I raised the .45 and shook my hand like I had palsy and he said
Cut it out, Pete, goddamnit.

Okay, okay, I said, here goes.

I fired dead-center into his chest and he flew backward like he'd
been yanked by a rope. He landed flat on his back and lay spread-
eagled without moving, his eyes closed.

John ran over and knelt beside him and shook his arm and said
Russ, you okay?

Russell didn't stir. He's not breathing, John said.

Oh Christ, Red said.

I really thought I'd killed him. Then his chest suddenly heaved
and he started pulling deep breaths and his legs twitched. Red squat-
ted on the other side of him and patted his face and said Come on,
buddy, snap to, man.

Russell's eyes fluttered open. Atta boy, Red said, you really got
the wind knocked out of you, son.

Jesus, Russell said. I thought you . . . were gonna *shoot* me . . . not
run over me . . . with a fucken train.

We helped him to his feet and he groaned like a decrepit old man.
I saw a bright light, he said, I swear.

Fat Charley said *he* saw a sweet chariot swinging low out of
heaven, coming for to carry Russ home.

Red used his pocketknife to dig the mashed bullet out of Russell's vest. We were so wowed with the vest's efficiency we decided we
had to get enough of them for all of us. John said he knew just the
place.

The next day the bruise on Russell's chest was the size of a dinner plate and purple as a plum. He said it didn't hurt at all except
when he breathed. It would be about a week before he could bend

over to tie his shoes without gritting his teeth, and the bruise wouldn't fade away for a lot longer than that.

But sore as he was, he was ready to do the job.

• • •

The heist was set for Monday. On Friday we left Chicago in three cars. John and Russell were with me in the Vickie, Knuckles went with Shouse in his Chevy, and Charley rode in Red's Auburn sedan. When we crossed the Iroquois I turned east but Red and Shouse kept driving south to Terre Haute, where an old M City pal of ours named Cueball Lucas was running a boarding-house, and where we'd meet up the following day.

I was headed for a town called Peru, about twenty miles north of Kokomo. It was the place John had been talking about when he'd said he knew where we could get more vests. He'd told me he had it on good authority that the cop house in that burg had a load of them. I asked what good authority he was referring to, and he hesitated before saying Homer Van Meter. He said he'd met up with the scarecrow after getting his parole, and they'd worked a few small jobs together. Van Meter had clued him to places where a guy could buy guns or get medical treatment on the QT. And he'd told John about the vests in the Peru Police Department, which the cops had gotten through some promotional deal with the manufacturer. The scarecrow had wanted the two of them to put a gang together, but John turned him down. When he told Van Meter he was arranging to bust some pals out of the joint, the scarecrow said I get it, you're throwing in with Pierpont. He told John the escape plan sounded like a pipe dream and to look him up when it failed.

John said he wished he could've seen his face when Van Meter got the news about M City. He said Homer was a good man to have on your team and asked if by any chance I'd changed my opinion of him.

I gave him a look.

Didn't think so, he said.

Anyhow, that's how we came to hit the Peru cop house. For all John knew, Van Meter had already heisted the vests himself, but we figured it was worth a look. In Logansport, a few miles outside Peru, Russ stole a Hudson and we left the Vickie parked behind a closed filling station.

We timed our arrival at around ten o'clock to be sure the sidewalks were rolled up and the citizens all in bed. The cops were sitting at a folding table playing cards when we strolled in. There were three of them. They looked up and saw us, and one said Holy shit, *you* guys.

Russell stripped them of their revolvers and John got the gun case key out of the desk. The case held six bulletproof vests—plus two Browning Automatic Rifles, a pair of pump shotguns, another two .38 six-shooters, and several boxes of cartridges and shotgun shells. We told the cops to spread their coats on the floor and place the guns on them and tie them in tight bundles with the coat sleeves. They were finishing up when somebody behind us said Say, what's going on.

I whirled around and aimed the cocked .45 in the face of a guy wearing an apron and holding two small paper sacks.

No, no, no, the guy said and dropped the sacks so he could throw his hands up.

He was from the restaurant next door, bringing the cops an order of sandwiches. I asked what kind and he said three roast beef and two ham.

Well hell, Russell said, give them here. The guy picked up the sacks and handed them to him.

John and one of the cops carried the guns out to the Hudson and then we ordered the bunch of them into the basement and said not to come out for half an hour.

We ate the sandwiches on the way back to Logansport, where we retrieved the Vickie and left the Hudson in the same spot we'd taken it from. I wonder if the guy who owned it ever found out it was used in a robbery by none other than the notorious Pierpont Gang.

We drove down to Kokomo and had a fine reunion with Pearl in the Side Pocket. I gave her one of the Peru shotguns in repayment for the one she'd given me earlier. I apologized that it wasn't cut down like the one she gave me, but she said she knew somebody who could take care of that. We caught up on things over a bottle of beer, then went to her place and we flipped coins to see who'd sleep on the sofa and John was the odd man and got it. Russ and I got the beds in the guest room.

In the morning Pearl made us a big breakfast while we read all about ourselves in the paper. Our second cop-house robbery in a week had of course made quite a stir.

Police departments all over the state were beefing up the security of their stations, putting bars on the windows, posting guards with machine guns at the doors around the clock. The warden at Michigan City said he was sure we were arming ourselves in order to raid the prison and break out more of our pals. The American Legion claimed to be rounding up a posse of twenty thousand men.

The *National Guard,* for Christ's sake, said it was ready to help law enforcement agencies with every weapon it had, including tanks, airplanes, and—get this—poison gas.

Poison gas.

And the newspapers called *us* dangerous.

That afternoon we joined the other guys at Cueball Lucas's place in Terre Haute, and there was a lot of whooping and backslapping when they saw the vests and guns we'd grabbed up in Peru. That night we kept to the boardinghouse and took it easy, playing pinochle and listening to the radio.

On Sunday we spent the day going over the plan again and again until it was coming out our ears. After supper me and John, Russ and Charley, took in a picture show. *King Kong.* What a great flick. We were all pulling for the ape, of course, though there was no question they'd do him in at the finish. Afterward, we went to a speakeasy for one beer apiece and kept talking about the movie. We loved the line at the end, that it was beauty killed the beast, and we had a lot of laughs joking about Kong having sex with the blonde. John said Kong could've asked me about all the best ways for a big galoot to make it with a little chick. I said Watch your mouth there, buddy, but I yukked it up along with the rest of them.

. . .

Cohen had said to hit the bank between two and three o'clock on Monday afternoon. After we'd cased the place and studied its routine, we decided on two forty-five. We got into Greencastle a little early, so we drove around some to keep our timing right. John and Red and I were in a Studebaker. Right behind us were Charley and Russell and Shouse in a Hudson. We'd stolen both cars in Clinton that morning, where we'd left Shouse's Chevy. Copeland was the switch driver, waiting for us in Red's Auburn in Mansfield, just the other side of the Raccoon River.

It was sunny but windy and nippy. The people on the streets walked with their heads down and holding on to their hats. We'd put the vests on before leaving Terre Haute almost an hour earlier and we were feeling their weight, especially in our neck muscles, but they were so expertly tailored you couldn't tell we were wearing them unless you looked really close. And since having seen how well they worked, not a man of us was about to go without one.

We were idling at a red light when a pair of young girls crossed in front of us and the breeze blew their skirts up and gave us an terrific eyeful of legs and garter belts and even a peek of white panties on one girl before she managed to clamp the skirt back over on her hips. Red gave a high wolf whistle and they hustled away, blushing like cherries.

Lamm used to say it was good luck to spot a pretty girl just before a heist, John said. That's what Dietrich told me.

Then seeing two of them must mean double good luck, I said. Especially getting a look at that much of them.

Piss on Dietrich, Red said. We make our luck.

We went around the block once more and then I pulled into an angled parking spot two doors away from the bank. Shouse parked a few spaces from us and stayed in the Hudson, and Charley and Russell came over and joined us near the entrance to the bank. Red was the outside man. He stood by the Studebaker to watch the street and the bank door and make sure nobody double-parked behind us and blocked us in.

Russell had the stopwatch. Punch it, I said to him, and we went in.

There were a dozen or so citizens in the place. Russell posted himself by the front door and kept an eye on the stairs to the basement, where we knew the guard had already gone to tend the furnace and have a smoke. If he'd been dumb enough to come back up with a gun in his hand, Russ would've shot him before he made it to the top step.

I pulled the .45 and called the stickup and said for nobody to press any buttons. Eyes went big and mouths fell open and a woman said My God, it's *them*.

Fat Charley brandished the stockless tommy gun and told everybody to keep their mouths shut and be reasonable, then bunched them all against a wall out of sight of the sidewalk windows.

Most of the good folk were terrified, but a busty brunette with a sexy mouth was staring at me like I was some movie star. I gave her a big smile and she blushed but couldn't keep from smiling back. I went into the cage by way of the door, but John did his Douglas Fairbanks number and vaulted over the railing, then looked at the brunette and winked—and she really lit up.

John ordered the tellers to get all their cash out on the counters and leave the drawers open, then he followed me into the vault. Cohen had said the vault door would be unlocked—and it was. He'd said the bank's own cash wouldn't be more than six or seven grand, that most of its holdings were in negotiable bonds and we'd find them in a file drawer labeled INSTRUMENTS on the left side of the vault—and we did. The cash drawer was directly below it and held packets of mostly twenties. John bagged the greenbacks while I grabbed up the bonds.

According to Cohen, the Quarry money would be in the bottom left drawer on the other side of the vault. We went over to the drawer and I opened it.

It was empty.

John swore and said it looked like somebody'd been pulling Sonny's dick.

I tried the drawer to the right. Nothing but ledgers. The next one was full of document files.

Hell with it, John said, we gotta get a move on. Let's clean out the cage and scram.

As he started for the vault door, I opened the drawer above the bottom left one. There was a black valise in it. I took out the bag and opened it and said Whoa there, junior, lookee here.

John came over and took a gander, and said Ooooh yeah.

The valise was filled with banded packets of cash. Packs of fifties and hundreds.

He held my sack open and I put the valise in it. It seemed like we'd been in the vault an hour. We hustled out with our sacks under our arms and Charley called out to get the swag on the counters but Russell was looking at the stopwatch and said *No*, let's go.

We'd planned it for five minutes but did it in four fifty-six. Not bad at all, considering the extra time we'd spent in the vault. That's what I mean about time losing meaning in a bank heist. Without somebody in the crew holding a stopwatch, you'd have no idea how long the job was taking. All you're aware of while you're pulling it off is the hard pump of blood and adrenaline. But like I said, we were one smooth team, the best there was.

Exactly four minutes after we'd entered the bank Red had got in the Studebaker and started the motor and then moved over to the passenger side. Shouse had the Hudson running too, and as soon as we came out he backed out of the parking slot and pulled up to us and John and I slipped Russell the money and he got in the car and Shouse drove away. Charley and John got in the back of the Studebaker and I slid behind the wheel again and I drove away nice and smooth and followed Shouse out of town.

By the time the cops showed up at the bank we were long gone. And by the time they put up roadblocks around Greencastle we were already way beyond them. I headed for Mansfield to dump the Studie and switch to the Auburn, and Shouse went to Clinton to pick up his own car.

As we whizzed down the highway we were whooping and laughing and slapping each other on the shoulder, making bets over how much the haul would total. Fat Charley said it was the neatest job he'd ever worked, notwithstanding the pirate-movie theatrics of an individual he would allow to remain nameless.

Red turned to glare at John. Goddamnit, he said, you pull that acrobat shit again?

The question caught John cold. What's eating you guys, he said.

I swear to God, Red said, if you'd busted a leg, I woulda been all for leaving your ass back there.

John said he didn't get what Red was bitching about. I ain't gonna bust a leg, he said.

What makes you so sure, Red said. You got steel bones? *Rubber* bones?

What the hell, John said, the jumps were just for fun, to give the rubes a show, give them something to tell their grandkids.

Red said to fuck the rubes *and* their grandkids, it was a dumb-ass risk.

Charley said he was logically obliged to concur with Red.

It wasn't just risky, Red said, it was showing off. It was kid stuff. Unprofessional.

Once again, Charley said, I must sadly agree with Mr. Three Digits.

John looked like he thought maybe they were pulling his leg. I kept my eyes away from his in the mirror, but I could feel his gaze boring into the back of my neck.

He said You too, Pete?

They're right, John, it's not smart.

He was quiet for another minute, then said Well hell, if that's the way you boys feel about it, I won't do it anymore. I sure don't want anybody thinking I'm un-*fucken*-professional.

Everybody laughed and Charley said he thought Red would feel better if John made that a promise.

It's a promise you can put in the goddamn bank, John said.

Red said In the *bank?* Not on your life, buster. Banks get robbed.

* * *

According to the next day's newspapers, the Greencastle bank said we'd made off with $76,000—fifty-six in negotiables and twenty in cash. The actual sums we counted out in the Terre Haute boardinghouse were ten thousand in bonds and fifty-five in cash, an even fifty of it from the black valise. A veritable trove, as Fat Charley phrased it. And a nice break for Sheetz, too, since it qualified him for a one-quarter cut.

The newspapers now called us the Terror Gang, which made it sound like we were burning and pillaging and raping instead of simply robbing banks. Damn newspapers always overplay everything, making mountains out of molehills and devils out of imps. They're never satisfied unless they're scaring the bejeezus out of the citizens, and they were doing a fine job of it in our case. The state was crisscrossed with roadblocks, vigilante groups were patrolling the countrysides, the National Guard was on high alert and ready for action.

Matt Leach was in the news again too. He called us the Dillinger Gang and said we'd make a bad mistake before long, and as soon as we did he'd come down on us with both feet. A photograph of him talking on the phone was my first look at him. Tall and thin and sort of pinched up, like both John and Mom had described him. He looked almost skeletal and gave the impression of a well-dressed undertaker.

Russell wanted to know what made Leach think we were the *Dillinger* Gang.

Red laughed. I bet John called him up and told him it was, he said. Who else in this bunch likes seeing his name in the papers so much?.

Go to hell, John said. The crazy bastard has it in for me is all. He wants me getting most of the heat.

It's that badman name, I said. It sells a lot more papers than any of ours.

Charley said I was right, but he thought there might be another reason too. He suspected Leach was trying to sow discord among us by means of his vaunted expertise in psychology.

By referring to John as our leader, Charley said, the good captain could be hoping to bruise Pete's pride and inspire friction in the ranks.

I said if that was so, then the man was even dumber than he looked. For all I cared he could call us the Mutt and Jeff Gang. I meant it. I never cared a crumb about celebrity. Red was right about John, though. He tried not to show it but you could see how much it pleased him to have us called the Dillinger Gang. That's how he was. Johnny Fairbanks.

But Red had given John an idea. We gathered around the telephone and he placed the call. He told whoever answered that he had a hot tip on the Dillinger Gang for Captain Matt Leach.

When Leach came on the line, John said This is Dillinger, you Hoosier bastard. The gang wants to send their regards.

He held the mouthpiece toward us and we all said in unison *Helloooo,* you b-b-b-bastard!

John held out the receiver so we could hear Leach stammering in a fury and we all laughed like hell. Then John said into the phone I'll keep in touch, pal, and hung up.

• • •

When we were ready to clear out of Terre Haute, Red's Auburn refused to start. Cueball was a pretty good shade-tree mechanic and thought the problem was a worn timing chain. He said he could make the repair but it might take three weeks or more to get the parts he'd need. Red said for Cueball to let him know when he got it running again and he'd come back for it, then had me drive him to a car lot where he bought another Auburn, a five-year-old green roadster in fine shape except for a slightly crooked front fender.

One thing I can say in favor of the newspapers: They were a big help to us by pointing out where the cops were setting up a lot of their roadblocks. We started back north by routes that would bypass them, the other guys heading back to Shytown while John and I made for East Chicago.

But of course the cops don't tell the papers everything, and the papers don't always get the facts right anyway, and we hit a surprise roadblock at a bridge over the Kankakee.

We didn't see it till we came around a curve in the road, and then it was too late. There were motorcycle cops posted near the curve, ready to brace anybody who pulled off the road and tried to turn around. There was nothing for it but to join the line of cars waiting to be inspected at the near end of the bridge. We were in our road disguises, and they'd served us well so far, but they suddenly felt inadequate.

We took out our pieces and thumbed off the safeties and held them hidden under our overcoat flaps, ready for come-what-may.

The first few cars in line got passed through, but the Dodge directly ahead of us had three guys in it, and the cop checking the car suddenly pulled his gun on them and called for the other cops to come over.

The guys in the car were ordered to get out and put their hands on the roof. Two cops kept them covered while two others patted them down.

After about ten minutes the cops realized they'd made a mistake, and they let the guys go. There was a long line of cars behind us by then and some of the citizens were leaning on their klaxons at the delay.

One of the cops signaled me forward, and I pulled up to him and said For a minute there, we thought you boys had your man.

The cop said yeah, he did too, one of the guys in the Dodge had been the spitting image of Dillinger. He bent down and peered past me at John.

Christ, he said, everybody's starting to look like that son of a bitch.

Then he stepped back and waved us through.

• • •

It was cold and drizzly gray when we got to East Shy, but Sonny Sheetz was in bright spirits. He congratulated us on a job well done. As always, Cohen and Captain Kidd were in the office too.

I opened my satchel and dumped the swag on the desk.

Yes, yes, yes, Cohen said.

I told them the Quarry cash had been in a different drawer than the one they'd said. Either Sheetz's man had been in error, or the Quarry's man had taken it on himself to put the valise in a different drawer for some reason.

Hazards of the trade, Sheetz said with a sad shake of the head. You simply couldn't depend on the accuracy of information or on people behaving predictably. He commended what he called our self-possession and initiative.

Neither he nor Cohen bothered to count the take. I told them it came to sixty-five grand. Sheetz said that was excellent, then looked up at the ceiling and did some arithmetic in his head, moving a finger in the air like he was writing figures, then said he figured his cut at $16,250.

That was the number I'd come up with. He nodded at Cohen, who raked all the bonds to his side of the desk and then counted some of the cash out of the pile and added it to the bonds, then pushed the rest of the cash over to us.

Our end was $48,750. Christ almighty, we were *rich*. And we hadn't been out of M City a month.

Feel free to count it yourself, Sheetz said. I won't be offended.

I would've counted it if John hadn't been so quick to say there was no need. You took our word, we'll take yours, he said, and started putting our money in the satchel.

It's always a pleasure doing business with you boys, Sheetz said. You're not only good, you're lucky.

We're the best there is, John said, clasping the satchel shut. We make our own luck.

We stood up and put on our hats.

Glad to hear it, Sheetz said, but just the same, you boys be careful out there. And do let's stay in contact.

Do let's, John said.

Captain Kidd watched us go out the door, his face as impossible to read as Russian.

. . .

We got back to Chicago late that night and cut up the take. The next day we went on a spending spree and John finally bought himself a car, a Terraplane coupe, and that night we all went out together and had a high time.

We dined in one of the finest steakhouses in the city and then hit a half-dozen clubs all over the Loop. *Jesus,* we were jazzed. We laughed like lunatics at every wisecrack everybody made. The girls knew all the latest dances, and before the end of the evening so did we. I was cutting a rug like a real smoothie. I couldn't get enough boogie-woogie. Patty, who was practically a dance pro, said all us guys were good, but she thought John was so good he could've done it for a living. John grinned and blew her a kiss across the table. Billie patted his cheek and said It don't mean a thing if it ain't got that swing, and this fella's got plenty of swing.

It was a night that had everything—even the pleasure of saving a lady in distress. That happened when I found out the cigarette girl had run out of my brand and I went out to the car to get a fresh pack from the glove box. I was making my way back along the rows of cars in the parking lot and I heard a guy saying something about stupid no-good bitch and then the sound of a slap and a woman started crying. I spotted them two rows over. The guy was holding her against the side of a car and smacking her good. She was whimpering with each hit and trying to protect her face with her hands. Another guy was standing there watching.

I cut over to their row, moving fast and quiet, and they never saw me till I grabbed the hitter from behind by the wrist and tripped him down to his knees and pivoted hard and wrenched his arm out of its socket with a pop he'll never forget. It's a pain that'll take your breath away, believe me—I felt it once in a fight with the hacks in M City. All he could manage was a raspy moan before I rammed a knee into his chin, cracking his teeth together and laying him out. The other guy hooked me hard in the ribs and I covered up and took the next one on top of the head and the way he yelped I knew he'd busted his hand. I grabbed him by the lapels and slammed him back against a car and pulled the .45 and whacked him on the head with it. He dropped to all fours and I hit him with the gun again and that was all she wrote. The winner and still champeen . . . me.

The woman wasn't really hurt—slightly bloody nose, puffed lip, that was about it. She was a leggy thing, but even without the bruises her face would've been a little blurred at the edges, like she'd had one too many rough nights. I holstered the gun and gave her my hanky to put to her nose and she thanked me, then spit on the one with the popped arm. *Bastard,* she said, I hope you're dead.

I assured her he wasn't and said we'd better amscray before somebody came along. She asked my name and I said Len Richardson. She said hers was Wilma or Willa or something and started telling me what the fracas had been about, but I didn't really care and didn't pay much attention. We went around to the front of the club and I put her in a cab and paid the driver and when the car drove off I threw away the little card she'd given me with her phone number on it.

When I got back to our table in a rear corner of the room and told the gang what happened, Mary's first impulse was to make sure I hadn't been hurt, and she gently felt the knot on my head and saw that it wasn't bleeding. Then she gave me a scolding for getting mixed up in something that didn't concern me and might've got me arrested.

The guys were sorry they'd missed the scrap. I mean to tell you, I felt *great*.

We drank more than we usually allowed ourselves and we all got a little buzzed—except for Copeland, who got plain drunk. He'd been trying hard to keep his word about taking it easy with the booze, but being so near to Patty when she was no longer his girl was eating him up. She had to turn him down three times before he got the message that she wasn't going to dance with him. But he kept giving her moony looks across the long table where we all sat, and even though she tried to ignore him I could see it was getting to her. So could Red, and he finally told Copeland to knock it off or they could go out in the alley to discuss it. I was hoping Knuckles would take the dare. I figured once he got his ass whipped he'd get over the whole business with Patty and pull himself together for good. But all he did was glare at Red and get up and leave.

Much later that evening—in the wee hours, to be exact—we had another minor set-to among ourselves, this time in a basement joint called the Tiger's Rag. This one started when the bandleader announced that the next number would be the last one of the night and Shouse asked Billie to dance. He was the only stag at the table, although he'd started out with a date, a blond looker named Greta Something-or-other who struck me as being too nice for the likes of him and proved me right about midway through the evening. They were slow-dancing together when Shouse must've said or done something real wrong because Greta suddenly pulled away and slapped him so hard his hair jumped. Mary and I were right beside them and we laughed along with some other dancers who saw what happened. Shouse stood there and rubbed his jaw as Greta went to the table to get her purse and vamoose. Then he looked at me and Mary and said There's plenty more fish in the sea, and moved away into the crowd. Mary rolled her eyes and said he'd never catch anything but trash with the kind of bait he used.

Anyhow, when the last dance was called, John and Billie, who'd been enjoying themselves for most of the evening, were in the middle of a hot-eyed, hissing spat that they were trying to keep from turning into a scene. Mary later told me it had to do with a soldier who'd cut in on John and then held Billie too close for John's liking. To make it worse, Billie didn't seem to mind. So John cut back in on them. The soldier looked irked and said something, but whatever John said in response was something the soldier wanted no part of and he hustled off. Billie was so angry she pushed John away and came marching back to the table with him at her heels. They'd been going at it in angry whispers for about ten minutes when Shouse asked her for the last dance. Billie jumped up and said You bet, Ed. She grabbed him by the hand and practically yanked him out onto the floor.

John lit a cigarette and nudged me and jutted his chin at a great-looking girl dancing near our table. He was trying to affect indifference to Billie and Shouse and not even glance their way, but his face was stiff as wood. Good thing he wasn't keeping an eye on them, because when I caught a glimpse of them through the swirl of dancing couples they looked like they were trying to have sex through their clothes. The stupid bastard had a hand on her rump and she was nuzzling his neck. Then I lost sight of them again. I was afraid if John saw them he'd lose his cool and flatten Shouse in the middle of the dance floor and then here came the cops.

I told him I hadn't had a dance with Billie all night and better do it before the number ended. As I got up I gave Mary a look and cut my eyes at John. She was quick to pick up, and she distracted his attention from the floor by asking if he'd been in touch with his family lately.

I made my way through the mob of dancers and tapped Shouse on the shoulder. He turned with a glare, then saw it was me and his expression eased up quick.

Ah hell, Pete, he said, you sure know how to break up a man's good time.

Billie looked at me over his shoulder and said Hiya, Pete, you wanna dance with me? She was drunker than I'd thought.

Shouse stepped back and said She's all yours, partner. I clamped one hand around his right forearm and grabbed him by the nuts with the other and gripped hard enough to stand him up on his tiptoes. His eyes bugged and he made a croaking sound and I told him to shut up and stay still or I'd crush them like eggs. I told him to quit bird-dogging our women if he didn't want his face to end up in pieces.

Okay, okay, he said, his voice cracking. His eyes were watery with pain. I unhanded him and he let out a quivering breath and hunched over slightly and gingerly felt his goods. The dancers around us were staring curiously and Shouse tried to smile like the whole thing was some kind of joke. I told him to get going, in case John had seen what he'd been up to, and he made his way off the floor and toward the exit.

Billie was looking at me like she didn't know whether to be mad or amused or what. I opened my arms to her and said I believe this is my dance, mademoiselle, and she laughed and said Well it sure is, Mon-sewer.

As we swayed to the music, I told her it was no skin off my nose what she did with who, but one stupid squabble in public by any one of us could bring the roof down on all our heads.

She asked why I was blaming her, she wasn't the one with the jealousy problem. Talk to *him,* she said.

I said I would, but it would help if she wouldn't give him reason to be jealous in the first place.

Yeah, yeah, she said, I hear you, big daddy.

Then she gave me a lazy-looking smile and said Tell me something, Petey, where you carry your gun?

I had to laugh, the question was so completely off the point.

Sometimes under my arm, I told her, sometimes at the small of my back, sometimes both places at once. Why was she asking?

She giggled and said because I'd swear you're carrying one right . . . *there,* and she pressed her belly hard against an erection which I swear to the living Jesus I hadn't been aware of. There are women who can do that—give you a hard-on before you even know it—and she was one of them.

My face went warm and I drew back from her a little.

Awwww, she said, I was enjoying that.

I took a gander toward our table but couldn't spot any of our bunch through the crowd. Then the number was done with—and none too soon—and it was time to go home.

On our way to the car, Billie had to step into an alley to throw up. She came back wiping her mouth with a handkerchief and said Well hell, no wonder I was sick, my stomach was full of puke. John was the only one who didn't think it was funny.

I had the Vickie's heater turned up high on the drive back, but there was a chill in the car that had nothing to do with the weather. I had a hunch John was angry with Billie about more than her drinking. He'd probably seen how she was dancing with Shouse.

Neither of them said a word to each other until they got back to their room in the apartment, and then oh man, did they cut loose. Mary and I could hear them all the way down the hall and out in the living room, where we were having coffee to take the edge off the booze. We didn't catch too many of the particulars, but they were chiefly along the lines of drunken squaw, stupid Hoosier, low-down tramp, jealous asshole, and so on.

Mary was big-eyed with shock at the names they were yelling at each other. I patted her leg and said people in love say the darnedest things. She hit me with the heel of her fist and said it wasn't funny and she'd be mortified if I ever spoke to her that way.

I said every couple had its own style, and John's and Billie's was simply a little *livelier* than most.

Mary said yeah, well, she'd thank me never to be so *lively* with her.

Oh no, ma'am, I said, I know what's good for me.

She scooted up next to me and gave me a hard kiss, then said You really are something, you know that?

Gosh lady, I said, what brought that on?

She laughed and kissed me again.

I mean it when I say I don't know why she was so tickled. Then again, I have to confess that even though I've known my share of women they've always been a mystery to me. They've always seemed a lot like the stars. You know how on a cold winter's night the stars can seem so beautiful and somehow comforting and at the same time make you feel really lonely? That's how it's been for me with women. So many times, even as I held them naked in my arms, they've felt as far away as the stars.

John and Billie were still at it when we went to bed. Then suddenly their squabbling stopped. Mary was holding me tight and we listened hard, and then heard a rising volume of familiar gruntings and gaspings and the creakings of their bed.

Well now, I said, sounds to me like somebody's kissed and made up.

Mary's laugh was low and lascivious. She said it sounded to her like a lot more than kissing, and she rolled up on top of me. And in a minute we were doing a lot more than kissing too.

• • •

The next day, we agreed that from then on nobody would have more than three drinks, including beer, when we did a night on the town. John laid down a tougher rule for Billie—no alcohol at all, nothing but soda water or ginger ale for her. Everybody knew Indians couldn't hold their liquor, he said. He didn't say that Billie had proved it at the Tiger's Rag, but we all knew that's what he thought.

Billie liked her booze and wasn't happy about John putting the clamps on her, but she didn't want to get into another big tiff with him. And although Mary thought John was being unfair, Billie didn't want her arguing with him about it either. But, Mary being Mary, whenever we were clubbing together and John went off to the men's room or onto the dance floor with Patty or Opal, she'd let Billie sneak a sip or two of her drink. Sometimes Billie had more of Mary's drinks than Mary did and would be obviously tipsy at the end of the night. John would say it went to show that an Indian could get drunk just breathing the whiskey fumes in a nightclub. It took a while for him to catch on to the game they were playing on him.

It was a funny kind of friendship between Mary and Billie. Billie was slightly older and a lot more experienced, but Mary was wiser in many respects and often acted toward her like a protective big sister. And like a spoiled little sister, Billie wasn't above taking advantage of it. During the first few days we all lived together, Mary made a big breakfast and John always joined us, but Billie wouldn't get out of bed till almost noon, after her breakfast had gone to waste, and she'd be hungry and asking when lunch would be ready. A few days of this was all Mary could take. The next morning when John came in the kitchen he found that she had made breakfast for only me and herself.

He grinned at me and said What's the gag?

I nodded toward Mary and said Ask her.

Mary said You want some breakfast, Johnny?

Well, sure, John said.

Then you better drag your girlfriend's lazy behind out of bed, she said, and have her make it for you. I'm not the household cook.

John stood there, rubbing his chin, then smiled and said, No, kid, you sure ain't. I'll be right back.

He returned in a few minutes with Billie in hand. Her robe was open and you could see her dark nipples pushing against the thin cotton undershirt. A few black curls of private hair were showing at the edge of her panties. She was rubbing her eyes like a drowsy child and grumbling about getting rousted from bed. What was going on, she wanted to know.

Time for breakfast, John told her.

I don't eat breakfast, Billie said.

I do, he said. And I'd be grateful as all hell, babydoll, if you'd make it for me.

Billie said *Me?* Jeepers, Johnny, I can't cook.

Time to learn, he said.

I'll teach you, honey, Mary said. She went around the table and closed Billie's robe and belted it, like she was tending a disheveled child, and I pretended not to see the scolding look she gave me.

In no time at all, Mary taught Billie her way around the kitchen, and from then on they took turns making breakfast.

· · ·

*B*reakfast was about the only meal we ever ate at home. Christ, we had it good in Chicago. We were loaded with dough and spending it hand over fist on restaurants and sharp clothes and good times galore.

It might be hard to believe that we could move around in public so freely without being recognized, but it's the truth. Like I said before, most people don't really *look* at others, and it's even truer in a big city than in a burg. Only cops pay close attention to the faces around them—but then so did we. We all had pretty good antennas for detecting cops, and we almost always spotted them before they did us.

It was funny to have the police in three states searching for us, and all the while we were right in the heart of Chicago, having a swell time, us and our girls. Even Charley, the last of the bachelor holdouts, got himself a steady girlfriend, a singer he'd met in a lakeside club. He insisted we had to hear her sing, so one night the bunch of us went over to the club where she was working. And Charley was right, she was a really fine crooner, and very pretty. She was Mexican—her name was Corazón or Concepción, something like that, I don't remember exactly because Charley had nicknamed her Tweetybird and then called her Tweet for short, and that's what we all called her too. She had a beautiful complexion the color of caramel, and gleaming black hair she wore in a braid down to the small of her back. After her set, she joined us at the table, and the way she and Señor Charles looked at each other it was obvious that amor was in the making. Any woman who could appreciate Charley's charms under his pudgy, middle-aged plainness was aces with us, but naturally that didn't keep us from kidding him about robbing the cradle and asking her what kind of mickey he was using to make a doll like her fall for an old fatty like him and so forth. Tweet had a great sense of humor, however, and took the ribbing as well as Charley did. She had come to Chicago from Tucson, where her widowed mother and younger sister still lived, and she was the only woman in the bunch who had never set foot among outlaws before throwing in with us. When we met her, Charley had of course already told her who we were.

The next day, when it was only us guys having a drink together, he said he'd told Tweet the truth about himself on their second date. He was afraid she'd be shocked, scared, maybe go running to the nearest precinct station to rat him out. To the contrary, he said, she was—to use his word—enrapt.

A gentleman does not kiss and tell, he said, but I *will* say that the remainder of that evening proved most exhilarating.

I laughed and said It's an old story, pal. Even the nicest girls can get all gooey about us gangster types.

That's a fact, Charley said. A man can only wonder at the fearsome mysteries of the female heart.

Hell, Red said, even women don't understand women.

Charley said some ancient sage once remarked that any woman on earth would willingly mate with the world's bloodiest tyrant in hope of bearing a son strong enough to murder the father.

What the hell did *that* mean, Russell wanted to know.

Charley said he wasn't exactly certain, but he didn't for a moment doubt the truth of it.

It means they got a chip on their shoulder, John said. Broads are pissed-off because men can kick their ass and fuck them by force if that's what it takes. The only way a broad can kick a man's ass is if another guy does it for her, but then she's got to fuck *that* guy, like it or not. They figure the only guy they can count on not to stick it to them is sonny-boy, so that's who they try to use to get back at all the other men in the world.

A provocative thesis, Jonathan, Charley said. You should be lecturing in philosophy at Yale.

You mean *jail,* Russell said.

Charley ignored the wisecrack and said the weakness in John's reasoning was that it didn't allow for such aberrant sonny-boys as Oedipus. As I'm sure you gentlemen recall, he said, Oedipus slew his father and had highly improper relations with his mother.

Red said With his *father's* mother? He fucked his *grandma?*

Charley gave him one of his reproving schoolmaster looks and Red laughed.

Russell said he'd always thought Oedipus was the French word for a guy who jazzed with his face. *Eat-*a-puss, he said. Get it?

Charley looked pained, but he'd asked for it with that *as I'm sure*

you gentlemen recall remark. He rarely got high-hat about his education, but whenever he did we were quick to jump on him for it.

Oedipus sounds like some raggedy-ass foreigner just off the boat,
John said. I wouldn't put a thing past some wop named Oedipus.

Russell agreed. He was sure Oedipus was a mug who once worked
for Capone.

I know the mug you mean, I said. Reggie Oedipus. Wrecking-
ball Rex they called him. Was doing thirty-to-life in Joliet for stab-
bing his old man and jazzing his mom. He spent so much time in the
hole it ruined his eyes.

That's him, Russell said. Old Rex didn't know the meaning of the
word *fear*.

Come to think of it, Red said, there were only about a dozen
words old Rex *did* know the meaning of.

Charley said a little learning was a dangerous thing and most dis-
maying to behold. But he was laughing too.

• • •

Except for Copeland and Shouse, we usually all had supper together and then went dancing afterward. When we didn't go
to a club we'd go to the movies, or now and then to the
prizefights, where we always got ringside seats.

The girls loved boxing as much as we did, and sometimes they
got so worked up at a fight it was more fun watching them than the
pugs in the ring. I mean, when they got blood in their eye the girls
were something to see. They'd holler for the boxer they were pulling
for to kill the other one. They'd shout Kill him, kill him!—only they
didn't say it like guys say it, they meant *kill* him. When they'd get
spattered with the fighters' blood they'd go even wilder. They howled
like wolves when their guy was landing some good ones, and when he
was getting the worst of it they'd turn the air blue with the profanity they used on the other guy. Tweet's Latin blood sometimes got so
steamed she'd cut loose in Spanish that didn't need translating but

surely would've made her momma's ears burn. And *Billie*—oh man, sometimes she looked like she was ready to jump into the ring and scalp somebody. At the end of a great round, Mary would be panting like *she'd* been fighting, her eyes blazing with a furious thrill.

One time during a terrific middleweight fight, we were all on our feet and yelling like crazy, and Opal got so carried away, flailing with her big fists, that she accidentally clipped Russell on the side of the head and knocked him down into his seat, and a guy in the row behind us started counting over Russ like a referee.

The girls' excitement, however, was why we didn't go to the fights more often than we did. Their screaming and carrying on drew a lot of attention, and compared to a movie house a boxing arena is pretty well lit up. There was too much chance somebody in the crowd would recognize us and blow a whistle, and how do you make a fast getaway from a ringside row in a packed house?

As for Copeland and Shouse, none of us had seen either of them since the night at the Tiger's Rag until one evening when Red and Patty ran into Shouse in the parking lot of a riverside club. He was driving a beat-up Model-T coupe with a missing front fender, and Red naturally asked him how come, a guy with his dough? Shouse said he'd bought a brand-new Lincoln the day after Greencastle, but inside a week he'd lost all the rest of his money at the gambling tables and had to sell the Lincoln and get a cheaper car. That was Shouse for you. He told Red he'd moved out of Copeland's place and was now living with a girl near the university, and he gave Red her phone number in case we needed to reach him. He said Copeland had taken up with some bimbo who worked the box office at a girlie club.

I had already decided that Copeland couldn't lick his booze problem and had to go, and John no longer had any objections. We went to Knuckles' place to pay him off, but he wasn't home, so we left a note saying to get in touch. A few days later he dropped by, and you could see in his face he knew what was coming. When I broke it to him, he asked for one more chance. He swore he quit drinking.

I said he'd had his one more chance.

He turned to John, who said Sorry, pal.

I gave him his share of the kitty money and wished him luck. He went out the door looking worn as an old man.

We didn't think he would rat us if he got collared and the cops leaned on him, but then again why take the chance? The next day we all moved to new apartments. Billie and John continued to live with Mary and me, but now Red moved in with Patty and Russ and Opal. Charley took a small place of his own in the same building as theirs, even though he was spending most of his nights at Tweet's place on the lake.

In only a few days, however, we'd all have to move again.

* * *

For all the fun we were having, we hadn't lost sight of business. Just as we were about to get in touch with Sonny Sheetz to see if he had something for us, Pearl Elliott came up from Kokomo, bringing us a half-dozen cold license plates and a big fat tip on a bank.

It had nothing to do with Sheetz and it wasn't a set-up. An associate of hers—Let's call him George, she said—had it on good authority that a certain bank not far from Chicago would soon be receiving a shipment of cash to finance federal work projects around the state, something in the neighborhood of twenty-five thousand dollars.

Twenty-five, Russell said, is that *all?*—and got a good laugh. Before the Greencastle haul, not a man among us wouldn't have drooled at the thought of a twenty-five-grand haul.

Most of the money wouldn't stay in the bank for long before being routed to its various recipients. In exchange for the name of the bank and the date the cash would be there for sure, this George guy wanted 15 percent of the take. Pearl's cut would come out of his.

It sounded too good to pass up, and the other guys were all for it.

I told Pearl she had a deal. It was the American Bank and Trust in Racine, Wisconsin, some sixty miles north of Shytown, and the cash would be there in eight days.

• • •

The next morning Charley and Mary and I drove up to Racine and spent two days doing the usual case—noting the bank's routine, diagramming the layout, coming up with three getaway routes to a lakeside camp a little north of Milwaukee, where we reserved a pair of cabins for three days in the coming week.

We were heading back into Chicago on an icy morning, the skyline coming into view, when we heard a radio report that on the previous evening John and two companions, a man and a woman, had been in a gunfight with more than a dozen policemen.

According to the report, the cops had set a trap for him outside an office building where they'd been informed he had a doctor's appointment. But John somehow managed to get to his car and take off before they could arrest him. One of the police cars gave chase through the city streets with the cops shooting at him as they went. They said they'd had to open fire and risk hitting bystanders because all three of the fugitives were shooting at them—Dillinger and the girl firing pistols from the windows, the other man shooting a machine gun from a porthole in back of the car—and they said they had a shot-up windshield to prove it. They claimed the fugitives' car had been made bulletproof. The chase lasted about five miles before John gave them the slip.

Holy Joe, Mary said.

Machine-gun fire through a *porthole,* indeed, Charley said. A *bulletproof* car. What patent nonsense.

Cops and newspapermen, I said. They have to pass a liar's test before they can get the job.

Charley said he'd wager the whole gang had already changed residences.

He was right. John was waiting for us at the apartment, sitting at the table and reading the newspaper, and when we walked in he grinned big and held it up so we could see the headline about his skirmish with the cops. He said we didn't live there anymore, everybody had moved to new places a few hours earlier. He and Billie had already transferred Mary's and my belongings, and Russ and Opal had taken Charley's stuff to a hotel apartment they'd got for him two streets over from the one they'd moved to with Red and Patty.

He tapped the newspaper and said You seen this?

I said we'd heard about it on the radio. I skimmed the report and saw it was much the same thing—he'd got away from sixteen cops while a *hidden machine gunner* shot at them from a *concealed porthole* in the Terraplane and a *gun girl* fired from the window.

As we drove Charley to his new place, John gave us the real story. He said it was an ambush, plain and simple. He was tipped off to it when the doctor happened to look out the window and said he wondered why there were so many police cars on the street. John took a peek and saw two squad cars parked about twenty yards ahead of his Terraplane, and another one at the corner of the intersection directly behind it. He could've left the building through a side exit and lost himself in the evening crowds except that Billie was waiting in the car. There was nothing to do but try to make it to her and play it from there. He walked out with his hand in his jacket pocket, gripping a .45.

When the cops didn't come at him as he walked toward the Terraplane, he knew they planned to wait till he got behind the wheel and then block him in with their cars and shoot him while he was hemmed in. Which meant the bastards were willing to kill Billie too, for no more reason than being in the wrong place at the wrong time.

He got in the car and Billie asked if he'd seen them and he said yeah and told her to hang on. Rather than go forward, as the cops must've been expecting him to, he put the car in reverse and floored it and went screeching backward and swung out into the intersecting street—causing cars to swerve and crash into each other—then he took off with the tires shrieking and gunshots cracking behind them. In less than a minute he was doing sixty and weaving through traffic with an unmarked car after him, a cop at one window shooting with a pistol and one at another window blasting with a shotgun, bullets and buckshot smacking the rear of the Terraplane and popping through the back window and one round spider-webbing the windshield.

He and Billie never fired a shot, never mind what the news reports said. He wished he could've shot back but he was too busy trying to keep from crashing the car. When the passenger side of the cops' windshield blew apart, John figured they'd either shotgunned it by accident or on purpose so they could claim they'd been fired on.

I couldn't believe those cowboys, John said. It's a damn wonder they didn't shoot each other, never mind some of the citizens on the street.

He managed to get in front of a truck that blocked the cops' view of him, then cut off his headlights and turned sharply into a side street. The cops went whizzing past. By the time they realized their mistake, he'd lost them.

He ditched the Terraplane on a back street in the North Side and stole a Lincoln—like switching from a speedboat to a barge, he said—and he and Billie went home to pack their bags. First thing this morning, he'd sent her and Opal with pursefuls of cash out to get new places to live, and well before noon everybody had moved. The others had apartments again, but Billie had rented a small house for the four of us a few blocks out of the Loop.

The police had found the Terraplane last night, and reporters on the scene said it had three or four holes in the rear window and more than twenty bullet and buckshot dents, but not one round had passed through the car's body. John said he was thinking about writing a letter to the Essex company and congratulating them on a terrific getaway car. He was high as a kite about the whole thing, and he couldn't stop talking about what a great little soldier Billie had been.

You shoulda seen her, Pete. Cool as ice. Not a nerve in her body.

Christ's sake, I told him, a guy couldn't leave town for two days without missing out on the fun.

It was no mystery, by the way, about who tipped the cops to his appointment with the doc. A scummy little fink named Artie. We'd known him few years before in M City, and John had been using him as an errand boy since before the rest of us busted out of the joint. There'd been rumors in M City that Artie was a fink, and even though there'd never been proof of it, I had a hunch the rumors were right. Not John. He liked Artie, and John being John, he trusted him far more than he should've. But the minute he saw the squad cars outside the doctor's office, he knew Artie had ratted. It was Artie who'd set up the doctor's appointment for him under a phony name after John complained about a neck rash that was giving him fits, and he was the only one outside the gang who knew about that appointment.

If there'd been the slightest doubt about Artie's guilt, it vanished along with him. We looked all over Chicago for him that night and couldn't find a hair of him anywhere. The chest of drawers and closet in his boardinghouse room had been cleaned out, and nobody at his usual haunts had seen him since the day before.

But every rat meets a bad end sooner or later, and about two months ago I got word Artie had taken a fall for—get this—robbing a bunch of old ladies at a bridge game. He got sent down to the Illinois state pen. The way I heard it, he'd been there only a few weeks when he was found in the shower one morning sprawled in his own blood. Somebody had cut his throat. Prison justice for a fink.

. . .

John's close brush with the cops didn't affect our plan for Racine. Neither did an incident with Ed Shouse a couple of days before the job. John had asked Shouse to check with the Essex dealers to see what kind of Terraplane models they had on hand and let him know, but when Shouse dropped by our house that evening to report what he'd learned, only Mary and Billie were there. John and I were still at Red and Russell's place, going over the heist plan with them and Charley.

Mary offered Shouse a glass of beer while he waited for us, and Billie insisted on having some too, even though John had forbidden her to touch alcohol when he wasn't around. The way Mary told it to me later, Billie was in a snit because John was supposed to take her to dinner that evening and there she was, all ready to go, and he still hadn't shown up.

They sat at the table, talking and drinking, and pretty soon Billie and Shouse were swapping dirty jokes. Mary told them they better take it easy if they knew what was good for them, but Billie paid her no mind. She turned on the radio and asked Shouse to dance. I don't know if he didn't take my warning seriously or if the combination of the beer and Billie's flirting simply got the better of him—but when John and I came through the door, they were dancing belly to belly, and the way Billie was laughing there was no question she was drunk. Mary was at the table and told me with her eyes she'd tried to keep this from happening. Shouse saw us and let go of Billie like she'd suddenly caught on fire.

John's face showed no expression at all as he started toward them. Billie put herself between him and Shouse, talking fast about how mad she was at him for keeping her waiting while he was doing who-knew-what rather than taking her to dinner like he'd promised—and that's as far as she got before John's backhand swat sent her sprawling over a coffee table.

He whaled into Shouse with both fists, driving him against a wall, and even if Shouse had been sober he wouldn't have stood much chance. John hit him with some terrific punches that spattered the wall with blood. Shouse slid to the floor and curled up and tried to protect his head with his arms as John started kicking him.

Mary said Stop him, Harry—not yelling but saying it with a frightened urgency. Billie scrambled up and grabbed John by the shirt and the sleeve ripped as he flung her hard enough to put her on her ass again. I bear-hugged him from behind and pulled him away, saying Enough, man, enough. I didn't care if he killed Shouse but I didn't want him doing in it the house. Then you had the problem of getting rid of the body and maybe the neighbors getting an eyeful when you lugged it out.

Okay, Pete, John said, okay. It was the first thing he'd said since we'd come in the house. I felt his muscles unflex and I let go of him.

Billie was up again, a small mouse swelling under one eye. You bastard, she said.

John grabbed her by the arm and pulled her down the hall toward their room, Billie kicking at him and cursing him like a dockhand as they went. He shoved her through the door and went in and slammed it shut.

I leaned against the wall and lit a cigarette and watched Shouse laboring to get up. His nose was pouring blood and was obviously broken. If the carpet he was dripping on had been mine I would've given him a few more kicks for messing it. His lips were bloated purple and one eye was nearly closed and he favored a leg. In less than a minute John had worked him over good, but he wasn't hurt that bad. He hadn't even lost a tooth. And he couldn't say he hadn't been warned.

You're gone, Ed, I told him, you're out. I said if he talked about us to anybody we'd hear of it and hunt him down and drop him into Lake Michigan with his legs chained to an axle.

He was a little shaky on his pins but was able to walk unassisted. Mary handed him his hat at the door just as Russ and Opal showed up. They were taking us to supper at some Chinese place across town they said was great.

Shouse didn't look at them as he left. Opal gave him a double-take, then turned to us all big-eyed with curiosity. Russell came in grinning and said to me *You* do that?

John, I said. Then told him what happened.

Russ was sorry he'd missed the show but was glad I'd booted Shouse. He guessed we'd seen the last of him. But of course we hadn't. We'd see him one more time.

We could hear John and Billie still going at it down the hall. If we'd been in an apartment and sharing walls with neighbors, I would've had to tell them to pipe down before somebody called the cops. The girls were worried about Billie and wanted to wait a little bit before we went out to eat, so I poured beers and we sat in the parlor. Mary was keeping up a good front but I could tell how much the whole thing had jangled her nerves.

A minute later we heard a door open and Billie's soft crying and then the door shut again. John came in the parlor and said Hey, kids to Russ and Opal and flopped down in an easy chair.

Russell said How's things, Johnny? He wasn't trying too hard to hide his amusement.

That bitch is gonna drive me crazy, John said.

You act like you're *already* crazy, Mary said. And you're driving *me* crazy. And Billie too.

I'd been hoping she'd keep out of it, but no such luck.

John said You defending *her?*

Mary said damn right she was. All Billie had done was get a little tipsy and ask a guy to dance. She hadn't been fooling around behind John's back and he didn't have any cause to get so jealous and no matter how jealous he got he had no right to hit her or even talk to her the way he did and if he couldn't take her as she is then he could tell her to go but no real man hit a woman and all real men knew that and John was acting like a stupid crazy jealous ignorant cowardly bully and a bully was the lowest kind of man there was in the world and if *she* was Billie she would've left his low-down bullying ass long before now—either left him or bashed his skull in with a frying pan while he was sleeping.

Boy howdy, did she let him have it. He'd sunk deeper into his chair as she tore into him, looking like a bad-behaved pup, and it was all Russell and I could do to keep from laughing. Mary cut a look at us and said What's so damn *funny,* and we shut up quick. She didn't seem to mind that Opal was grinning like she was at a Chaplin flick.

You owe her a *big* apology, mister, Mary said, and you damn well better give it to her. But to tell you the truth, I hope she tells you to fold your lousy apology four ways and stick it where the sun don't shine.

She stood and picked up her purse and said she was ready to go and headed for the door with Opal right behind her and laughing.

We watched them go out. Then John turned to me and Russ and said in a low voice Bash my skull while I'm *sleeping?* Jesus. I hope she doesn't give Billie any ideas.

Russell said Ain't love grand?

As we headed for the door I told John to try not to shoot her or get himself scalped while we were gone.

Oh, go to hell, he said.

After you, sir, I said, after you.

He faked a punch that made me flinch and said I'd get there long before him, watch and see if I didn't.

The girls were waiting for us on the sidewalk. Opal said Guess what?

Russell said Where's my car?

I asked where he'd parked it.

Here, Opal said, gesturing at the curb in front of us.

Russ looked up and down the street and said Where the *hell's* my car?

Gone, Opal said.

Gone? Russell said. Whaddaya mean *gone?*

Well, honey, Opal said, you see, it *was* here, but now it's not. It's what's called gone.

Parked across the street was a Model T with a missing front fender. I pointed at it and said I believed it was Shouse's car.

Russ looked at it for a moment, then looked up and down the street again. Then looked at me and said The bastard stole my car. He said it like he couldn't quite believe it, the way a guy might say he just got the word his mother died. He *stole* my goddamn car.

Sure looks it, I said.

My car, Russell said. John's the one who kicked his ass, why didn't he steal *his* car? Oooh, that low son of a bitch. He stole my *car*.

Yeah, I'm pretty sure he did, I said.

Jesus, he said, world's *crawling* with fucken thieves.

Watch your language, babydoll, Opal said—ladies present.

Russ was still swearing about it when we got to the restaurant, and he swore about it periodically during the meal, and he swore even louder when we got back to the house and he had to crank up the Model T by hand.

Mary and I entered the house quietly, listening hard for sounds of battle. We didn't hear anything until we were down the hall and caught the huff and puff of lovemaking coming through their door. Mary smiled and squeezed my arm. We went in our room and undressed and slipped into bed.

You did good, kid, I said, and she held me closer and giggled against my neck.

• • •

The next day's paper brought the news that Knuckles Copeland had been collared. He'd been in his car parked outside a hotel over on North Avenue and having a loud, drunken wrangle with some hooker when the cops showed up in response to the desk clerk's call. Next thing they knew they'd caught themselves *a member of the notorious Dillinger Gang,* as the newspaper put it.

Copeland wouldn't be able to tell the cops anything except where we'd been living the last time he'd seen us, although as I said before, we didn't think he'd ever rat us. But none of us trusted Shouse, and that afternoon we all moved once more, Billie and Mary renting another house for us.

• • •

Racine, oh man! It wasn't the hairiest job we ever pulled—that was the East Chicago heist that was yet to come—but Racine was a close one. A real kick.

We decided we didn't need anybody to replace Shouse, that the five of us could handle the job okay. We stole a new blue Buick in Highland Park. John and I tossed to see who drove and he won. We left my Vickie and Red's roadster in a garage in Waukegan.

We got into Racine at half past two. It was sunny but chilly and a wind was coming off the lake. We knew the fed money had been delivered that morning and that the bank would be at its fattest shortly before closing, after taking in the day's deposits. There was no parking on the street in front of the bank, so the plan was to park in the lot behind the building and then make our getaway through the back door.

If I had it to do over again, I'd work out the getaway a little better, especially the part about the back door.

Red had the street, and the rest of us went in. Russell had the stopwatch again and stuck close to the front door. John strolled over to the bank president's desk and Charley went to the table in front of the teller cage and pretended to fill out a deposit slip while I went up to the big front window with a Red Cross poster rolled under my arm and a little spool of tape in my coat pocket.

I shook open the poster and exchanged smiles with a middle-aged couple seated on a couch waiting to see someone. As I taped the poster to the glass, blocking the view of passersby on the sidewalk, I said Don't forget to give generously. The man said he always donated to the Red Cross. It had been real nice to him and his buddies during the war.

John and the president, a good-sized guy, went into the cage together without anybody paying them much mind and the big man started working the combination on the vault. Charley was looking at me, ready to move. There was a short line of customers at the only teller window open for business. At the far end of the cage a teller behind a window with a little CLOSED sign on it was counting a stack of greenbacks.

Ladies and gentlemen, I said, your attention please. The citizens all looked at me and I pulled the .45 and said This is a robbery. You know who we are and you know we mean business.

There was the usual big-eyed astonishment and a few little squeals and I told them to button their lips and get down on their stomachs, *now*, and they dropped like they were doing a group exercise. A plump brunette with her hair in a bun lay down on her back with her eyes closed. I tapped her leg lightly with my toe and said On your *stomach*, honey—this is a holdup, not a meeting with the board of directors. One of the other women snickered, a looker in a red dress. The brunette blushed and rolled over.

Fat Charley had the tommy out and was at the window of the money-counter, saying something I didn't catch except for the word *reasonable*. But that moron teller made a grab under the counter—and *bam*, Charley shot him off the stool.

Women screamed and some of the men started to raise up to see what happened. I yelled for everybody to stay down and shut the hell up or we'd shoot them all.

The teller had hit the alarm. We could hear it ringing outside the bank and I knew it was sounding in the police station. According to the plan, as soon as we'd been in the bank for three and half minutes Red was to go back to the car and have it running and ready to roll when we came out the rear door. But if the alarm sounded sooner, he'd get back to the car immediately.

I went into the cage where John was swearing at the bank president for still twiddling with the vault combination. The prez looked up at me and said Did you hurt someone out there? Like he was going to do something about it if I had.

I asked him his name and he said Weyland. Mr. Weyland, I told him, you have exactly ten seconds to open that vault or we'll blow your brains out.

I took a flour sack from my pocket and started cleaning out the cage drawers while John held his .45 to the back of Weyland's head and counted One . . . two . . . three. . . .

The teller Charley shot was lying on the floor, holding his bloody arm and looking at me like I was Satan in the flesh.

On the count of seven John cocked the hammer, and on the count of eight, abracadabra, the vault came open. He shoved Weyland in there ahead of him.

Yes, John would've pulled the trigger. Me too. It's a matter of maintaining authority as well as your self-respect. If you want to make idle threats, be a schoolteacher, be a preacher, be a newspaper editor. Do not carry a gun.

A police siren was closing in. Bystanders were crowding at the sidewalk window, peeking around the edges of the poster. Everything's a show to the citizens, everything's an entertainment.

I was emptying the last of the cash drawers when the cop siren sounded directly in front of the bank and I caught a glimpse of a squad car.

Russell had put away the stopwatch and was standing off to the side of the front door, ready for them. A uniformed cop came ambling in and said loudly All right now, people, who set the darn thing off *this* time?

Then he saw everybody on the floor and stopped short and tried to unholster his gun but Russ grabbed him from behind by his Sam Browne, yanked him off his feet and sent him skidding on the polished floor. He stripped the cop's revolver from him and pulled him upright and slammed him against the wall and said to stick his hands in his pockets and leave them there or he'd shoot him in the eye.

Then another cop came in, dangling a tommy gun in his hand like some woodchopper taking a break. Russell yelled Get him,

Fats—and before the cop could raise the tommy, *bam-bam,* Charley shot him in the leg and he went down in a holler. Now the women couldn't keep from screaming and the place became sheer pandemonium with all that shrieking and the squad car siren still going and the alarm jangling and jangling. Russell grabbed up the cop's tommy and dragged him away from the door.

John came out of the vault with a sack of money in one hand and his .45 in the other.

Let's amscray, I said. Russell ran over to the cage and covered the entrance from there while the rest of us made for the back door.

Which we found locked. The lock was the size of a brick and the key wasn't in it.

One of them out there's got the damn thing, John said.

I said forget it, we didn't have time to shake everybody down for it while more cops were on the way. We'd go out the front and shoot what we had to.

The cop on the lobby floor was holding his bloody leg and crying like a baby. I grabbed Weyland by the collar and said he was coming with us and I told Russell to bring the other cop. John pointed at the woman in red and said You too, sister.

She said Who, *me?* He snatched her by the arm and pulled her along.

The mob on the sidewalk scattered as we came out into the louder clamor, moving fast and holding the hostages close.

On the right, Charley, John hollered.

Charley fired a long burst at a pair of guys across the street with guns in their hands. People screamed and ran for cover and the two guys disappeared around the corner as bullets ricocheted and punched holes in parked cars and brought down a show window in a rain of glass.

We ran around the corner, pulling the hostages along, Charley bringing up the rear and covering us. He fired another burst and I heard more glass crashing but nobody shot back.

Then we were at the car and Red was revving the engine, saying Let's go, let's go, let's go!

John told him to shove over and got behind the wheel. I slid into the backseat directly behind him. We made the hostages stand on the running boards and hold on to the window posts and I said if they jumped off we'd shoot them. Weyland was at John's window and the woman at mine. The cop stood next to the front passenger seat and Red gripped him by the Sam Browne. Charley and Russ were in the backseat with me, Russ in the right-hand jump seat.

Hang on, kids, John said, and he gunned the Buick out of the lot.

He laid on the klaxon and we went barreling down the streets in a steady blare, weaving through traffic and zooming past gawking bystanders and taking corners so sharply the car leaned hard and the tires howled and it was all the hostages could do to keep from flying off the running boards. I had my arm around the woman's hips and held her tight against the door. Her dress was thin and she wasn't wearing a girdle and didn't need one, I can tell you. She let out a little screech every time we rounded a corner, but she was a good soldier, and Weyland held up well too. On one of the turns John scraped the right front fender against a taxi and the cop on the running board came *this* close to getting squished like a bug between the cars. He probably wasn't even aware of the tears blowing off his face.

A motorcycle cop coming from the other direction slowed down when he saw us, but I stuck the .45 out the window and he hunched down on the cycle and kept going the other way.

In minutes we were in the clear. Charley was watching behind us and said there was nobody in pursuit. I had John pull into a side street and stop the car, then told the cop to get off and Weyland and the woman to get in with us and make it fast. Weyland wedged in between me and Charley and I pulled the woman down on my lap.

See you suckers in the funny papers, Red told the cop and the by-standers, and off we went.

John took a few side streets to shed the last of the gawkers, then

got on a highway leading west out of town. He glanced down at the
seat beside him where Red had opened the map with the getaway
routes we'd laid out. Once we ditched Weyland and the woman and
got out of their sight, we'd cut north and head for the hideout cabins
by way of Waukesha and Menomonee Falls. All they'd be able to tell
the cops is that we went west.

We rolled past the city-limit sign and Russell hollered *WAAAA-
hoooo,* giving the woman a start, and we whooped it up big.

Weyland and the woman weren't sharing in our high spirits. Now
that they were in the car and the gunfire was done with and nobody
was chasing us, they had to be wondering what came next.

I asked her name and she said Ursula. I told her not to be afraid,
we'd be releasing them soon. She said she wasn't afraid, she was
cold—it had been freezing out on the running board but she hadn't
realized it while she was hanging on for dear life. She was hugging
herself in her short-sleeved dress and her arms had goose bumps.
Weyland said she wasn't kidding about the cold, his bald spot felt
frozen. I gave him my hat and then worked out of my coat and draped
it over Ursula's shoulders. As I did, my hand brushed her breast and
her face went rosy. The blush might've also had something to do with
the erection I'd sprouted under her ass.

Charley commended both her and Weyland on how well they'd
handled themselves and thanked them for their assistance in our
quest to achieve a more equitable distribution of America's wealth.

Red laughed. Fucken well said, pal.

Hey Jack, lady present, I said. He turned to Ursula and touched
his hat brim. Pardon my Portuguese, ma'am.

John glanced at Ursula in the rearview and asked if she knew how
to cook. She said of course she did. He waggled his brows and said
maybe she'd like to tag along, hire on as our cook, see to it we got the
proper nourishment to keep up the good work.

She got rosy in the cheeks again and said she didn't think her husband would like that. My stiffie was really nudging her bottom now.

She shifted her weight to try to ease herself off it, but I had my arm around her and she only managed to position herself on it more snugly. I don't think I could've smiled any wider.

Red pointed at a dirt cutoff up ahead and John nodded. He slowed down and turned onto it and drove into a grove of trees hung heavy with red and yellow leaves and stopped the car. Without letting Weyland or Ursula get a look at it, Red took an Indiana license plate from under the front seat and got out to swap it with the one on the car.

End of the line, folks, I said.

That's what they say when they're about to bump off somebody, Weyland said. He was trying to make it sound like a joke, but his smile was stiff and I think he was afraid it's what I had in mind. I pointed my index finger at him and said *Bang*. He flinched slightly and then everybody laughed, including him and Ursula.

Bumped off, Charley said. Those ghastly cops-and-robbers movies have the whole world talking like gangsters.

As Ursula started to step down from the car, I ran my hand over her rump—it was a sweet one, take it from me. She cut a look at me over her shoulder and I winked, and she showed that lovely blush again.

I hated to make it worse for them in the cold by asking for my hat and coat back, but hey, the coat was custom-tailored, and it was my favorite hat.

Red got in the car and John backed us toward the highway so Weyland and Ursula couldn't get a look at the new plate. They watched us turn onto the road in reverse, and as we headed off, she gave us a little wave goodbye.

John said he bet she wasn't lying about being a good cook.

Red bet she was good at a lot more than cooking and that her husband had no complaints about his love life. Right, Pete? I saw the fun you were having with her.

I gave him the two-finger Up yours sign.

Yeah, he said, that's what I'da liked to do to her too.

Russell thought it wouldn't have taken much to talk her into joining us. She's got the leaning, he said, I could tell.

All the best ones got the leaning, John said, and got no argument from any of us.

We made it to the cabins without incident. Even the weather was in our favor—a cold wind gusting off the lake and making it natural for everybody to stay indoors and out of sight.

The take came to a hair under $30,000. Forty-five hundred went to Pearl and her informant and we took cuts of five grand apiece and put the remainder in the common kitty. On top of the money we still had from Greencastle, we were feeling like fat cats.

We laid low for the next three days, enjoying the commotion we made in the news. Wisconsin lawmen promised to bring us to justice and blah-blah-blah. As we moseyed back to our cars in Waukegan by way of meandering back roads, the newspapers were still peddling panic to the citizens. As always, though, some of the letters to the editor made it clear that not everyone was howling for our scalps. There were plenty of citizens who didn't think we were much worse than some civic officials and probably a lot less worse than most bankers.

· · ·

After the Racine job we took it easy for a while. John bought a new Terraplane, a sedan this time, so the car had room for a few pals. It was a deep blue color like none of us had ever seen on a car before, and he christened it the Blueberry. Red ponied up a hefty $2,600 for a new brown-and-yellow Packard coupe with white-walled tires, spoked chrome wheels, and tan leather seats. He also let us guys in on a secret—he'd recently taken up with a hotel waitress named Elaine Dent Sullivan Burton DeKant, a moniker that got the laugh from us he expected. He said he'd asked her name one morning as she served his coffee at the restaurant and by the time she got done saying it he was ready for a refill. She told him she was divorced but she continued to call herself Mrs. DeKant because it sounded more respectable. In addition to the apartment he and Patty shared with Russ and Opal, Red had rented himself another place under the name of Orval Lewis, and that was where he was putting the blocks to the respectable Mrs. DeKant. He said she had the best melons he'd ever seen—out to here and with nipples that stuck up like thumbs. She was giving him such a good time that when he bought himself the new Packard, he made her a present of his green roadster and even promised to get the crooked fender fixed. We got a kick out of his monkeyshines, but Russell warned him that if Patty found out what he was up to she was liable to go at him *and* the respectable Mrs. DeKant with a butcher knife.

We didn't have any real close calls for about two weeks after Racine, not until the end of Prohibition—the fifth of December, who could forget?

On the first night of legal boozing in fourteen years, all of Chicago went on a toot. Every nightclub and neighborhood beer bar was packed to the gills. People drank in the streets, dancing and singing, offering toasts to each other. I'd never heard a louder night, not even on New Year's Eve. Drunks yahooing and klaxons honking and firecrackers blasting and—just like on New Year's Eve—gunfire sounding all over town as citizens took the opportunity to try to shoot down the moon from their windows and backyards. The city put extra cops on the streets, but most of them got pretty drunk themselves.

All our favorite speakeasies were now legitimate drinking joints, but with the heat on us more than ever after the ruckus we'd made in Racine, we hadn't been sure it was a good idea to show ourselves in public on a night when half the city would be out carousing too. John suggested we go to the Silk Hat, a black-and-tan club with a great jazz band over on the south shore that he and Billie often went to and that he'd been recommending to the gang for weeks. None of the rest of us had gone there because we didn't see any sense in driving that far for a drink and a dance when the Loop was full of great clubs. John and Billie liked it because even though it was spacious and drew big crowds its lighting was really dim—except for up on the band-stand—and couples could get pretty intimate without attracting at-tention. John told me Billie once blew him at their table and not even the party sitting next to them was the wiser. Besides, the Silk Hat was also dark in another respect—most of its crowd was Negro, and spooks weren't inclined to blow the whistle on anybody. So that's where we went to celebrate.

The club staff all knew John—Mr. Sullivan to them—and knew him for a big tipper. We were given a choice table at a front corner of the large dance floor. It was a swell band and the service was good, and like John said, the lighting was so low it was hard for anyone to get a good look at your face unless they were right next to you.

In honor of the occasion, we'd loosened our drinking rules, boost-ing our limit to four drinks apiece—except for Billie, of course. John had finally wised up to how she'd been managing to get buzzed whenever we all had a night out together even though nobody ever bought her a drink. He gave Mary a lecture about it and Mary lec-tured him right back, saying she could share her drinks with anybody she wanted to without his permission, thank you very much. Since then he'd kept a closer eye on both of them. But on this special night he let Billie have three drinks on her promise to space them at least an hour apart and not to sneak sips from Mary's glass.

Anyhow, what happened was this. Sometime around midnight, as I was making my way toward the gents' through the raucous mob and a haze of blue smoke so thick you could feel it on your face, I spotted John coming out of the wide entrance to the men's room. I was about to go up and ask if he could direct me to the local temperance hall, but at that moment a pair of palookas, white guys in overcoats, closed on him from either side. The taller one in a pale fedora grabbed his arm and John tried to pull away but the short one in the brown hat got hold of his other arm and John suddenly went still and I knew

Shorty was holding a gun on him through his overcoat. All I could see of their faces were their grins, like they'd just run into an old pal. Pale Hat slickly took John's piece off him and put it in his own coat pocket. I figured them for cops trying to make an arrest without exciting all the drunks around them.

With a hand on John's shoulder Pale Hat spoke to him with his mouth almost at his ear. I didn't know if John had seen me, but if he had he was being careful not to look my way. There wasn't fifteen feet between them and me, but the milling crowd made for good camouflage. I slipped a .38 out of the holster at the small of my back and held it under my coat flap, wishing I hadn't left the .45 in the car. It was the .38 I'd taken from the sheriff in Lima. For some reason its grip felt perfect in my hand, and it had become my favorite backup piece.

Now Pale Hat stepped back from John and said something more. John shook his head, and the guy took a look around. I sidled over some to keep a screen of people between us. Pale Hat then put a chummy arm around John's shoulders and was yakking into his ear again as the three of them headed for the side exit. I couldn't see our table from where I stood, so I couldn't signal for help before following them outside.

The side door opened into an alley crammed with cars parked at all angles. The night was still clamoring with car horns and fireworks and random gunshots. A faint scent of burnt powder mingled with the reek of garbage. About ten yards to my left the alley abutted a street and was illuminated by a streetlight. To the right the shadows were deep and long and it was a good thirty yards to the next street.

And there they were, maybe twenty feet away, the three of them standing next to a sedan facing in the other direction, its motor idling and its lights on. There were two vague figures in the car, at the front window and at the wheel.

As the short one started to open a back door, the tall one said Hey, and they all turned toward me.

Because of the streetlight, I was showing them a clear silhouette, but I knew they couldn't see the gun I held against the front of my thigh as if I had my hand in my pants pocket. And against the cast of the headlights down the alley behind them, their shapes stood out too. I could tell John was the one in the middle.

They didn't know who I was or they wouldn't have just stood there. Like skating on thin ice, speed was everything, and I was already moving toward them as I said in a buddy-buddy tone Hey guys, which way she go?

The short one said *What?*

The blonde, I said, closing in on them, hoping John was set. She come this way?

No blonde come out here, Mack, the tall one said. Beat it.

Shorty put his hand in his coat pocket and took a step toward me.

There the bitch goes, I said, and pointed down the alley with my left hand.

It put them off balance for half a second but that was enough. I was three feet from Shorty and shot him in the face, the bulldog sparking bright. John pounced on him as he fell and I shot the tall one twice and his gun clattered on the pavement and he staggered back and crashed into the garbage cans. The guy behind the wheel was halfway out of the car when I shot him in the head and he lurched against the door and slid to the ground in an awkward fold.

I spun toward the one still in the car as he was bringing up a shotgun and *bam,* John let him have it in back of the head with Shorty's pistol. The guy pitched over on the seat and John poked the gun through the window and shot him again.

It was over just that fast. My ears rang and the gunpowder haze stung my nose.

Brother, John said, and blew out a breath like he'd been holding it for an hour.

Bastard cops, I said. Even through the garbage stink and the gunsmoke I could make out the smell of their blood. A dark puddle of it was spreading around Shorty's head.

Cops, my ass, John said. These are the Quarrys. Let's scram.

We ran down the alley to the far end of the block and then tried to look casual as we walked out onto the street and up around the corner and ambled down to the club's front entrance. I can't speak for John, but my heart was going like a jackhammer and it was hard to draw an even breath and my legs were a little feathery and I had a strong urge to piss and I'd never felt more . . . *alive* . . . in my life.

We went in the club and rounded up the others and got out of there. As we headed for our cars parked a block away we gave the other guys a run-down of what happened. As we were driving off, a squad car with its light flashing but its siren mute turned onto the street flanking the club and stopped next to the alley entrance.

• • •

Red and Russell walked Patty and Opal to the front door of the apartment house while Charley put Tweet in a taxi for home. Then the guys followed me and John over to our new house. When we got there, Billie and Mary excused themselves and went to the bedrooms so we could talk in private.

John said the tall one in the pale hat was Art Quarry and the shorty was named Bud. The two in the car were their brothers. The Art one told John they'd been hunting him ever since he stole their money out of Greencastle. Then they got an anonymous telephone tip about his fondness for the Silk Hat. They'd been there every night for a week, waiting for him to drop by, posting themselves by the men's room because sooner or later every man's got to water the lilies. They were about to give up on the Silk Hat for good when they spotted him. If he'd waited five minutes to take his piss they would've missed him. The Art guy thought that was funny. He called it a quirk of fate.

I said the Art guy didn't know the half of it. If they'd left five minutes earlier they wouldn't be lying in the morgue.

They told John they were taking him where nobody would hear

his screams while they discussed how he would repay their fifty grand.

I have to tell you, boys, John said, I was never so glad to see anybody as when Pete came out that door.

They couldn't hear enough about the fight. After John told it, they had me tell it, and both times Russell asked the same thing: They never got off a shot? Not *one* shot?

Never had a chance, John said, not against Pistol Pete.

Or him, I said. The shotgun might've nailed me if John didn't nail him first.

Red said the whole thing sounded fucking outstanding and goddamnit why did he always miss out on the fun.

Charley asked if all four of the miscreants were expired.

I told him I thought so but we hadn't bothered to make sure. We'd see what the paper said in the morning.

Russ wondered why the Micks had been hunting for John in particular and not for anybody else in the bunch. I asked who he'd look for if he'd read in the paper that the *Dillinger* Gang stole his money.

Quite so, Charley said—he who basks in the limelight shall attract the most attention, for worse as well as better.

John said if Mr. Makley's crack about basking in the limelight was some kind of snide reference to the way he *used* to enter a bank's cashier cage—and he hoped Mr. Makley noticed that he did *not* use that method in Racine—then Mr. Makley could go to hell.

I indubitably shall, Mr. Fairbanks, Charley said, and hard upon your heels, I'm sure.

As for the phone tip the Quarrys got about the Silk Hat, they might not've known who gave it to them, but we did. Ed Shouse, no question about it. He tipped the Quarrys to get back at John for the ass-kicking he gave him. John said he was putting the bastard at the top of his list.

After we all had a nightcap beer and the others left and it was only the two of us, John told me he'd never killed a man before. He said it like he was unsure of how he felt about crossing that particular line.

Well, I told him, he sure killed that one tonight, and as far as I was concerned he couldn't have picked a better time to bust his cherry.

Listen, I said, it's them or us. Simple as that. Them or us.

He gave me a poker-faced stare for a moment—then that crooked smile. Well now, brother, he said, that's a true fact, isn't it?

The next morning he read the newspaper report to me. Three of the Quarrys were found dead at the scene and the fourth died in the hospital three hours later without naming his killers. The paper called it a *gangland slaying* resulting from a *turf war* and said it was fitting that the death of Prohibition was marked by the deaths of men who'd prospered from it. The cops had identified the four as members of a family of St. Louis bootleggers who'd probably gotten on the wrong side of the Chicago mob.

It's what they get, the cop in charge told reporters. Sooner or later it's what every one of these mugs gets.

John put the paper down and ran a finger around his collar and made a big mock gulp—and then grinned his cocky grin.

* * *

A few days later the Chicago P.D. announced a list of its ten most-wanted fugitives. All of us were on it, including Mary and Pearl.

Yikes, Mary said, when she saw the list, I've been promoted from a moll to a desperado like you boys.

John told her she wouldn't think it was so damn funny if she got arrested as a desperado.

Ooooh, Mary said, I'm *so* scared. She was trying for a laugh from us and she got it.

I didn't know if Pearl was aware of the Chicago heat on her, so I phoned her at home in Kokomo. When she answered by saying Paulette Dewey residence, I knew she was aware, all right.

She didn't know how the cops had connected her to us but figured it could've been anybody who'd ever seen her in our company.
The world's crawling with rats was her simple explanation. She wasn't
worried about the cops tracking her down, not under the Dewey
name. As for the Side Pocket, the building was leased to Janet Cody,
who didn't exist, and Pearl had put Darla Bird in charge of the place.

• • •

The following day Cueball Lucas called to tell us he had finally repaired Red's Auburn sedan and it was ready to be
picked up. Red had forgotten about the car by then, he was
so delighted with his fancy new Packard. When he heard the Auburn
was fixed, he said he didn't care, he didn't want the car anymore, and
he was going to tell Cueball he could have it for a hundred bucks. I
said at that price I'd buy it myself. My brother Fred's beat-up old
Chevy was on its last legs and he was in bad need of a better car.

Sold to Mr. Pierpont for a C-note, Red said.

The title to the sedan was in its glove box, and Cueball assured
me he could have it put in Fred's name with no problem. I thanked
him and said I'd send the money for the repair work, then called Fred
and told him he now owned a new Auburn and all he had to do was
get Dad to drive him to Terre Haute to pick it up. Fred was tickled
pink but said Dad was under the weather with a bad cold and Mom
would take him to Terre Haute. My mother came on the line to say
hello, and I told her I wanted to pay a visit. She said no, the cops were
still watching the place, to wait till she gave me the all-clear.

Three days later Cueball telephoned to say that my mother and
Fred were on their way back to Ohio with the Auburn, but not without running into a little trouble first. My mother had told Cueball not
to say anything about the matter, but he didn't want me to hear about
it from somebody else and get mad at him for not having told me.

What happened was that in addition to Ohio cops, some of Matt
Leach's men had been keeping an eye on my parents' house too.

When my mother and Fred drove off to go get the Auburn, the Leach men tailed them into Indiana and all the way to Terre Haute in the belief that they were being led to me. When everybody arrived at Cueball's, the cops barged in and searched the place from top to bottom, then arrested Mom and Fred and Cueball and hauled them off to jail. A few hours later Leach himself showed up and released them and apologized to my mother, saying it had all been a bad misunderstanding. Cueball said my mother used some unladylike language on Leach and told him he deserved to get cancer for persecuting her son. Cueball wanted me to understand that my mom hadn't been harmed.

I said he'd done the right thing to let me know and asked if he knew where Leach was.

He'd heard him say he was going back to his headquarters in Indianapolis.

Mary was sitting in a chair across from me, and my face probably showed what I was feeling because she looked alarmed and asked what was wrong. John and Billie had gone out for a late breakfast and hadn't come home yet. I went in the bedroom and holstered the .45 under my arm and the .38 on my right hip and put on my coat. I took the .30-06 Enfield from the closet and strapped it into a suit bag and put a full five-round clip into the bag too. I told Mary I had to go to Indianapolis, and she said she was coming with me. I said no she wasn't and she said to try and stop her. I was in no mood to argue so I let her suit herself.

I didn't say anything during the three-and-a-half-hour drive. I think Mary talked every now and then but I wasn't listening even a little bit and couldn't have told you then or now a word of what she said. I wasn't thinking of anything except Matt Leach having abused my mother and the pleasure it was going to give me to kill him.

We got to Indy at midafternoon. There was a hotel directly across the street from a municipal building annex that contained the headquarters of the Indiana State Police. I parked in the lot behind the

hotel and got the suit bag from the backseat and we went in and I
booked us a room on the third floor, facing the annex.

The window gave me a clear view of the three doors to the state
police offices. If Leach was in there, it was ten to one he'd come out
through one of those doors. And if he wasn't there, that was okay
too—I'd wait in that room until he showed up the following day or
the day after that or whenever he finally did.

I took the Enfield out of the suit bag and pulled the bolt open and
set the clip in place and thumbed all five rounds into the magazine,
then tossed the empty clip back into the suit bag and slid the bolt
home to chamber a bullet. I positioned a chair near the window but
far enough back from it so that the rifle muzzle could rest on the sill
without jutting out into public view.

And then I waited for Leach to come out.

Maybe Mary had been talking all along, but like I said, I don't remember. I didn't really hear anything she said until I was watching
for Leach. I kept my eyes on the office doors while she sat on the bed
and spoke to me in a low voice, spoke low and with restraint and a
little nervously, the way you might talk to a large growling dog, or
to some guy standing on a window ledge twenty floors up.

She talked about how shooting him wasn't a smart thing to do,
how she understood why I wanted to kill him but he wasn't worth it,
how maybe we'd be able to get away before every state cop in that
building came charging into the hotel but the odds were they'd kill
us both before we made it halfway across the lobby. She talked about
how everybody in the gang believed in me and even though nobody
ever said it out loud the plain and simple truth was they all looked to
me as the leader and trusted me never to put them in danger simply
to settle some personal score and blah-blah-blah. She kept saying the
same things over and over, phrasing them a little differently each
time, but still the same things.

And all the while I was watching cops going in and out of the
annex, waiting for Leach to show himself.

I don't know how long we'd been there—twenty minutes? an hour and a half?—when one of the doors opened and out came two guys in suits and one of them was him.

I leaned forward and snugged the rifle butt into my shoulder and placed my cheek lightly against the stock and directly behind the humpback sight. He even did me the favor of stopping on the walkway to light a cigarette, making a still target of himself.

I laid the front sight directly over his heart and my finger tightened on the trigger.

That's when Mary said: He'll never know it was you.

Leach started walking again and I slowly swiveled the barrel on the sill to keep the sight blade on him.

What satisfaction could there be in killing somebody, Mary said, if he never knew what hit him or why.

I kept the sight on him as he came down to the sidewalk.

My mother would think it was a damn dumb way to get myself killed, Mary said.

Now Leach was at his car and he laughed at something the other guy said. I raised the sight to his grinning skull face.

Mary said she could be wrong but it didn't seem a very self-respecting way to even the score.

He got into the car and I sighted on him through the windshield.

Then the car drove away and he was gone.

To this day he's got no idea he came *this* close to getting his clock stopped.

Lucky b-b-bastard.

I worked the bolt to empty the magazine, and then picked up the rounds and put them in my pocket and set the Enfield against the wall. Then I looked at Mary for the first time since we'd come into the room.

She was wiping tears off her face and laughing her wonderful laugh.

Then we were out of our clothes and on the bed and having so much fun we were probably breaking a dozen laws.

• • •

We spent the night in the hotel and slept late. We had a room-service brunch and then took in a movie—*Duck Soup,* a new Marx Brothers that made us laugh so hard our stomachs hurt. When Groucho told a guy You're fighting for this woman's honor, which is more than she ever did, I thought of John and Billie for some reason.

We headed for home around midafternoon. In Lafayette we ate an early supper and lingered a while over coffee and cigarettes. Shortly before sundown, as we were going through Rensselaer, we heard a radio report that I'd killed a cop in a Chicago garage and made a clean getaway.

Holy Joe, Mary said, next they'll be accusing you of shooting Abe Lincoln.

We were almost to Shytown when the news item was repeated, once again in the breathless, rat-a-tat, edge-of-your-seat style the radio guys love to use in reporting violent crime—but this time with a correction. The slayer of Police Detective Somebody-or-other was *not* Harry Pierpont, the fugitive Michigan City escapee, murderer, bank robber, and member of the Terror Gang. It was *another* member of the gang—John Hamilton, also known as Three-finger Jack Hamilton. The identity of the cop killer had been confirmed by Hamilton's woman companion, one Mrs. Elaine DeKant, whom Hamilton deserted near the scene of the crime and who'd been arrested by police. Mrs. DeKant positively identified Hamilton's photograph at police headquarters and confirmed that he was missing two fingers, which he'd told her he'd lost in the war. She claimed she knew him only as Orval Lewis, an independent investor. Mrs. DeKant led police to the apartment Hamilton had been renting under the name of Lewis and the landlord also identified his picture. Mrs.

DeKant was being held in the Cook County Jail on charges of accessory to murder and abetting a fugitive.

The report went on to say that citizens all across the country were outraged by the Terror Gang's second killing of a police officer. Acting on information that the gang was in their city, Chicago police were on a rampage, pulling raids all over town and snaring dozens of crooks in the process.

• • •

As soon as Mary and I got home we called the gang together at our place. Opal came with Russell and Charley, but Tweet was working, and Patty had stayed at the apartment in case Red showed up there. Nobody'd heard a peep from him since the news of the shooting. We figured he might've skipped town, but even so, he'd get word to us as soon as he could. Russ and Charley said they'd never seen so many squad cars prowling the streets. It was no night to venture outside, so we stayed put, playing cards and keeping an ear to the radio for news about Red.

Around ten o'clock there was a knocking at the door—two slow raps, then three quick ones, our call sign. John opened up and there Red stood, smiling sort of hangdog and sporting a badly swollen eye that was shaping up into a world-class shiner. John tugged him inside and closed the door and we all gathered round and slapped him on the back, happy as hell to see him.

The girls ran up and gave him hugs. They'd been worried about him, of course, although they hadn't been pleased to learn of Mrs. DeKant. According to Opal, Patty didn't say anything about the woman when she heard the news, only that she hoped Red was safe, wherever he was. But it was obvious she was both hurt and furious.

Charley asked what happened, and Red said he'd tell us the whole story if somebody would get him a goddamn drink. I poured everybody one while Mary got a piece of steak from the icebox for him to hold on his eye, then we all settled ourselves in the living room.

Man gave me no choice, Red said. Which none of us had doubted for a minute.

He and the respectable Mrs. DeKant had taken the roadster he'd given her to a garage that morning to get the fender straightened out. The mechanic said the job wouldn't be difficult and the car would be ready by one o'clock. They took a taxi to his secret apartment and cavorted for a time, then had a late lunch at a café and went to a movie. It wasn't till after four that they got back to the garage.

There was no one around when they went in, but the roadster was in a garage bay, the fender nicely straightened. Red and Mrs. DeKant were admiring the fine job when two men came out of the office—one in overalls and obviously the night garage man, and the other one as obviously a plainclothes cop. Whatever tip he was acting on, the cop didn't know Red by sight, that was obvious too, or he wouldn't have come out of the office without a gun in his hand.

The guy flashed his badge and asked Red if the car was his. Red said no, it was his wife's, and asked Mrs. DeKant to show the man the registration. She gave Red a look but dug the paper out of her purse, and as she handed it to the cop Red said he'd show him his driver's license and reached into his coat.

The cop said to keep his hands out of his pockets and was fumbling for his gun when Red pulled a pistol and shot him twice. He fell on his ass with thin streaks of blood spurting from his chest and he tried to plug the wounds with his fingers, then babbled something and fell over and shut up.

Bastard got blood on my shoes, Red said. Did I get it all off?

I didn't see any blood on either shiny shoe, but he took a hanky from his jacket and gave both another wipe.

If he hadn't gone for it, Red said, he could be having a cold beer right now. But no, he had to go for it.

What could've happened did, Charley said.

The garage man had thrown up his hands and backed away, saying Not me, not me, and then ran out of the place as Red got behind the wheel of the Auburn. But the keys weren't in the ignition so he grabbed the woman by the hand and they hustled out to the street. He was impressed by the respectable Mrs. DeKant—she didn't let out a squeak or cry or in any way lose her nerve. She looked scared, Red said, but she kept her mouth shut, and despite her high heels she was moving right along with him as he fast-walked toward an alley halfway down the block.

Then somebody with a gun was hollering at them from across the street. Red made him for another plainclothes and figured the only reason the guy didn't shoot was the risk of hitting the woman. The cop ran into the street without looking and a car braked hard and swerved to keep from clipping him and the cop jumped back and fell down.

Red hated to leave Mrs. DeKant to the wolves, but you do what you have to. He said So long, baby, and sprinted off around the corner and into the alley. He came to an intersecting alleyway and turned into it and ran past several back doors before entering one with a green dragon on it. There were so many back doors along there the cops couldn't know which one he went into.

He'd figured the place for a Chinese restaurant and it was—and that was good because Chinks generally know how to mind their own business. He went through the kitchen, giving hard looks at the cooks and dishwashers like he was an immigration man on the prowl and they got out of his way fast. Then he ambled out into the crowded dining room and nodded pleasantly at the few people who looked at him in passing. He walked out the front door and flagged down a taxi and went to his Orval Lewis love-nest to retrieve the Packard. He knew Mrs. DeKant would describe it to the cops, so he switched the plates on it and drove down to a certain auto shop in Hammond and left it there to get a new paint job.

He returned to Chicago on an interurban. The sight of all the cops on the streets made him jumpy as hell and he rode the trolley to the end of the line, then caught a cab to a hotel eight blocks from the

apartment he shared with Charley and the girls. He waited till the
taxi was out of sight, then walked home.

Opal said You've been *home?* You seen Patty?

Red gave her a glum look and nodded and took the steak off his
eye. How you think I got this shiner?

Opal said *Ha!* and clapped her hands, and Billie and Mary
laughed like happy kids. Actually, Red was the only one in the room
who didn't look amused.

Tell us, Red, Billie said.

It's humiliating, he said.

I hope so, Mary said. So tell us and take it like a man.

He figured Patty had heard about the shooting on the radio news
and was probably a little put out by the mention of Mrs. DeKant, and
so he'd been cautious in approaching their apartment. The door was
deadbolted from inside, so he tapped the call sign on it, ready to run
if she should greet him with a weapon in her hand. But when the lock
turned and the door swung open he saw that she'd been crying and
that her hands were empty. She opened her arms wide to receive him
saying Baby, baby, are you all right, I've been so *worried,* and he figured true love had the upper hand, that his minor indiscretion meant
little to her compared to the danger he had so narrowly escaped.

They hugged tight and he told her he was fine, just fine, there
was no need to worry anymore, Daddy Red was home safe and sound.
He was thinking he was a pretty lucky fella to have such an under-
standing woman.

She wanted to have a look at him, so he took a step back and that
gave her all the room she needed to swing the rolling pin she'd picked
up from the table by the door.

That first one caught him on top of the head and his legs nearly
buckled. He fell against the doorjamb and she was hollering something
but all he understood of it was *low-down bastard* and *DeKant cunt*—and
wham! the pin caught him on the eye like a Dempsey haymaker.

I tell you, boys and girls, he said, I saw some stars. A goddamn *rolling pin*. I felt like one of those dumb bastards in the funny papers. Pardon my Japanese, ladies.

The girls were grinning like keyboards.

She barely missed him with the next swing or she would've busted his skull into as many pieces as she did the poor lamp she hit instead. And then he was outside and hightailing it, not catching what she said as he took his leave but fairly certain that it wasn't endearments.

I'm lucky I'm alive to tell the tale, he said. You think this eye's bad, look here.

He bowed his head so we could see a purple lump the size of an egg showing through the thin hair near his crown.

He wondered if anybody had a sofa he could borrow use of for a while. Mary said he could use ours, even though somebody who two-timed Patty didn't deserve any kindness.

Maybe not, he said, but I sure as hell deserve another drink.

I thought he did too, and I poured him a big one.

So here I am, he said. This morning I had two girlfriends and now I've got none. Don't tell *me* how fast things can change.

Opal said she knew for a fact that Patty had never liked a fella as much as she liked him, and if he played his cards right he might be able to wheedle forgiveness from her. But brother, he better be serious about it because if he pulled a stunt like this Mrs. Whoever again, he'd have Patty *and* her to deal with.

Mary stuck a finger in Red's face and said Me too, Jack, you hear me?

Yeah-yeah-yeah, Red said.

Considering the size of that knot on your head, Russell said, I'm surprised you can hear anything but bells.

Red cupped a hand to his ear and said Come again?

• • •

The next day's papers gave front-page play to the shooting, of course. The Chicago P.D. declared all-out war on the Terror Gang and formed a special squad whose sole mission was to hunt us down and take us in, dead or alive. Considering that they called themselves the Shoot-to-Kill Squad, there wasn't much question about which way they preferred to do the job. The special outfit was headed by some hotshot captain and was composed of fifty hand-picked guys, the toughest mugs on the force. *Fifty* guys. Man, that's an army.

In a related report, all charges against Mrs. Elaine DeKant had been dropped and she had been released from custody after the state attorney determined that she had been duped by John (Three-finger Jack) Hamilton and absolved her of any complicity in the murder of Detective Sergeant Somebody-or-other.

An editorial said that the plague of foreclosures and loss of property across the country in these hard economic times made it possible to understand—but certainly never condone—the anger that prompted so many citizens to cheer our depredations against the banks. But murder was another matter. Murder was indisputably beyond the pale and could not but outrage all moral men. Especially heinous was the killing of a police officer. The police were, after all, the sanctioned defenders of the social order, and to take sides against them was no less than to side with the forces of anarchy and etcetera, etcetera.

Charley said the piece was so moving he had half a mind to turn himself in.

We kept off the streets for the next few days. John dyed his hair red and Red dyed his black, and both of them were growing mustaches. Russell had Opal buy him a pair of phony specs like mine and John's. I did drive Red down to Hammond one night to pick up his Packard, now painted a solid black. He switched the plates on it again and stored it in the same parking garage where John and I kept our cars.

Every night we met at our place to discuss our next move. It was time to clear out of Chicago for a while, on that we all agreed. What we needed was a vacation, and we preferred someplace warm. We decided on Florida, and the next day Mary and Billie went to a travel agency to see about rentals and got us a huge beach house in Daytona Beach.

The only ones not going were Red and Patty. Russell brought Red fresh clothes from their place and he bunked on our sofa for three days. He called Patty several times a day before she finally accepted the phone from Opal and talked to him. They were on the line for half an hour before he joined the rest of us in the kitchen and said that all was not exactly forgiven but at least she'd said he could come home and they'd see how things went.

I called Pearl and told her we were going to lay low for a while at a hiding place in Michigan, all except for Red. If she needed to get in touch she could do it through him. She said she didn't blame me for not being more specific about where we'd be holing up, that if she had the same kind of heat on her she'd be extra careful too, even with her trusted friends. I said I knew she'd understand and we both laughed.

We were packed and set to go when we got the news that Matt Leach and his boys had collared Ed Shouse in Paris, Illinois. Acting on a tip from some stoolie and working in partnership with the Paris police, Leach set up an ambush outside the hotel where Shouse was staying. When Shouse came out, accompanied by another man and two women, Leach yelled for them to surrender—which Shouse, yellow bastard that he is, immediately did. The other guy made a run for it and the cops opened fire. Somehow the guy got away, but in all the shooting, one Indiana cop was killed by another, taking a bullet through the eye. Must've been some show for the neighborhood.

When he was grilled, Shouse gave the cops a lot of cock-and-bull about how we slept in bullet-proof vests every night and held daily combat drills in preparation against a sudden police attack. He said he'd left the gang because—get this—we were all too *kill-crazy* for his taste.

He'd been identified as one of the men who delivered John from the Lima jail, and he stood charged as an accessory to murder. He admitted he'd been in on the break, but said he'd been assured by none other than yours truly that nobody would get hurt, never mind killed, never mind the county sheriff.

Russell said he'd pay a thousand dollars for five minutes alone with that bigmouth, car-thieving son of a bitch before they shipped him back to M City.

Charley said Shouse lacked the sand to ever try a breakout on his own, and he believed we'd seen and heard the last of him. But like I've said before, we hadn't.

John telephoned Leach and told him what a good laugh we'd got out of his Keystone Kops caper in Illinois, but didn't anybody ever tell him the police were supposed to shoot the bad guys, not each other? Maybe Santa Claus would bring him a shooter's manual and an instruction book on police work.

Christ, it was *so* easy to get the guy's goat. He started st-st-stuttering and we all yelled Merry Christmas, Dick Tracy! Then John dropped the receiver in its cradle.

* * *

We left town in a four-car caravan—John and Billie in the Blueberry, Charley and Tweet in his Terraplane, Russ and Opal in the Hudson, me and Mary in the Vick. Tweet was going with us only as far as Nashville, where she would catch a train to go visit her mom and sister in Arizona. She'd renewed her contract with the club and had a six-week break before going back to work. Charley offered to go pick her up in Tucson at the end of January so they could drive back to Shytown together, and she wasn't the only one who thought it was a great idea. We decided we'd all make a grand-tour of it and go to Arizona from Florida, then cut back around to Chicago by way of Santa Fe, Denver, Kansas City, and St. Louis.

In Indianapolis the others went on ahead while Mary and I

stopped to visit with her mother and Margo. I'd wanted to go see my mother too, but the cops were still keeping an eye on the place and Mom didn't want me to risk it.

Mary's mother greeted her with so many tearful kisses you'd have thought she hadn't heard from her in years, even though Mary made it a point to phone her at least once a week and it hadn't been three months since they'd last seen each other. During dinner at a restaurant, she told us Jocko was in prison in Danville, Illinois, on a two-year rap for receiving stolen property. Mary gave me a look that said *Same old thing.*

Margo was now divorced from her jailbird husband and was dating several fellows, but complained that she still hadn't met a guy worth keeping. She had quit her waitressing job a few days earlier because the boss refused to keep his hands off her, but she'd be starting as a hostess at another restaurant in two weeks when the woman she was replacing left to get married. She jumped at our invitation to go with us to Florida and come back to Indy by train.

I slept on the sofa that night and Mary shared Margo's bed, and after an early breakfast we shoved off. It was cold and gray all the way into Nashville, where we checked into a downtown hotel, Margo in her own room next to ours. The next morning was slow-going over foggy mountain roads winding through dense pine forest, but once we got down from the hills it was all blue skies and sunshine, although still a little chilly, and we picked up some speed. At Margo's request I bought a pint of bourbon at a roadside store somewhere in Georgia. She wanted it for later that evening—to take the chill off before bedtime, she said—but by the time we pulled into a motor court near a little place called Jessup, she and Mary had finished off more than half the bottle.

Margo said she'd been lonely by herself the night before and asked if we could get one cabin with two beds. I said it was okay with me if it was okay with Mary. Mary ribbed her for being a big baby and said she sure knew how to cramp a big sister's love life. Margo said she certainly didn't want to do that and for us not to pay her any mind. You two go ahead and do whatever you feel like, she said, like I'm not even here. Mary told her don't think we won't.

Well, let me tell you, both of them meant what they said. While Mary was soaking in the tub with a drink, Margo wasn't the least bit bashful about changing into her nighty in front of me, stripping down to her panties with no more concession to modesty than turning her back. I was under the covers in my Skivvies with a book of short stories and I couldn't help peeking while the peeking was good. She had a rump almost as fine as Mary's, but she had slightly larger breasts, and I caught a side view of one as she raised her arms to slip on the nighty. As she turned around I cut my eyes down to my book, but her giggle as she got in bed made me suspect she knew I'd been watching. When Mary came out of the bathroom in her camisole I was reading a story about two gunmen waiting in a diner to kill a guy when he showed up, but Margo had ruined my concentration and I'd been on the same page for ten minutes. Mary must've given her some kind of look, because Margo said Oh now, he didn't *see* anything, he's had his nose in that book. I looked up all innocent and saw them both smirking at me. Mary turned the book in my hands so she could see the title. *Men Without Women,* she said—well, that's certainly not *your* problem at the moment, is it?

The minute the lights went out Mary started fooling around, which was a little surprising, given that we weren't alone. But I'd be lying if I said it wasn't extra exciting making love in the dark while her sister was in the next bed. Mary must've thought so too, and made no effort to mute her pleasure. We went through a lot of happy moaning and groaning and finished up breathing like we'd run a race. Margo said Boy oh boy, did *that* sound like fun—and we all giggled like school kids.

Sometime in the middle of the night Margo got under the covers with us and hugged up against my back and whispered that she was cold and her blanket wasn't warm enough and don't mind her. Mary raised up on the other side of me and said not to try anything funny, and Margo said Not me, sis. I don't know how I got back to sleep, snuggled between a pair of nearly naked women, but when I woke in the morning I was spooned up against Mary, and Margo was still cuddled to my back with her arm around me and a hand on my stomach, and I had an erection so urgent it ached.

The girls came awake and Mary felt my horn nudging her and asked what I thought I was going to do with *that* big idea in the bright light of day and her sister right there.

Margo slid her fingers down to me and said Oh my word. Mary rolled over, saying Hey you, that's private property, and pulled her sister's hand off me and out from under the blanket.

I was on my back now, my stiffie poking the covers up like a little tent. My grin felt idiotic but I didn't care.

Margo asked if she could have a look at it, and Mary said certainly not.

Margo said Pretty please, and Mary said *No,* it wasn't a damn sideshow.

Margo said Well, okay, then—and yanked down the blanket to expose my pecker sticking out of my shorts.

Woweee she said, and grabbed it and gave a few quick squeezes, saying Honk-honk.

Mary yelled *Mar-GO!*

The thing twitched like it was having a seizure and . . . *bang,* the spunk shot out in filaments and the girls shrieked and scrambled off the bed. Margo ran for the bathroom as Mary flung a pillow at her, both of them howling with hilarity.

I wasn't having such a bad time myself.

Those Northern girls . . . oh, man.

• • •

Driving into Florida was like flipping several pages ahead on the calendar and entering late spring. A few miles north of Jacksonville we heard an excited radio report that John and Red and I had been killed by the cops in Chicago.

Acting on a tip, the Dillinger Squad had stormed into a north-side apartment and shot the three of us before we could pull a gun. The reporter promised more details as soon as they were available.

Mary said it was terrible news, she was going to miss me. Margo said I didn't look half bad for a dead man. I said if God ever made anything stupider than cops and news reporters I hadn't met it yet. I wondered who the three guys were.

We had an early lunch in a Jacksonville café. The girls were wild for a side dish called grits, which looked like warm white paste mixed with sand and pretty much tasted like it to me. Mary said to try them with butter, so I did, and she said isn't it better, and I said yeah, now it tasted like buttered sandy paste. The cornbread was another story, though, and I had several helpings of it with my barbecued pork ribs.

At a tourist shop next door we bought sunglasses and straw hats, swimsuits and suntan lotion that smelled like coconut. And I got a short-sleeved shirt I couldn't resist—bright green with yellow parrots all over it.

None of us had seen the ocean before, and it was wonderful to drive along the open road for mile after mile with all that blue Atlantic on our left. The view was broken now and then by sand dunes and sea oats or by a town or a cluster of resort cabins. At a roadside stand we bought a sack of oranges and a bag of boiled peanuts—goobers, the woman called them. A horde of seagulls was swooping and screeching overhead, and we flung goobers for them to snatch on the fly.

We rolled into Daytona Beach late that afternoon. We got a local map from a filling station and Mary figured out how to get to the house and directed me to it. When we pulled up in front of the place we could hardly believe the size of it. It looked like a small two-story hotel, which we came to find out was exactly what it had been once upon a time. The yard was large and deeply shaded with huge oaks hung with Spanish moss. The gang's cars were in the driveway. As we were getting the bags out of the Vickie, the front door opened and they came rushing out to greet us, all open arms and happy laughter.

I introduced Margo all around. A surpassing pleasure, my dear, Charley said, and kissed her hand. Margo batted her lashes like some coy thing in the movies and said Goodness, what a charming assembly.

The house was even bigger than it looked. It had twelve rooms, including a huge parlor, a dining room, and a big kitchen. A gallery ran along both sides of the house and connected to a screened back porch that overlooked the beach and opened onto to a wide wooden sundeck furnished with lounge chairs, a picnic table, and a barbecue grill. The rushing surf was a hundred feet away. The first time the tide came in, Charley said, Opal thought it was going to carry them all off, but it crested about fifteen yards from the sundeck. John said he'd never really known what a great night's sleep was till he'd snoozed under a window open to the salt breeze and the sound of breakers.

They'd heard about me and John and Red getting shot dead by the Shytown cops. John said he'd been thinking of sending Matt Leach an invitation to the funeral, but then the afternoon paper had said it wasn't us, after all, just three small-time crooks.

In the words of the great Mr. Twain, Charley said, the reports of your deaths were greatly exaggerated.

* * *

We were in Florida for the next three weeks or so and had a terrific time. Except for the business with Billie, that is, and I'll get to that.

It was perfect weather, the days toasty but not hot, the nights cool but not quite cold. For the first two days, we spent the mornings walking on the beach and splashing in the surf, then lazing on the sundeck. I never got tired of watching the pelicans dive for fish. Despite the lotion we slathered on ourselves, all of us got sunburns except for Charley, who never stepped outside without his wide-brimmed straw hat and a long-sleeved shirt buttoned at the neck and cuffs. He'd wear bathing trunks but never went in the water, preferring to sit on the sundeck with a towel over his legs. After lunch we'd go Christmas shopping.

There was a seafood diner called the Mermaid within walking distance of the house, and we ate lunch there almost every day. The first time we went there, Charley recommended we all try the raw oysters on the half-shell. He was the only one of us who'd ever eaten them before, and I asked what they tasted like. Well, he said, they're fleshy and slick and juicy, and they have a salty, pungent flavor.

Everybody grinned big and John said You know, if Red was here he'd want to know if you were talking about oysters or, ah . . . something I won't mention in front of the ladies.

Even the girls cracked up. Billie said she wasn't sure she should try them. What if she liked them so much they turned her into a lesbian? John said that would be okay with him, since he was sort of a lesbian himself.

On Christmas morning we all exchanged presents in the parlor. Mary was wowed by the diamond necklace I gave her, and I loved the gold ring she gave me. It looked a lot like a wedding band and naturally I got ribbed by the guys. John gave Billie some sexy lingerie, and she held it up for everyone to admire. Russell wolf-whistled and Charley and I applauded and she asked if we'd like to see her model it, but John didn't care for the joke and told her to put it away. He got over his pique, though, as soon as he unwrapped Billie's gift—a silver St. Christopher medal he'd admired in a Chicago jewelry store window one day.

Old Saint Chris will keep you safe, baby, Billie said, and blew him a kiss across the room.

I'd promised Mary we'd spend some time by ourselves while we were in Florida, and the day after Christmas we tossed our bags in the Vickie, told the others we'd be back in time to celebrate New Year's with them, and drove down to Miami on a road called the Dixie Highway.

We stayed in a fancy hotel overlooking the river where it empties into Biscayne Bay. The park across the street was deep green and shady with palms and had a band shell and fronted a charter boat marina, and there was a long pier with a three-story building containing an amusement arcade and a dance hall. We went to the horse races at Hialeah, where hundreds of flamingos roosted on a lushly landscaped lake in the center of the track, and each time the birds flew from one spot to another they became a huge cloud of shimmering pink under the deep blue sky. We went to the jai-alai fronton and marveled at the speed of the game and the grace of the players as they whipped the ball against the high court wall and raced and leaped and dove to catch the rebounds in their cestas and keep the ball in play. We bet solely on players in red jerseys and won two hundred bucks. We took walks in the bayside park and fed popcorn to the pigeons and strolled along the fishing docks and admired the catches the charter boats brought in, including a shark almost twice my size that could have swallowed Mary whole and was scary even dead. We went dancing every evening in the hotel ballroom, except one night when we went to the pier dance hall and then had fun at a shooting gallery in the arcade, the only time Mary fired a gun in her life. We made love under the open window of our room with a fat gold moon beaming on us.

We hired a taxi to drive us around in the adjoining municipality of Coconut Grove and fell in love with the place, with its jungle greenery and salty air, its narrow streets and quaint houses and sailors' taverns, its bohemian character. Mary said she wouldn't object if I wanted us to move there when I finally called it quits in the banking trade.

It was the first mention she'd made about me quitting the business, and I reminded her that she said she didn't want a normal life. She said she doubted that life in Miami could be called normal. I said she was a pretty slick debater. She gave me a happy smooch and said yes she was.

• • •

On the last day of the year we left Miami before the sun was above the palm trees and were back in Daytona by midafternoon. The girls boiled ears of corn and made a salad and seasoned a platter of steaks while John got a charcoal fire going in the grill. Russell and I filled a washtub with bottled beer and crushed ice and set it on the back porch.

One of the girls had found a jump rope in the house, and they took turns with it. It wasn't at all surprising that Billie and Mary were such nimble skippers, but even big Opal was an agile jumper. They all went at it as happy as schoolgirls. It was fun to watch them and listen to the jump rope ditties they'd learned as kids. Mary sang:

> Cinderella, dressed in yella,
> went upstairs to kiss her fella,
> Made a mistake and kissed a snake.
> How many doctors did it take?
> One . . . two . . . three . . .

Opal said she bet there weren't many girls who hadn't made the mistake of kissing a snake sometime or other. Russell flicked his tongue at her and she took a playful swat at him. Billy's ditty got a big laugh too:

> Oh my back, I'm so sore,
> ain't gonna do it for a nickel no more.
> Fifteen cents, that's the price.
> Give me a quarter and I'll do it twice.

Christ, John said, who taught you to jump rope when you were a kid? The girls at Mabel's whorehouse?

I *thought* you looked familiar, Billie said. You always went in there on Dollar Night, didn't you.

Mary and Opal laughed and blew raspberries at John.

Somebody tuned a radio to a big-band station and we danced on the deck while the steaks sizzled and the sun went down on the other side of the house. It was another of the few times we relaxed our rules on drinking, and Russell had bought a couple of bottles of Scotch in case anybody wanted something with a little more kick than beer. We were all happily buzzed when we sat down to eat.

Nobody could get over the fact that we were barefoot and in shorts while back in Chicago they were shoveling snow. Mary and I weren't the only ones who'd given thought to moving there—Russ and Opal had talked about it too. Charley said he had a hunch that we might sing a different tune in the middle of a Florida summer, which he'd been told was as humid as dog breath and ten times as hot, not to mention the hordes of mosquitoes. John and Billie liked Florida too, but for some reason John had it in his head that Mexico was the place to retire for keeps. He'd never been there, but he knew that was the place for him. Billie said she guessed she'd have to learn Spanish. John said *Sí, sí, señorita.*

Margo wanted to go dancing again at a beach club they'd been to the night before. Charley said sure, and Russ and Opal said they'd go along. Margo had confided to Mary that she had tried getting Fat Charley into the sack, but the man was in love with Tweet for real, and he wasn't the kind to fool around behind her back. So Margo settled for the pleasure of his humorous company and the fun they had in dance clubs. They all got cleaned up and changed, then wished the four of us a happy new year, said not to wait up, and went off in Russell's car.

The moon had come up and the ocean gleamed silver. The tide was in and the waves were breaking big, the surf rushing up to within forty feet of us. The beach was pale and smooth and deserted in both directions except for a large bonfire at a far distance where a party was going on. We could faintly hear the singing and laughter. We tuned in another musical program on the radio and did a little more danc-

ing and had another drink or two. Then Billie said she wanted to go
swimming. And right there in front of us she stripped to her black
underwear. She skipped down the deck steps and stumbled slightly,
then ran shouting into the surf and dove into a wave.

John took a pull off his bottle of beer and stared out at her, then
smiled and said Drunk redskin. None of us was more than vaguely
sober at that point.

Mary said Oh quit, Johnny, she's having fun.

And then *she* took off her shorts and shirt, even though she wasn't
wearing a bra, and ran off to join Billie. She whooped at the coldness
of the water as she plunged in, and Billie took off her bra too and
flung it away with a shout.

John's smile had gotten wider at the sight of Mary's breasts. I
have to say, Pete, that little girl of yours has got a side to her I never
would've guessed.

I'd been thinking the same thing ever since the escapade with
Margo. Yeah she does, I said.

The girls stood in water to their tits and held hands and yelled
like kids on a carnival ride as a large swell lifted them and carried
them on its crest before breaking and tumbling them in the surf.
They came up spitting water and laughing and pushing their hair out
of their eyes.

Come on in, boys, Mary called out, the water's fine.

John said he bet it was colder than a witch's cunt.

I said I was game if he was.

A moment later we were racing into the water in our undershorts
and we yelled at the coldness of it, but after a few minutes of horsing
around and splashing at each other and diving into the waves it
wasn't too bad. Then Mary got on my shoulders and Billie mounted
on John's and we had horse fights, the girls trying to wrestle each
other off into the water as John and I tried to trip each other down.
As often as not, we'd all go tumbling when a big wave hit us. We'd
roll and bounce off each other in the surf and get dragged a few yards

by the undertow before coming up spluttering and laughing and everybody claiming victory.

The undertow kept yanking down everybody's underpants, and then Billie said Ah hell, we're all among friends, and took her panties off and tossed them away. Mary laughed and took hers off too and sent them sailing.

Well now, I said, I feel way overdressed. I crouched in the water and took off my shorts and balled them up and tossed out to sea. Then John took his off and swung them around his head on one finger like a lasso and flung them at Billie, who laughed and ducked underwater to dodge them, and a wave carried them away. I wondered what a fisherman would think if he reeled in somebody's underwear.

Billie asked Mary if she wanted to switch horses for a few rounds and Mary said why not. I didn't mind, but to tell the truth I was surprised John didn't either. But like I said, we were all a little tanked. It was obvious he was having fun, judging by his stiffie when he stood up with Mary mounted on him, his hands high on her thighs and her ankles crossed over his chest. I confess I was sporting a pretty happy hard-on myself, what with Billie's ass wriggling on my shoulders and her bush rubbing the back of my neck and her tits jiggling against my head as she and Mary tried to unseat each other. Every time a wave knocked us tumbling, I'd cop feels off Billie and she'd laugh and give my twanger a pull or goose me good. Judging from the happy shrieks Mary let out as she and John rolled around in the surf, I suppose they were having the same sort of fun. I can't speak for the others, but I felt like a kid in a swell new playground.

I want to make it clear that play is all it was. Nothing more than a lot of sexy teasing fun among pals, without any of it getting out of hand. But booze always brought out Billie's most dim-witted devils, and in the middle of all our fooling around she said she never thought she'd see a cock as big as Johnny's, and whose did Mary think was bigger, his or mine.

I thought Oh, Christ.

Mary gave a shaky laugh and said *Bill-ie*, for God's sake.

Billie wanted to use a measuring tape to see who was champ.

Mary said the water had got too cold for her and started trudging through the surf back toward the beach.

Yeah, Billie said, let's go measure them right now.

The moon was bright enough for me to see that John wasn't smiling anymore, and I sensed his anger like a drop in the temperature. It wasn't that he gave a damn which of us was bigger, believe me. What galled him was Billie talking about another guy's dick, never mind that it was all in fun among best friends. Like I said, he was cool with everything except women. With women he was as big a sap as most guys.

As we waded out of the water, Billie still hadn't picked up on the dark change in John's mood and she was babbling about how thickness mattered as much as length and she'd have to measure both how long and how big around they were. I tried to make a joke of the whole thing and told John I'd be damned if I was going to let either of these sex-crazy broads measure my dick like it was a carpet sample or something. Billie laughed and slapped me on the ass and said for me not to go getting all bashful on her.

Mary had hustled into the house and came back to the porch in a robe and with towels for us. John and I tied ours around our waists, but Billie simply held hers over her breasts with one hand and poured herself a drink with the other. John watched her a moment and then slapped the glass out of her hand and said You drunken bitch.

He grabbed her arm and she dropped her towel and beat at him with her fists, cursing him as he dragged her naked into the parlor and up the stairs. Mary started after them but I caught her hand and said to keep out of it. We heard a door slam and then didn't hear them anymore, one of the blessings of that huge house and its thick walls.

Mary said how dare I stick up for him. I said I was only minding my own business and she better do the same. She was as steamed as I've ever seen her. She said John was an utter asshole to get so worked up just because Billie noticed a dick. What the hell did he think people were going to see when they went skinny-dipping? He thought he was so sophisticated but he was nothing but a rube, a goddamn bumpkin. She went on like that for a while, and then we went to bed in one of the downstairs guest rooms. She lay with her back to me, so I let her be and went to sleep.

She woke me in the night when she snuggled up to me and hugged me close. She said she was sorry but she couldn't stand it when he treated her that way. I said I knew that and she had nothing to be sorry about. John was the one who was going to be sorry. I knew him, and it might take him a while to cool off, but when he did he was going to feel bad for behaving as he had. We held each other without talking for a while and I thought she'd fallen asleep. But then she said in a whisper that, in case I'd been wondering, she thought John's pecker was impressive but he had nothing on me. I said I hadn't been wondering. Good, she said. Besides, I said, I'd seen right away he had nothing on me. We stuffed the sheet in our mouths to muffle our laughter.

She wasn't in bed when I woke at sunrise, the first one of 1934. I found her in the kitchen having coffee with Billie, who was nicely dressed and wearing makeup that didn't hide her fat lip. John had also given her a thousand dollars and the keys to the Blueberry and told her to get the hell gone, he didn't care where. She told us she'd probably go home to Wisconsin for a while till she made up her mind what to do.

Her suitcase was by the front door and I carried it out to the car. Russell's Hudson was in the driveway but I hadn't heard them come in. Billie said to tell them all goodbye for her. She gave me a hug and peck on the cheek and wished me a happy new year again, then she and Mary hugged hard and both of them started to cry. A minute later she drove off around the corner and was gone.

● ● ●

*L*ater that morning Mary and I took Margo to the train station and kissed her so long and she headed home to Indy. When we got back to the house, I went and sat on the beach and tossed pieces of bread to the gulls. John came out and joined me and said he should've known better than to let Billie have any damn firewater. I said none of us should've had any damn firewater.

For the next few days Mary gave John the silent treatment, even at the supper table, and the others got a lot of chuckles out of it. One night John finally caved in, as I'd known he would, and told her he was sorry, he swore he was. He said he knew he'd been a stupid bastard and that he missed Billie more than he'd ever missed anybody in his life. He had already phoned Red and Patty in Chicago and asked if Patty knew how to get in touch with Billie on the reservation. She didn't, but she said she'd try to find out and would let him know.

Mary told him he didn't deserve another chance, but Billie would probably give him one because she loved him, which was a *lot* more than he deserved.

John said he knew that.

We *all* know that, Opal said, and everybody laughed.

Another week went by without word on Billie, and John was undecided about going with us to Arizona or going to look for her in Wisconsin. We did, however, get some interesting news by way of a Chicago paper several days old. The cops had been tipped that a gangster named Jack Klutas was hiding in a house in a little burg outside of Shytown, and two carloads of cops had gone there to take him in, dead or alive. They busted into the place and collared a pair of guys without a fight, but neither of them was Klutas, who happened to be away at the time. One of the guys was a nobody, but the other was our old pal Walt Dietrich. As we were reading all about it, Dietrich was already back in M City and probably swapping stories with Okie Jack Clark. As for the Klutas guy, the cops set up an ambush at the house, and when he got back and tried to make a fight of it they shot him more than a dozen times.

John thought Klutas had been stupid and Dietrich played it smart. The way he saw it, if the cops had the drop on you, the thing to do was surrender. I hated having to agree, but the simple truth is that dead men can't try jailbreaks.

Russell remarked that Dietrich was the third guy in the M City breakout bunch who was back in stir. And Jenkins was dead. Besides us, the only ones still at large were John Burns and Joe Fox, and he wondered where they were.

Fat Charley said You do?

• • •

We sold our cars and bought new ones with Florida plates. I went for a black-and-yellow Buick and Charley got himself a tan Studebaker. John sprang for another Terraplane, a pale blue sedan. Russell sold his car too, but decided not to buy a new one till he got to Tucson. Charley wanted company on the long drive to Arizona and had invited Russ and Opal to ride with him.

Two days before we intended to leave for Arizona, John still wasn't sure what he was going to do. And then we received a phone call from Red at five o'clock on a Sunday morning. John got down to the phone ahead of me, thinking it might be about Billie. In part it was—Patty had finally made telephone contact with her in Wisconsin. Red gave him a number where she could be reached, then said to put me on the phone.

Pearl had called him fifteen minutes earlier with an offer of a bank job for us from Sonny Sheetz—and Sheetz wanted our answer within the hour. Pearl didn't know why Sonny was so desperate, but the bank was in East Chicago, right in his front yard, and her guess was he'd got wind of an audit about to happen that could tie him to some shady bookkeeping. She said the guaranteed take would be at least fifteen grand. To show his appreciation to us for accepting the job on short notice, Sonny wouldn't take a cut. The short notice was the catch—the heist had to be done on Monday, and the bank closed at three o'clock.

We're talking about *tomorrow*, Red said.

Pearl had told Sheetz we were in Michigan, and Red didn't disabuse her of the notion. If they'd known where we really were they surely wouldn't have bothered to offer us the job, figuring we could never make it up there in time. Red didn't think we could, either, but he didn't want to tell Pearl no without first checking with me.

I told him to hold the line and quickly laid the thing out to John. We'd been spending fast and loose, all of us were getting low on funds, and we'd been thinking about pulling a job on the way to Arizona. Now here was a fat one dropped in our lap. Fifteen thou would keep the wolf a long way from the door while we lazed around Arizona.

John liked the job, but he was as doubtful as Red that we could get up there in time. Chicago was more than a thousand miles away and God knew how many towns in between to slow us down. Before three o'clock tomorrow?

I said, You and me? *We* can do it.

He arched an eyebrow. I gestured with a hand like it was a speeding car and said *Zoooom*. And he laughed.

I told Red we'd take it. He gave a low whistle and said You *know* the kind of trouble we got if you guys don't make it?

I said not to fret, we'd make it, and in the meantime he should get us a car for the job. We'd see him at his place.

We were on our way in the Terraplane before sunrise. John had talked with Billie on the phone and of course been forgiven. He told her to take the Blueberry to Chicago and meet him in the parking lot of some tavern on Byron Street where they'd been a few times, to be there no later than three o'clock and wait for as long as it took. She said sure, no questions asked.

After the job, John would be taking Billie to meet his family in Mooresville before heading for Arizona. I'd drive the Blueberry to Indianapolis and sell it to our ex-con pal Elmore Brown, then check into a hotel and wait for Mary to get to Indy with my Buick. Maybe we'd visit my mother, depending on whether the cops still had the place under surveillance. Charley and Russ and Opal would go on to Tucson ahead of us. We all had Tweet's phone number to call and find out where everybody was.

* * *

*Y*owsa, what a drive! I have to tell you, that Terraplane could *move*. John had first turn at the wheel and we barreled up the Florida coast at sixty-five miles an hour with hardly a stoplight along the way except for St. Augustine and Jacksonville. Then we were roaring over Georgia clay roads, passing farm trucks in clouds of red dust, honking slowpokes out of our way, slowing only as we went through the burgs. We didn't get chased by a cop till after I took the wheel and we flew through a stop sign going through Macon. I gave him the shake as soon as we cleared town.

What we mostly talked about as we went along was Mary and Billie. He asked if I was serious about going to live in Miami and settling down and I said I was. Was he serious about settling in Mexico? He said he sure was. He wanted to know when I was going to do this settling and I said I hadn't exactly decided yet. When was he going to do his settling in Mexico? He hadn't exactly decided yet either. I said I didn't know about him, but I found it very comforting to have such solid plans for the future. We were both grinning to beat the band and he asked what was so damn funny. I said what did *he* think was so funny. He said I asked you first. We laughed so hard it was all I could do to keep the car on the road. It took us a while to get ourselves under control, then nobody said a word for the next hour.

Sometime during that drive he told me a story about Billie I've never forgotten. Back when they were on their first date, she told him she'd had a lonely childhood on the reservation, she never had many friends. Her only steady company for years was a cat she'd found by

the side of the road and named Ling Ling. The name sounded Orien-
tal to John, and he asked if it was a Siamese. Oh no, she said, nothing like that, it was just a regular cat with one head.

In Atlanta we bought a sack of burgers and bottles of cola and
then went winding up into the mountains. We had to turn the
heater up high against the increasing cold. I was wowed by how well
the Terraplane held the road as it leaned through the curves, John
grabbing tight to the dashboard whenever the tires let a little
screech and the car started to drift before I muscled it back under
control. Still, the mountains slowed us down and they strained me
to the bone. By the time we hit Chattanooga that evening I was glad
to let him do the driving again.

I snoozed in the backseat as we sped through the night, then
somewhere near the Kentucky line I woke to a siren and a flashing
red light behind us. They stuck with us at over seventy miles an hour
down a straight dirt road in country so dark we couldn't see a thing
outside the headlight beams. If a cow had stepped out in the road,
that would've been all she wrote. I picked up the Thompson from
under a coat on the floorboard and leaned out the window and fired
a bright yellow burst over their roof. They must've hit the brakes
with both feet, they faded out of sight so fast.

Around four in the morning we crossed the river into Indiana. I
took the wheel and John curled up in back. Come daybreak my eyes
felt red as the sunrise, like they had sand under the lids. I stopped in
Terre Haute for gasoline and another refill of the coffee thermos. John
woke up and asked if I wanted him to spell me, but I said I was doing
fine and go ahead and sleep some more.

And we did it. We rolled into Chicago shortly before noon. It was
cold but sunny and bright. The car was gray and brown with mud
and dust but the engine still purred like a happy cat. We parked in a
public garage at the end of the block from Red's place.

Patty answered my knock and threw her arms around me and
smooched me all over the face, then gave John the same swell welcome.

Red stood there beaming at us and said Bedamn if you boys didn't get here with time to spare. Hell, we got most of three hours yet.

• • •

P atty made us a lunch of ham and cheese sandwiches, potato salad and Cokes. All was well between her and Red, and we were glad to hear they'd decided to join us on the Arizona trip and were packed and ready to go. We ate, then showered and put on fresh clothes. Red kissed Patty at the door and said he'd be back in no time.

He'd swiped a Plymouth in Naperville the day before and swapped its Illinois plates with a set of Ohio tags he'd got from Pearl. The car was in the parking garage, next to his black Packard. We got the guns and vests out of the Terraplane and put on the vests. All of us wanted to go in the bank but somebody had to drive and stick with the car, so we did a three-way coin toss. Red and John came up tails and I showed heads. I got behind the wheel of the Plymouth and we headed for the First National Bank in East Chicago.

If you ever need proof that you should never hit a bank without casing it first, this job is it. We didn't even know what the parking situation would be like. I figured that if I had to, I'd double-park in front of the bank. If a cop came by and told me to move along while John and Red were inside, I'd fake motor trouble till they came out, and then I'd deal with the cop any way I had to. It wasn't the kind of planning that would've made old Herman Lamm tip his hat to me.

As luck would have it, there was a parking place almost directly in front of the place. I slid into it and cut the front wheels away from the curb, ready for a fast getaway, and I left the motor running.

They might as well put up a sign saying Reserved for Bank Robbers, Red said. I tell you, boys, this is getting *too* fucken easy anymore.

Maybe we should tie one hand behind our backs, John said. Or wear a patch over one eye.

Yeah, Red said, like pirates—*Arrrgh*.

John slipped the Thompson under his overcoat and Red checked the chamber of his .380 and put the pistol in his coat pocket. I had my .45 beside me on the seat.

We'll be right back, John said. And they got to it.

They'd been inside less than three minutes when a uniformed cop came down the street, walking in my direction. We wouldn't know until we read the papers the next day that the police station was only a block away. I didn't hear an alarm, but we knew some banks had alarms that sounded only in the police station, so as not to tip off the robbers. The cop didn't look too concerned, though. If he was responding to an alarm, it was another case of thinking it wasn't for real. Then he pushed open the door and froze, and I figured John or Red had seen him coming and got the drop on him. He went inside and the door closed.

But somebody had hit a silent alarm, all right, because here came more cops running my way, all of them with guns in their hand. Eight of them, maybe ten, some in uniform, some in plainclothes. I watched through the windshield as they shooed pedestrians away from the bank and took cover behind cars or in store entrances. None of them was aware of me. It was like watching a movie. I set the .45 between my legs and eased the car into gear, ready to boom us out of there the instant the guys made it into the car.

I felt my heartbeat in my throat. It seemed a long time before the bank door opened and out they came. John was holding some citizen in front of him as a shield, and Red had the money sack in one hand and his pistol against the ribs of the cop who'd gone inside. As they started toward me, a uniformed cop stepped out from the recessed entrance of the store next door and yelled something and the citizen dropped to the sidewalk, giving the cop a clear shot at John, and *bam-bam-bam-bam*—he popped him four quick ones.

John took them all in the chest, staggering back against the bank's brick wall, then cut loose with a rattling blast of the tommy that sent the cop jolting backward like he was having a fit and dropped him to the sidewalk in a bloody heap. John scooted up beside Red and the hostage cop and I reached over the seat and pushed open the back door as the three of them hustled up to the car in a tight knot. Somebody was yelling *Don't shoot Hobie, don't shoot Hobie* but some of the cops started shooting anyway. As John dove into the car the hostage cop broke free and all the cops opened fire. Red grunted and sat down hard on the sidewalk with the sack of money tight under one arm and then the other arm jerked and his gun went skidding under the car. Bullets were cracking off the sidewalk and chipping the brick wall and punching the car. John rolled out and grabbed Red and heaved him up and into the car and tumbled in behind him, and how he didn't get hit I'll never know.

I gunned the Plymouth away from the curb with the tires squealing. The open back door struck a parked car and crunched half off its hinges as we tore through a huge clatter of gunfire, bullets thunking into the car and making starbursts in the windshield. Then we were around the corner and out of sight of the cops, and John was able to wrench the broken door nearly shut and tie it closed with his belt.

I took a lot of lefts and rights through the back streets. I don't know if anybody tried to chase us, but if they did, we sure lost them. Then I doubled back to the main highway and mixed into the traffic heading for Shytown. Nobody around us seemed to pay any attention to the holes in our car or the mangled door. God bless the average Joe and his lack of interest in anything but himself.

Red was slumped on the seat, swearing and groaning as John checked his wounds. The front of his pants was soaked dark red. He had two bullets high in the leg, and John said none of the blood was from an artery and the wounds were nothing to worry about.

Fuck you, nothing to worry about, Red said. It ain't *you* bleeding like a stuck hog.

Either bullet hit any higher and it would've been your jewels, John said. You're damn lucky, man.

Oh yeah, Red said, I'm luckiern shit. Look here, Pete, how god-damn lucky I am.

He held up his right hand for me to see in the rearview. The tip of his ring finger had been shot off.

Looks like you're *Two*-finger Jack from now on, I said. I was still riding high on the adrenaline charge.

John said Two-Finger Jack was a hell of a lot better than No-balls Jack, and we both went into a laughing fit.

Ha fucken ha, Red said.

At the saloon on Byron, Billie was parked to the side of the building. She lost her big smile quick when John and I helped Red out of the Plymouth and she saw his bloody pants and the red-stained hand-kerchief around his hand. We eased him into the Blueberry and I sat in back with him. John got behind the wheel and told Billie it was good to see her. We left the Plymouth where it was.

Billie was big-eyed with concern about Red, who was sweating hard despite the cold weather. Oh God, she said, how bad is it?

I'll be okay, Pocahontas, Red said, but there goes my Arizona vacation.

Doc Moran's is where we were headed. He was a good surgeon who'd taken a fall on an abortion rap. He'd managed to get his license back and still had a public practice, but prison had altered his atti-tude toward the law, and nowadays the biggest part of his income came from treating wounded fugitives on the QT. He received his of-ficial patients in a fancy office in a downtown hotel, but he also had a little clinic out at the edge of town where he tended to girls in trou-ble and guys like us.

We parked in the alley behind the clinic and took Red in through the back door. We were in luck and Moran was there. He was a little edgy about having us in his place and kept asking if we were sure we hadn't been followed. As always, a handful of hundred-dollar bills did wonders to settle his nerves. He examined the wounds and confirmed John's opinion that they weren't as bad as they looked. Red swore and said don't try telling him they didn't *hurt* as bad as they looked.

The doc said he'd have him patched up in an hour or two, and I gave him Patty's number to call when the job was done. We told Red so long, we'd be back in a few weeks. He said to get him an arrow-head for a souvenir, and I said sure thing. But I'd never see him again.

We went back to his place and broke the news to Patty. For a minute she looked like she might cry, then took it like a good soldier and said Just our luck. She had the keys to Red's car and would col-lect him when Moran called.

We dumped the money out on the table and tallied it. Sixteen thousand and some change. I gave Patty three grand to tide her and Red over and said I'd call every few days to see how he was doing. She said she didn't really want to go to Arizona anyway. Who the hell wanted to risk a winter sunburn when you could stay nice and cool in Chicago?

I asked John if he wanted to hold half the take till we got to-gether in Tucson and divvied up with Russ and Charley, but he said no, Mary was the company treasurer, give her the swag for safekeep-ing. We had a beer for the road, then John and Billie said adios and they'd see me in Tucson, and they left for his dad's farm in Mooresville.

* * *

That evening I drove to Elmore Brown's garage a few miles south of Indy and sold him the Blueberry. He paid even less than usual because he'd have to replace the blood-stained seat before he could resell the car. One of his mechanics gave me a ride back into town and dropped me off at a hotel overlooking the river park.

As soon as I checked in, I called Margo to let her know where I was and that I was registered as Harry Roark. I told her Mary would probably arrive in town the next day unless she ran into bad weather or some other slowdown on her way from Florida. Margo had heard the news about the robbery and that one of the bandits had been shot, and she'd been worried sick. I assured her we were all fine, that Red—the only guy in the gang she'd never met—hadn't been hit as bad as they said and was being well tended.

I slept late and then ate a large breakfast in the hotel dining room and read the newspaper versions about the East Shy job. The cops had recognized John and Red but not me. They'd found the shot-up Plymouth and said that judging from the blood-soaked seat they were sure they had *mortally wounded* John Hamilton. Good. If they thought he was dead they wouldn't be searching all over Chicago for him.

The cop John killed was named O'Malley. The story mentioned more than once that he had a wife and kids, and it used the word *tragic* at least a half-dozen times. As if having a family was supposed to give a cop some kind of special protection from harm. As if we weren't supposed to shoot back if a *family man* shot at us. Christ, where do people get such loony notions? If a cop doesn't want to risk making his wife a widow or leaving his children fatherless, what's he doing being a cop? Awfully irresponsible, if you ask me. There oughta be a law.

In spite of the cold wind, I took a stroll through the riverside park. The trees were skeletal and the sky had no color at all. The buildings looked like huge gray tombs. People were bundled deep into their coats, their faces muffled to the eyes and their hats pulled down tight, and they walked with their heads bent to the wind. My memory of Florida seemed unreal, Miami like something I'd dreamt.

In the afternoon I went to the movies, a double feature—*Gold Diggers of 1933* and a Mae West flick with angels in the title. I'd seen the Gold Digger one before, together with the other guys, and we'd argued about which of the dancers was the best-looking. But there was no disagreement with Red's idea that a wonderful way to die would be to smother under a pile of the entire long-legged, bare-assed gang of them.

I missed Mary bad. I hadn't spent much time alone since getting clapped into Pendleton nine years before, and the solitude felt strange in a way I can't explain. Back at the hotel I telephoned my mother and said I wanted to pay a quick visit. She said she hadn't spotted any cops for the past few days, but that didn't mean they weren't watching, so be careful.

It was already dark outside when there came a knock at the door and a husky female voice said Telegram for Mr. Roark. I figured it was from Mary and thought maybe something had gone wrong. I was digging in my pocket for a tip as I pulled the door open—and there she stood, holding her overcoat closed around her, a small travel bag dangling from her shoulder, and smiling the greatest smile I've ever seen.

Actually, sir, Mary said, it's more a special delivery than a telegram. She glanced up and down the hall, then said *Ta-daaa* and threw the coat open to show me how terrifically naked she was underneath it.

I pulled her into the room and shut the door and she shrugged out of the coat and jumped on me and we tumbled to the floor, laughing and grabbing and smooching. Our first go of the evening was there on the floor with my pants around my ankles and my knees getting rug burns.

* * *

We were at my mother's for two days and saw no sign of police lookouts. My dad and Fred took turns going for casual walks to scout the property line. Mom told us about her and Fred's run-in with the law in Terre Haute and their four hours as jailbirds. Her description of the dressing down she gave Matt Leach made Mary laugh, but I felt a touch of the anger that had taken me to Indy to shoot him for the bullying bastard he was. We told them about our Florida vacation, and they marveled at Mary's descriptions of Miami and said the place sounded too good to be true. I said it did to me too, and I'd seen it with my own eyes. We caught up on our sleep and went for walks in the woods behind the property and had fun sliding around on the frozen surface of the creek. And on a Friday morning before sunrise we said goodbye and promised to visit again as soon as we got back from out West.

It was cold but mostly sunny as we angled down through the bare cornfields of Illinois, and crossed the river into St. Louis. If you've never seen the Mighty Mississip, brother, you've got a treat in store. Then came the rugged Ozark country of south Missouri and northern Arkansas, the roads winding through dense thickets and around deep ravines. We went through the Indian Nations in Oklahoma and through oil field country where the earth was stained black for miles and miles.

We crossed the Red River into Texas and spent a night in Dallas. While we were taking supper in a café, I saw in a newspaper a few days old that Clyde Barrow and Bonnie Parker had busted a partner of theirs out of an East Texas prison camp in broad daylight and killed one guard and wounded another in the process. We'd been hearing things about those two since the spring and summer before we broke out of M City. They'd been in some bad shootouts with the cops, and I recalled that Clyde's brother had been killed in a police ambush sometime the previous summer. John thought they were nothing but triggerhappy, harebrained hillbillies, but I always admired their moxie. The only picture I'd seen of Bonnie Parker was the one almost everybody had seen, the one with a cigar in her mouth, which as much as anything else established her newspaper reputation as a rough, queer hardcase. But the farther south we went, and especially once we got into Texas, the more we heard the rural folk speak of them in the same admiring way a lot of Midwest working people spoke about us—not to mention a lot of people who were *out* of work. When folks see the Law siding with those who make life hard for them, they're just naturally going to root for the outlaws.

Anyhow, the picture of Bonnie that ran with this story was a different one. She was posing against the back of a Ford and smiling at the camera with her hip angled sexily in a clingy black dress and her blond hair showing under a sassy beret. I'd had no idea she was so pretty, or so small. It wouldn't be till I was on death row and heard the news of her and Clyde getting ambushed by a posse—a bunch of goons so scared of a pair of kids they had to shoot them more than 150 times to be sure they were dead— that I'd find out she was exactly the same size as Mary. Four feet eleven and ninety pounds. Mary took a look at the picture and said Bonnie was wearing really nice shoes, a detail that had escaped my notice. In the interest of sticking with the whole truth, I'll confess that after I saw that picture of Bonnie Parker I had dreams about her. I'll even admit some of them were a little racy—like the one where we were sharing a tub filled with bubble bath in some luxury hotel and she said she never imagined anything could be so grand and Chicago was like a dream come true. She was excited about our plan to rob a bank together. She was smart and funny and had a Texas accent that knocked me out. I have no idea what she kissed like in real life, but let me tell you, the kiss she gave me in that tub was the kiss of all time. In most of the dreams, though, we had our clothes on and were either walking along the lakeshore or sitting at an outdoor café table and laughing about something. When I'd wake up I could never remember what we'd been laughing about. And I'd be holding on to Mary and feeling guilty as sin.

We drove across dusty brown North Texas plains that stretched to the horizons, and I bought some arrowheads for Red at an Indian curio shop. We entered New Mexico and took a look at Albuquerque, then turned south along the Rio Grande. The river was the color of rum and ran past yellow hills and green pepper fields and red and blue mountain ranges under thunderheads and faraway purple rain. We stopped for the night at a motor court in Las Cruces, and we made love at sunset in an unreal ruby light flooding the cabin through an open window. Then we got dressed again and walked to a Mexican restaurant down the road and had a supper of roast kid and rice while a small brown man in a white suit sat in a corner playing a guitar and singing softly in Spanish. When we walked back to the cabin the sky was packed with stars, and a copper crescent moon was low over the mountains. I can close my eyes and still see it all as clear as a snapshot.

Mary phoned Tweet and they chattered loud and all excited for a while in the way women friends do. Tweet gave her a telephone number for Charley and Russell and one for John. She said Russ and Charley had stayed in a hotel their first few days in town, but the night before last the place caught on fire. Lucky for them they'd rented a house the day before and it was ready to move into. They were using the names Davies and Long. As for John and Billie, they'd arrived yesterday and were staying in a tourist-camp cabin until they could find a house too. She gave Mary the name and address of the camp and said John was registered as Frank Sullivan.

We had an early breakfast and then headed west. At daybreak the Buick's shadow reached way out ahead of us. We passed through landscapes marked by buttes and mesas, low dark mountains and flat stretches of scrubland. We rarely saw another car. By midmorning we were in Arizona and the mountains grew higher and more jagged. We started seeing a lot of those big cactuses with their arms up like they're being robbed. We drove through narrow red canyons and thickets of scraggly trees with bright green bark.

All in all, I liked the desert country, but Mary wasn't keen on it. She preferred places with tall leafy trees. As far as she was concerned, a mesquite was nothing but a big thorny weed, and the wide open spaces made her nervous. She wished we'd never left Florida, and her heart was set on Miami more than ever. I said we'd be back there soon enough—and for some reason thought of the big laugh John and I had on the drive from Daytona when we'd asked each other about our plans for settling down.

I don't even bother trying to imagine the life we could've had in Florida. It'd be like trying to imagine the life we could've had on the moon. Because once we got to Tucson, the life I could've had was all decided.

IV

The Falls

It was a small, pretty town with mountains on almost every side, and I hadn't seen so many people in cowboy hats except in movies.

The Wild West, Mary said. *Yeeee*-haw.

I said not every town could be as sophisticated as Chicago.

For God's sake, Harry, she said, this burg makes Indianapolis seem sophisticated.

We stopped for lunch at a chili parlor, then found the tourist camp and I registered us as Harry and Mary Thompson. I asked if my friend Frank Sullivan had checked in, and the clerk said he sure had, yesterday, and he kindly assigned us the cabin next door to John's. As soon as I parked the car, John and Billie came rushing out their door to greet us and there was a lot of back-slapping and hugging and laughing and how-about-this-town and so on.

We had a beer and told each other about the family visits and our drives west. After visiting his dad, John and Billie had gone to Kansas City for two days and had a great time in the jazz clubs, which he said could hold their own with Shytown's. We begged off joining them for lunch and a movie since we'd already eaten and wanted to shower and rest up, but agreed to supper at seven o'clock at a steak house Russ and Charley had recommended. He wrote down the address and said he'd stop by their place later and ask them to join us.

I joined Mary in the shower and we fooled around some and did each other's back, then took turns drying each other off, then flopped on the bed and had a nice quickie. After napping a couple of hours, we decided to go out and have a drink somewhere before meeting the others at the steak house. It was another beautiful desert sunset as we drove out of the tourist camp and turned toward downtown.

When I stopped for a red light at the end of the block, a cop car pulled up behind me. I checked them out as I pretended to adjust my phony specs in the rearview. There were two of them in the car, a uniform behind the wheel, a plainclothes in the shotgun seat. The driver tapped his horn lightly and the plainclothes guy stuck his head out the window and smiled and waved us over to the curb.

I gave him a friendly wave in return and pulled over, and the cops parked behind me. I thumbed off the safety on the .45 under my arm and drew the .38 from its belt holster on my side and held it in my left hand, against the door. Be ready, I whispered to Mary.

She was looking back at them and said she didn't think they were wise to us. They didn't seemed scared enough.

The one on the passenger side got out with his hands empty and came up to my window all smiles. Nice brown suit. He said he was sorry to trouble me but apparently I wasn't aware that visitors with out-of-state license plates were required to register their vehicles with the city police. I said I'd never heard of any such ordinance anywhere, and he said neither had he. It was intended to cut down on smuggling cars across the Mexican border—a pretty useless law, if you asked him, but what could you do? Every officer on the force—uniform *and* plainclothes, mind you—was under orders to strictly enforce the ordinance or lose his job.

I thanked him for letting me know about it and promised to take care of the registration first thing in the morning. He said if I didn't take care of it right away, I'd be getting pulled over every few blocks, and as much as he hated to admit it, there were fellows on the force darn quick to ticket an out-of-state car if it didn't have a registration decal—and even to impound the car if they got an argument. That's what happened to his own cousin visiting from Oregon two weeks ago, believe it or not. His cousin swore never to set foot in Tucson again and who could blame him. Wait till enough tourists got mad and stopped coming to town, see how fast they got rid of the stupid law then and quit wasting police manpower. Meantime, the best thing was to get my car registered right away. Wouldn't take two minutes, and he'd even ride with us to give me the quickest directions to the station and make sure we didn't have to wait around when we got there.

I had to decide fast—shoot him and run, or play it like a good citizen and see what happened. If he was on to me, he was cooler than any cop I'd ever come across. But for weeks I'd been going unrecognized by cops all over the Midwest, so how could this hick be wise? Not likely. I turned to Mary and she made a face and said she wasn't the least surprised about the dumb law and let's just get it over with.

Hop in, officer, I said, and slipped the .38 under my belt at my side.

He directed me to the station, chatting like an old buddy, asking about Florida, saying he'd always wanted to take a vacation there. I said he should, it was a great place and I ought to know, having lived there for the last ten years. We pulled up in front of the station and I told Mary I'd be right out. The other cop had followed us, and he parked in back of me and got out of his car too. He was bigger than Brown Suit and came ambling behind us.

Brown Suit said the registration forms were in the chief's office and led the way through the door. The chief was standing beside his desk. His eyes widened when he saw me—and I saw Russ and Charley's luggage piled against the wall behind him.

The next few seconds were pretty much a blur. I grabbed for the .45 but the big cop got me in a bear hug from behind and I couldn't pull the piece out of the holster. Brown Suit tried to get my hand off the gun and I kneed him in the balls and sent him banging into the chief. I bucked and twisted, trying to shake the big one off me, and there was a lot of shouting as we crashed around the office and lost our hats and my glasses flew off and then Brown Suit and the chief were on me too and the four of us went down in a struggling heap. I got the gun out but couldn't cock it because the big guy had his hand around the hammer. Then here came more cops, cursing, kicking me in the ribs, stomping on my head. Somebody wrenched my arm hard enough to make me holler and the .45 dropped out of my hand and the .38 was yanked off my belt. They wrestled me onto my belly and somebody sat on my head and somebody else pinned down my legs and they got the cuffs on me. And that was all she wrote.

They pulled me up on my feet and the chief grabbed me by the hair and said Oh yeah, oh *yeaaah*—we got us Mr. Handsome Harry here. You're under arrest for a whole bunch of shit, Pierpont. And you're gonna *burn* for killing that cop.

Christ on a crutch, I *walked* into that jail! I should've let that cop have it the second he stepped up to my car window, then jumped out and let the other one have it, then made a run for it.

Shoulda, woulda, coulda. . . . What could've happened did.

I'd been a free man exactly four months.

• • •

They hustled me off to the county jail, which was bigger and more secure than the city lockup. When we got there the cops had to clear a way to the doors through a crowd of reporters shouting questions and popping flashbulbs. I couldn't believe how fast they'd got the word about me, but a cop said they'd been hanging around the jail since my buddies got brought in a couple of hours earlier. They were all locals so far, he said, but reporters were on the way from every corner of the country.

They took my prints, then sat me in front of the mug camera. I closed my eyes before the shutter clicked, so they tried again and I did it again. The booking sergeant said Piss on it, who cares? And they took me up to the cell block.

Charley and Russ were in adjoining cells and didn't look happy to see me. Russell's face was beat up and he had a bandage around his head like a big turban. They put me in with Charley, who quick stuck his hand out said The name's Charles Makley, sir, what might yours be?—letting me know he'd been made, but he didn't know if I had. We shook and I said I was Harry Thompson. He introduced Russ as Mr. Clark. The cops at the bars laughed at us and said we could quit the act anytime, that as soon as my prints were run they'd have me cold too. I asked what became of my lady friend and they said what did I think—she was under arrest for aiding and abetting. So was Opal, who in addition had been charged with assault.

When the cops moved out of earshot, the guys told me the sad story. Charley had been collared around two o'clock. He and Tweet were shopping for a radio in a store when suddenly there was a cop on either side of him and a gun in his ribs. One of them grabbed him by the hand and took a look at his mutilated finger and said Got you, fatso. They weren't interested in a thing he had to say. The last time he saw Tweet, a cop had her by the arm out on the sidewalk, waiting for a squad car to come for them.

Russell they took at the house, but not without a scrap. A guy in a Western Union cap came to the door with a telegram for Mr. Long. He was such a shrimp Russ never suspected he was a cop. When he opened the door to sign for the message, the guy went for a gun under his jacket. Russ grabbed him and yanked him inside and they wrestled for the gun all over the house. The guy was little but he was a bulldog. Two more cops barged in through the back door and there was a lot of swearing and yelling and Russ caught a glimpse of Opal swinging on them with both fists. Then he was on the floor with three guys on him and one of them whacking him on the head with a pistol like he was driving a nail. Next thing he knew they were dragging him out in cuffs and he could hear Opal cursing them but he could hardly see for the blood in his eyes. Later he found out that another cop had come running up to the front porch and Opal slammed the door on his hand and broke one of his fingers.

Our undoing, as Charley called it, was on account of the hotel fire. He'd awakened to the sound of an alarm and the smell of smoke and he ran out of his room just as Russell and Opal came rushing out of theirs, all of them in bathrobes. They got downstairs before remembering they'd taken all their guns out of the car and put them in one of the suitcases and the suitcase was up in the room. Except for a twenty-dollar bill Charley had in his robe, all their cash was in their bags too. They tried to go back upstairs but the firemen wouldn't let them. Charley offered them the twenty if they'd save their luggage, and the firemen did it. He and Russ considered themselves lucky, not only because of the bags, but because they'd rented a house the day before and had been assured it would be ready to move into that morning. Russ took charge of the suitcase with the guns and Charley got some money from his bag and paid a hotel worker to take the rest of the luggage to their new place.

That, Charley said, was a stupid move on his part.

I didn't see the need to say how much I agreed with him.

The way the cops told it to Charley, the two firemen had raved to everybody in the firehouse about the double sawbuck tip. Somebody wondered what the luggage contained that was so important, and somebody joked that maybe the big tippers were gangsters, and somebody said maybe they really were. They started going through a stack of true-crime magazines, and *bingo*—there's an article about John and his pals, and it's got mug shots of all of us. The firemen called the cops. The cops interviewed the hotel staff. And soon enough they talked to the guy who'd taken Mr. Davies' and Mr. Long's luggage to their new address. They staked out the house, then followed Charley to the store and pinched him, then pulled the phony telegram business to get at Russell. In addition to all the guns and cash they found in the house, they came across a piece of paper with the address of a local tourist camp. Thinking John and I might be staying there, they'd sent a couple of men to scout it.

And now here *you* are, Charley said. It boggled his mind that a bunch of cowboys had apprehended the three of us with not a shot fired or an injury among them except for a fractured finger.

Listen, I said, as long as John's still out there, this ain't over, not by a long shot.

Ten minutes later here came John—wearing cuffs and leg irons. They'd laid for him at Russ and Charley's, hoping he'd drop in. And he did.

. . .

We were allowed a phone call but it had to be local, so Charley called Tweet. Her mother answered and he identified himself as Leo Davies and the old lady gave him an earful before Tweet was able to get the phone away from her. Tweet said the cops had grilled her for two hours before she convinced them she'd had no idea of his real identity and let her go. Was there anything she could do? There was indeed, Charley told her. She could call Paulette Dewey, our attorney in Kokomo, Indiana, and tell her we were in severe need of legal representation. Charley didn't enlighten her as to who Paulette Dewey really was—the less Tweet knew, the less legal risk she ran. We figured Pearl would call Sonny Sheetz, and he would either do something for us or he wouldn't. Charley told Tweet that after making the call to Kokomo she was to stay out of the whole business and not contact him in any way. If she ever claimed she knew him as anyone other than Leo Davies, he would say she was a lying, publicity-hungry bimbo. She cried but said she'd do as he asked. As far as I know, they never exchanged a word again after that phone talk.

At our arraignment the next day we had a lawyer, a guy from Los Angeles named Van Buskirk who we nicknamed the Dutchman. By that time I had been positively identified too, but not John. When they called his name in court and he was told to stand up, he said why should he, he wasn't Dillinger. He insisted he was Frank Sullivan right up until his prints proved otherwise later in the day. The girls were in court too, all three of them charged with abetting us in some way or other. I didn't get a chance to talk to Mary, but I gave her a wink and she managed a little smile in return.

During the next few days we were besieged by reporters at our cell doors. Russell said he now knew what the animals in a zoo felt like and all that was missing was peanuts for them to throw at us through the bars. One idiot asked Charley his opinion of the jail, and Charley said he had been in better bastilles. The guy started to write it down, then looked confused, and Charley spelled it for him. Another newshound turned out to be the son of an old friend of Charley's back in St. Marys, and they chatted about mutual acquaintances and the old home ground. The kid couldn't understand why a man as highly educated and well mannered as Mr. Makley would choose to become a gangster. Charley told him the reason was quite simple— because as a gangster he lived more in forty minutes than his old man had lived in forty years. The kid said Oh, I see. But you could tell that he didn't see a thing.

For the most part I ignored the reporters, and whenever they came with a camera I'd turn my back to the bars. But of course just because I didn't say anything didn't stop them from quoting me. According to one guy, I said the first thing I was going to do when I broke out was kill the cops who caught me. Another one said I bragged about paying a thousand dollars a week in protection to the Chicago mob. You'd think they got paid by the lie.

Fortunately, most of them wanted to talk to John—after all, it was the *Dillinger* Gang. At first he ate up their attention with a spoon and yakked like a magpie, though most of what he told them was bullshit of course. Like the sad information that our partner Jack Hamilton was dead. He gave them the story we'd agreed on to try keeping the heat off Red back in Chicago—that we had dumped Hamilton's body in the Calumet River after he died of wounds he received during an East Chicago bank robbery the week before last. John was quick to add that none of us had been on that job with Hamilton, but we got the word from friends. When a reporter said that various eyewitnesses had identified John as the man who killed Officer O'Malley during that very same robbery, John got peeved and said most so-called witnesses couldn't identify shit from brown sugar and the guy could quote him on that.

Even the governor dropped by for a look at us. I said it was the first time I'd seen a governor where he really belonged—although that's not the way I was quoted in the papers. We also got a visit from the cops who'd rounded us up. John posed for the cameras with them, but I said Sorry boys, no pictures. I did tell them they were the best cops I'd ever run into. The cops in Indiana and Ohio, and especially in Chicago, would've bushwhacked us the first chance they got rather than try to take us alive.

We'd been in that cow town jail about three days when Matt Leach showed up. I was sitting at the rear of my cell and heard somebody say Well, Johnny, we meet again—say now, that's a nice mustache.

I stood up and saw him in front of John's cage right next to mine, with his hands in his pockets and looking smug. And I couldn't help it, I saw red. I sprang to the bars and grabbed for him, intending to break his neck or strangle him, whichever came first. He barely managed to jerk away in time. He went white as a sheet and I wouldn't be surprised if he pissed his pants. I cursed him up and down for a low son of a bitch who bullied women and a lousy coward who jailed my mother. I said the only thing I was sorry about was that I hadn't killed him when I had the chance. Which of course only confused him, since he never knew I'd had him in my rifle sights.

J-j-jesus, he said, you're ins-s-sane.

My rant got the other inmates all worked up and the whole cell block was in a clamor. The jailers hustled Leach out of there, but it still took a while for the joint to settle down.

. . .

Leach had come to Tucson with a bunch of other officials who wanted to extradite us to Indiana. They wanted John for killing the O'Malley cop, and the rest of us for busting out of M City and the Greencastle heist. But Ohio wanted us too—John for robbery, and me and Charley and Russell for killing the sheriff in Lima. And then Wisconsin jumped into the fight and said it wanted all of us for the Racine job.

There was no question where we preferred to go to—Wisconsin was the only one of the three states without capital punishment. The Dutchman brought the Wisconsin prosecutor to see us, a man named John Brown. I said he certainly didn't look as if he had been a-moldering in some grave, and John Brown nodded and gave a tired little smile, like it was the thousandth time he'd heard a joke about his name. We signed the papers Brown put in front of us, and the Dutchman said all we needed now was a something-or-other writ that he'd have ready to put before the judge in the morning. And then we'd be off to Cheeseland. We thought we'd pulled a slick one.

But the Arizona governor made some kind of underhanded deal with Indiana, and that night the Hoosiers came in and grabbed John. He put up a fight but didn't stand a chance. They pried his fingers off the bars and dragged him out of the cell by force and clapped him in irons. He hollered he was being shanghaied and we were swearing and raising hell as they muscled him out of there. The way we heard it, they had him in an airplane and out of Arizona in less than half an hour.

The Dutchman didn't find out about John's abduction until the next morning, and he was outraged, for all the good it did. The rest of us then went before a judge who released Billie and Opal but not Mary, who'd been charged with helping us bust out of M City. He denied the Dutchman's writ and handed us over to Matt Leach and the state of Indiana.

As we were leaving the courthouse a mob of reporters swarmed around us, yelling questions and taking pictures. I ducked my head to hide my face under my hat brim, but some of the cops pinned me between them and one snatched my hat off and two others forced my head up and all I could do to defend myself against the cameras was close my eyes. I heard the shutters snapping like jaws and the bulbs popping. One of the hounds yelled Make him open his eyes, willya? A cop said The hell with these leeches, and they shoved my hat back on my head and hustled me out of there.

An hour later, we were in a special car on a train bound for Chicago, each of us sitting in a different row, all of us in cuffs and leg irons and surrounded by armed guards.

For some reason—and without me asking for the favor, since I wouldn't have asked the son of a bitch for the time of day—Leach told the policewoman in charge of Mary to let her sit beside me for the whole trip. I don't think she and I exchanged a dozen words during those two days. There was nothing to say we didn't already know. We simply held hands and gave each other a look now and then. I could see she was scared about what might happen to her. The way it went, she'd do almost a month in the Indytown jail before they dropped all charges against her—but that little stretch would have its effect.

The only kiss we had on that train ride was when the policewoman came to take her to another car a few minutes before we pulled into Chicago. It hadn't occurred to me until then that I might never see her again.

•   •   •

*T*here were a hundred cops waiting at the station, and God
knows how many gawkers. They put each of us in a separate
car and we drove off in a motorcade a block long. We crossed
the state line into Indiana and sped through East Chicago. I caught a
glimpse of the Indiago Industries building over by the lakeshore and
I wondered if Sonny Sheetz was in there at that moment, maybe
counting money. It was a cold gray morning and the windblown lake
looked like crumpled tin. Nobody talked as we rolled along, drawing
curious looks from everyone we passed.

We knew where we were headed, but still, it's hard to describe
how I felt when we came in sight of the M City walls. Like for a
minute I forgot how to breathe.

As they marched us toward the gate, Charley said if anybody
would care to shoot him in the head before we passed through those
portals, they would be doing him a colossal kindness: Better a quick
death than what awaits us within those walls, he said. A cop told him
to shut up.

You can imagine how the warden and his hacks were slavering
over having us back in their power. We had humiliated the bunch of
them, and they meant to make us pay for it. Half an hour after getting to M City, we were stripped and in the hole.

I sat with my back against the wall and hugged my knees to my
chest, shivering in the freezing darkness. I pretty much succeeded in
not thinking about anything except that as long as you're alive there's
hope for escape. I had no doubt whatever that the M City goons intended to kill us, one way or another, and they probably wouldn't
take long to get to it.

After a few days, though, they came for me and gave me a set of
grays to put on, then chained me up and took me to the warden's office.

The room was crowded, what with the guards plus the warden
and some guy in a pinstriped suit, plus Russ and Charley, who were
in chains too. Charley grinned at me and Russ gave me a nod. Charley

had never done time in the hole before, but he looked all right. A little less corpulent than I'd ever seen him, since the whole time we were in solitary we got nothing to eat but a few slices of bread. Russell still had the bandage on his head but it was now filthy brown with black patches of dried blood. None of us had shaved or washed since we'd been on the train, and it was amusing to see all those faces pinched up at the smell of us.

We were in the warden's office because Indiana and Ohio had made a deal—the Hoosiers got John and Ohio got the three of us. Mr. Pinstripes had papers that would send us to Lima to stand trial for shooting the sheriff. The odds in Ohio didn't look good, but they were better than our chances of staying alive in M City.

None of us hesitated to sign the waivers. The warden looked like a kid who's just been told there's no such thing as Santa Claus.

* * *

As you'd expect, defense measures at the Allen County jail were a whole lot beefier than they'd been the last time we were there.

They had round-the-clock guards, a pair of them with Thompsons at the entrance to the building, two more with twelve-gauge pumps in the corridor between the office and the cell block, and two guys armed with clubs in the cell block runaround. We were the only prisoners in there—all the local miscreants had been transferred to other jails. The cells were partitioned from each other by bars, not solid walls, and we were kept in separate cells with an empty one between us. It was impossible to talk without the guards overhearing, so we mostly kept our mouths shut. They can take away your privacy but they can't get in your head. During our first weeks in Lima I constantly racked my brain for some way to escape. Every morning I'd look at Russell and Charley in hope of seeing some sign that maybe one of them had come up with an idea. But none of us came up with anything, not in that tight little lockup and under constant watch.

We hired a team of lawyers to represent all three of us, the main one being a woman named Jessie Levy, as good as any mouthpiece I ever met—and by far the best-looking. I had the feeling that if she ever took off those glasses and let down her hair she'd be a ball of fire.

She told us John was in jail at Crown Point, Indiana, and the joint was being guarded by cops, posse men, and the National Guard.

I said maybe they better put a net over the place too, to make sure he didn't fly out of there.

We were arraigned in the middle of February. Each of us would be tried separately for the murder of Allen County sheriff Jess Sarber, me first. My trial was set for the sixth of March.

Sad to say, but by the time of our arraignment Russell was showing clear signs of defeat. It sounds harsh, but the truth's the truth. Charley saw it too. No question in my mind it had to do with the daily letters he was getting from Opal. I don't know what she was writing to him, but each letter seemed to diminish his spirit a little bit more. I finally asked him one day how she was doing. But he only shrugged and lay on his bunk and stared at the ceiling.

I got letters from my mother and Mary. My mother said for me to have hope, I would beat this thing yet. That was Mom, the eternal optimist. Mary was staying put at the Indianapolis apartment she shared with her mother and Margo. She hadn't come to see me because she was afraid. The month she'd spent in the Indy lockup had spooked her bad, and she was terrified of going back to jail. She said she loved me and was praying for me. I wrote back that I loved her too and she was doing the right thing by staying away.

I'll confess that my own spirits weren't exactly sky-high while we were waiting to go to court. I kept as active as I could—I did push-ups, sit-ups, I ran in place till I was exhausted. I was hanging tight to the hope of breaking out even though I had no idea how it might happen. Still, when you feel like you're about to drown, you hold on to anything that might keep you afloat.

And then, three days before my trial began, John escaped from Crown Point.

• • •

We got the news from Jessie Levy. It explained why the guards had been glowering at us even more than usual all day. Charley said he'd have to stop calling him Johnny Fairbanks and start referring to him as Johnny Houdini. One of the guards said it wouldn't be long before everybody would be calling him Johnny Dead.

Everybody knows the Crown Point story. Christ, they'll still be telling it years from now. They had him behind bars and under the heaviest guard in the world, and still he got away. And the kicker is that he did it with a fake gun. They say he whittled it out of a chunk of washboard frame and painted it with black shoe polish and then used it to force a guard to unlock his cell. He rounded up more than a dozen guards and jail employees and locked them all up, taking his sweet time about it, singing and making jokes. He took up a collection from them so he'd have a little traveling money, then rattled the wooden gun along the bars and laughed at them for being suckered by a toy. He snuck down to the jail garage and got in the sheriff's car—the *sheriff's* car, I love it!—and drove out of there as casually as you please. Drove right past all those cops and soldiers standing guard outside the joint and armed to the teeth. He was long gone before they knew he'd made the break.

It's a great story, and all of it true—except for the wooden gun. I knew that part was bullshit the minute I heard it, and one of our lawyers said I was right. Never mind which one—Mr. X, let's call him, though maybe it wasn't a *mister*—and never mind how he got the story.

Oh, there was a wooden gun, all right, but John wasn't the one who made it, and it's not what got him out of there. The toy was a cover for the real piece that was smuggled in along with it. A lot of money changed hands to arrange the break. Some of it went to cer-

tain jail guards and officials, some of it to a judicial authority, as Mr.
X phrased it, who made sure John wasn't moved to another jail.
Where the dough came from, Mr. X didn't know, but my guess was
Sonny Sheetz. John had been doing business with him since before I
got out of M City, and he trusted Sheetz more than I ever did. The
wooden gun—which he'd made sure to show to the guards after he
locked them up—was what kept the inside guys off the hook, no
matter how much suspicion fell their way, and no matter that several
guards insisted it was a real gun John stuck in their face before locking them up. The plan was smart and worked smooth as Vaseline, but
I hated to think of the price John must've paid for it. I had a feeling
that anytime Sonny wanted to find John from then on, all he'd have
to do was reach in his hip pocket.

All the same, when I heard he was out, I didn't have a doubt in
the world *we'd* soon be out too. How could it go any other way? He'd
helped us bust out of M City, and then we'd busted him out of jail,
and now he'd busted out of a lockup everybody said was escape-proof.
Escape-proof for ordinary guys, maybe, but not for the likes of us.
Whatever his deal with Sonny Sheetz, I knew he wasn't going to leave
us to the wolves.

Not him. Not us.

Naturally Charley and I couldn't talk about it, not with the
guards right there in the runaround. But he could read my face from
his cell. He cut his eyes around at the bars and at the guards in the
runaround and made a gesture indicating all the guard-power posted
outside the jail—and he shook his head and made a face that said *I
don't think so.*

The guards weren't looking, so I raised a fist and shook it and
nodded hard—*Yes, yes.*

He shrugged with uncertainty. Then showed a small smile. Then
made a face: *Maybe.*

Russell was watching us from his cell. I shook my fist at him too.
Yes . . . yes, goddamnit.

He seemed to sigh and his shoulders sagged. He stared at me without expression for a minute, then lay down and turned his face to the wall.

I wanted to yell, to throw something at him.

• • •

Word of John's escape put Lima in a panic. Every cop and citizen out there was as certain as I was that he was rounding up a gang to come and liberate us. Overnight the town turned into a National Guard camp—and those soldier boys were not in a good mood after the way John had embarrassed their Indiana comrades.

They built a fence around the jail and strung rolls of barbed wire around it. They swept searchlights over the streets and alleyways all through the nights. They had machine guns in sandbag emplacements at each corner of the courthouse and on the rooftops of neighboring buildings. They even set up a machine gun *inside* the jail, at the end of the corridor in full view of our cells. The officer in charge said if anyone tried to free us, the first thing to happen is we'd get shot into hamburger.

I said it looked like they were expecting an invasion by the Prussian army. Charley laughed along with me, and I was glad to see Russell smile. The officer told us to shut the hell up, and Charley and I grinned and grinned.

Matt Leach arrived with a warning. He'd received a tip that Dillinger and his confederates were planning on sneaking into town in National Guard uniforms. Another rumor had it that John intended to kidnap the governor of Ohio and use him to ransom us. Every day a team of mining experts checked the grounds around the jail for signs of tunneling. Every day an army airplane scouted the local roads and rail tracks.

Jessie Levy brought word from Mary that she was thrilled to hear of John's escape but was awful glad she'd been sticking close to home and that the cops had been keeping her under surveillance. Otherwise they would've accused her for sure of abetting John in some way or other.

• • •

I went to trial shackled hand and foot, the cops shoving a path through the rubbernecking yokels and bellowing news-hounds mobbing the front of the courthouse. I held my cuffed hands up in front of my face as the cameras snapped all around me. Some of the papers described the atmosphere of the trials as carnival-like, but nuthouselike would've been closer to the mark.

The courtroom was packed, of course. Every spectator was patted for weapons before being allowed to enter, and a dozen men with shotguns were positioned around the room. Two guards, one in front, one behind, led me to the defense table. A man seated in a nearby chair held a submachine gun and stared hard at me. One of the cops said he was the son of the man I'd killed. He'd replaced his daddy as the high sheriff.

I never killed anybody, I said. I was damned if I was going to make it easy for them.

Not that the verdict was ever in doubt. The sheriff's widow and the deputy who'd been on the scene each pointed at me from the stand and said I was the one who pulled the trigger.

And then they brought Ed Shouse from the Michigan City pen. He'd agreed to testify against us in exchange for Indiana dropping all charges on him pertaining to the killing. I wanted to jump up and throttle the bastard with my manacle chains. He never looked my way as he testified about being part of the crew that busted John out of Lima, not until the DA asked him if the man who shot Sheriff Sar-ber was present in the courtroom. Shouse pointed at me and said That's him, Harry Pierpont, and he quick cut his eyes away again. I yelled out he was a low-down yellow liar, which of course is what he was, never mind that it was true about the sheriff—everybody already

knew that was true. The judge banged his gavel and said to strike my
remark from the record. Shouse didn't look at me again before they
took him out. They would've nailed me even without his testimony,
but that's hardly the point. There's nothing lower than a guy siding
with the law against somebody he partnered with, no matter what
kind of personal bitterness there is between them.

My defense was that I wasn't in Lima on the day in question, that,
in fact, I'd never been in Lima in my life. So how did I explain that
the revolver taken off me in Tucson belonged to Sheriff Sarber? I'd
had no idea it was Sarber's gun—John had given it to me after someone else, I didn't know who, had given it to him in Chicago. The
widow Sarber and the deputy who said I shot the sheriff were simply
mistaken. They'd been subjected to a terrifying experience and their
memories couldn't be trusted to recall the details of it accurately. Besides, there were thousands of men who looked like me. As for
Shouse, you couldn't believe a word out of his mouth. He was bitter
because John beat him up and we kicked him out of the gang for trying to poach his partners' women. He even stole a car from one of us.
On top of all that, he was insane and everybody knew it. Ask Charles
Makley. Ask Russell Clark.

Not much of a defense, I'll be the first to admit, but it was all I had.

My mother took the stand and swore I was having supper with
her at the farm in Leipsic on the day the sheriff was killed. She said I
hid in a secret nook in the attic when the cops came searching for me
a couple of hours after the jailbreak. The jurymen looked at her like
she was saying she could fly. I wanted to kick hell out of all of them.

Like I said, the verdict was a foregone conclusion, and there was
really no need for me to take the stand. But I did. I wanted to have
my say. That gave the DA the chance to try to get my goat, but if you
want my opinion, I got the better of him. The bastard said the only
reason I'd agreed to stand trial in Ohio is that I wasn't tough enough
to take the hole at Michigan City. I said I'd been in the hole more
times than he'd been kissed by women who weren't his mother—

which got a small laugh from the crowd. I said I'd done stretches in the hole so long that I couldn't stand up when they took me out, that I couldn't see straight and it took days for my eyes to adjust to the light. I said a guy like him would bust into hysterics before he'd been in the hole an hour.

When he said we'd taken more than $300,000 from banks since breaking out of M City, I said if that was true I'd be retired in Miami Beach right this minute, sitting in the sun and sipping rum cocos. That got another laugh from the spectators and the judge warned them to keep order.

The DA said I couldn't deny robbing several banks since my escape from Michigan City—there were dozens of eyewitnesses who'd identified me. I said I wasn't denying it, but I was honest enough to do my robbing with a gun and man enough to take my chances against anybody who tried to stop me. At least I wasn't a two-faced, double-talking, hypocritical bank president who used crooked books to rob widows and farmers of their property and life savings. *That* one got a big roaring laugh, and had the judge banging his gavel like a carpenter in a hurry.

I told the DA that men like him hated men like me because they knew damn well they didn't have the daring to do what we did. It was that simple. Every time you look at me, I said, you see what a coward you are.

He acted all indignant, of course, but you could see in his face how hard the truth hit. I felt great, never mind that at the defense table Jessie Levy had her head in her hands.

It took the jury about forty minutes to convict me of murder in the first degree. The only question was whether they'd recommend mercy and spare me a mandatory death sentence—*and,* I might add, give me another chance to bust out of whatever joint they put me in. But when they came filing back into the courtroom I knew the answer before they gave it. One or two of them couldn't even look at me, but the others, oh man, you could see the pleasure in their eyes.

A few of them were smiling at me the way sissies smile when the teacher pinches the ear of some classmate they're all afraid of, some kid they show a completely different kind of smile to when it's just him and them. I never smiled at *anybody* the way they were smiling at me. I wouldn't be able to keep my self-respect.

Guilty and no mercy. The judge said I'd be sentenced after all three trials were concluded, but that was a mere formality. I couldn't help thinking that if it hadn't been for Shouse, the jury might've made the mercy recommendation. Then I thought *If, if, if,* and had to laugh out loud—which got me a lot of horrified looks.

The reporters swarmed up to the table, their flashbulbs popping. Mom rushed over to me and did her best to shield my face from them. She was crying and called them cannibals. I kissed her and whispered in her ear to not let them get her goat, to be strong. And then they took me away.

Charley's trial was next. A half brother I didn't even know he had came to testify that Charley was with him in St. Marys at the time of the Sarber shooting. The trial ran four days and then his jury was out all night, which Jessie said was a good sign—somebody was obviously arguing for mercy. As Charley left for court the next morning, I wished him luck. He grinned and said Seven come eleven. He wasn't grinning when he came back. I asked what he got, and he said The kit and kaboodle. And didn't say another word the rest of the day.

Then it was Russell's turn. His disposition by then can be described as sheer indifferent gloom. He'd been sleeping eighteen, sometimes twenty hours a day. Jessie said he even nodded off in court a time or two. When they'd bring him back at the end of the day, we'd ask how it was going, and if he bothered to answer at all, he'd only shrug and stretch out on his bunk and be asleep as soon as his head was down.

But he got the luck. The verdict was guilty but with a recommendation of mercy. That was as it should've been. He never laid a hand on the sheriff.

The judge rejected Jessie's motion for new trials, and we all got the sentences we expected. Russell drew life. Charley and I got the chair. We were scheduled to ride the lightning on a Friday the thirteenth less than four months away.

· · ·

All during the trials, I kept an eye out for John. But the news always had him a long way from us. He robbed a bank in South Dakota, of all places, *three days* after breaking out of Crown Point, though we didn't hear about it till well after that. Mr. X told me there'd been a lot of shooting on that job and somebody wounded a cop. He said the gang took hostages on the running boards for the getaway, and I was reminded of Racine.

A week later, during Charley's trial, they hit a bank in Iowa, and it was a wonder they got away. There was more wild shooting and the cops used tear gas and some of the citizens joined the police in taking shots at the robbers. To top it off, although they got around twenty grand, they left behind more than $150,000. Christ almighty. The whole thing smacked of bad comedy. I was sure Red was working with John on those jobs and I couldn't believe they were capable of such sloppy work. But when I found out Homer Van Meter was in with them, plus that trigger-happy runt named Nelson or Gillis, whichever it was, it was clear enough to me why the jobs were going rocky. Still, I figured John was working on a plan for our deliverance, and I kept watching for him.

And he did show up. On the day we were sentenced.

We were being led back to the jail, shuffling in our shackles between two rows of National Guard riflemen forming a wide corridor across the street and holding back the crowd of spectators braving an icy wind to have another look at us. The three of us were bareheaded and the wind whipped our hair. It had the cops holding on to their hats. And as we started up the jailhouse steps, I spotted him.

He was well beyond the crowd, standing at the foot of a monument in front of the courthouse, bundled in an overcoat and with his hat low over his face—but I knew it was him. It was only a few seconds, but long enough to see him raise his fist.

I'm out here, brother . . . hang on. . . .

I laughed as I went through the door. Fat Charley arched his brow at me like I might be losing my grip, and I shook my head and laughed some more. I never did tell him about seeing John that day. I was afraid he'd say I couldn't be sure it was him, not at that distance, and my disappointment in Charley would've been hard to take.

• • •

We were transferred to the Ohio state prison in Columbus on a frigid morning of blowing snow, once again in separate vehicles and accompanied by a caravan of cop cars. We sped along country roads and barreled through town after town, and even the bad weather didn't keep the folk from gathering on the sidewalks, huddled in their coats, to squint at us as we whizzed by.

At one point, the car I was in fishtailed for a moment as we went through a curve, and I said to the driver What're you trying to do, kill me? A couple of the cops snickered. One said it was too bad I was such a crumb or I might've made a good cop. Not on your life, I said—too many rules and too many bosses. I was sure right about that, the cop said.

Another crowd was waiting in front of the prison. Those good citizens were taking a chance. In addition to the riflemen up on the walls, there were National Guard machine guns aiming at us from the backs of trucks. If anyone had made a wrong move, we wouldn't have been the only ones to get all shot up.

They processed us into the joint and then led Russell off in another direction and took me and Charley to the death house.

We passed through gate after gate as we went down one corridor after another, with armed guards at each gate except the last two, where the guards carried only clubs. The last corridor ended at a heavy steel door with a small barred window. A guard peeked out at us, then unlocked the door and swung it open and said Welcome to the Hot Seat Hotel, gents.

The front of the row was an open area with a desk near the door, a small shower room on one side and a set of stall lockers on the other. The cells ran down both sides of a center aisle, separated from each other by stone walls and fronted with bars. They put us in adjacent cells.

When they turned the lock on me, I felt like I was buried under the ocean floor.

• • •

Charley and I never saw each other except when one of us was taken out to go to the shower. It was easy to talk through the barred doors, but of course you didn't have any privacy. Because we were in neighboring cells, though, it wasn't hard to exchange notes. You balled up the paper tight and small, checked the hallway with your little shaving mirror to make sure nobody was watching, then quick reached out and flicked the little ball through the bars of the other cell.

The other inmates on the row were all as dumb as dirt if not outright deranged, and we generally ignored them. Two of the cells across the aisle faced directly into ours, but one of those guys spent most of his time sleeping or jerking off and didn't seem to recognize our existence, and the other was the looniest guy on the row, always babbling to himself about who-knows-what. The guards said he'd chopped up both his mother and his wife with an axe. Everybody called him the Bug.

The only visitor we could meet in private—that is, without a double layer of steel mesh between us, and with the guard required to stand far enough away that he couldn't overhear us—was our lawyer, Jessie Levy. She came to see us fairly often. She was working on another motion for new trials.

At first my mother came to visit too, about every other week, but I had to put an end to that. She'd always been a good soldier, but my being on death row was too much for her. Each time we faced each other through the thick steel mesh in the visiting room she ended up in tears. I couldn't take it. I told her not to come see me again until I got off the row.

As for Mary, she wrote me every day during my first weeks in Columbus. To avoid the prison censors, she'd send her letters to Jessie, who would slip them in among legal papers she'd give me to review in my cell. The truth is, except for some pretty explicit sex stuff, most of what she wrote me would've passed the censors with no trouble. She'd always say she loved me and missed me and hoped I was doing well. She'd tell me about her waitressing job at the same restaurant where Margo was a hostess, and about the garden she was raising in the backyard. She hoped I understood why she hadn't come to see me, but she didn't want to make the police more suspicious of her than they already were. I supposed that was also why she never mentioned John in any of her letters—she was afraid of what would happen to her if the letters fell in the wrong hands. She said she was sorry she was such a sissy, but jail had been awful, and she didn't believe she could bear it again. Besides, she said, she had spoken with my mother and knew how her visits had affected me. She didn't think she could keep from crying any more than Mom could, so it was just as well she didn't come see me. She was sure I agreed.

I didn't agree at all, but I didn't say so. I wanted to see her, never mind how bad I'd feel when she went away again, or that we couldn't even touch fingertips as we did through the wire mesh at M City. But it wouldn't be the same if I had to *ask* her to come. Besides—and Christ, I hate to confess this, but why not?—I couldn't help wondering how much she and John were seeing of each other. I mean, what could be more natural? They trusted each other, they liked each other, they'd played together naked in the surf at Daytona Beach. I'm not saying I thought they were fooling around. But *if* they were, it wouldn't have surprised me.

By the end of my first two months on the row, her letters had become a now-and-then thing. I didn't complain to her about it. Under the circumstances, I didn't have much to say either, other than what I'd said to her a hundred times before.

I heard from Pearl Elliott once. A brief note saying she thought of me often and wished she was more of a religious person so she could pray for me without feeling like a sap. She was still laying low, but if there was anything she could do, say the word.

* * *

We weren't allowed newspapers or radios, but the hacks kept us up on the news about John, and what we didn't hear from them we got from Jessie Levy.

We hadn't been in Columbus a week before he and Billie shot their way out of a police trap in St. Paul. A week later they paid another visit to his dad in Mooresville, twenty miles from Indytown. They spent *two* days there, even though the entire region was crawling with federal cops hunting for him. Most of the neighbors knew he was there and nobody gave him away. Newspapers ran headlines about it. The feds had a fit. Jessie told me a gang of cops barged into Mary's house, waving warrants and making threats, but the bullying bastards hadn't harmed any of them, not Mary or Margo or their mother. Mary made no mention of it in her letters.

Then came the bad news of Billie's arrest. She was caught in a Chicago bar where she and John had gone to meet someone. She told the press that as soon as they got there John excused himself to go to the men's room, and while she was waiting in the foyer the feds rushed up and collared her. Some fink had tipped them to the meeting. She said when John came out of the gents' and saw the situation—and that there were too many cops for him to rescue her— he wisely walked out, passing within a few feet of the cops and giv-

ing her a wink of encouragement. Her account enraged the feds. They
insisted she was lying, that John couldn't have been in the bar or
they'd have spotted him. She laughed at them and stuck to her story.

The next thing we heard was that John and Homer Van Meter
had robbed the police station in Warsaw, Indiana, and made off with
a load of guns and bulletproof vests. It irked me to hear he was part-
nering with the scarecrow. Then again, with us out of the picture, it
was only natural he'd turn to Van Meter.

Then came a hell of a shootout with the feds in Wisconsin that
made headlines from coast to coast. John and the gang had been laying low at a vacation lodge up there called Little Bohemia, but once
again somebody ratted. More than a dozen federal agents snuck up in
the middle of the night and opened fire with machine guns and shot
the place to pieces. The gang fought back, killing one fed and wound-
ing another, plus a local cop—and every man of them got away. The
feds managed to kill one citizen and wound two others. Their only
captives were three of the gang's women. John had made the federals
look like fools before, but Little Bohemia was the capper.

Within an hour of getting the news of the battle in Wisconsin,
the warden doubled the guard in the death house. The papers re-
vived the rumor that John and his gang were in Ohio with plans to
snatch the governor and his family and hold them as hostages till we
were released. We heard that the governor's yard looked like an army
outpost, there were so many soldiers posted around the place.

* * *

The more I heard about what John was doing out there, the
smaller my cell got, the deeper I felt buried. Time turned
strange—the days dragged by even as the day of execution
seemed to be coming at me like a train. I had a recurrent nightmare
in which I'd see myself strapped in the electric chair. There'd be a
burst of blue-yellow sparks from under the steel cap on my head and
I'd feel my eyes bulging from my skull and I'd smell my roasting

blood and feel my muscles wrapping tight around my cracking bones. I'd bolt awake in a terrified sweat, choking on my heart, biting my tongue to keep from screaming.

To get hold of myself, I'd think hard about the last time I'd seen John—outside the Lima courthouse, his fist raised high.

Hang on, brother, hang on. . . .

. . .

Our appeals for a new trial kept getting turned down. Jessie was quick to file a new motion on the heels of every rejection, but her services didn't come cheap, and Charley and I started getting worried about how we'd continue to pay her. We'd both had some cash hidden away and we had let her know how to get it, but it wasn't much and we figured it would soon run out, if it hadn't already. When I brought up the subject the next time we met, she said we didn't need to worry, that John had given her enough money to keep her retained and working on our case. Mary had delivered the cash to the Indianapolis office of one of Jessie's associates.

It was nice to know we didn't have to worry about losing our lawyer, but I had a bad feeling that John was putting up all that cash because it was *all* he could do for us.

. . .

We didn't get the news about Red till almost a month after it happened. Jessie got it from Mary, who heard it straight from John. I don't know why he took so long to tell her.

John and Red and Homer Van Meter had escaped from Little Bohemia in the same car, but hours later they ran through a roadblock and the cops went after them. There was a lot of shooting and Red was hit in the back. Nobody thought it was serious at first, and after they lost the cops they ditched the getaway car and hijacked another. That's when they saw how bad Red was bleeding and that the hole in

his back was the size of a silver dollar—which Jessie said was how
John described it to Mary. They treated the wound the best they
could, but Red got worse as they pressed on to Chicago, and by the
time they got there, he was delirious. The entire Chicago Police Department was scouring the city, and every crooked doctor in town was
too scared to tend to Red, including that bastard Moran. They were
on their way to try somebody else when Red died in the car. They
buried him out in the countryside, but John didn't tell Mary where.

When I told Charley the news, he didn't say anything for about
an hour. Then he came up to the bars of his cell and said poor Red
got shot more often than anyone he'd ever known.

No, wait, he said, permit me to restate that in the man's own
mode. I mean the *fucken* guy got shot more often than anyone I know.

Yeah, I said . . . fucken guy.

· · ·

In late May, Billie was convicted of harboring and got two
years in the federal penitentiary at Milan, Michigan. A week
later, Patty and Opal were arrested in Chicago on the same
charge, and ended up in the same pen with her on two-year jolts of
their own. I bet those three ruled the joint like queens.

About a month after Billie's fall, John and his cowboys hit a bank
in South Bend, and it was another crazy mess. The cops shot some of
the citizens the guys used for shields. Van Meter shot a cop. Then
some citizen shot Van Meter in the head and they say the scarecrow
went down like he'd been pole-axed. Then he got back up and got in
the car like all he'd done was trip on his own big feet. A dozen people witnessed it and none of them could believe it. I can believe it—
hell, you can't hurt a dummy by shooting him in the head. Another
citizen shot Nelson point blank but the runt's vest saved him. And he
shot the hell out of the citizen. Then a high school kid jumped on
Nelson and rode him piggyback all over the sidewalk, trying to take
him down like it was some kind of rodeo event. The runt finally man-

aged to throw the kid off and gave him a burst from the tommy gun
and managed to hit him *once*. In the hand. And the kid fainted.

One hit with a tommy gun. Jesus, what a bunch of clowns. I don't
know how they managed to keep from shooting themselves in all
those left feet.

Nevertheless, they got about thirty grand in South Bend. John
dropped down to Indy and gave Mary another couple of gees toward
the Pete-and-Charley fund, as he called it. He also said that if some
stranger came up to her on the street some day soon and gave her a
little goose in the behind, not to be too quick to slap the mug, because it would probably be him. He was going to see a plastic surgeon.

● ● ●

When the court pushed back the date of our execution so
it could consider Jessie's latest motion for a new trial,
Charley and I joked about dodging a live wire and so
on. But Jessie said she was running out of ideas.

I was still hoping against all reason that John would think of
some way to deliver us. I kited a note to him through Jessie, who
passed it on to Mary. It included a diagram of the row. I said he didn't
owe me a thing—he'd helped us bust M City and we'd busted him
out of Lima and the scales were all even. Just the same, I'd sure appreciate it if he could come up with something. And if he couldn't,
that was okay, no hard feelings, and I'd see him in hell.

He sent back a note. Before she gave it to me, Jessie made a point
of letting me know that as far as she knew it was just another love letter from Mary. I said I understood completely.

It was short and to the point. Columbus couldn't be cracked.
He'd paid a bunch of ex-cons who'd done time in the place to draw
him a detailed map of the prison, and he'd personally cased the outside of the joint twice. He'd probably been within fifty yards of me,
he said, but I might as well have been on the moon. He'd gone to

S.—meaning Sheetz, of course—and told him to name his price for getting us out. Sheetz told him there was no way, not at any price. It was one thing to buy off a few people at Crown Point in order to sneak in a gun, but it was something else entirely to try buying somebody out of the death house. John said it looked like snake eyes, no matter how we rolled the dice. If he got to hell first he'd save me a spot next to his in the mess hall.

I read the note twice, then put a match to it and watched it fall apart in flames over the toilet, then flushed the ashes away.

• • •

When I whispered the news to Charley the next day, he was quiet for a minute. Then, so softly I barely heard him, he said: Well, they can only hang us once.

He was right about that, I said, only they weren't going to *hang* us, that was the trouble. I could face a noose, but the electric chair . . . oh man.

Indeed, Charley said. It's embarrassing.

That threw me a little. Embarrassing wasn't what came to mind when I thought of the chair.

• • •

Shortly after lights out on a hot night in July, a bunch of howling, laughing hacks came barging into the row and the overhead lights blazed on and the hacks stomped up to our cells, whooping and hooting and rapping their clubs along the door bars as one of them yelled *Extra, extra, read all about it! Dillinger deader than a fucking doornail!*

Everybody knows how it went. The feds ambushed him in Chicago. They lay for him outside a movie theater he'd gone into with those two double-crossing cunts. When he came out, the cops came up behind him and shot him a half-dozen times as he tried to run for it into an alley. One of the whores admitted she ratted him, and you know damn well the other one did too, no matter how much she denies it.

They say the street turned into a circus midway. Men dipped handkerchiefs in his blood, women stained the hems of their skirts. Some woman snipped a lock of his hair and some guy was trying to pull a ring off his finger when the cops kicked his ass away. One of the cops shook John's dead hand and said Real pleased to meet you like this, Johnny-boy. A parked car with Indiana plates was taken apart by souvenir hunters before they found out it wasn't John's.

The next day the hacks brought newspaper pictures for us to see. One showed a mob standing around the blood-stained spot where he went down. Some of the people looked heartbroken and some were grinning like ghouls. Another photo showed him on a morgue slab and covered with a sheet to his neck as a line of gawkers filed by. His forearm was bent upwards under the sheet, forming a tent and giving the impression of a huge erection. Later editions retouched the shot to get rid of the tent, but the alteration only convinced everybody it had been a hard-on for sure. That's what started all the talk about John's big dick. I hardly recognized the close-ups of his face for the plastic surgery. He had a trim little mustache and puffy cheeks with cuts and scratches and a hole under one eye where a bullet had come out. And there was a picture of the soles of his bare feet with his name on a tag on both big toes.

That afternoon they chained us up like King Kong and took us under armed guard into a large room two gates removed from death row, and there a bunch of reporters asked us about John. I agreed to do the interview only after the warden promised to keep cameras out of the room. Charley and I stayed cool and answered their questions, most of which were naturally pretty stupid, and we turned the tables as much as we could. When they asked if we thought it had been necessary for the feds to kill John or whether he would've surrendered if he'd been given the chance, I said they had to kill him so he wouldn't tell the truth about how he'd bribed his way out of Crown Point.

He'd busted out of Lima the same way, I said, only it was supposed to look like he'd been delivered, but somebody, I couldn't say who since I wasn't there, had panicked and shot the sheriff. They asked if it was true that John had recently sent us each ten thousand dollars to keep paying for our appeals. Charley said don't make him laugh, he would've been happy if John had sent five bucks to keep him in cigarettes. One of them wanted to know what I felt like when I heard John was dead. Imagine asking such a thing. Mom was right, reporters are cannibals. I asked the guy if he had a brother and he said yeah he did. I said Well, think how you'd feel if somebody came and told you your brother had fallen into a huge meat grinder.

Some Hoosier in the crowd wisecracked *My* deadbeat brother, I'd do a jig. And got a lot of laughs.

Cannibals.

What the warden didn't know was that I would've submitted to the questioning even if he hadn't given in on barring the cameras. It was a chance to get another look at the security set-up outside the row, which I'd seen only once, back when they first brought us into the death house. I needed that look. Because the night before, Charley and I had made a decision.

The hacks who'd awakened us with the news had whooped it up a while in front of our cells, having a high old time, and I guess Charley did what I did, simply sat there and took it. When they finally went away and the other inmates settled back into their bunks again, I stepped up to the corner of the cell where the bars met the wall between me and Charley and checked the row with my mirror. The guards were bunched around the desk at the far end of the row, still cracking each other up with jokes about John.

Hey, I whispered.

Charley came up to the corner on his side and I saw his hand mirror stick out to check the guards. Sir? he said low.

Let's bust it.

He chuckled and said That would be grand.

No kidding, I said.

I see, he said. He stuck his mirror out for another check on the guards. How?

John's trick, I said.

Charley reminded me that Mr. *S*. said it couldn't be bought.

John's trick for real, I said.

He didn't say anything for a minute. Then: A real *fake?*

A *real* fake.

He laughed low and said the word *optimistic* didn't even begin to suffice for such an idea.

I said to consider the alternative.

He said he wanted to think about it.

I said sure.

He said Okay, I'm in.

* * *

We wouldn't have had the time to try it if we hadn't gotten another postponement in the execution date. Jessie was straightforward about this one being it, the last shot. If we didn't get a new trial on this motion, well. . . .

We told her we understood and we were grateful for everything she'd done, and I meant it. Jessie Levy is as good as they come. And I want to make it clear that she had absolutely no knowledge of what Charley and I were up to. Neither did Mary. Neither of them ever did anything more than kite letters for us. I want that understood.

Another thing we had going for us was that they never pulled shakedowns on death row. I bet they will from now on.

The first one took me almost two weeks to make. Charley kept a lookout for me with his mirror. I heated several bars of soap and pressed them together into a larger block and let it harden. Then I started carving with a tin spoon and a safety-razor blade. I never worked on anything as meticulously as I did in making that gun. I cut the soap into the basic shape of a bulldog revolver and then started in on the detail work. I took special care in forming the cylinder and its grooves, the chambers, the bulletheads in them, but it still took me several tries to get them right. I was careful as a surgeon in carving the ejector rod, then the trigger guard and trigger. I used a pencil to bore a sleeve into the barrel, and for an even more realistic look I fit a fountain pen cartridge into the sleeve. I used tin foil from cigarette packs to make the front and rear sights. I made the handle grips out of the cardboard cover of a jigsaw-puzzle box and even carved checkering into them. Then came the coloring. Using the ink I'd drained from the fountain pen, I did the grips in solid black, then experimented with diluting the rest of the ink until I had exactly the right shade of bluing for all the metal parts. If I say so myself, Michelangelo couldn't have made a better-looking piece.

I let the ink dry, and after lights out that night I passed it around the bars to Charley. A minute or so after the lights came on the next morning, he stood at the bars and said softly Most impressive, sir, most impressive.

That was the day we got the news that Homer Van Meter had been killed by the cops in St. Paul. The way Jessie Levy told it, somebody—maybe Van Meter's girlfriend, maybe Nelson the Runt, *somebody*—had ratted him out, and the cops laid a trap for him. They say he was shot so many times that when the smoke lifted he looked like bloody sticks and rags. I think I've made it clear I didn't care for the guy, but he was on our side of the law and he was John's friend. So it counted as bad news.

• • •

I made the next one an automatic—a little thing about the size of a .25 caliber. It was much simpler to carve and only took half as long, and Charley was just as impressed. I suggested we make our move the next time they took me out for a shower, in two more days. He said the date caused no conflict on his social calendar.

That afternoon Jessie Levy came to tell us what we'd known all along—there would be no new trial. The courts had rejected her last appeal. She said she was sorry, she'd done all she possibly could, she wished she could think of something more, and so on.

I said to forget it, I had no complaints about her efforts on our behalf. I slipped her a note to give to Mary the next time she saw her. The note told her she was the love of my life all the way to the end and I hoped she'd never regret a thing.

I didn't.

• • •

The shower guard was an old wiry little hack Charley and I had nicknamed Curley in honor of his total baldness. He'd been a prison guard since 1900 and had been on death row for twenty years. He'd seen it all, and he didn't mind talking about it—except for the executions, and I knew he'd witnessed plenty of them. The first time I asked him what it was like to die in the electric chair, he said he didn't know, he'd never died in one. Come on, I said, you know what I mean. Yeah I do, he said, but you don't want to hear about it. And that was that. Every time I asked again, he'd only shake his head and clam up.

He was a widower whose only three children, all sons, had been killed in the world war. His people were from Missouri, and he was proud to say both his daddy *and* his granddaddy had ridden with Bill Anderson's guerrillas during the War Between the States. Charley once asked him how a man from such a notorious line of desperadoes had ended up as a prison guard. Curley said it was simple, that from the time he was a young man he'd realized he was sure to wind up in jail, one way or another, and it was better to be on his side of the bars than on ours. Just the same, I had a feeling the choice hadn't done away with his desperado leanings.

When he came to take me to the showers, I was holding the fake revolver under my change of underwear. The idea was that as soon as I stepped out, I'd give him no more than a glimpse of the gun as I grabbed him, then I'd hold it under his chin where he couldn't get a better look at it.

He put the key in the lock and said Okay, Harry, hose-off time. Then looked at me and stood there without turning the key. Maybe the old rascal saw it in my eyes, I don't know, but I could tell that he knew what was up.

I was standing far enough back in the cell so that the hacks by the desk couldn't see me. I dropped the underwear and pointed the gun at his face and gestured for him to open up.

He cut his eyes over to Charley, then glanced toward the front of the row, then looked back at me and said in a normal voice Hurry it up with those shoes, Pierpont, I ain't got all day. Then whispered: You'd never make it, son, not even if that thing was a real McCoy. His expression was hard to read. He might've been sad or he might've been about to bust out laughing.

Charley's whisper—*So what?*—sounded like a piece of prayer.

Curley took another look at him. And smiled. And then unlocked my door.

I stepped out and grabbed him from behind with an arm around his neck and jammed the toy to his ear. The guy in the cell across from mine started screaming and yanking on his bars like the loony he was.

The two guards at the desk near the door to the row were staring at us big-eyed. I shouted for them to freeze or Curley was finished.

Where the *hell,* one of them said, although I barely heard him over the shrieking lunatic. I pulled Curley over to Charley's cell and said to unlock it and he quickly did. Charley jumped out and pointed his toy with both hands at the two guards and yelled for them to come over and get into the cell.

One of them glanced toward the door and Charley hollered *Be reasonable or be dead.* Judging by his face, I think he was as close as I was to laughing at the thought of them running out the door and locking us in while we yelled Bang-bang.

They came over with their hands half raised and Charley ordered them into the cell and took the keys from Curley to lock it. I said to hold on a minute and surprised the hell out of Curley when I pushed him into the cell and pulled out a squarehead hack who thought he was tough. Oh God, the squarehead said, not *me*. I told him to shut up or I'd shoot him in the pussy.

Curly wanted to argue about it too, saying Me, goddamnit, *me*. I gave him a little so-long salute and started for the door, pushing the squarehead hack ahead of me.

The rest of the guys on the row were clamoring to be let out and Charley was already turning their locks as he went down the aisle. We figured that the more guys we set loose the better our own chance once we got outside the row.

Somebody in the outer corridor shouted What the *hell's* going on. A freckled face appeared at the door window for an instant before the Bug crashed into it, howling like an Indian and trying to grab the guy through the bars. In a minute there were a half-dozen guys at the door, beating at it with their fists.

Charley had to shoulder through them to get to the door and unlock it. We let the others charge out ahead of us, and they tore after the freckled hack, who was already at the far end of the corridor and going through the gate. Another guard slammed the gate shut behind Freckles and turned the lock and they ran for the next gate, where whistles were shrilling and other guards were hollering.

We didn't have the keys to the second gate, but there were wooden benches along the wall and several of the cons picked one up and started ramming the gate with it. The Bug climbed halfway up the bars and was jerking and shrieking like an enraged monkey.

Riflemen were lining up at the other gate.

I held the squarehead hack in front of me and yelled Don't shoot or I'll kill this bastard!

In those narrow corridors the sudden rifle fire was like a chain of dynamite blasts. The squarehead hollered *No-no-no*! as bullets sparked and rang against the gate bars and ricocheted off the walls. One of the guys battering with the bench grabbed at his belly and went down screaming. Blood flew off somebody's head. The bench crashed to the floor and the cons went racing back to the row. High on the bars the Bug was still screaming, and then he spasmed and dropped like a sprayed roach. The hack in my arms slumped into a dead weight and he slipped out of my grasp. I felt a hard shove on my shoulder and staggered halfway around and saw Charley slumped against the wall with his hands to his bloody chest. He grinned at me and started to say something—and his mouth blew apart in a red spray.

And then I was facedown on the floor and feeling the life draining out of me, and I knew another minute would be all she wrote.

But, as you know, it wasn't. . . .

OCTOBER 17, 1934

 So.

It's past midnight, and they're a little tardy, but here they are at the door.

The warden says something and then the guy with the Bible says something.

I've been shaved above the ankle and at the top of my head. They have to help me up, they have to hold me. Two big hacks position themselves close on either side of me and support me under the arms and by the back of my belt. They're very strong, and from even a small distance it probably looks like I'm walking mostly under my own power and they're simply holding tight to me. In fact, I'm hardly bearing any of my weight as we go out of the ready room and into the death chamber.

There are reporters but no cameras. All of them look like somebody just drew the curtain at the side show and they're by God getting their two-bits' worth.

And there it is. . . .

Every picture I'd ever seen of one of them has scared me nearly witless, and for the last three weeks I've been as afraid as I've ever been.

Now here it is for real.

It's smaller than I'd expected.

And much odder than it looks in pictures. Like something some crackpot put together in his garage.

The straps, the wires, the little metal cap. . . .

The thing suddenly seems, well . . . funny.

Comic.

Silly as hell.

No. More than that. It strikes me as truly and hugely ridiculous.

To think that this . . . this contraption . . . is the best they can come up with.

This is *what I was afraid of? Christ, what a waste of good fear.*

The thing isn't frightening, it's . . . embarrassing.

Charley was dead right. It's embarrassing *to be killed this way, to be killed by people who think up shit like this. How can you think up something like this and have any self-respect?*

On the other hand . . . it's pretty amusing to see how pasty-faced serious they are.

I give a big smile to one and all as I'm strapped and buckled down. The reporters are scribbling like mad, and not a one of them smiling back.

The metal clamp closes around my ankle.

The metal cap clutches to my head.

The warden asks if I have anything to say.

I almost say Yes, would you please hold my hand?

But it doesn't seem worth the effort. Not for this knock-kneed, worm-dick bunch. I go on smiling and shake my head.

They put the hood on me, and I hear them all back away a little.

Like they do when you pull the pistol and announce the stickup.

Jesus, it was grand.

It was always so grand . . .

Under the hood my grin grows and grows and feels like it's going to—
WOOOOOOooooooooooooooo. . . .

Author's Note

It may be of interest to the reader that all of the central characters in this book were real people and most of its major events actually took place. It should be noted, however, that much of the pertinent historical record is vague, contradictory, or in error. In any case, this book is a novel, and as such its chief allegiance is not to the fact but to the truth of its story.

BOOKS BY JAMES CARLOS BLAKE

HANDSOME HARRY
A Novel
ISBN 0-06-055479-7 (paperback)
A retelling of the John Dillinger story through the eyes of Handsome Harry Pierpont, a key player in the notorious "Dillinger Gang" and the only member to die by electric chair.

UNDER THE SKIN
A Novel
ISBN 0-06-054243-8
(paperback)
Jimmy Youngblood spends a good bit of his time doing what he does best— murdering men. But when he meets and falls in love with the beautiful, bold Daniela Avila, his life suddenly turns upside down.

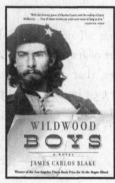

WILDWOOD BOYS
A Novel
ISBN 0-380-80593-6 (paperback)
From the raw clay of historical fact, Blake has sculpted a powerful novel revealing the heroic and unsettling saga of "Bloody Bill" Anderson, a fearsome guerrilla captain of a band of Kansas "redlegs."

A WORLD OF THIEVES
A Novel
ISBN 0-06-051247-4 (paperback)
Eighteen-year-old Sonny LaSalle is a top student and champion amateur boxer. But with the sudden death of his parents, he is drawn into his uncle's profession of crime and treachery.